I0637574

DANCE WITH THE DEVIL

OCEANFRONT PUBLISHERS • ISBN 0-9648389-0-6 • $6.95 U.S.A./$8.95 CANADA

by J. C. ARLINGTON

DANCE
with the
DEVIL

DANCE
with the
DEVIL

J.C. Arlington

Ocean Front Publishers
Venice Beach, California

DANCE WITH THE DEVIL © 1996 by J.C. Arlington

If this book was bought without a cover it is stolen property, and may have been reported to the publisher as "unsold or destroyed." Neither the author nor the publisher has received any payment for this "coverless book."

All rights reserved. No part of this book may be reproduced or transmitted in any form or by any means, electronic or mechanical — including photocopying, recording, or any information storage and retrieval system — without the written permission of the publisher, except where permitted by law. For information address: Ocean Front Publishers, 13428 Maxella Avenue, #243, Marina del Rey, CA 90292.

Library of Congress Catalog Card Number: 95-70446
ISBN: 0-9648398-0-6

Printed in the United States of America
10 9 8 7 6 5 4 3 2 1

This book is a work of fiction. Names, characters, and episodes are the product of the author's imagination and are used fictitiously. Any similarity to actual events or persons, living or dead, is entirely coincidental.

THIS WORK OF FICTION IN NO WAY SHOULD BE VIEWED AS DEROGATORY TOWARD ANY ETHNIC GROUP OR RELIGION. WHEN READ IN ITS ENTIRETY, EACH READER WILL SEE THAT THE GOOD IN ALL PEOPLES AND RELIGIONS OUTWEIGHS THE BAD.

For Linda

"Manslaughter is forbidden by Him."
— *The Qur'an* (25:68)

"Thou shall not kill."
— *The Torah*, and
The Bible (Exodus, 20:13)

1

*T*he hot desert sands of the Libyan desert can not only scorch the human shell, but they can wither away the soul. This day was no exception as the sand blew across base camp, and the trainees, who were hard at work, prepared for their calling. With more than two dozen tents set up, civilian Toyota trucks converted into military vehicles coming and going at all hours, and abundant hardware stockpiled, this training base was well equipped. There were AK47's, M16's, crate after crate of corresponding ammunition, and plastic explosives. Looking at this weaponry, this camp had firepower enough to take on at least an infantry company. It was a highly mobile base when it had to be, and that was usually twice a week. They could pack up, move out, and be secured in a new location within a few hours. They had to be ready because they knew that the sky had eyes. Satellites above could electronically record their camp in detail. Those photographs could then be quickly disseminated throughout the Great Satan's massive intelligence apparatus.

Amad and Mahmud, two young men in their mid-twenties, were among the dozen men standing around atop a hill a quarter mile from base camp. They were there to witness the demonstration. Below them in the valley sat a rather unusual oblong-looking structure, hastily built out of wood and coated lightly with concrete. The men, ranging in age from early twenties to mid-thirties, wore dated and faded former East Block military fatigues. They were heavily armed — some with AK47's, others with M16's — and had belts of ammunition strapped to and draped across their bodies. There was no doubt they were ready to defend themselves here and now, if need be. But that wasn't the case at present. They all focused their attention upon the fabricated structure in the valley about a quarter of a mile away.

The next moment, a young man with a hand radio approached from the rear. "We are ready," he said in Arabic.

The men put on clear plastic goggles.

Within moments the structure in the valley exploded into a massive fireball. Thousands of fragments from what had been the structure scattered in all directions. The fragments fell from the sky, strewn like confetti.

The men took off their goggles and congratulated themselves. They turned and walked jubilantly back toward their base camp, in a mood that bordered on the kind of excitement little children have when playing with their Lego toys.

Abdul Kasim was there to congratulate the men on their successful experiment. He was in his late forties with a medium build and the semblance of a leader. He had a full beard and was dressed like the other men, except he wore a black beret. He said to Amad and Mahmud, "We proceed as planned." He put on a pair of dark Western-style sunglasses, got into his Toyota truck, and drove off towards camp.

Every agency in town that had a satellite detected the explosion. Photographs were made, compiled, and analyzed by the Central Intelligence Agency, the Pentagon, and the National Security Agency. All photographs were classified accordingly and passed on to their respective intelligence departments. Having kept close watch on these camps for some time now, the next step was to take more pictures, do more analyses, and pass the information on to political operatives. The President instructed everyone to keep a close watch and try to predict what all this meant.

The sun was always up before he could convince his body to move. Peter Murray liked late, lazy mornings that way now, simply because the warmth of the sun's rays at mid-morning were always so soothing. And for how many years did he get up at four in the morning anyhow, when the sun had yet to appear? Too many to count. Why should he get up any earlier, when in fact everything was looked after? Maria had already been up for a few hours. She had already opened Maria's Cantina for the breakfast customers, and Oscar had everything well in hand down at the shop. By this time, he had already taken out the first group of scuba divers, usually a dozen or so, who came from the States this time of year to escape the El Norte which was about to begin its plunge into winter.

Oh well, his stomach was growling anyhow, and when it did, watch out. He loved to eat, but he was not one of those who lived to eat; rather, he ate to live. This was one of those influences that had carried over from his military days when he had participated in specialized campaigns and other top secret missions with the Defense Intelligence Agency and the National Security Agency.

He rolled onto the other side of the bed, where he could still smell the sweet aroma Maria had left behind on her pillow. If it weren't for food, he could just stay in bed all day and await her return; but no, there was too much work to do, or so he thought. Actually, there wasn't. However, he had to putter about at the scuba shop with the gear and the books to give himself something to do. So he got up and made his way to the bathroom and into the shower. If there was anything that could still jump-start him in the morning, it was a refreshing morning shower. At least it had worked during those dark mornings in his past.

Coming out of the shower with a towel wrapped around his waist and a toothbrush stuck in his mouth, he pulled some clean clothes from the dresser and tossed them onto the bed.

Peter was a handsome, rugged-looking ex-Marine. Forty-eight years old, tall at six feet two inches, lean, with broad shoulders, he looked well-worn and experienced. His brown hair was more sandy now after these last few years in the sunshine.

The bedroom was taken care of by him, not Maria. Another military influence in his life, a fastidious environment. It did have that Caribbean touch, however. There was scuba gear in the corner, a fish net draped for effect in the other, seashells, a shark's jaw, and a few local Mexican paintings depicting the sea.

Peter got dressed in shorts, sandals, and a T-shirt. He didn't shave this morning. Actually, he now went for several days before shaving. He let the stubble grow and, just before it became scraggly, he would shave it all off. Peter had grown laid back since his forced retirement from the government. He was not exactly a hermit, since he operated the scuba shop and hung out at the restaurant with local friends drinking late into the night, but he was close to hermit-like, living where he did and taking life slower.

He strolled out of his small Mexican house and into the mid-morning sun. Their house was well kept, in contrast to some of the others in the area. Then again, that's the way it was in most parts of Mexico, and Cozumel Island in particular. The Mexican people did what they could, when they could, to fix up and maintain their casas.

Living close to the restaurant, in the center of San Miguel, where all the tourists shuffle through after they disembark from their cruise ships, made it quite convenient for Peter to move about and provided for good business. Their restaurant, or cantina, was only a block away from the house on the opposite side of the street. Maria's, as it was called, was totally financed and maintained with Peter's money, although for legal reasons, and reasons of anonymity, Maria was the registered proprietor. The same arrangement with the scuba shop and diving company was in effect, so that made Peter's life less complicated.

Peter walked into Maria's, and was greeted by Alberto, or Al as Peter referred to him. Alberto actually told Peter a few years ago, "Call me Al." Peter got a kick out of Al's sense of humor.

"Buenas dias," Al said to Peter.

"Same here," Peter responded. "What's the word?"

"Breakfast will be ready in five minutes, Master." Al said the last word like Peter Lorre would say it. Al was a huge fan of American movies, especially the old ones. Though only in his mid-twenties, Alberto could name for anyone who asked him the titles of movies, their directors and stars.

"Knock it off. Business looks good. How's Maya?"

"She wants a baby."

"So give her one," Peter said as he headed for the office, Al in tow.

"She works too hard at the travel agency. I might have to stay home and raise it. By the way, she's got more referrals for business." Al stopped at the kitchen door while Peter kept going.

Peter called over his shoulder, "Thanks, Al. Anyway, having a baby, and having the father stay home and raise it, are honorable these days. Times have changed."

Al shook his head and darted into the kitchen.

Peter sneaked up behind Maria, who sat at the desk doing bookwork. She was absolutely the most beautiful woman Peter had ever known. She was five feet six inches, and had what most men would consider well-rounded bosoms. She had medium-length, shiny black, bushy hair that was full of body. When she smiled, the dimples in her cheeks accentuated her youthful demeanor. At the age of thirty-seven, she was the most adorable woman anyone could ever want, thought Peter. Having been all around the world, seeing and dating women of all nationalities, no one had ever been more enchanting than Maria. During the nine years they have been together, Peter had fallen deeper into true love, more and more so every day. He had never before felt for a woman like he felt for Maria. Not even Katharina, his ex-wife. Although at the time he thought he was in love with Katharina, apparently it wasn't true love. With Maria he had found his soulmate.

"Morning." Peter snuggled with her from behind.

She tilted her head backwards to get a full passionate kiss. "Um. I just can't stop thinking of you," she sighed. "I have to pull myself away from you each and every morning and force myself to come to work."

"Then don't. We'll hire someone." Peter sat on the desk and watched her work. Maria was a driven woman. She had her business law degree from Harvard and had practiced in D.C. That's where they had met.

"I must say, this recession isn't over, and we are still feeling the brunt of it," Maria said.

"Oh, we'll weather it. Besides, we're in this for the fun, not the money." Peter fidgeted. "What do you say we take the day off and go to the beach?"

"Oh, not today, Peter. We have all weekend. Besides, you have a scuba run this afternoon."

"Well, maybe Al would take it."

"I gave him the afternoon off to be with his wife. They want a baby, you know."

"Come and get it," Al said through the open door. Peter followed Al out after kissing Maria on the head.

Breakfast at Maria's offered an extensive variety of choices — everything from traditional Mexican to American and a myriad of international fare. That way the tourists had much to choose from, just in case they wanted a taste of home. After all, besides Americans, there were many Germans and other European tourists who had in recent years discovered Cozumel.

Cozumel, a small island, lies just off the eastern coast of the Yucatan, and boasts some of the best coral reefs for scuba diving in the Caribbean — or the world, for that matter. The main town of San Miguel offers the typical tourist entrapments, and the always-warm tropical breeze and idyllic water temperature make it one of the most alluring getaways in the Caribbean. This is precisely what had attracted Peter to San Miguel, where he opened Maria's Cantina and a scuba diving rental and excursion shop.

Maria joined Peter during coffee, just moments after he had gulped down his delectable Spanish omelette. "Business will pick up," he said.

"Yes, I'm sure it will," she answered. As Peter sipped his coffee, she looked at him reflectively. "I only wish Father and Mother were here to see us now. Father would get such a kick out of how you've changed." She smiled and

went back to her papers, jotting down numbers, trans-
ferring their balance total on a pad.

Now it was Peter's turn to be reflective. He said, "There
are still some stories I must tell you one day about how
much of a hard-ass your father was."

"You know those old war stories don't turn me on, Peter.
Tell 'em to Rolf."

"Fair enough." Peter smiled and looked past her into
the street.

Maria's was a quaint little cantina in the center of a
block just off the main plaza. An elongated rectangular
building with a small courtyard at the back, patrons could
eat outside and catch a warm breeze on a cool night or,
depending on the season, catch a cool breeze on a warm
night. The place was decorated very Caribbean-style and
had an area where the customers could watch their food
being prepared. Cerveza was plentiful, with brands from
all around the world, so that, again, the weary tourist
might have some variety with which to quench a thirsty
palate.

Al handed Peter a copy of the *Miami Herald.* Peter took
out the sports section and handed the rest of the paper
back to Al, who promptly returned to the kitchen. Peter
was only interested in the sports section. He reviewed the
most recent scores and highlights. This was his only contact with what was happening in the outside world. In the
past, he has been an enthusiastic reader of most major
newspapers, and national and international magazines,
depending upon where he was at the moment and what
was available. He had read them from cover to cover, concentrating heavily on the political coverage. Now, ever
since the politicians had sold and forced him out, he
couldn't give a crap.

Though he looked very young for a man in his late forties, Abdul Kasim was adept in the ways of the world. He was respected by his peers, and trusted completely by his superiors. He carried out his orders and participated in assignments without question. Tonight, he stood ready to assist in the cause.

He stepped out of his safe-house and into a dusty Cairo street. The night was warm and begged for justice, he thought. Kasim had in his possession fabricated passports and related documentation.

At the airport in Cairo, he boarded an American carrier. He was clean-shaven and dressed in Western attire: jeans, a dress shirt, and light jacket. He'd always preferred American carriers because their safety standards were better than any other, despite the occasional bombing or hijacking. The jet lifted off and carried Kasim towards his rendezvous with Allah's soldiers.

Reclining in his seat after takeoff, Kasim watched the in-flight movie. Tonight the film was a recent American western. Why were westerns having this surge in popularity recently? He couldn't help but wonder why it was that these funny Americans were so wrapped up in their past. Why did they glorify the violent and unjust raping and stealing of the land, he wondered. Although, as the film progressed, he couldn't help but become caught up in the emotion of the story. He had to hide his reaction so that fellow brethren aboard wouldn't notice that he was enjoying the movie. Kasim corrected himself in his mind, and thought, how clever those Americans were with their modern propagandistic methods!

Jack Dugan was a veteran political and intelligence mastermind. He had served in numerous government posts throughout his illustrious career, including deputy positions at State, Defense, and the National Security Agency. His ROTC experience landed him in the military at an early age, where he quickly climbed the ranks until he resigned his commission to work in the intelligence community. At fifty-two, and as head of that Cold War relic in Langley, the CIA, Dugan had earned the President's full faith and confidence. In fact, they knew each other from their law school days at Georgetown University. Although Dugan knew how to politically handle a nod of the head and a wink of the eye, he served his government post with absolute distinction, doing what he believed was in the best interest of the United States.

Dugan arrived at his desk at 6:00 A.M., where voluminous stacks of documents, binders, and folders already awaited his attention. He had been up for at least two hours, and had already jogged with the President and eaten breakfast with Mrs. Dugan, his wife of thirty years. He took his seat and began to finger through some papers that lay on top of the stack.

Ian Conrad slipped into the room. Conrad was the Chief of the Directorate of Operations — the person in charge of covert operations around the world. He had only recently celebrated his forty-sixth birthday, but was beginning to show his age; at least, his head was balding faster since he took this job.

"Jack?" Conrad asked, knowing full well what was to follow.

"Close the door," replied Dugan. "I've read your brief. What happened?" Dugan asked this in a soft tone. However, Conrad knew that this tone was an agitated one.

"We lost him in the Metro, while switching trains."

"Paris again. Damn French." Dugan shifted in his chair. He didn't like what he was reading or hearing.

"Those assholes live and move around there like it's their own personal campground. Damn haven for those bastards." Dugan dropped the papers back down onto the desk. He rose from his chair and walked to the window, where he stared out. "They're making a move, Ian."

Conrad thought it through as he talked. "He's certainly not a principal, just the delivery boy."

"But, Kasim the delivery boy? Why?"

"The magnitude of the operation, perhaps."

"Information, Ian. We need more to go on."

Conrad didn't say anything. He understood the task at hand. He pivoted around on his heel and started to make a quick exit from the room.

Dugan called after Conrad: "I don't care where I am. I want to know when you know." Conrad closed the door gently.

Dugan sat back down and pondered this distressing information. Abdul Kasim, thought Dugan. He scanned Kasim's file and the file on his organization, The Army of Allah. The Army had had an American businessman assassinated in Egypt two years ago. Of course, their claim to fame was the New York Trade Center bombing. Beyond that, they'd been quiet for a while. Dugan feared the worst scenario: another high-profile domestic hit.

She could barely walk around now. Although her mind was as sharp as ever, she couldn't command her body to do what she wanted, especially without argument. It felt as if the pain was to remind her that she wasn't in charge anymore — as if she really needed reminding from her unruly, decrepit body!

"Dammit," she mumbled under her breath, as she struggled to maneuver her walker around, almost tipping over as the edge of it caught in the corner of the door frame. At the age of seventy-seven, still as stubborn as ever, Helen maintained her own house and took care of herself as best she could.

Truth was, even though she wouldn't admit it, her son Harry, Peter's brother, really took care of her. He lived only a quarter mile down the road and saw her every day. Dividing the chores between himself and his wife Joan, they maintained their sanity as well as they could while they cared for her. They couldn't fathom the thought of putting Helen in one of those convalescent homes, and they knew she wouldn't agree to it. Peter even sent Harry money to help maintain her home care, which included a nurse three times a week and a cleaning crew twice a month for the hard-to-reach areas, though Helen did push the vacuum around a bit with her walker. What a sight. But then again, it gave her exercise and some self-worth — worth that many elderly people no longer experienced.

She made her way into the kitchen. This kitchen, so much a part of her life, was now very difficult to navigate. Simple chores exhausted her. She used to host parties, family get-togethers, and just plain cook up a good dish for her late husband. Now she barely had the strength to put a frozen dinner in the microwave or heat some soup.

After making her way over to the cupboard, Helen got some bread and shuffled to the kitchen table, where she laid the bread down. She struggled back to the refrigerator and located some cold cuts. While she made her way back to the table, she thought about the cooler weather that had been settling in lately. She dreaded the long cold winters that were usually an absolute given in this part of western New York.

Finally, Helen made her way towards another cupboard where she withdrew a jar of mayonnaise. On her way back to the table for the third and final time, Helen stopped a minute to catch her breath. She breathed erratically, and was not able to catch her breath. She clutched her chest, dropping the jar of mayonnaise. It broke when it struck the floor. She stood, clutching her chest with one hand and wincing in pain. She couldn't move. She was frozen as the level of pain increased. This was pain like she had never felt before. Finally, she decided that she must make it back to the table where she could sit. Struggling against the pain, Helen barely made it. She slumped into a chair.

Memories flashed through her mind. She remembered the day when her youngest son, Peter, had gathered her along with her eldest son Harry, and her late husband. Peter shocked them all when he told them he was accepting a commission with the Marines to go fight Communists. No one knew what to say. Harry wasn't required to go. The draft board denied him service because of his asthma. Thank God, thought Helen. Peter had disappointed them. They thought he would certainly attain higher achievements when he finished college. After all, he was very bright, and his grades were impeccable. In Peter's mind, however, he thought that joining the Marines was a high achievement, and he still thought that way. In his mother and father's minds, however, why would Peter risk his life and throw away an education — an education his shopkeeper father had worked so hard to pay for — when he could get a continuing college deferment and stay out of that stupid war?

While she tried to catch her breath, more memories surfaced and passed through Helen's mind. She thought she saw Peter standing there before her. She was thankful that he had survived Vietnam, but somewhat disappointed that he wanted to make a career out of the service.

How many wars had she lived through? There were always wars, no matter what the politicians said, and there would be another for Peter, she thought. Of course, Peter never really informed her or anyone else of exactly where he was, or exactly what he did during Vietnam, or thereafter. He used to tell her that he was doing spy work, and that if they needed him for anything, they were to go through the Red Cross, or a contact at the Pentagon he had given her. She used to ask him what kind of spy work, and he would say looking at pictures or listening to messages, to keep her at ease. In fact, it was illegal and too dangerous to tell her more than that. She had finally accepted his career choice, but not his divorce. That had hurt her badly, and she had never really gotten over it, in part because she blamed Peter for the break-up.

Helen clutched her chest at the kitchen table. Now pleasant thoughts passed by gently. She saw her husband. She smiled slightly. Finally, she fell forward onto the table. Her hand fell to her side. There was no more pain.

It was another one of those perfect days. The sun was up, the tourists were out. Occasionally Peter would do a night run for the tourists who were adventurous and experienced, but for today, an afternoon run would suffice.

Peter readied the boat while Oscar got the divers situated. Not a bad showing at all. Ten divers was a good number, although they could accommodate up to twenty. Peter didn't make that much profit anyway — just enough to pay the staff, maintain the boat and equipment, and have a little left over for a drink or two.

Oscar was one of Maria's distant cousins. At twenty-two, he was one of her youngest. He was always very enthusiastic about each excursion he led. Whether with Peter or on his own run, Oscar had a good time. He truly enjoyed scuba diving, as well as helping around the restaurant when necessary.

"Ready," announced Oscar.

Peter waved his acknowledgment, and Oscar cast them off. Peter accelerated slowly, just enough to clear the dock. A couple of hundred yards from shore, Peter sped up, and they were off for a few hours of enjoyable and educational scuba diving.

The Paris streets were always crowded. Everyone was going somewhere or, as Kasim believed, many were going nowhere. He wore a light jacket in the cool October air, a jacket that seemed a little bulky. Nevertheless, the Western world was doomed, he thought, and would sooner or later crumble in upon itself. With a little push from organizations such as Kasim's, preferably sooner. After all, France was one of those Western countries that had such a low moral and spiritual standard, according to Kasim and his people, it was only a matter of time before Allah called it home. In the meantime, however, there were more important targets, more immediate concerns directly affecting his group.

He walked amidst the crowds with such ease. No one paid him any attention. He laughed at how easy and lax the French were. Freedom, such as that found here in France, created an atmosphere that terrorists like Kasim found tempting. He believed that if they wanted to, they could blow up the whole city in the name of Allah's army. At least, Kasim believed, they would be saving the French from themselves. He prayed that the American mission he was helping to execute would be so easy. It would be a daring one, indeed.

Kasim darted off down an alley near the Left Bank, and entered a flat. Inside, he walked down a hallway and stopped at a door near the back of the building. He knocked at the door, striking it in an unusual way, with what appeared to be a prearranged code: three taps, followed by two, then three more, then four.

A voice from within, in Arabic, asked, "Who is there?"

Kasim replied, "It is I, your brother." After a moment, the door opened and Kasim entered.

Inside, he was greeted by Amad and Mahmud, who had last seen Kasim in the Libyan desert at their demonstration two weeks before. They were well armed with automatic weapons, and prepared to shoot it out if the wrong man was at the door. Kasim embraced them both. They were dressed like Westerners in order to blend in.

"Brothers," greeted Kasim. He unzipped his jacket and pulled out a large manila envelope. "Everything you will need is here. All of the arrangements have been made and we proceed as planned."

Amad took the envelope and opened it to study the documents.

"I am honored to be chosen for this," said Mahmud.

"Allah has picked you because you are ready."

"I hope I will see you again."

Kasim seemed agitated. "Nothing will happen to you. We are doing Allah's work, against the Great Satan. Allah will be with you."

Mahmud nodded his head and grunted agreement. Mahmud had been taken in by Kasim as an apprentice when he was a young man. They were like brothers, and Kasim couldn't begin to imagine the plan failing.

So sure of himself, Kasim said, "I will see you upon your return." He zipped up his jacket, embraced Mahmud, and left the apartment.

Mahmud stared after Kasim. He knew that the task ahead would be one that required discipline. He was well trained. The Army of Allah was trained in the deserts of the Middle East under protection from and financing by friendly governments and an assortment of special interest groups. They had received the best training a warrior could have, with some of the best equipment money could buy. Everything was now in place. All that was left was to execute the plan. It was time.

2

Maria usually took a siesta by mid-afternoon. She had to, considering how early she got up and how late she stayed at the restaurant. So today was nothing out of the ordinary, except when a loud knocking was heard on her outer door. Awakening from a dead sleep, she felt disorientated at first. Now, a second loud knocking was heard at the door. Who could that be, she wondered. She got up from the bed and answered the door.

"Who is it?" she asked.

"Maria, it's Al."

She opened the door, and Al stood there looking forlorn. He seemed nervous and upset.

"What's wrong, Al? What's happened?"

"Harry called. Peter's mother died this morning."

"Did he say how?"

"Yes, he thinks it was a heart attack. Joan found her sitting at the kitchen table. She'd been dead for a couple hours or so."

"Okay. Let's not call Peter. I'll meet him at the dock. What time is it?"

Al looked at his watch. "Already four."

"You okay at the restaurant?"

"We're fine. You go."

"Thanks, Al."

Al turned and left the house. Maria closed the door. She went back into the bedroom, sat down, and put on her shoes.

Maria thought about Peter and his mother, Helen, whom she had never met. Maria knew that Peter's mother had taken his divorce painfully, and in a way had never forgiven him for it.

Down at the dock, Maria waited. It was almost five o'clock and the boat was due to arrive soon. She remembered when her own mother had died of breast cancer. It had been a horrifying experience. At least Peter's mother had lived a full life, and death was not that unexpected for a woman of her age. Maria's mother had suffered through a long and painful illness. Certainly, her death was not entirely unexpected, but there had always been a glimmer of hope with each round of treatment. When death finally came, Maria had been somewhat prepared and had had time to say goodbye.

Maria debated over whether she should go with Peter to the funeral. In a way, she wanted to accompany him for support, but it might not be such a good idea for the rest of the family, considering that Maria and Peter were not married. She'd never met Katharina, and didn't think this would be a good time to meet his ex-wife.

Finally, Maria saw the boat arriving, right on time. She waited quietly, deep in her own thoughts.

As Peter approached, he could see Maria standing at the dock. He knew something was up, since she had never met him there before. She was usually at the restaurant by this time, and Peter never asked her to meet him here.

The boat slowed and pulled up to the dock. Oscar jumped out and secured the boat. By now Peter suspected that something serious had happened. He cut the engine and waited until Oscar escorted the scuba divers off the boat and collected their gear. He followed Oscar off the boat and walked over to Maria, who waited calmly.

"Your mother passed away," she said, hugging him.

"How?"

They eased from their embrace, but stayed close.

"Apparently a heart attack. It happened quickly." She took him by the hand as they walked up the dock.

"I'll go. You stay here and take care of business," Peter said.

In a way, Maria was relieved, but she also wished she could be by his side. She agreed that this was best, and squeezed his hand as they walked.

Peter didn't say anything. He had seen men die violent deaths, some by his own hand. However, this was his mother and, although they had their differences, she was still his mother, the woman who had given him life. This was certainly different.

"I checked on flights," said Maria. "You'll have a hop because they're completely booked out of the island."

"What's the best way?"

"There's a flight from Cancun to Atlanta. From there it makes a stop before arriving in Buffalo. It's the quickest I could find."

"Okay. I'll get Oscar to take me to the mainland. You meet us back at the house. Go ahead and make the arrangements, and we'll be right there."

They embraced. Finally, Maria let go, and Peter somberly headed back toward Oscar to fill him in.

Jack Dugan got into the back of his limousine that was waiting in a special parking spot in the basement garage at Langley. His driver, Kenny, started the engine and was ready to drive off when Conrad came running up.

"Hold it, Kenny." Dugan lowered his window slightly, just enough for Conrad to speak through it.

"We need to talk, Jack," Conrad huffed, winded by the run.

The door lock popped up. Conrad opened the door and got in the limousine. "A surveillance camera videoed Kasim leaving Paris, and an agent confirmed his arrival back in Cairo," explained Conrad.

"They couldn't apprehend him?"

"The French didn't get all their officials informed in time."

"Damn it, Ian. This is not enough." Dugan was not pleased that this was all the information Conrad had to offer.

"We've also confirmed the trace on the C4 to Libya. Two-thirds of that shipment is missing. Where it's going is not known. We don't believe these two occurrences are mutually exclusive," said Conrad, shifting in a concerned manner.

Dugan looked straight ahead and thought it over for a long moment. "This has to be domestic, Ian. I'll call Pritchard."

"And Cairo?"

"Get the son-of-a-bitch." Dugan knew how that sounded. It was a good thing these conversations weren't recorded. "Pritchard can alert everyone down the line from his end. I'll call the President and tell him what we have. You call State and Defense and do the same. We'd better have a national security meeting as soon as everyone can get there. Let's be overly cautious about this one." Dugan picked up his car phone and pushed an automatically programmed number.

Conrad exited the car hurriedly. He walked intensely toward the elevators at the Central Intelligence Agency.

Dugan responded quickly when the secretary to Victor Watkins, the White House Chief of Staff, answered the phone. "Barbara? It's Dugan. I need to speak with Vic."

Dugan's limo sped away from Langley.

Taking the boat over to Playa Del Carmen late this night was no problem for Peter or Oscar. They both knew their way around the channel very well. They could maneuver blindfolded. While waiting at the dock for Peter and Maria, Oscar had prepared the boat.

Maria and Peter pulled up shortly thereafter, and walked down the dock to Oscar. There was no exchange between Peter and Maria. They both had their own, related thoughts.

"I'll call you with my flight information just before I return," said Peter. "You better give me three or four days." He hugged and kissed Maria goodbye.

She responded in a concerned way. "Everything will be fine. Say hi to the children for me."

Peter's children had visited the island a couple of times. Sarah never accepted Maria. She was cool and distant in Maria's presence. Peter sensed this, but let it be. He figured that Sarah would grow out of it.

Paul had handled the divorce, and Maria, much better than Sarah had. Because of this, at times Sarah could be cruel to Paul. When Sarah saw Maria being kind to Paul, she would cuss at him — though for what, he never knew. For the most part, Sarah kept her anger inside, still critical of her father, because, as the newspapers had said at the time, "COLONEL MURRAY IS HAVING AN AFFAIR WITH MARIA RIVAS."

Maria and Peter ended their embrace. Peter climbed aboard the boat while Oscar prepared for departure. Maria stood and watched as Oscar untied the boat and motored out. Peter stowed his two bags below for the short trip across the channel to the mainland.

Maria watched from the dock. A moment later she saw Peter return topside to the deck, to assist Oscar and to watch her as the boat pulled away.

Peter worried about Harry, his older brother by five years. He knew that Harry would take Mother's death hard. Harry had been much closer to the folks than Peter.

In Playa Del Carmen Peter left the boat and headed for the taxi stand, where he found a cab to take him to the Cancun airport. It was usually a 35- to 40-minute ride by car, depending upon the traffic and how fast the driver went. Nonetheless, Peter thought he should make his flight with plenty of time to spare.

John Perkins always worked late at the State Department. He had a small office at the end of a long corridor, near several larger offices. Katharina had recently begun to compare his long hours to those worked by Peter. The only difference between the two men's jobs was that Peter had disappeared for a week or more at a time. Katharina had usually learned of Peter's missions from a superior, with very little detail, for obvious reasons.

Perkins had climbed in the ranks since Peter and he had last spoken, shortly before the divorce had been finalized. Peter actually had no sour feelings toward Perkins — it wasn't his fault.

At forty-three, Perkins was now a middle manager, or some might say, a bureaucrat. He had been educated at Princeton and was a career diplomat. His area of expertise was the Middle East, and therefore he was assigned to the Middle East bureau. One of his several duties included shuffling papers and communicating between embassies and the Department in D.C.

As Perkins prepared to head out, he was stopped by Patrick O'Reilly, a senior State Department official. "We have a situation, John," O'Reilly said. "Let's go into my office."

Perkins followed O'Reilly into an office down the hallway from his own. O'Reilly's office was spacious and well kept. His desk, however, did have the omnipresent stack of files and documentation. O'Reilly spoke slowly and deliberately. "We have to get out a cable. The Army of Allah may be executing a terrorist incident. Analysts believe it may be a domestic target, perhaps another American landmark. Intelligence reports confirm that a high-level operative, believed to be Abdul Kasim, was spotted in Paris and made some sort of a hand-off. To be safe, I want all embassies in the Middle East on high alert, as well as all of our allies informed immediately. I want you to handle that."

Perkins responded without any hesitation. "Done." He rushed out of O'Reilly's office and returned to his own. He began to scratch out a memo for the encoded message that would be sent immediately.

There went his exit home. The downside of working in government was, of course, the long hours. He'd call Katharina and tell her he wouldn't be coming home for at least a couple of hours or more, depending on when he confirmed that all embassies had received and decoded the message. He typed out the message as three staffers entered. Perkins informed them of the situation as he wrote the communique. "We have an important transmission."

Peter arrived at the airport in Cancun and checked in. He had only one carry-on bag containing enough personal items for a short stay and one garment bag containing his suit. The attendant checked in the garment bag and put a tag on it. He tore off the end of the tag and handed it to Peter. The attendant said, "I see you don't have your address on your garment bag. Would you like a tag?"

"No, that's fine." It was one of those things that Peter had carried back with him to civilian life. He didn't like to have his name or any other identifying marks on items out of his immediate control. It didn't really matter, now that he was a civilian — it was just habit. He preferred it that way. Peter believed that if the bag got lost and he really needed it, he had the tag which he hoped would be enough to trace it. If the bag got lost and could not be found, so be it. He could always replace it.

He made his way to the gate, where he would now have several hours to wait. This would give him time to get started on that book Maria had given him. It was an international spy novel. Having been in espionage himself, Peter always liked these books best, although the life wasn't as glamorous as novelists made it out to be.

Most of the air travelers who walked about the terminal were tourists from the States. There were, however, a few European and Asian travelers as well.

Cancun had grown considerably over the last dozen years or so. Only a short hop from Atlanta, Miami, and other southern U.S. cities, Cancun's popularity had recently skyrocketed, attracting many with its impressive sandy white beaches, warm water, and adventurous scuba diving. Cozumel, in turn, had also grown in size and popularity, since many Cancun hotels and travel agencies offered short excursions. There always seemed to be just enough tourists to maintain the economy; in fact, a sizable share of them were coming and going through Cancun's airport at the moment.

Time passed. While Peter read his book, passengers for his flight began to gather. Now and then he glanced around and surveyed the other passengers. It appeared that it would be close to a full plane, at least 125 people. There were several young and middle-aged couples, and a few senior couples. Peter seemed to be one of the few people traveling alone.

Kasim walked through a crowded marketplace in a heavily congested area of Cairo. He maintained a brisk pace. He sensed that someone was following him, but he could not be exactly sure who. After he turned onto one street and then quickly down another, Kasim believed he had made his getaway. He slipped into a home just off the street. Inside, he sighed with relief. He was greeted by several men who wore automatic weapons like jewelry. He walked into the back room.

A split second later, the front door was violently broken, smashed into pieces. Five specialized Egyptian commandos burst into the room. They were instantly met by a hail of automatic gunfire from the men within. The commandos kept up their rate of fire, but not before two were hit, falling to the floor dead.

Kasim, who had gone into the back room where he was met by two other brothers in arms, managed to blast his way through the back door, where half a dozen other commandos had taken positions outside. In an instant, several other men, apparently civilians just standing about, took out automatic rifles and began to pin down the commandos. An all-out front and back battle was now under way.

Kasim and his two compatriots managed to get just enough cover from the surrounding civilians, who were on rooftops and porches, to crawl away and disappear into a house across the alley. The men from the rooftops and porches rained a hail of bullets down on the surrounding Egyptian commandos, until most of the commandos' lives were extinguished. A few wounded Egyptian commandos retreated.

Kasim and his associates had made another successful escape. They were smuggled out by friendly acquaintances in a van that had been parked near the rear door.

Back at the scene of the first house, additional Egyptian commandos arrived and finally overwhelmed the remaining gunmen. Managing to apprehend only four, the rest were killed or had fled.

Two Egyptian Special Agents dressed in civilian clothes (one named Qadir) waited on the street outside, a short distance from the front of the house. They had taken up defensive positions after the battle had ensued, but now grew impatient and distressed while watching the activity from their position. They realized they had underestimated the support that Kasim had in the area. They exited the scene in haste and were sorely disappointed when told, over handheld radios, that Kasim had not been apprehended with the rest.

In the dead of night a Mexican man drove to the rendezvous point in the jungle just outside Cancun. The moon was high in the sky, and the jungle was thick. The route was along one of those Yucatan roads where the jungle actually creeps right up to the edge of the roadway. The Mexican road officials had to constantly machete the jungle; otherwise, it would overtake the road in less than a month.

Miguel, as he was known to those who employed him, was a fit and rugged-looking man in his mid-forties. The headlights of his Nissan Sentra coupe illuminated the long stretch of roadway in front. He pulled off the main road from Cancun and drove for a quarter of a mile, until he saw the aircraft food service truck parked where he had been told it would be. He pulled alongside the truck and cut the engine of his car. He got out and went over to the front of the truck where he felt the hood. It was still warm; the truck had been delivered recently. Miguel was an operative for hire and didn't ask questions, so long as the money was substantial and deposited in his account prior to the job. He knew his agent, who handled his set-ups, but beyond that, the details didn't concern him. A large sum of money had been deposited for this operation. He did only what he was paid to do. If he failed in any way, they knew who he was and where to find him for retribution. He, on the other hand, didn't know who they were or where they could be found.

Miguel walked to the back of the truck and opened the service door. He slid it up. Inside, he found the clothes he had been instructed to wear. He dressed in the food service clothing and checked his cargo. The cargo was airplane food service carts, one of which was a fake. The phony one obviously held the cargo that he was to deliver. It was authentic-looking on the outside, but the interior was hollow and contained something other than food.

Miguel exited through the rear of the truck and closed the door. He walked to the front, and was about to get into the driver's seat when he heard a small rustling noise coming from the jungle just a few feet away. He froze and listened, but heard nothing more. Just to be sure, he carefully crept around the side of the truck, wielding his small, strange-looking plastic handgun. He deciphered the commotion. Five feet from the dirt roadway, lying in the brush, was the now-deceased body of the original driver of the truck. The man had been shot in the head, and was still lying there, dressed in his company's food service clothing, identical to Miguel's. Apparently a small lizard or other jungle creature had been investigating the dead body. Miguel shrugged it off and got into the truck, fired up the engine, and drove away.

At Cancun's airport, he sailed right through security with the phony identification he had been given. He got the necessary clearance and waited to drive to the gate where InterAir Flight 243 was being readied for takeoff.

Miguel acted the part well. No one suspected anything out of the ordinary. He appeared to be a delivery man. He actually had been one in the past, which was one of the reasons he had been hired to do this job. He promptly got to work and handled the aircraft food service carts that were in the truck. He transferred one cart from the truck to the aircraft, guiding it over the ramp. There was an aircraft employee there to check the inventory. Miguel then inserted the food service cart into a holding dock near the rear of the aircraft while the airline employee watched and checked off the items as they came aboard. The man asked in Spanish, "You have the papers?" He inspected the first cart that Miguel brought onboard.

"Si," Miguel answered. "It is on my clipboard in the truck."

Miguel returned to the truck, then reappeared with another food service cart and his clipboard.

"All in order?" asked the man.

"Exactly what is on the paper," replied Miguel.

Miguel handed the man his clipboard. The man bought it. After all, what was there to suspect? Everything was in order. Miguel continued loading the food carts into their respective holding slots. The man watching Miguel didn't bother to inspect the other carts. He inquired, "All the same?"

"Si. I checked it all off."

The man scanned the paper on the clipboard, signed it, and handed it back to Miguel. Then the man walked down the aisle of the aircraft to inspect something else while Miguel finished securing the carts in their places.

A few other technicians were working around the area, but none had any cause to do anything different. All of the technicians and ground crew were Mexican workers, as was the food service deliveryman.

Back in his truck, Miguel drove into the Cancun jungle. After he was deep in the jungle, he turned off the main roadway and drove down a dirt strip. A quarter mile later, he pulled over and stopped the truck near a car parked at one side of the road. This was a different location from where he had picked up the truck. The new car was a Ford Escort. He got out of the truck and walked to the car. After tossing the truck keys into the jungle, Miguel opened the rear door of the car and took out a duffel bag containing civilian clothes. He changed into them, then hurled the duffel bag into the jungle. His job now complete, Miguel got into the Escort and drove off.

Dugan had slept at the office; however, he hadn't gotten much sleep. Now it was early morning, and he was talking on the phone heatedly and pacing in front of his desk. "That's not the issue, Dave. We need more to go on than that. I still say it has to be a civilian target. There's too much security everywhere else. Unless, of course, it's suicide. We can't rule that out either."

Conrad dragged into the office. He still had on the clothes he had worn the previous day, only without the sport jacket. His shirt was wrinkled and slightly soiled.

Dugan hung up the phone. "Whaddaya have?"

Conrad explained rather grimly, "Egyptian secret police took four of the group into custody. Kasim was not one of them. The Egyptians are working on them now."

Dugan sat down at his desk and rubbed his eyes with both hands. He sighed, "More, Ian."

Conrad turned to go. Dugan called after him, "Put on a clean shirt for chrissake!" Conrad then slipped out of the office.

Dugan looked around his office in despair. He knew something was going down, but where? What was the target? All the indicators of a move by this dangerous terrorist group suggested something was about to happen. He knew that in this business they could have all the latest and most reliable intelligence almost instantaneously, but it was still not enough. Prediction was something for a sorcerer, but wasn't that what his organization was supposed to do? Sure, they could gather data and offer the President advice, but predict? Events were about to unfold any minute, and he could do nothing. Dugan, all the men and women around him, and the American people could only react to the coming events. All the king's horses and all the king's men were helpless to stop the Army of Allah. Perhaps he didn't have the right people working on this, or they hadn't paid the right price. Perhaps his agents hadn't tried hard enough, or they had been sloppy. Certainly the Egyptian informant who had infiltrated the organization some time ago, and who was later killed, wasn't cut out for the job, or had had bad luck. Human nature was to second-guess. Damn! If only this! If only that!

3

"Ladies and gentlemen, we will begin boarding Flight 243, nonstop to Atlanta, momentarily," announced the gate attendant. "Please have your boarding passes ready," she said in English with a heavy Mexican accent.

Peter stashed his book in his carry-on and decided he had better visit the restroom before boarding. On the way, he passed Amad, who was heading in the opposite direction. Amad was dressed casually, in Western attire. He was well groomed, and there was nothing about him that would cause suspicion. Peter saw him, but didn't think anything of it. Amad carried his jacket in one arm and a book in the other, nothing else. He headed in the direction Peter had come from.

Peter returned from the restroom and waited in line to hand his ticket to the boarding agent at the gate. The couple in front of him was young, in their early twenties. They were obviously returning from a vacation, and seemed very much in love by the way they held onto each other. Peter could have picked the young man out at one hundred yards just by the way he stood and conducted himself, and by his haircut, and his total politeness and respect for others. He was Marine. Yes, he was dressed in civilian clothes and on leave, but he was one hundred percent U.S. Marine. The couple handed their tickets to the boarding agent and walked through the gate. Peter did the same and followed them.

"Welcome aboard," said the attendant at the door to the plane.

The plane appeared to be about three-quarters full. Peter followed the young couple for a few rows, until they took their seats. As he passed their row, sitting just two rows behind them was Amad. Amad was settled in and appeared calm. He was reading the airplane's magazine, the complimentary one that was readily available to every passenger. Peter saw him, but again thought nothing of it and scanned past him for his own seat. He found it half a dozen rows beyond Amad. Peter had an aisle seat. One passenger was sitting at the window seat, and the seat between them was vacant. That would be perfect. Peter could put his carry-on bag on the middle seat and rest his arm upon it. The woman at the window was middle-aged and minded her own business, as did he. She had her nose buried in the latest issue of *Vanity Fair*. He settled in and resumed reading his book.

A few more passengers drifted onto the plane, the usual late arrivals. Among them was Mahmud. He made his way to a seat near the front of the plane. Like Amad, he was dressed in Western clothing, wearing a dress shirt and jeans. Mahmud got situated in his seat and then watched the activity around him. Unlike Amad, Mahmud was a little tense, and looked around more than a normal passenger would. Clearly, he was anxious for the plot to begin, but he had to wait until they were airborne. Pulling off this great plan in the face of the Americans, he thought, would be the greatest honor for his cause, Allah's cause. Like Kasim, he truly believed it was the Americans who were destroying the world with greed and pornography.

They were a godless people who believed a prophet was
the son of Allah, or at least the majority of them did. They
were, he believed, controlled — or better still, ruled — by
Israel. America would soon get what was coming. They
were about to have all of Allah's wrath unleashed upon
them for their sins.

The crew went about its business. One crew member
secured the front door while others helped some passengers
get situated. The plane began to taxi shortly thereafter.

Peter was very relaxed in his seat. He read his book
intently. The woman at the window seat was immersed in
her magazine. Amad calmly scanned the American "propaganda magazine" he was reading, while Mahmud nervously watched those around him. The crew took their
places and the plane lifted off, America-bound.

Shortly after liftoff Peter became drowsy. He hadn't
slept much the night before, so he rested his book against
his chest, leaned his head back, and succumbed to unconsciousness.

The crew was up and about a few minutes after liftoff,
getting ready to pass out breakfast. By the time the passengers had eaten breakfast, it would be time for the descent.
It was just a short hop across the Gulf of Mexico before
landing in Atlanta.

Anxiously, Mahmud got up from his seat. He pivoted
toward the aisle and walked to the rear of the plane, as if
to go to the restroom. He tried to keep his adrenaline in
check. Amad also got up from his seat and followed Mahmud after he had passed. They both walked past Peter,
who was snoozing.

At the rear of the plane, in the galley, three crew members prepared for the breakfast service. Mahmud quickly
approached and before the stewardess could say "May I
help —" he had delivered a thrusting blow with his right

hand, crushing her larynx. She suffocated as she fell to the floor, clutching her throat. Before the other two steward-esses could react, Amad had kicked the one who was kneeling square in the head, causing her neck to snap backwards and break. Amad and Mahmud were experts at what they were doing. With such precision, and quick and effective maneuvers, Amad and Mahmud had the situation under control before anyone knew what had happened. Mahmud didn't have to finish off the third crew member, because she fell to the floor to shield herself. He stepped back and watched her as Amad quickly unsecured the fake food cart.

A male passenger sitting in the last row got up to see what the commotion was. "What's wrong? Everything okay?" Mahmud, reacting spontaneously, kicked him in the gut and knocked him onto the floor.

By this time Amad had extracted two plastic handguns from the fake food cart. He tossed a handgun to Mahmud, who caught the pistol and covered the aisle. Amad acted quickly. He pulled out some other plastic paraphernalia. Included were two strange-looking belts, wires, and some other plastic devices. They began to secure the equipment to their bodies.

The explosive hardware and weaponry was some of the best in the business. It was high-grade C4 from a stockpile originally manufactured in the former Czechoslovakia. It came from the same batch that had blown up the simulated aircraft fuselage in the desert just weeks before. It took Amad and Mahmud only seconds to completely strap themselves into their respective plastic monsters.

By this time the man who had been kicked in the gut was helped up by another passenger, an older man whose wife had stood up in her seat to see what had happened. Several other passengers at the rear of the plane became concerned and looked around, talking among themselves.

Amad and Mahmud were ready to proceed. They had obviously practiced this to perfection. Every detail was performed in rhythmic precision. Amad turned to the remaining stewardess and commanded: "Sit down in that seat over there." His English was quite good. The accent was there, of course, but his diction was eloquent; his words were clear. He had obviously studied well.

The stewardess, extremely nervous at best, did as instructed. Although she had shielded herself from Mahmud out of self-defense, she sat in fear, thinking the worst was yet to happen. She knew that she had been spared for the time being. It could have been her dead body on the floor in the galley instead of her colleagues. It was because of some small twist of fate that she was alive. She could only do as she was instructed now and suffer through the course of events. She sat down in the last seat of the last row on the plane.

Amad and Mahmud quickly made their way down the aisle, stepping around the fallen man. Amad, leading the way, pushed the old man back down into his seat. Next, he instructed the passengers on what to do. "You have been hijacked. This is a high matter. Everyone will keep their head down upon their own upper legs at all times. Anyone trying anything foolish, will die." He said "die" very bluntly.

Peter was groggy, coming out of his snooze. The event hadn't yet registered.

The steward who had greeted Peter at the door came forward and demanded, "What do you think you are doing?"

Amad stepped forward, smashed the steward across the face, and sent him crashing to the floor. He then reached down and put the barrel of his plastic handgun against the steward's forehead. He admonished the passengers, "This is what will become of you." He pulled the trigger, sending a bullet smashing into the steward's brain and exploding out the back of his head.

After hearing the gunshot, Peter was fully awake.

Amad stepped over the body. By now, most of the passengers had figured out what was going on. They had put their heads down on their laps in total terror, some shaking, some sobbing. A few passengers, however, had not. They were looking around as though what was happening was all an illusion, a movie. They didn't quite get it yet.

Peter did get it. He put his head down as instructed.

Confusion and affliction ran rampant through the minds of most passengers.

Peter tried to control his thoughts. What could he do? He saw Maria sitting with him at the restaurant, saw them sharing a laugh at the beach. He thought of his mother, waiting for her son to come home and say goodbye. His children danced in his head. He saw them grown up and married, with families of their own. Their careers he would not know, because, as it seemed, he was not sure he was going to live to see anything more.

Mahmud covered the aisle while walking backwards, following Amad, who covered the front. By now most of the passengers had complied with Amad's demand and had put their heads down.

Amad opened the door to the cabin and announced himself to the cockpit crew, "You have been hijacked by the Army of Allah." The crew turned and looked in shock, although they remained focused. Amad stormed in and put his pistol to the copilot's head. "In the name of Allah, we have already killed three people aboard your aircraft. We have high-intensity plastic explosives strapped to our bodies." He said this as though reading it from a prepared text. In fact, he was recalling it as it had been written and rehearsed during their preparations. He deserved an Oscar for this performance. So far, it was flawless. "You will inform Atlanta of the situation. You will fly to Havana and wait for instructions. If you try anything, you will end up like your steward out there in the aisle. We have enough plastic explosives on our bodies to completely destroy this aircraft. Your instructions will be short and clear." He took out a piece of paper from within his pocket. "You are to read this to Atlanta." He handed the paper to Captain Green.

Captain Green was fifty-four years old. He had flown in the Air Force during the Vietnam War. His record was impeccable, not a blemish. He had never had an incident, while flying for the Air Force or for the airline. Now, as then, he remained calm.

"Does everyone understand the instructions? I want everyone to respond with a simple 'Yes' and a nod of the head," conveyed Amad.

"Yes," nodded the captain.

"Yes," said the copilot.

Amad then backed away from the copilot. "Inform Atlanta. Put it on speaker and don't use headphones." He looked squarely at the captain while Mahmud covered the passengers outside the door from behind.

Captain Green made the call himself. "Atlanta, this is InterAir Flight 243."

A moment later a voice from within the console answered, "Two-four-three, Atlanta, go ahead."

"Atlanta, Two-Four-Three." Captain Green read from the paper and spoke slowly so that he was clearly understood. "We ... have been ... hijacked ... by ... the ... Army ... of ... Allah ... We ... are ... being ... instructed ... to fly ... to ... Havana ... We ... are ... changing ...

our heading ... and ... plotting ... a course ... to Havana ... at ... this ... time."

There was a long silence. The cockpit grew tense. Amad studied the crew carefully. A bead of sweat rolled off the temple of the copilot, Jorge Luna. Although only in his late thirties, Luna's heart rate had increased dangerously close to a heart attack.

The captain concentrated on a scenario that was beginning to play out in his mind. Vietnam had taught him to remain clear-headed in times of crises. He had had a few close calls, like the time anti-aircraft fire rocked his jet and almost sent him out of control in late 1970. Through it all, his mind remained clear, his thoughts carefully calculated.

Finally, the voice box answered, but with a different voice coming on, perhaps a supervisor. "Two-four-three, this is Atlanta. We read, have been hijacked. En route to Havana. Is that correct?"

"Roger. This is Flight 243 en route to Havana," answered the captain. Reading from the prepared paper in his hand he continued, "Will advise of the situation and instructions upon arrival to local authorities. Two-four-three ... out."

Amad took out a second paper and handed it to the captain. "Read this to your passengers."

Green took the paper from Amad, but not before giving his copilot a concerned glance, checking to see if he was all right. So far, his copilot seemed fine, although more sweat was building upon his brow.

Green read the note to the passengers. "This is your captain. We have been hijacked by the Army of Allah. Your hijackers have weapons and highly dangerous explosives strapped to their bodies. Any foolish acts will be met with death. The Army of Allah seeks only justice against the forces of evil. Justice is something not at all easy to obtain. Evil cannot be trusted. The government of the United States is evil incarnate, but the people of those United States are not necessarily so. However, they are more than ready to sacrifice any citizen of the United States to achieve their goals. They are also more than willing to die for Allah's cause, that which is good. They will blow up this aircraft if anyone tries anything against them."

In the first-class section, a middle-aged couple sat listening. The man said to his wife, "Take off your jewelry. Hide it in your shoe."

The young Marine, Dion Robinson, and his wife, Maxine, sat in coach class, holding each other's hand tightly. Their heads rested upon their respective laps. He whispered to her, "I feel helpless."

Maxine answered, "I don't want you doing anything. I love you too much for that." She seemed even stronger emotionally than he. Dion squeezed her hand.

Peter, head resting upon his lap, listened to the message being read by the captain. The woman sitting at the window seat near him was whimpering softly to herself, obviously in terror. More reflection exploded in Peter's head. Memories seemed to run, amalgamate, then disappear, only to re-emerge. Like the Marine, he knew he was helpless, but he wanted to act.

The hijackers' message continued. "Mr. Lincoln, one of your new hosts, will walk down the aisle with a trash bag. Each of you will deposit all your personal identification papers into it. You will place the items in the bag, pass the bag, then put your head back down. The passengers in first class will clear out at this time and find a seat in the coach area."

The passengers who were in first class quickly obliged. The captain's voice continued. "Now, we repeat, they have high explosives. Either of your new hosts can blow this aircraft into a raging fireball. What they have strapped to their bodies is highly sensitive and can be detonated at the slightest jarring. They can detonate these devices from many external sources, quickly and efficiently."

Truly, Peter could do nothing but hope, or find religion like many would at this particular and precarious time. He remembered how he had "found" religion in the past, too many times to care to recall. In the jungle, on helicopters, in the rainforest, in Middle Eastern deserts. In the past, during those moments his attitude had been different. Although then he had been as afraid of death and the unknown as anyone on either side of him, now it was different. Back then, he had a fatalistic disposition. He figured that if his time was up, so what? Now he had someone to live for. He could not die on her, or himself for that matter. He was the happiest he had ever been. But now there was absolutely nothing he could do except sit and wait it out like the rest. He couldn't risk anything and get all these people killed.

In the cockpit Amad stood over the flight crew as he dispatched Mahmud with the garbage bag. "Go." Mahmud departed from the doorway where he had stood guard on the passengers.

It was a helpless dilemma for the passengers, thought Peter. There was no place to run while flying thousands of feet off the ground. They were literally sardines in a flying can. Here stood these two preposterous terrorists, with complete control over the fates of 125 people. So what if they were at the front of the plane and you were at the rear, thirty rows or thereabouts from them. It was not as if you could jump overboard and swim to shore. There was nothing anyone could do. And most certainly no one had a weapon aboard, except Amad and Mahmud.

Mahmud walked down the aisle and passed the garbage bag to the passengers. He watched as the passengers began placing their driver's licenses, passports, and other identification papers into the bag. Some passengers were extremely nervous; others were calm but concerned. Everyone did as requested, hoping for a miracle that they would somehow emerge from this horrible nightmare. Mahmud made his way down the aisle towards the young Marine and his wife.

Robinson slipped his military identification card into his shoe. He figured that he could stall them if they wanted to single out any representative of the United States government. Maxine looked at him in grave concern because she knew that his wallet held no other identification. He had no need to carry his driver's license, so he hadn't carried it.

Mahmud was now at their row, passing the bag to the opposite side of the aisle first. The three passengers sitting there swiftly deposited their wallets into the bag. The bag was given to Dion. He dropped his wallet into the bag, as did Maxine. Mahmud moved on, not noticing Dion's high and tight haircut that would have given him away to most.

The airplane banked to the right. Everyone, including Peter, knew it was obvious they were changing course. But to where? No one could do anything but sit back and ride it out. Peter felt completely helpless, like the rest of the passengers of Flight 243.

4

*F*ederal Bureau of Investigation Director Eugene Pritchard took the telephone from his wife. The Pritchards had been enjoying a quiet breakfast together in their home just outside Washington, D.C.

"Speaking," he answered. As Pritchard listened, his face changed from an expression of routine to one of anxiety. He had a tough, angular face. At forty-nine, he was a no-nonsense, accomplished, and pragmatic director. He got right to the point and made decisions quickly.

"Where?" He listened. "Over the Gulf right now?" He got up from the breakfast table. His wife, the same age, watched as he looked her square in the eyes and shook his head slowly. She knew something terrible was happening.

Finally, he spoke again, "I want the squad activated and brought in ready to go. Havana," he said, half to himself as the wheels turned in his head. "Damn. Call State and get the diplomatic channels activated. I'll call the A.G. Any demands made? . . . Nothing? . . . Okay." He hung up the phone. He wanted to make the call right away to the Attorney General, but he stopped, thought a moment, and rubbed his face with his hands. "An American airliner was hijacked out of Cancun," he said to his wife.

"The President's in Europe," said his wife.

Pritchard sighed. "Yes, politically, it's an important trip. However, that's his call." He walked to the window and tapped lightly on the pane. "I think I know what this is about. That's gotta be it."

His wife sat up slightly, leaned forward, and asked, "What?"

"CIA informed us that a Middle Eastern extremist group was planning a hit. This may be that hit. Damn it. Cancun, Mexico?" He shook his head.

"American tourists are all over the place down there," said his wife in disbelief.

Pritchard picked up the phone and dialed a number. It rang a couple of times, then someone answered, and Pritchard spoke. "This is Eugene Pritchard. I must speak with the Attorney General at once, please. Yes, I'll hold." He was always polite, even to secretaries and phone operators, for he knew all too well that they were the power behind any successful leader.

It was a chilly fall day as Katharina walked away from the house with Sarah and Paul. Katharina was an attractive German-American woman in her mid-forties. Peter certainly knew how to pick women. She carried some luggage and hurried the children into the car. John left the house and locked the door after them. He carried more luggage, one suitcase in each hand.

The house was very conventional-looking for Chevy Chase, Maryland. It had that suburban look, albeit on the higher middle-class scale. Their neighbors in the area ranged from Supreme Court justices to assorted government workers. Sarah and Paul both looked a lot like Peter. At thirteen years old, Sarah had her father's dark brown eyes, and Paul already had his build, though he was only eleven. Everyone was in a somber mood. No one spoke to anyone else. John put the luggage he was carrying into the trunk and got into the driver's seat. He started the car and headed toward the airport.

Peter got a good look at Mahmud when he dropped his passport into the garbage bag. He had his old passport that was about to expire, the one he had gotten just before resigning his commission. He hadn't planned to have it renewed, since he now lived full-time in Cozumel and was considering getting his Mexican citizenship.

Peter couldn't be certain how the explosive devices on Mahmud's belt worked. Mahmud was carrying his plastic handgun wedged in between his belt and the small of his back while he moved the garbage bag from row to row. There was still nothing Peter could do, he thought to himself.

In the cockpit, Captain Green looked over some maps and charts while his copilot monitored gauges. Green's own scheme was playing out in his head. He had to do something, but would they know? Could they tell? Had they ever been to Havana before, and would they know if they saw it from an airplane window? How would the air traffic controllers respond? Sure, it was risky, but he knew that Havana might be a tough and untrusting negotiator. He decided to follow his plan. He had flown the route hundreds of times before and knew the layout very well. He believed it was worth the risk.

Green continued checking instruments and flight books. He corrected the plane's direction according to his plan. Amad watched him carefully, but saw nothing to worry about. Green increased the plane's speed in order to compensate for the time differential. Again, as he slowly increased the speed, almost to full capacity, Amad paid no undue attention. It would be a longer flight than they expected, but would they notice? Green would know soon enough. He turned to Amad slowly and said, "I must call the tower now."

"Proceed. I want it on the speaker," said Amad. Green switched over the radio frequency for his new destination.

"Havana, this is InterAir Flight 243, originally bound for Atlanta. We have been hijacked and diverted to your location. How do you read? Over." Unbeknownst to Amad, Captain Green kept the line open, not releasing the transmitter button.

In the control tower, the air traffic controller was stunned. She knew what she had just heard. Diane Becker was in her early forties, astute at her work and fast on her feet. She had to be. That was her job. At any given time she could be talking with a dozen flights. She yelled across the room to Horacio, who supervised the tower this day. "Horacio, quick!"

Horacio was in his mid-fifties, a Cuban-born American. Although he had been in the U.S. for more than thirty years, his accent was still there, much to his own pride. "What is it?"

"Listen to this."

They could hear the open line directly into the cockpit of Flight 243. They heard the hum of the interior of the plane, that hum most passengers can hear while flying. Horacio, puzzled, looked at Diane.

Diane looked back at Horacio and said, "Flight 243 to Atlanta says it has been hijacked and is en route to Havana."

"He can't be mistaken about the channel," worried Horacio.

Amad's voice could now be heard over the open line, "What is taking them so long to answer?"

Green could be heard saying, "Let me try again."

Diane said, "He wants you to play along."

"This is dangerous — get me another channel," instructed Horacio.

Diane looked in her radio log and scribbled down some numbers for Horacio.

Captain Green's voice could again be heard over the open channel. He talked slowly, in order to give his unknown associates time to take in what was happening, "I repeat, Havana, this is InterAir Flight 243 originally en route to Atlanta. We have been hijacked and have been diverted to your location per hijackers' instructions. How do you read?"

In the cockpit, Captain Green now risked it all. He released the open line.

Horacio, in the tower, responded in English with his Cuban accent — since English was the international language used for air travel. "Two-four-three, this is Havana." He looked at Diane with concern. Continuing, he said, "I fully understand your situation. We must go to channel five-eight-eight to continue our delicate communications. We have other flights airborne with, how should I say. . . ?" — he was playing right along, cleverly — ". . . priority."

In the cockpit, Captain Green felt greatly relieved that his gamble had thus far paid off, but there was a long way to go. Through it all, he maintained commanding composure. He looked at Amad, who nodded permission with his head. Another obstacle overcome. If Amad had said no, and Green had to keep the line open over the speaker, other approaching flights would have given away their true destination and probably have gotten someone killed for the stunt. So far, it was working.

Captain Green responded to Horacio, "This is Flight 243. We understand and are switching to five-eight-eight.

Out." He turned the radio frequency to five-eight-eight. Only now did the copilot understand what Green was doing. He kept his discovery to himself and focused straight ahead, wondering if Green was going to get them all killed. Surely, these two terrorists would know the difference when they landed. Although, he contemplated the fact that Havana was a coastal Caribbean city, as was Miami. How would Green handle the approach? Luna tried to think it through. Terror and uncertainty were visible in his eyes.

In the tower Horacio took the controls from Diane, who called the number for the Federal Aviation Administration. Horacio switched radio frequencies and waited. Everyone was well trained and knew what to do. By this time the other air traffic controllers, while still at their posts, sensed the urgency in the unfolding affair. As Diane waited for a reply, she called out to an assistant nearby, "Randy, call airport authority. We have a hijacking. We go by the book."

Randy, slightly younger than Diane, promptly went into action and punched the numbers into his telephone.

Horacio instructed Diane, "Get me a map of the Caribbean. Let's give this courageous captain room to maneuver." He waited for Flight 243's call.

Captain Green's voice was soon heard on the new frequency. "Havana, this is Flight 243."

"Flight 243, this is Havana," said Horacio, "We will be clearing a flight plan for your approach. We need a few minutes to clear the ground here. We'll keep a close watch on screen and guide you in."

Green acknowledged, "Roger. Over."

"We will make the necessary preparation at our end," Horacio responded. "Do you have any other information for us at this time?"

In the cockpit, Captain Green looked over his shoulder at Amad. Amad stepped forward with his handgun ready, and took the headset with the microphone. He spoke into it, reading from a prepared statement. "This is Mr. Washington of the Army of Allah. We will state our demands when we have landed. We want to inform the government of Cuba that we wish no harm to come to the people of Cuba. We feel that Havana is a safe and neutral city where we can have our demands met. We will be making demands on the government of the Great Satan, the United States of America. We will make those demands known. We must stress that we have highly dangerous explosives strapped to our bodies, and we are prepared to blow up this aircraft and kill all those onboard if any attempt is made to interfere with our objectives. We are prepared to die for our cause, that which is right. You will have the area cleared for us. We may depart if we feel events are not in our favor. Do you understand these instructions?"

After a pause, Horacio answered, "We fully understand your position. We will not attempt to interfere, but will negotiate in good faith. We will have a runway assignment ready for your landing shortly. Over."

Amad handed the headset back to Captain Green, who spoke into it, saying, "We copy and will await your assignment. Out."

Captain Green's heart was racing, but from his external calmness, you couldn't tell. Could this scheme of his really work? He realized his first responsibility was for the safety of his passengers, but he also realized the dilemma they were all in. He now prayed that his gamble would pay off.

Coolly, Amad spoke to Captain Green. "So far, captain, you have done what is in the best interest of you and your passengers. Now, for your sake, you had better hope that your government does as we wish; otherwise, we will kill everyone, one at a time. I will kill you last, so that way you can watch each of your passengers die before you."

FBI Director Pritchard and several of his assistants were greeted at the Bureau's emergency command center by CIA Director Dugan, who had with him an assistant. They all entered the room and closed the door.

Pritchard, in command, spelled it out. "Just moments ago, the FAA in Miami informed us that InterAir Flight 243, from Cancun to Atlanta, was headed their way. The pilot has tricked the hijackers into believing they are bound for Havana. It's a wild card that will either work or get everyone killed. It just might work. The FAA is diverting air traffic from the Miami area and sending the flights to Orlando, Jacksonville, and other airports. The local airport authority is clearing all ground traffic away from runway. Let's see . . ." He looked at his notes. "Runway two-seven-left. The hope is that they can keep the plane at enough of a distance so the hijackers cannot recognize where they are. Certainly this pilot is taking a big risk, but I'm more at ease that we will be able to control events on our soil rather than Castro's."

A young female Special Agent burst into the room and said, "Sir, they're on approach. Flight 243 should be on the ground in about thirty minutes."

Pritchard responded, "I'm on my way as soon as we conclude here. Jack, I'd appreciate all the background you have and any assistance you can lend."

Dugan offered, "Here's the complete file." He shoved several large, bulky, rubber-banded manila envelopes across the table to Pritchard. The envelopes were marked CLASSIFIED: TOP SECRET.

The Special Agent who had just burst into the room interjected an annoying comment they didn't want to hear but knew was coming, "The press has got wind. They're storming around outside."

"Stall them," ordered Pritchard angrily.

The Special Agent departed quickly. Pritchard wrapped up the briefing, "A few minutes ago our anti-terrorist intervention expeditionary force departed for Miami. The A.G. is being notified and will call the White House. That's it, folks. Everyone knows S.O.P."

Pritchard darted out of the room, followed by the others. They went their separate ways in the hallway. Pritchard was followed by two Special Agents who would accompany him to Miami. He moved with a sense of urgency. His assistants had to race to keep up with him.

Dugan shuffled out with his assistant in tow. He yelped, "We screwed this one up. Get someone on this in Miami. Have them hang out there. I want to know everything from that angle. Those bastards are not going to get away." There was tense anger in his voice. He was thinking that he could have prevented this. This type of activity was, in part, his responsibility to help prevent. "I don't want another Pan Am 103 or Beirut on our hands," Dugan declared angrily.

Harry Murray was up early, as usual. It was going to be a long day, and in ways he had yet to discover. He had already begun the necessary arrangements for his mother's funeral. So many decisions to make.

Harry was slightly shorter than Peter, about five feet nine inches, and, at close to fifty, had more beef about him. Having taken over the family business after Father had his "businessman's heart attack," Harry had added a few pounds himself and was beginning to look like his dad. Joan and the children, one boy and two girls, ranging in ages from 15 to 20, were still in bed.

Harry poured some breakfast cereal into a bowl and splashed on some milk. He clicked on the morning news and settled down to eat at the kitchen table. His house was decidedly middle class. There was nothing extraordinary about it, suburban America at the dream's best.

When the television came on, a female anchor was on the air. Harry noticed immediately that something was unusual, because the anchor was holding her earpiece tightly in place and listening to what was being said. There was dead silence as she did this and Harry wondered what was up.

Finally, the anchor transmitted the information she had received in her ear. "Okay, let's bring everyone up to date as to what we know at this time." She read from her notes, not the TelePrompter, which indicated the rawness of the information. "We have unconfirmed reports that early this morning an American jetliner was hijacked over the Gulf of Mexico. The details are sketchy, and we want to be as accurate as we can. We don't know the flight number or where it — " She stopped and put her hand up to her earpiece and listened again. "Just a moment." She continued, "The Associated Press is now reporting that an American jetliner has been hijacked over the Gulf of Mexico early this morning." She waited a moment, apparently transmitting the information as it came in over her earpiece. "The airplane was bound for Atlanta, but has been diverted to Havana, Cuba. It originated in Cancun, Mexico," she said slowly.

Harry's interest was peaked, but the thought that it could be Peter's flight had not even crossed his mind yet. He crunched away at his cereal.

Joan entered the kitchen. She was up unusually early. Because of her mother-in-law's death, she couldn't sleep very well. She was the same age as Harry, and was beginning to show it. After three kids, who wouldn't? — although she maintained an active schedule. She joined Harry for breakfast. "What's going on?"

"A hijacking," answered Harry. "They don't know much yet."

The Boeing 737 carrying the 125 passengers was only a few minutes from landing. So far, while Amad remained in the cockpit and Mahmud kept busy with the passengers, neither had bothered to look out the windows to see where they were. It never crossed their minds that what was now happening could occur. Also, realistically, they couldn't glue their eyes to a window while leaving their backs exposed to a hostile takeover attempt from a passenger or crew member.

"Flight 243, this is Havana, over."

"Havana, this is Flight 243."

"We are not clear on the ground here. You will have to make a pass. Turn heading eight-one, over."

Green responded, "Roger, heading eight-one."

Green understood the move. Buy time and disorient Amad and Mahmud if they knew the layout. Green began a hard long bank to the right. After a couple of minutes, he banked hard to the left.

Amad studied the moves and said, "I don't like this delay." He grabbed the headset from Green and spoke into it. "Havana, we will make only one pass. You will permit us to land immediately. Over."

There was a long pause, then Horacio came on. "We thank you for your understanding. We had to clear the ground traffic here," he lied. "You will be allowed to land after your passover."

Everyone on the plane remained seated with their heads in their laps. Many wondered about the peculiar turns the plane was making, because the turns were hard one way, then hard the other. Even Peter was confused about their location. Green's plan, aided by a clever tower supervisor, was working thus far.

Looking from the back of the plane forward, it appeared to be a ghost plane; there were no heads of passengers visible from that angle. It looked deserted. Mahmud sat in a galley seat that had been designed and reserved for a flight attendant. Actually, there were two dead attendants on the floor near his feet. It didn't seem to disturb him. He had seen death many times.

In the cockpit, Amad sat on the floor, bracing for the landing. He sat with his back to the cabin door while he guarded the cabin crew. From his vantage point, and because of his attention to security of the cabin crew, he couldn't see anything but sky beyond the cockpit windows. Therefore, Green hoped that upon landing Amad would still see nothing until they had stopped at the far end of the runway. And then, had Amad or Mahmud ever been to Havana? If so, did they know the layout? From the end of the runway, would they be able to distinguish between Miami and Havana? The similarities were all there, of course — from the climate and the coast to the palm trees — but to the trained eye, Havana was certainly distinguishable from Miami. From the window of a plane far down the runway, away from everything, could you tell? Green would know soon enough.

He made yet another hard banking turn, which confused Peter and the others once more. Peter thought this was certainly unusual. They were not making an exact circle of anything, but they were changing directions somehow.

Finally, Green leveled out and slowed the airspeed down considerably. This must be their approach, reasoned Peter.

That particular bump that most passengers are aware of when the landing gear is lowered was felt. At least it was felt by Peter. He knew that Mahmud was in the galley about ten rows behind him, guarding the passengers from the rear, so he couldn't raise his head too far to see what was going on outside the window. He did turn his head to the side and faced the window, but could see only the weeping woman and the sky beyond. She looked at him as tears rolled down her face. He stretched out his hand to her, a total stranger, who was unsure what to make of his gesture. He whispered to her, "It will all work out. I promise you."

She took his hand reluctantly, and he held her hand tightly. His outward strength calmed her somewhat, but the tears still flowed. If she had known the uncertainty that was within Peter's mind, she would have probably lost all control. He was just as worried as she was. And he knew that events were beyond him, that their fates were in the hands of these lunatics. In fact, he knew very little of the situation. Not knowing, being out of control, trapped within the confines of this sardine can, was accentuating the terror. At least for the passengers aboard Flight 243, the terrorists had achieved their immediate but subtle goal: terror.

Flight 243 touched down smoothly. It was a perfect landing. The plane's forward motion was slowed rapidly when the engines reversed their thrust. Peter could see through the window now, and watched as the wing flaps did their job. Beyond them, he could see a few palm trees and an adjacent runway. That was it. He couldn't make anything else out.

The plane slowed at the far end of the runway, and came to a complete stop. It didn't turn to taxi like a normal flight. From Peter's vantage point he still couldn't see much. There were more palm trees and a grassy area just off to the side of the runway but, beyond that, nothing to indicate where they were.

In the cockpit, Amad stood, as Captain Green shut the engine down. What was visible outside the cockpit's windows was similar to what Peter saw. There was a fence just past the end of the runway and some palm trees beyond it. Clearly, they had touched down in an area not normally used for regular airliners. Captain Green kept his sense of relief to himself.

Mahmud dumped the garbage bag full of passports and ID's onto the floor in the galley, some scattered near one of the dead flight attendants. He began sifting through the passengers' identification, making two piles: one for American passports and driver's licenses, and the other for those who were not American. He came across Dion Robinson's wallet, searched through it, and discovered it had no photo identification. He set it aside in a pile of its own. After completing the separation, he then looked more closely at the pile containing the American identification. Clearly, this pile was larger than the non-American pile. He began to separate women and children from the men. He came across Peter's passport and placed it in the appropriate pile. Although the American adult male pile was smaller than the rest, it contained a good supply of candidates to use as collateral.

Peter noticed the faint smell of urine. A woman in her early sixties, sitting two rows in front of him, was extremely upset and couldn't hold it any longer. He could hear her whimpering softly. Peter felt emotionally shaken, as he began to comprehend the loss of human dignity. He had experienced worse things in the deep jungles of South East Asia, letting go from all orifices possible — many times out of terror, sometimes from disease, often simply because nature called at an odd time. At least he was either by himself or around a few buddies who understood. This poor woman, however, lost it surrounded by more than 125 strangers, though no one really felt embarrassed by it, for many knew that they would have to release soon enough themselves.

In the cockpit Amad stood over the crew. He told the captain, "Radio now."

Captain Green spoke slowly and cautiously, "Havana, this is Flight 243. We have landed safely."

"Two-four-three, this is Havana," answered Horacio. "You are cleared to stay at your present position. All air traffic has been diverted. We await your demands."

Amad took the headset from Captain Green. He spoke in an authoritative tone, again reading from a prepared text. "This is Mr. Washington of the Army of Allah. You will inform the government of the United States that we are well prepared to blow up this plane if our demands are not met, and that we will kill one passenger each hour. We wish no harm to the people of Cuba. However, we will blow up the entire aircraft if the government of Cuba tries to take this aircraft by force. We have enough highly explosive material strapped on our bodies to carry out our threat. Do you understand this communication, Havana?"

"We understand fully," replied Horacio, who was now transmitting from a different room, a central command center one floor below the main air traffic control area. Around him were several officials, including the local airport authority, a Special Agent from the FBI, and an official from the FAA. They all had binoculars around their necks and could see Flight 243 at the end of the runway off in the distance. A man took notes and an electronic device recorded the transmissions. Horacio instructed Mr. Washington, "Go ahead with your demands, Flight 243."

Amad read from a list. "Our first demand is that the government of the United States release the political prisoners connected with us. These prisoners are well known and are being held by the American government. We have a plan that will allow us to confirm their release. Our brothers who are being wrongly and unjustly imprisoned in America will be flown together in an official United States government plane immediately to Beirut, Lebanon. They will be picked up by an unmarked, white, enclosed truck." He was interrupted by some commotion taking place in the coach area.

"Stop!" yelled Mahmud. He ran down the aisle toward a male passenger, about thirty years old. The passenger was sitting at one of the emergency exits and had managed to partially open the emergency door. He was frantically trying to get it completely open when Mahmud arrived on the scene.

Amad stepped out from the cockpit to see what was happening. He continued to cover the crew, while backing out and looking in the direction of the action.

Mahmud had taken his gun from his belt and, rushing up to the passenger, discharged two quick rounds into the man's chest. He lunged forward and put a third bullet into the man's head. Several passengers nearby screamed in horror as the man's blood splattered about them.

"Shut up and sit down!" screamed Mahmud.

"Back in your seats!" Amad shouted angrily. "You see, you will die if you pull a foolish stunt!" He was very heated. He yelled at Mahmud, "Drag that man up here!" He pointed to where he stood, in first class near the front door. He turned to the cabin crew. He pointed to Luna and said, "You, come here."

Luna jumped at Amad's command. He was trying to stay calm, although his hands trembled a bit. He entered the first-class section as many passengers throughout the coach area trembled and sobbed.

Amad barked at him, "You reassemble that door." He pointed with one hand while covering Luna with his plastic pistol in the other. Luna moved too slowly for Amad. "Faster! Move faster!" His English slurred a little under the stress he was now feeling. Although Amad and Mahmud were well trained at their task, both were certainly feeling the heightened sense of urgency of their plan. Neither would hesitate to kill again, and quickly, if need be.

Nervously, Luna tried to put the door back into place. Amad stepped aside as Mahmud dragged the dead passenger's body up to the front door of the plane. Amad told Mahmud irritably, in Arabic, "Get back there and cover the passengers. Scare them back into their seats!"

Mahmud quickly returned to his post. He shouted at the passengers as he walked past them, "You will meet the same fate if you try anything like that! Your blood will be on your own hands!"

Mahmud passed Luna, who had managed to secure the door. Luna's uniform was soaked with the dead man's blood. He was all the more shaken, but managed to get a grip on his emotions. He walked back towards Amad, who followed him into the cockpit after they both stepped over the bloody corpse.

Mahmud walked past Peter, who had peeked around the edge of the seat to witness the aftermath of the passenger's actions. He had returned his head to his lap, when he heard and felt Mahmud move past him.

Peter was as shocked as the other passengers. He had seen death before, and had, like Amad and Mahmud, initiated it, but that was in war. He wondered now if there was any differentiation. He could say that he had killed only soldiers, opposing warriors, and not civilians. Still, he had seen civilians die in war. But this, aboard an airplane, was this war now?

Peter continued to debate this issue in his head. What was war actually? War, in Peter's sense, had always been interpreted as between nations, opposing ideological camps, factions — the final act of political interaction. The group now in control of his fate was not a state, only an armed radical terrorist faction, a faction, like a gang... declaring war on a sovereign government? And were these aircraft passengers ambassadors representing the sovereign government that this faction was opposing in war? If so, the passengers *were* their government, in a sense, because in a democracy the people are the government. Then this was a war that this faction had declared upon them.

Peter could only think that he was not, and had not been for some time, a representative of the American government. He no longer had any connection with his former government, only a pension, which in fact he had given to his children's trust funds. The only tangible connection he had with the government was through his extended family living in the States. Peter was not so sure what his connection to the U.S. government was to him now, although in the terrorists' minds, he was an American, holding an American passport. "Damn it, I don't belong here," complained Peter to himself.

In the cockpit, Amad and the crew listened intently to Horacio's voice over the speaker. "Flight 243. Come in, two-four-three."

Amad picked up the headset microphone to answer. "Havana, this is two-four-three. We had a minor interruption. Do you understand our instructions?"

Horacio acknowledged, "We have recorded your instructions, Flight 243. We will contact the American government through diplomatic channels. We assume you know that we cannot go through normal diplomatic agencies, and that this request will take some time to establish and confirm. Over."

"We are aware and have prepared for this," Amad replied. "We will give you two hours to inform us of the official American response. If, after two hours, we have not been answered, we will begin to torture, then kill one American on the hour, every hour thereafter. By my watch, the time is thirteen minutes until the hour. You have two hours and thirteen minutes until we begin our first sacrifice. Do you understand, Havana?"

There was a short pause. Then Horacio was heard saying, "We understand. We will contact you well before that time."

Because of the way in which their plane was positioned, Peter could not see any other airplanes coming or going. None of the passengers knew where they had landed, including Peter. He was aware that the plane had initially made a hard bank to the right, which meant east. They were obviously still in the Caribbean. Much of his and the others' frustration was not knowing the details of their predicament. Then again, what good would it do to know those details if you were helpless? Nothing to do but affirm your faith in your creator, if you happened to believe in one, and sit back and let the events unfold as they might.

Peter had sat it out many times before in the jungle, waiting for the enemy amidst rain-soaked vegetation and hiding in painfully small places. These past experiences made it possible for him to temporarily control his stress and anxiety, but for how long? With one passenger already having lost it, Peter wondered how much longer it would be before another did the same. Many around him were huddled tightly in their seats, shaking and whining softly to themselves. For their sake, Peter hoped no one else would try anything, himself included.

Onboard the FBI Director's plane, Eugene Pritchard talked on the phone as three male assistants worked other phones nearby. The hum of the jet could be heard faintly in the background. "Get everyone into place and stand by." He pushed down a button on the phone and looked at one of his assistants.

"The President on line two," said assistant Roth, who was a quick and promising Special Agent.

Pritchard punched another button on the phone. "Yes, Mr. President. Yes. I have the squad in place and ready to go . . . I understand . . . Nightfall would be preferable . . . I can't predict that they won't, but where to? I couldn't guess . . . We can't rule that out either. This group, as you well know, is suicidal . . . Well, the pilot took a big gamble . . . I hope so too . . . Yes . . . Yes . . . I'll call you back." Pritchard hung up the phone. He looked over at Roth. "We need to get that link-up with the Pentagon and have a reconnaissance jet on standby. Let's hope it doesn't come to that."

5

Harry and Joan had dropped off their children at Joan's sister's for the day. They were on their way to the airport to pick up Katharina and her kids.

In the car, the mood was somber. Harry, closer to his mother than Peter, certainly was taking her death quite hard. Yes, she had lived a long and fortunate life, but she was still his mother. The silence in the car was too much for Joan. She turned on the radio.

"I have to break the silence, Harry. Maybe some music?"

Harry nodded in agreement. Joan found an oldies station playing one of those good old '60s songs. The song was ending at the top of the hour. The disk jockey came on and said, "It's on the hour, folks. We'll be back in five minutes, right after the news."

Neither Harry nor Joan seemed to be listening at this point; rather, they had drifted off into the fading tune of their past. The news anchor came on with the top story. "This is Donald Shelby. CNB radio network has just confirmed moments ago that an Atlanta-bound flight from Cancun, Mexico, with approximately 125 passengers and crew aboard, has been hijacked. Preliminary reports indicate that the plane has flown to Havana, Cuba. We have confirmed that the President, who is traveling in Europe, has interrupted his schedule and is back on Air Force One. We have received unconfirmed reports that the hijackers are making some demands related to United States foreign policy. Beyond this information, details remain sketchy. We will keep you informed as developments arise." The radio went silent for a few moments, then a commercial came on.

Harry looked at Joan, who looked back at him, both with their thinking processes on overload.

Joan asked Harry, "Did you hear that?"

"I'm not sure," responded Harry in a subdued tone.

"I have just been handed the following information and therefore it is unedited. It's just coming off the wire as I read it," continued Shelby after the commercial. "What we now know is that InterAir Flight 243 from Cancun, Mexico, en route to Atlanta, with more than 125 passengers and crew, has been hijacked over the Gulf of Mexico. It has apparently landed in Havana, Cuba, although the Castro government has not yet given confirmation."

Harry turned the radio off. "There is more than one flight out of Cancun, right? I don't recall his original flight number before his transfer, but — "

"Let's not jump to conclusions just yet. We'll check at the airport," Joan said to calm Harry's worst fears, although she shared the same anxiety.

At the Greater International Airport in Buffalo, they quickly parked the car and rushed into the terminal. Joan ran to keep up with Harry. They rushed down a corridor and to the counter, which alarmed the ticket-taker. A security guard came over to investigate.

Harry threw out his words while panting from the run. "My brother . . . I think . . . he was to be . . . on Flight 243 from . . . Cancun to Atlanta."

The ticket-taker, a little more at ease now that she knew what this was all about, and a bit concerned for Harry as well, said, "Won't you please come into our office?" She led Harry and Joan into the office just behind the counter. The security guard followed them.

Harry and Joan watched the arriving passengers get off the plane from D.C. Harry, obviously distraught, paced back and forth. Joan was worried for him. She could not believe what was happening to his family. His mother had passed away, and his brother had been hijacked. Ever since she had married Harry she had feared Peter's death, seemingly inevitable because of his profession. Although Peter had never gone into detail about his around-the-world adventures, Joan suspected that they were dangerous. After Peter's forced retirement she had thought, at least the family could rest a little easier. But hijacked? And on the way to his mother's funeral? Finally, she spotted Katharina and the kids in the crowd of arrivals. "Katharina!"

Katharina spotted Harry and Joan, and walked over to them, followed by Peter's children, Sarah and Paul. Joan intercepted and greeted the children so they would not overhear what Harry was about to tell Katharina.

Harry took Katharina by the arm. Katharina could sense shock in Harry's behavior. His voice cracked slightly as he said, "Peter's plane has been hijacked."

Katharina's face lost its color. Like Joan, she had always half-expected news like this while she was married to Peter. She had had terrifying visions of Peter's death. She had imagined him being killed in action, taken hostage, or blown up somewhere, but now, to be hijacked in retirement, as a civilian? She harbored no animosity towards Peter. He was, after all, the father of her children, and she did, in her way, still care about him.

"What do they know?" she asked.

"Not much right now. We better stick to our plans and take the kids to Jackie's. We can watch the news and work the phones. The airline people say they know very little, and that the news will get the information first."

"Okay. We won't tell the children about this until we know more," agreed Katharina.

They both turned back to Sarah, Paul, and Joan. Harry greeted them, but it was clear that he was taking this hard. This was too much for him.

Mahmud was studying the male American passengers' identification documents. So far he had seen nothing unusual. Then he remembered the wallet he had set off to the side. He grabbed Dion Robinson's wallet and opened it. It contained thirty dollars in cash and one credit card. Mahmud realized that this meant someone had not surrendered their identification. He took off down the aisle towards the cockpit.

After Mahmud passed by, Peter couldn't help but peek around the edge of his seat. He watched Mahmud carefully and sensed his agitation. When Mahmud approached the cockpit and announced his presence to Amad, Peter pulled his head back out of Amad's view.

Peter still didn't know what was happening and, along with the rest of the passengers, he was frantic and tense. Although able to control his stress, he still felt very anxious. Unlike the man who had met his fate at the trigger of Mahmud's gun, Peter understood that there was nothing he could do. It would be suicide for him — and maybe unnecessary deaths for the others — if he tried anything, he told himself over and over again. He could only wait and let the authorities work things out. Though it would be unbelievable to most, he still had faith in the system because, having been a part of that system, he knew that things did work out in the end.

Mahmud informed Amad of the suspicious wallet. Amad seemed impatient with this news. "Separate the Americans now and find this person," Amad told Mahmud. "Find this person and find out what he hides."

Mahmud turned and moved back down the aisle with a sense of urgency. He was still high from killing the disobedient passenger, and now he had a new mission. This one would be even more enjoyable because he would get to play detective. Once he found out who this person was, and hopefully it was an American, he would exact due punishment.

Mahmud had been recruited at age thirteen into the Army of Allah, much like American inner city youths are conscripted into their gangs. They become proselytized by their respective causes and thus fatalistic about their lives. It was always the youth who were the most impressionable. Like young American kids, Mahmud quickly fell into the quandary of discontent, poverty, and hopelessness. Unlike his American counterparts at that age, however, Mahmud was taken in by elders who must have young recruits to further their cause. In his mind he saw himself as a warrior, different from American youths who see themselves as survivalists in a war without any direction except survival. In a larger sense, although this would probably not happen within his lifetime, Mahmud reasoned that he was working to save his American counterparts from themselves.

Mahmud instructed the passengers, "I will now call out names." He shouted this order so that all of the passengers could hear him, from one end of the plane to the other. "When I call out your name, I will instruct you to go to the front or the back of the airplane. If I instruct you to go to the front, you will sit just behind first class. You will take up another seat there. I will shoot you dead if you try anything foolish, just like I sacrificed the other passenger." His English was as good as Amad's, albeit his accent was not as heavy. Peter, at his seat, thought that both men had been taught well. They must have had good teachers. In fact, they had both studied and prepared thoroughly for this great day. Of course, it helped to have watched many American movies, like their friend Kasim, who, along with brothers in the cause, sat around for hours at a time watching CNN in international hotels throughout the Middle East. Anyone who had watched CNN as they had, could learn American English.

"Tony Miller!" shouted Mahmud. A moment later a scared, balding, middle-aged man stood up midway in the cabin with his hands in the air. Good obedient passenger that he was, thought Mahmud. "To the front of the plane!"

The poor man shook and sweated profusely. He had a slight spare tire about his waist, and if this situation became any more stressful, Mr. Miller would be a likely candidate for a heart attack. He made his way to the front of the plane and took a seat there.

Peter thought about what was to transpire. The men, all American, would be moved to one area, readied for slaughter. With every passing moment, Peter wondered what this Army of Allah wanted. He hadn't followed current events lately, so he searched his mind for clues to the history and makeup of this group. He couldn't recall anything, and this frustrated him. "Damn," he mumbled softly to himself. "What the hell is the Army of Allah?"

At one of the more popular international hotels in Giza, under the shadows of the great pyramids, Kasim sat in the Intercontinental Room watching as the events of the hijacking unfolded on the Ted Turner show, the Cable News Network. Several tourists — some European, a few American — had gathered to watch the program. If Kasim could have it his way, his people wouldn't be subjected to the Great Satan's propaganda network which misdirected their lives. Nonetheless, for the time being, he tolerated the existence of these intruders.

A familiar male anchor came on the all-potent idiot box and reported, "In case you have just joined us, this is what we know so far about the hijacking of InterAir Flight 243 from Cancun, Mexico, en route to Atlanta, Georgia. The flight was hijacked over the Gulf of Mexico early this morning by a group calling themselves the Army of Allah. The pilot radioed Atlanta and informed them that they were flying to Havana, Cuba. However, the Cuban government has not confirmed this."

The anchor was handed a note from off-camera. "I have just been given this update." He read from the typed note, "A Miami-bound flight from New York has landed in Orlando, Florida. Passengers disembarking from that flight do not know the reason for the diversion and have been told only that flights into Miami International Airport have been cancelled."

Kasim perked up a little after hearing this. The anchor continued, "We will have more information as it becomes available. For now, we will take this short break."

Kasim stood up, more than a little concerned about that last message. He wondered if there was a connection and what it might mean. He paced back and forth behind the other television watchers for a few minutes. Finally, he left the hotel.

In the air, above Florida, FBI Director Pritchard's plane was on final approach to Miami International Airport.

From his window Pritchard could see the hijacked Boeing 737 jetliner at the far side of the airport. It just sat there at the end of the runway, lifeless, pointing in the direction of a palm tree. From what he could make out, the immediate area surrounding the aircraft was wide open. Access to the plane would be easy. Concealment, however, would not.

Peter heard the faint sound of a small jet landing. Mahmud was busy calling out names, and Amad was not trained in discerning the different sounds of aircraft engines. Neither paid the noise any attention.

The wheels spun in Peter's head. Since their landing, he hadn't heard another plane land until now. He though a small jet had landed somewhere off the port side, not far away. They must be in the States somewhere! Probably in the south, he figured, because of the palm trees. Maybe Florida. The plane sounded like a Lear jet. It must be a government aircraft, with someone important onboard. Hopefully, Peter now prayed, this nightmare would soon be over.

Peter thought about Harry, and what Harry would do with Mother. Would he keep her on ice until Peter got up there, God only knew when? How would the children react when they heard that their father was a hostage in a ridiculous political drama? Damn it, Peter thought, as he pondered his sad state of affairs. And Maria? He only hoped that this was over before she heard about it. He knew she was strong under pressure and that she would jump into action, perhaps getting on the phone and pushing people along.

"Peter Murray," called Mahmud, "To the front of the plane."

Peter looked over at the terrified woman next to him. She was shaking intensely and clutching the crucifix around her neck. Peter stood up, his hands in the air. He made his way into the aisle and didn't look at Mahmud. He figured he had better not look, so as not to draw unwanted attention. He knew not to look a scared animal in the eyes, nor a high-strung human. He couldn't do anything, anyhow, he kept repeating to himself in his head. Besides, he again rationalized, Harry was burying his mother — why should the poor bastard have to bury his only brother also? So Peter did as he was told. Still, he felt ashamed.

Most of the American men had already been called. They now filled many of the seats near the front, so Peter took a seat almost a quarter of the way behind first class. There couldn't be more than eight or nine others who would follow him. Peter took an aisle seat again. This time there were two men sitting to his left, one at the window and one in the middle.

The man by the window, Mr. Simon, was a recent retiree on vacation with his wife. The man sitting in the middle was thirty-three years old, and had been vacationing with two buddies who were sitting a couple of rows in front of Peter. Peter noticed that the two men, although in fear for their lives, were handling the strain as well as he was. They, too, hoped that those on the outside had things under control and would end this nightmare soon.

After settling in and putting his head back down, Peter heard Mahmud call a couple more men. They took their seats to Peter's right, just across the aisle.

That was it. The remaining passengers were sitting behind Peter at the back of the plane: all the women and men who were not Americans.

Dion Robinson remained in his original seat, with his wife, Maxine, a few rows behind him. The row he was in was now empty, except for him. The male American passengers were sitting in front of him, and the rest of the passengers were behind him.

Mahmud had conducted the entire cattle call while standing in the aisle at the back of the plane, so he hadn't detected Robinson, who remained seated. However, it was clear that as soon as Mahmud inspected his rearrangement, Robinson would stick out like a sore thumb, and God only knew what would happen then. Robinson took out his military identification and put it in his shirt pocket. When discovered, he would proudly surrender it upon demand.

Dugan was back in his office working the phones when Conrad entered, carrying some papers. "Okay, and only use this secured line." Dugan returned the receiver to its cradle.

"This is our operative that I've dispatched to Miami," said Conrad, handing a file to Dugan. "Agents in Cairo spotted Kasim in Giza, but lost him somewhere in the crowded street. They're keeping a close watch and looking for the first chance they have to apprehend him. If anything breaks, you'll be the first to know." He stormed off with an urgency and determination to see this through.

Dugan scanned the agent's file. Although the agent answered to numerous names, he was officially known in the Agency as Jim Shell. That name might just as easily have been John Doe, because Jim Shell was born outside of Havana, Cuba, forty-three years ago. His Cuban name had been Rafael Castillo. As a young boy, Shell-Castillo fled Cuba with his family just after the revolution and settled in southern Florida. He grew up in that proud anti-Castro environment, and through contacts with the community and his father, he worked his way into the CIA, where he had been an agent working the Caribbean for twenty years. Although highly dependable and forever committed to his adopted government, after the counter-revolution that was sure to come, Shell-Castillo would most certainly return to his homeland like so many others who held the same dream.

Dugan flipped through Shell's binder, then put it off to one side as the phone rang. He lifted the receiver quickly, almost jamming it into his cheek. "Dugan," he answered urgently. "Yes, Mr. President . . . You know where I stand on this . . . No deals . . . Yes . . . That's what I would recommend . . . They see this as war, so we should treat it as such. I recommend Pritchard be given the green light . . . The White House at six. Okay." Dugan hung up the phone, grabbed his jacket, and stormed out of the office.

Katharina was on the phone with John, who was at his desk in the State Department. Harry paced in front of the television. Joan came out of the bathroom, where she had already gone twice since arriving home after dropping off Peter's children at her sister's house. During the car ride from the airport, Katharina and Harry said not one word as they thought about this crisis that was still developing. Joan had amused Sarah and Paul with small-talk about school and life in D.C., although her mind was elsewhere.

Katharina repeated out loud what she was hearing from John. "President's on his way back to the White House. State Department knows very little. Can't go beyond that much more anyway. Okay." To John, " 'Bye." She hung up the phone and turned to Harry and Joan. "I'm sorry he doesn't know any more than that," she apologized.

"Forget it," Harry told her.

"Can I get you anything, Katharina? Something to drink?" asked Joan.

"No, I'm fine. Thanks. I'd be running to the bathroom like you."

They watched as the television anchor reported, "We have now confirmed that the President is en route to the White House, having departed Frankfurt, Germany, just moments ago. We are also receiving word from our affiliate in Miami, Florida, that there is indeed a major disruption going on at the airport there. They inform us that incoming flights are being diverted to other airports throughout central and southern Florida. The officials at the airport in Miami have no comment at this time. We are also told that FBI Director Pritchard left Washington soon after the hijacking, but the FBI is not commenting on where he has flown. We are standing by, awaiting official word from either the White House or other government sources. We also must note that the Cuban government continues to deny that any American flight has landed in Havana. We don't want to speculate at this early stage. When we have confirmed our sources, we will immediately pass any information to you."

Harry, his face showing the stress, turned to Katharina and Joan and asked, "Why would they say they were hijacking a plane to Havana and land it in Miami?" He said this not so much as a question, but as a statement to himself.

"That's what it sounds like," said Joan, trying to agree as well as comfort him. "But let's not jump to conclusions just yet."

There was a tense silence as they waited for more news. "Harry, are you going to call the funeral director?" asked Joan gently.

"Yeah. Thanks." Harry went to the phone and dialed, while Katharina and Joan remained transfixed at the television. No new information was offered, and that only added to their tension. For Peter's family it was anxiety at an unbelievable level — a horror movie.

Pritchard was escorted, along with his assistants, into a conference room where central operations had already been set up. Greeting the newcomers was Theodore Berry. Berry was a tall, clean-cut man in his late thirties, dressed in a freshly pressed, immaculate, black SWAT team outfit. As the field commander for the FBI's anti-terrorist intervention squad, he had already spread out a map of the Miami airport on the large conference table and was studying it when the Director arrived. Berry straightened when the Director entered the room. "Mr. Director." He extended his hand to Pritchard, who responded with a quick, businesslike handshake.

"Ted. How are the wife and kids?" asked Pritchard.

"Fine, thank you, sir."

Berry introduced those who had gathered around them. "This is Captain Hernandez with the airport authority."

Pritchard shook his hand. Hernandez was in his late fifties and wore his airport police uniform proudly.

Berry continued, "This is Martin Fowler with the FAA."

Pritchard shook his hand. To Berry, "What's your assessment?"

"Classic operation, by the book." Berry pointed to the map and indicated where he had already highlighted the plan. "We'll approach the aircraft from the rear. Whatever direction they might turn it doesn't matter — we can still get up through the wheel well and baggage hold. The equipment will be ready momentarily, so we should have a good read on how many hostiles there are and where they are concentrating their activity." He gave Pritchard a concerned look and continued. "The friendly kill ratio could be high. As you know, it all depends upon the element of surprise, the number of hostiles, their position at the time of infiltration, and their immediate capability to self-detonate, assuming that's not a bluff."

There was a long pause. "This is war, Ted," Pritchard revealed in a most straightforward manner. "The friendly kill ratio will be one hundred percent if they find out that they have no deal. The President said there is absolutely no way that he would make a deal, and that we are to proceed with discretion."

"I understand," acknowledged Berry.

Pritchard understood clearly the political ramifications of seeing Americans killed and thrown from a plane. He felt compelled to explain it to Berry and the others. "It's the basic law of supply and demand," said Pritchard. "If these terrorists get what they want, then they, or others who could follow, will be back for more. If these bastards see that it's futile, then hopefully our actions here will deter future terrorism. Get me a two-man detail dressed in ground crew garb, wired and ready to recover any deceased that are thrown from the plane. They must be Cuban-Americans. Get a good look at the situation from that angle. That's it. Get your men briefed and readied for the go. You'll have little advance warning."

Berry picked up his personal gear that was lying beside the door. He departed, knowing clearly that this operation was a green already. Now he had only to give his squad of twenty men their final briefing on the specifics of the plan.

Pritchard knew what had to be done, and gave the orders like a general heading into battle. "Captain Hernandez. This is the situation. We are going to stall them until our squad is in place and ready to go. You heard

Berry. We will surround the plane and have high-powered listening devices and television cameras set up here and installed shortly." He pointed on the map to where the equipment would be placed. "I want the whole airport secured and your officers on a perimeter of five hundred meters surrounding the plane. No one in, no one out." He paused a moment, then said, "We expect there will be some casualties. Get a temporary morgue set up. Let's hope, in the name of God, there won't be many dead. I'm sure the press will be all over the place soon. Keep them out and say nothing. They could blow this whole thing, for chrissake. Mr. Fowler, let's get to the tower."

Fowler trailed Pritchard out. Pritchard's assistants followed, hot on their heels. They headed toward the tower where Horacio and the other officials had gathered.

Dion Robinson was as worried as anyone else, but he had more reason to be. He knew that Mahmud was inspecting the new seating arrangements, identifying the passengers row by row. He had started his inspection at the rear of the plane, where he matched up the non-Americans and women with their identification. As he got closer and closer to Robinson, Maxine began to shake with fear.

Mahmud stopped at Maxine's row. She was beyond nervousness as he asked the woman next to Maxine for her name. The woman responded; Mahmud found her passport and handed it back to her.

"Your name," Mahmud demanded of Maxine.

"Maxine Robinson," she answered, her voice cracking slightly.

Mahmud dug through his pile of female identification. Finally, he found hers and tossed it at her. She took it slowly and didn't pay any attention to the woman sitting on her other side. She focused only on what was in store for her husband.

Mahmud completed his inspection of the women and non-Americans. At last he had only the American men to inventory. He gathered up the remaining identification cards and passports.

In the cockpit, the first deadline had arrived. Amad was resting against the wall just inside the door. He kept his plastic handgun trained on the crew. Amad glanced at his watch, then looked back up at the captain. Green was feeling much calmer now. Luna had also settled down and they were totally focused on their deception.

Amad jumped to his feet. "We must radio now." He said this with such force that it almost caused Luna to lose control of his bowels. Amad moved toward the captain to take the headset.

"Havana, this is two-four-three."

In the control tower, Horacio responded while looking up at Pritchard. "Two-four-three, this is Havana. Go ahead."

From the cockpit, Amad instructed, "The two-hour deadline for the American response has come. Do you have any information for us? Over."

"Uh, two-four-three, this is Havana," Horacio continued. "We have made contact with the Americans through diplomatic channels. We have relayed your demands to them. The Americans tell us they will do what is necessary to cooperate, but that it will take time to respond to your demands."

Amad had expected this answer. It amounted to nothing more than typical government stalling. However, he would not fall for it. He spelled it out, saying "Okay, that leaves us no choice. We will begin to execute — one passenger on the hour every hour. The first execution will commence now. We will throw the body from the plane. You may send two men to retrieve the body. You will inform the Americans and allow the international press to videotape the body as it is tossed from the plane. Remember, we have eyes all over the world and will know full well if our demand is not met. Do you understand, Havana?"

Horacio looked up to Pritchard, who began to fume slightly under that Teflon exterior. Of course, he thought, that was just what they wanted, a world audience for which the press could sensationalize this madness.

Pritchard turned to one of his assistants and barked, "One pool camera. Set it up per my instructions." Roaches, he thought to himself. The media would get us all killed in order to get a story. He nodded to Horacio.

Horacio notified Amad, "We understand, Flight 243. We will have a camera set up and inform the Americans. We are doing our best to accommodate your demands, Flight 243. The people of Cuba are a peaceful people. We would only ask, in the name of humanity, that you release the women and children."

There was a long silence. Pritchard and the others grew tense waiting for the reply, but it finally came. Amad informed them, "We are sorry, Havana. We will save the women and children for our protection, and will execute them after the others, assuming that our demands have not been met by that time. You will inform the Americans and tell them that the blood of all those onboard will be on their hands. All they need to do is release our political prisoners and we will fly to an undisclosed location and release everyone. There will be no further discussion. You may retrieve the first body in about five minutes. Again, we must warn you to try nothing foolish. We have enough plastic explosives onboard to completely destroy this entire aircraft. We will not hesitate to do so, and plan to keep a close watch on the area around this aircraft. Two-four-three, out."

Pritchard nodded to Horacio again. Horacio said, "We understand, two-four-three. This is Havana. Out."

Horacio had a look of terror on his face. Everyone in the room knew the plan. They all began to mentally calculate how many people would die before the assault took place. One on the hour, every hour. Could they stall these terrorists?

Mahmud approached the row where Dion Robinson sat all alone. Suddenly, Amad appeared at the cabin door. He called for Mahmud, "It's time." He looked squarely at the passenger sitting in the first row of coach class. Michael Collins, in his late forties, of medium build, was terrified. "You!" Amad scared Collins half to death. "Drag that man to this door. Do it now!" Amad was pointing at the dead steward's body. Collins, who was shaking, stood and walked back to the steward's body. Mahmud covered the man from the other side of the steward's body. Mahmud had passed Robinson, but hadn't noticed him yet.

Collins dragged the body to the front of the plane. Amad instructed Luna to assist by opening the door, which he did. Collins stopped at the door, while Amad stood clear. A businessman from Atlanta, husband, and father of two young children, Collins was about to lose it. He wanted to vomit. He had been on a business trip to Cancun and couldn't believe what was happening.

"Throw him from the plane!" ordered Amad angrily.

Assisted by Luna, Collins tossed the steward's body from the open door. It fell with a loud thud that those seated in the front of the plane could hear. It was a sickening sound. Collins was frozen in shock for the few seconds it took the body to crash onto the tarmac. It was a good thing the crew hadn't had the opportunity to serve anything to eat; otherwise, Collins most certainly would have upchucked it by now.

"Back to your seat!" yelled Amad.

Collins awoke from his lifeless stare and hurried back to his seat, where he put his head down and drifted off into relative obscurity once again. It was a good thing Amad had yelled at him, or Collins might have passed out and fallen from the plane.

Luna closed the door and returned to the cockpit. Amad blared at Mahmud in Arabic, "Back to your post. Get your business cleared up."

Mahmud quickly obliged. He passed Peter once again. Peter watched Mahmud's feet pass by as he walked down the aisle. Mahmud got reoriented quickly to what he was doing. He continued to inspect his arrangement, especially the American males now herded together like cattle for the slaughterhouse.

"Sir?" A weak voice called out from behind him by about ten rows.

Mahmud turned around angrily. "Who said that?"

"Back here, sir."

Mahmud saw a hand raised above a seat in the female section. He walked over to it, quite annoyed by the interruption. "What do you want?" he asked the frightened woman in her late fifties. She was shaking and crying.

"I have to go to the restroom."

Now, if that didn't piss off Mahmud! He got right into her face, pointed his plastic handgun at her forehead, and screamed for all to hear, "No one does anything but sit in their seat. No one gets up for anything. If you must go, do it in your seat. I will shoot anyone who moves out of their chair. Do you understand me?" He demanded an answer not only from her, but from everyone around her. "Do you all understand me?"

Those who were brave enough answered with a mumbled, "Yes."

Mahmud stormed back up the aisle. He had more important business to attend to: the work of the Almighty. Minor distractions such as this were meant, he believed, to divert his calling. Mahmud wouldn't tolerate this. He decided to shoot the next person that pulled a stunt like that.

The woman, who was now sobbing softly, was comforted by the women sitting next to her. She didn't know what to do. It's not a natural thing, she thought, just to sit there and let go, so she held on, hoping this ordeal would soon end. She had always used a bathroom. Sure, she'd been sick in the past — with diarrhea, in fact — but she had always made it to the bathroom in time. However, her stomach was so upset now that she couldn't hold it. It was humiliating, this natural act. Those sitting immediately around her understood and sympathized with her. There was nothing she or anyone else could do. Unable to wait any longer, the woman defecated in her clothing and cried uncontrollably.

6

Pritchard, Horacio, Fowler, and a few other assistants and officials, all with their binoculars raised, watched as two Special Agents, both Cuban-Americans dressed like ground crew, placed the steward in a body bag, set it on a flatbed truck, and drove it back across the tarmac toward the makeshift morgue, inside a nearby hangar.

Pritchard turned to his assistant, Roth, and barked, "Get the medical technician on it. We haven't detected a shot since putting our mikes in place. I want the probable cause and time of death ASAP."

Roth sprinted off. Pritchard said to the others, "My guess is that we have fatalities already. Probably from the initial takeover, so they're bluffing the first executions."

The others around the room looked at Pritchard with concern. "It's revolting enough," said Pritchard. "Although I trust the American people will, in the end, understand."

Ironically, what the American people would not understand, when it was revealed, was that one of the men who had indirectly helped sell these terrorists their weapons was on the airplane, too. Events do come full circle. Life was indeed an absurd merry-go-round.

Everything was in order. His credentials, which were pinned to his lapel like the others who had gathered there, were inspected. Shell, although now his name was Martinez, slipped through security and into the press lounge like the other reporters. His credentials identified him as a reporter for *Cuba Today*, a Cuban-American newspaper based in southern Florida. How did these CIA guys do this? That was part of his job: to know how. He mixed in easily with the dozen or so TV reporters, producers, and camera operators who had begun to set their equipment up. Shell had been instructed to just gather data and report what he found when he found it.

Shell watched the press and listened to the buzz. The pool camera was now in place and on the monitor in the press lounge, so they all could see Flight 243 parked on the tarmac at the far side of the airport. The picture came on just after the two Special Agents had removed the steward's body, so the press was still in the dark about that incident.

"What's the latest?" Shell asked another reporter sitting nearby, who looked anxious to get more of the story than she had so far.

"Nothing, except that the Director will be down in about ten minutes to give us the usual 'No comment' or 'That's all we have at this time,'" she replied.

"You think the terrorists will want to talk to a reporter?"

"God, let's hope so. That could be just what I need to put me up there with the rest of them," she said in a calculating way. "But they'll want one of the biggies, so you and I don't stand a chance."

Her disappointment was obvious. Damn, Shell thought. What bloodsuckers. People were probably dying on that plane, and all she cared about was getting the story. He shook his head and thought about what would have happened if television had been invented during the American Civil War. Lincoln would have probably been thrown out of office, and there would be a United States of North America and a United Confederate States of North America. "Damn," he said to himself softly. After the bodies of loved ones started piling up on the tarmac below, most Americans would just want to end the ordeal and give the terrorists what they wanted, regardless of the repercussions. God, he hoped the FBI had its shit together. Shell knew how they'd screwed things up in the past . . . harsh criticism, coming from a CIA man.

Maxine Robinson wondered what they would do to her husband when Mahmud discovered him sitting in the wrong place. She prayed they wouldn't kill him on the spot. His military identification would almost certainly get him killed.

She started thinking about what she might do to protect her husband. She knew that the ideas that ran through her mind would probably get her killed, or critically injured at least. Could she do it? If no one else stood up and tried to stop this madness, she might. Maybe there was a chance that, once she made a move, others would follow. Hopefully, this suicide thing was just a bluff anyway. She wondered if anyone could really do such a thing? Wasn't suicide against the will of God — anyone's God? Didn't we all share the same God anyway? This whole terrorist concept of "in the name of God" confused her. Why would this God, our God, want someone — whether they were acting in his name or not — to terrorize people who were, by and large, good people?

Finally, Mahmud discovered Dion Robinson sitting alone in his original seat. At first he didn't know what to make of it. "What is your name?"

"Robinson," Dion said reluctantly.

"I have your identification?" Mahmud demanded.

Robinson thought it through. He now got a good long look at the man who was wrapped in wire and plastic and appeared to have detonating devices all about him. Robinson figured that Mahmud would eventually beat it out of him, so he decided to take his chances. "I gave you my wallet, but not my ID."

"Why would you do this?" Mahmud asked angrily.

"May I?" Robinson indicated that he had something to reveal from his pocket.

Mahmud nodded his approval, but with his gun ready.

Robinson took out his military identification card. He handed it over to Mahmud.

Mahmud took it and figured out what it was after a moment. Abruptly, he said, "Get up there," indicating where he wanted Robinson to sit.

Robinson moved up a couple of rows and sat across the aisle from Peter.

Mahmud continued his inspection. He didn't think much of Robinson at this time. He treated the Marine as just another American foe.

Maxine had peeked over the seatback in front of her to witness the event. She seemed relieved at this point, but how much longer would this ordeal continue?

In the cockpit, Amad was growing impatient, with no news from Havana tower control. His ire began to show in his face. Green and Luna kept to themselves. Green was thinking of scenarios about what could be waiting for them. He knew about the FBI's counter-terrorist intervention unit, and could only hope that it was on its way and that they would be able to infiltrate the aircraft without too many passenger casualties. If only he could alert Miami control about the number of terrorists onboard.

He certainly couldn't risk that with Amad watching his every move. So he continued to wait.

"Give me the headset," Amad instructed Green.

Green passed it to Amad. Amad spoke into it, "Havana, this is two-four-three."

A moment later Horacio replied, "Go ahead, two-four-three."

"We want to know what the Americans have said." Amad's voice sounded anxious.

In the tower, Horacio, surrounded by Pritchard and half a dozen other suits, read from a paper handed to him by Pritchard. He said, "We have received word from the Americans that they want to avert any more loss of life."

That was just what Amad had expected. Those Americans were so concerned about the loss of just one American life. He knew that the most important weapon, television, was doing its trick. However, Amad was not easily convinced. He had been trained to handle this mission in a certain way. He would proceed as planned, regardless of what they told him. Those Americans were very tricky and could be stalling, he thought. Amad listened.

Horacio continued, "The Americans are prepared to exchange the passengers for your prisoners. They are prepared to meet your demands and are working out the details at this time. Over?"

Amad said, "We understand. However, to underscore our position, we will proceed to execute an American on the hour, every hour, until we have received confirmation that our demands have been met."

Horacio looked at Pritchard, who looked withdrawn. Pritchard knew, as did everyone in that room, that what he was doing was all a set-up to buy time. Time they all wished would pass more quickly. Most of the people in the room were past middle age, and all would, in truth, rather have time to do just the opposite: slow life down. At this moment, however, time was the counter-enemy, the invisible force over which they had no control.

Pritchard said, "I wonder how they plan to make the confirmation. Maybe they have a radio or portable TV."

"Director Pritchard," said Roth, re-entering the room.

Pritchard turned on a dime and said, "Yes?"

"We have our agents at the Federal penitentiary in New York getting dressed up and made to look like the Army of Allah prisoners. It's being staged for the media now. The counterattack will occur well before any plane could have made it to Beirut."

"Good."

Amad's voice was heard squawking over the speaker. He continued, "Havana. Are we to understand that flights in and out of this location have been cancelled?"

Horacio responded, "That is correct, two-four-three. We have given this situation top priority."

"Why did he ask that question," thought Pritchard aloud, "unless they're planning a takeoff? Damn it!" Pritchard snapped at Roth, a man who was used to taking orders and providing a quick response. "Tell Berry we may need to accelerate this."

Another of Pritchard's assistants entered the room and informed him, "The pool camera's been fixed."

Pritchard nodded his understanding.

Onboard the plane, Amad entered the doorway of the cabin and called out to Mahmud in Arabic, "Number two now, Mr. Lincoln."

Mahmud understood what Amad meant, as did Peter. Once again, Mahmud interrupted his passenger rearrangement and stormed up the aisle, passing Peter along the way. Peter saw his feet pass by again.

Mahmud yelled at the terrified Mr. Collins, who was trying to be inconspicuous in his seat, "You — again!" Collins jumped up. His heart was racing, his mind was exploding with memories of his life. His life was, as they say, "passing before him," and he acted like a robot on automatic.

"And you!" Amad ordered Luna, who, though calmer than Collins, appeared sweaty and slightly trembling. "Drag that man's body to the door," Mahmud ordered Collins, pointing to the body of the passenger he had killed earlier. Luna opened the front door as he had before so the body could be thrown out.

In the tower, Pritchard, Horacio, and the others simultaneously raised their binoculars to watch the horror unfold as the plane's front door opened again.

In the press room, the video monitor, which was hooked up to the pool camera, continued to show the plane at its resting spot. The door remained closed. No activity could be seen, except the palm trees beyond the plane swaying in the gentle breeze. However, what Pritchard, Horacio, and the other suits observed was not what the press saw. Shell sat there, watching the pool camera. He grew restless.

From his position about a hundred yards from the opened door, Berry could see into the plane's interior with his high-powered, helmetlike surveillance headgear. His assistant lay in the grass right beside him. Berry could see Collins and Luna struggling to get the dead body through the door. He could also see Mahmud standing slightly off to the left side. Berry's surveillance gear did double-time photographing the event before him.

Collins didn't know what he was doing. He was thinking, but not about anything in particular. Images flashed through his mind so rapidly that he could not focus on what he was doing. He had the body by the feet, while Luna had it by the hands. Collins stared vaguely at the poor man's grotesque-looking face that just hung there like a drooping rubber plant. Half of the man's head was gone. His brain was missing.

Mahmud shouted, "Throw him out. Now!"

Luna looked at Collins, who did not look back at him. What they did was mechanical. The old one, two, three, heave-ho. It came so naturally, like throwing a sack of sand.

Luna did his part and let go at the precise moment when the momentum and gravitational force of the dead body passed the point of no return, but Collins didn't. He just didn't let go. The weight of the dead body pulled Collins right off his feet and out the door. Mahmud shoved past Luna after he realized what had happened. Luna was shocked and showed it. He felt nauseous and wanted to vomit, but couldn't.

Collins held onto the dead body all the way to the tarmac. The body hit hard, with a thump, and as soon as his plump frame crashed onto the tarmac a second later, Collins lapsed into unconsciousness. He actually bounced slightly from the impact and rolled under the plane. His right shoulder was crushed, his right arm broken, and most of the ribs on his right side had multiple breaks, but luckily, Collins' head bounced — albeit violently — off the dead man's left thigh.

From his position, Mahmud couldn't get a shot at Collins. The body was just under the plane, so he could only shoot at Collins' feet, which were slightly visible, but why waste the ammunition? Collins must have died from the fall. From what Mahmud could see, his body was lifeless.

Still, Amad was angry — not necessarily at Mahmud, but at the Americans. How dare this American take his own life and deny them the opportunity to kill him like the rest? That was one of their human shields down there now, Amad thought.

"Close the door!" Amad yelled to Luna. "Back to the plan," he screamed at Mahmud in Arabic.

Luna re-secured the door and returned to the cockpit, followed by Amad. Mahmud went back to his business of identifying the captives. As he walked down the aisle, he shouted militantly, "Another fool has died. You cannot escape the anger of Allah! I will kill you all for him!"

Peter watched again as Mahmud's feet passed by. Mahmud was extremely angry at the stunt Collins had pulled. He felt Collins had outsmarted him — although, in truth, he hadn't. Collins wasn't in control of his faculties when he fell. He didn't know what he was doing. An escape had never crossed his mind; it had just happened by accident.

It didn't matter. Mahmud was steaming. He stopped just past Peter's row, then pivoted abruptly. Mahmud thrust himself back to Peter's row and lunged towards Robinson, who sat across the aisle from Peter. Mahmud bent over and shoved his plastic pistol into Robinson's face. He shouted, "You are an American soldier?"

"No sir," replied Robinson.

This answer angered Mahmud even more. He pistol-whipped Robinson on the side of his head. Robinson barely flinched, which angered Mahmud still more. "What are you, then?"

"I'm an American Marine. My Geneva convention number is five, five, five, dash — "

"Shut up!" Mahmud cut Robinson off. "I do not need to know that. There is no Geneva convention here." Mahmud pressed the gun up against Robinson's head.

Robinson's heart beat faster and his palms got sweaty, but he didn't move an inch. This made Mahmud angrier.

Peter tilted his head slightly at an angle to see what was going on. Out of the corner of his eye he could see Mahmud's back to him. Peter studied his plastic explosives and corresponding wiring. He could see that Mahmud had multiple detonators attached to him. They appeared to be simple switches, connectors of some sort. Peter knew very little about explosives. What he did know, however, was that people who were trained the way Mahmud was, were serious about what they did. Once again, he reasoned that he couldn't take that gamble and get everyone killed, so he sat still.

When Robinson didn't respond, Mahmud slapped him upside the head with an open hand, just to anger him and test his resolve. It didn't work. Robinson took the slap and swallowed air. Mahmud screamed, "To the front — now!"

Though Robinson did as he was told, he wanted to strike back at Mahmud. He deliberated, but decided against what would be a rational move under normal circumstances. For these were certainly not normal circumstances; one act of counterstrike and he could receive a bullet between the eyes *and* be responsible for the destruction of everyone on the plane.

Peter watched helplessly as Robinson got out of his seat and shuffled toward first class. Mahmud had found a catch to toy with, like a cat with a mouse. He couldn't wait to inform Amad that he had found an American military man to torture and murder to further their cause. The others were only American taxpayers and, although they helped finance the government his group wanted to overthrow, an American military man represented the machine directly, a machine that helped prop up his own secular government.

From her seat, Maxine couldn't see what was going on. She had to stand up to see Dion walking to the front of the plane. Now she began to consider desperate measures. They had caught him. She knew they had already killed, and would not hesitate to kill Dion and delight in the fact that he was an official member of the U.S. government.

Pritchard finally had a remote hooked up to monitor Berry's operation. Pritchard and the rest of the officials in the tower watched as the two Special Agents went to retrieve the bodies that had fallen from the plane.

Berry radioed in, "Fox, this is Mole. We have seen two hostiles. They are wired and have what appears to be plastic explosives. Small handguns in possession. Will keep you posted. Snake one, this is Mole. Keep slithering in. Mole out." Berry's assistant, next to him in the grass, clicked away with a high-powered telescopic camera. He got about three dozen pictures of Mahmud and Amad. They watched as the two Special Agents on the tarmac approached the bodies.

The first agent almost vomited when he saw the corpse that was missing most of its head. Sometimes it didn't matter who you were or what your background was, the effect could be the same for anyone.

As the other agent got closer to Collins, he could see shallow breathing. "He's alive," he whispered. "Let's get 'em and get out of here."

They quickly lifted the dead passenger onto a small airport flatbed truck. As they did the same with Collins, they could hear broken bones grind and crunch. It didn't cause Collins any pain; he was out cold. No one knew what life-threatening dangers this maneuver would cause. One of those broken ribs could puncture Collins' lung, or rupture an artery. Under normal situations, a medical professional would immobilize the body before moving it. But this wasn't a normal situation, and the number one priority was getting the bodies back to the hangar, dead or alive. If Collins was lucky and survived, and if they could revive him soon, he might be of some use. Then again, he probably couldn't help, as the shock was likely to be too traumatizing.

The agents drove back to the hangar/morgue with their passengers.

In the press lounge, Shell and the reporters were beginning to get restless. On the monitor before them the pool camera hadn't revealed any of the events that had just happened.

The longer he sat there, the more suspicious Shell became. The FBI was taking too long to brief the press, and the plane looked too calm. He couldn't see any activity. Even from the camera's distance of three hundred yards, they should have been able to see shadows moving around the plane, he reasoned. Instead, all he could see moving was the same palm trees.

Shell got up and slipped out. He figured he had better try a different approach.

Harry paced in front of the television set as Joan returned from another trip to the bathroom. Katharina was on the phone again with John, who had nothing new to offer in the way of information. Only moments earlier Katharina had confirmed with the airline that Peter was indeed a passenger on Flight 243, but the airline couldn't provide any more information.

Katharina ended her conversation with John and hung up. Immediately the phone rang again. Joan answered it. "Hello . . . Maria."

Harry and Katharina both looked at Joan as she tried to calm Maria.

"Yes," continued Joan. "He is . . . They don't know . . .

Okay. I understand, you're at the restaurant, watching CNN . . . Yes. You want to speak with Harry? Okay." She handed the phone to her husband.

"Maria?" asked Harry. "Yes . . . I would have never thought it could come to something like this . . . You think so? I can't imagine them doing that though . . . Right . . . There's nothing we can do here but wait. John is calling here every thirty minutes . . . Okay, sure. Every hour . . . Okay." He hung up and turned to Joan and Katharina. "She thinks the government is just stalling and won't agree to whatever it is that the hijackers want. She thinks they may try to take the plane by force."

Just then the television anchor came on. "We are going live to a briefing by the Director of the FBI."

A moment later Pritchard appeared on screen in the small press room. "I have just a brief comment to make. I cannot and will not answer any questions at this time because of the sensitive nature of the situation." He paused and shuffled some papers. "InterAir Flight 243 from Cancun to Atlanta was hijacked early this morning over the Gulf of Mexico. The hijackers are representatives of a Middle Eastern group known as the Army of Allah. They are a radical religious group that advocates the overthrow of the secular government of Egypt. We are engaged in highly delicate negotiations with the terrorists onboard Flight 243, and I cannot discuss anything in more detail. We have about 125 passengers onboard, and their safety is our primary concern at this time. The pool camera will allow you to view the situation as it unfolds from there. Thank you." He turned and walked away, but not before several reporters shouted the usual ridiculous questions that could not be answered, lest the whole affair be jeopardized. Vultures, thought Pritchard. He had to get out of here before they ate him alive.

The anchor came back on and summarized what Pritchard had just said. Harry turned to Joan and Katharina and said, "I have to get to the funeral home."

"I'll go with you," said Joan. "You can stay and wait by the phone if you like," she said to Katharina.

"Yes. Yes, you go on ahead," answered Katharina.

"Here's the number. We shouldn't be an hour," Harry said.

Harry knew that he would have to hold off on Mother's funeral until this ordeal was over. He certainly couldn't bury their mother while Peter was being held at gunpoint somewhere over the Caribbean. Poor Mother, lying in a refrigerated compartment waiting for her boy to come home. Mother was gone, he reassured himself, but Peter wasn't — not yet, anyway. Mother's funeral could wait.

Kasim was in a rush. He walked clandestinely around the Cairo streets, watching his back at all times. He knew that Egyptian and American intelligence agencies were looking for him. However, he had been at this cat and mouse game for more than fifteen years, and he was very good at it.

It looked like there was a disastrous snag in the plan. It appeared to all, except those onboard Flight 243, that the plane was not in Havana. How could Amad have let that happen?

He turned and walked casually down a busy street, then slipped into a nondescript house. Inside, half a dozen men were gathered, all in their middle to late years. They had agreed, as part of their initial plan, to wait out the event in locations scattered around the city. But now, because something seemed to have gone wrong, they had gathered to talk this through.

They greeted one another and settled down as Kasim called them to order. An older man sat off to one side and listened. He was in his seventies, grey and frail. He still had a keen mind and waited for the debate to materialize. Everyone was dressed in native Egyptian attire: Gallabia gowns and Ghoutra headcloths.

"It seems that the Americans have stolen our hijacked aircraft," Kasim said in his native language, not realizing the absurdity of the statement. "The FBI said they are negotiating, but we can't trust them. I think the Americans will attempt to wear down Amad and Mahmud and take them out. We should inform the Americans that we will escalate this war all over the earth if they do not comply with our demands."

The older man spoke up. "I agree with Abdul. We must threaten the Americans, to let them know we mean business and we are a force not to be ignored. Allah is on our side. He will not let our brothers Amad and Mahmud fail. They will stick to their plan and blow up the plane if there is interference. The Americans should stall long enough for Amad and Mahmud to execute Phase Two of the plan. The Americans are predictable. A single human life to them is important. They should give over our brothers, however. The American people won't stand for Americans being killed for something they don't understand. The government is accountable to the people. The American president cannot risk the death of all those Americans. Our cause is just, and larger than one life, two lives, or a hundred and fifty. Proceed." He waved his hand at Kasim and the rest, got up from his chair, and slowly left the room. His aging and tired body moved along with the aid of an assistant and a cane.

"Then it is done. We cannot control the events on the plane, but we will exact the total wrath of Allah upon them and unleash all at our disposal if they prevent us from succeeding. I think we should consider moving up our date for the Mother of All Battles. Praise Allah," yelled Kasim. He was immediately echoed by the others.

Amad stood at the door while Mahmud briefed him about Robinson. Green and Luna could hear them talking, but they couldn't understand Arabic.

Elatedly, Amad told Mahmud, "I'll inform the Americans. Perhaps we can hit home with the American public. We could execute this Marine in the doorway on camera. That might speed up the release of our prisoners. You keep a close watch on him."

Mahmud nodded and grunted his agreement. Amad went back into the cockpit to further antagonize the Americans. He snatched the headset away from Green and spoke to the tower. "This is two-four-three."

"Go ahead, two-four-three," said Horacio, quick on the trigger.

"We have an American Marine onboard, and we intend to torture him to death and hang him from the door of the aircraft."

In the tower, Pritchard gave a distressed look to Horacio.

"Do you have any additional information from the Americans regarding the release of our prisoners?" asked Amad.

There was a slight pause, then Horacio answered, "Yes, we do, Flight 243. We have just received word that the prisoners you want are being prepared for their release. They should be airborne within the hour."

In the cockpit, Amad listened intently. In a way, he believed Horacio, yet part of him didn't. He believed he was in Havana — he had no reason to suspect otherwise.

Horacio sounded Cuban. There had been no attempt to pressure Amad.

Unbeknownst to him, Amad was being watched through the cockpit windows by a squad from Berry's unit with high-powered telescopic binoculars. Photographic equipment recorded the activity.

The cockpit images were being viewed in the tower by Pritchard and his staffers, seated near Horacio.

"That's it, sir," reported a technician sitting next to Pritchard with a headset on, listening to sounds from within the airplane. "Only two hostiles." The field unit had set up highly sensitive electronic recording devices with directional microphones. Pritchard's electronic technician now listened to the voices of Mahmud and Amad, and recorded Mahmud's footsteps as he walked up and down the aisle. The technician continued, "We're not picking up any other movement except the two we have confirmed."

"Okay. We'll have their exact whereabouts pinpointed as we go in. Let's go, now," Pritchard said, then spoke into the microphone to Berry. "Mole, this is Fox."

"Fox, this is Mole, over."

"Proceed and accelerate." Pritchard's voice had a sense of urgency.

"This is Mole. I copy. Proceed, over."

"Affirmative. Be advised, we confirm only two hostiles, over."

"I copy, two hostiles. I read their positions and have them locked in, over."

"Roger. Fox out."

Pritchard and the tower crew could see the men crawling slowly up the runway toward the tail cone of the airplane. They could hear Berry give the final order to his unit. "Snake, this is Mole."

A man answered, "Mole, Snake. Over."

"Proceed and accelerate."

The man had already heard the order given by the Director, but it made it official when Berry called it in. That was proper chain of command. The man answered, "Roger, Snake proceeding."

"You copy, two hostiles? Over."

"Roger, two hostiles, Snake, out." Snake's unit consisted of two men, both in their late twenties and ex-Special Forces, who now worked for the Bureau and were good at what they did. They moved slower than turtles. Each wore a small earphone, and a microphone in front of their mouth — like a telephone operator — so they could communicate with Berry and Pritchard.

Pritchard explained the procedure to Horacio and the others as they watched Berry and his men move in. He said softly, "They'll reach the tail cone within a few minutes and then be under the belly of the plane. Shortly thereafter, some will climb up through the front wheel well, the others up through the baggage hold. The whole operation will be slow going at first. They will methodically dismantle the obstacles in their paths — namely, parts of the wheel well and the fuselage — in order to get in. At the last moment, they will have to rely on the element of surprise and blast their way in. We'll be able to pinpoint the exact location of the two hostiles and inform the unit. They should be able to terminate the hostiles as they blast their way through. The final blast-through should last only a few seconds. Hopefully, as our team enters, the two hostiles will be in the process of dying." Pritchard looked down at Horacio, whose face expressed the same anxiety Pritchard was feeling.

7

S he had the day off and was not in tune with the world at large. After awakening she had made breakfast for herself, and was now reading the morning paper, *her* paper, the *Washington Sun*. She had worked for the paper for fifteen years, and was the best investigative journalist in the business. Ann Howard got any story she wanted.

Howard was certainly a Washington insider, having investigated some of the all-time biggest political stories during her tenure. She had written extensively about Iran-Contra, Whitewater, the Abrams CIA case, Pentagon procurement fraud, high-profile political scandals, and other stories that exposed government waste, mistrust, and abuse. She took on human interest stories that involved ordinary people caught up in extraordinary events. Many of those who became involved in her stories ended up bitterly resenting her attitude that the public's right to know and freedom of the press took precedent over an individual's right to privacy.

Her phone rang as she read the *Sun* and sipped her coffee. "Howard," she answered. "No, I haven't . . . You're kidding . . . In Miami . . . Who? . . . I'll be there in thirty minutes." She hung up the phone and sprang into action.

Ann was in her mid-forties, slender, and had hair the color of the sun. An attractive woman, men often found her intimidating because of her intelligence.

Well, as it turned out, this was her story, literally. She had interviewed one of the Army of Allah's prisoners in the federal penitentiary located in upstate New York just a year ago. Much of her article had focused on how the prisoner felt about his treatment during the trial, and subsequent claims of mistreatment in prison. Only during her introduction, in passing, had Ann referred to the man's crime: the cold-blooded murder of several American citizens in a well-publicized bombing on American soil. Needless to say, the story upset the families of the victims. But controversy sells, and her coverage of the story had made news on a national level. Though many Americans were outraged, the marketplace ruled, and the *Sun's* editors and owner counted their sales.

Shell (his name tag now read Estevez) made his way through the hangar with the other airport workers. He was dressed in ground crew garb, down to the grease, and had the necessary identification. Shell was carrying some tools and plastic tarpaulins. He blended in with the roughly thirty officials, including FBI agents, airport workers, and crew members from the medical examiner's office, who were standing around in a sloppy circle on the hangar floor. Shell stood at the back of the circle and watched as a medical technician attended to Collins, the barely breathing passenger of Flight 243. They were immobilizing his broken bones. The two other casualties — deceased, of course — were also being examined. Just as Shell had figured, the pool camera was showing the same video picture over and over again. Ingenious, he thought. How long before the media figured it out and went ballistic?

The deception was perfectly understandable, though. Shell would later discover that the government had no intention of releasing any convicted terrorists.

Peter had been in worse situations. Once, during a raid into Laos to destroy some Vietcong middle management, he had to lie low in the bush, not moving for almost a whole day while the enemy walked about him and his small assassination squad. If you had to urinate, you just did it. The jungle smelled strong enough already, so the smell of human urine didn't bother him or alert anyone else. Another time, while providing service to his country in much the same manner, he lay still while a large brown snake — they all looked the same to him — slithered across his legs. It had to be eight or ten feet, he thought at the time, because it took forever to go on its way. Nevertheless, he did as he was taught: just lie there, don't move, and it won't bother you, because snakes are more afraid of you than you are of them — or so they said!

Nevertheless, Peter was rather uncomfortable. If he was getting restless, those around him must be ready to jump for it like Mr. Collins had. Come to think of it, they weren't even in the air, and everyone was getting sick.

Mahmud found a small transistor radio that had been stowed in the phony food service cart, grabbed it, and stormed back up the aisle. Nobody dared move. Again Peter watched Mahmud's feet pass. Mahmud approached Amad, handed him the radio, and scurried back down the aisle.

Amad turned the radio on. He tuned in a station blasting American rock and roll music. Another of the Great Satan's tools, he thought. He fidgeted with the dial and found another American music station. Amad figured that, since Cuba was so close to Florida, the poor Cubans must get a lot of American radio stations. Next he found a

station playing Cuban music, although unknown to
Amad, it was a Cuban-American station transmitting out
of Miami. Finally, he tuned in a Miami-based news
station that wasn't talking about the hijacking. Amad
decided to leave the radio on this station in hopes that he
would soon hear mention of the story in which he was a
principal player.

Pritchard and his crew picked up the radio signal on
their electronic eavesdropping equipment. They feared
that the hijackers onboard would soon discover what was
really happening. "Can you jam that?" asked Pritchard.

"Give me a few seconds," said the electronics specialist,
as he struggled with his dials and switches.

"Buy me just a little more time," Pritchard thought out
loud. "Just a little more time." Pritchard always got his
man. In more than twenty-five years of law-related en-
forcement, he had always cracked the case and put the
lawbreaker behind bars. Whether they stayed there or not
was not his fault. Some criminals had even been captured
two and three times by Pritchard.

In the cockpit, Amad continued to listen to the
American radio station. Finally, the anchor came on and
identified the radio station. Sure enough, it was based in
Miami. No, they didn't block those American radio stations
anymore, thought Amad.

The anchor said, "Next up, more on the breaking story
of hijacked InterAir Flight 243. This is Stefani Browner."
The station went to commercial.

More than the usual amount of perspiration began to
run down Green's face. His heartbeat quickened. He knew
what he had heard, but didn't know what he should do. A
lousy little transistor radio, he thought. The American
media was, in part, helping to deliver their fate. What

could he do except wait it out like the rest? He glanced over at his worried copilot and held his breath.

The radio station finished its commercial, and the anchor returned to say, "For those of you who have just joined us, we will now bring you up to date on what we know so far of InterAir Flight 243, hijacked from Cancun to Atlanta earlier this morning. A flight carrying more than 125 passengers has been hijacked by a Middle Eastern group calling itself the Army of Allah. Their demands have not yet been made public."

Amad became a little agitated by the report.

"Atlanta control reports that the flight was headed for Havana, Cuba, but the Cuban government will not confirm that the plane is there. We are now going live to our man, Troy Cannon, who is out at Miami's —" The radio fizzled out at that point. Amad furiously attempted to re-tune the station, but got static.

Simultaneously, Green noticed that his flight instruments began to dance around in their dials. Luna also noticed the instruments and felt a slight reprieve.

Amad failed to regain the station's signal, or any radio station for that matter. He threw the radio onto the floor and grabbed the headset. He spoke into it angrily, "Havana, what is going on? We demand to know the status of our situation!"

A moment elapsed before the line was clear.

Horacio answered, "Two-four-three, this is Havana. What do you mean? We do not understand, over." As he said this, Amad's transistor radio began to squelch.

Amad turned to look at his transistor and said to Horacio, "We want to know what is happening with our political prisoners."

"We have told you that they should be airborne within minutes, over."

Again, Amad's radio was receiving the Miami station, although he couldn't distinguish what was being said. He threw the headset down and lunged for the radio.

Instantly, watching on screen in the tower, the electronics specialist scrambled to jam the signal again. Pritchard and the others could see Amad's aggravated reaction on the video monitor in front of them.

In the cockpit, a second after Amad tried to tune the station, it turned to static again. This infuriated him more. He again tried to re-tune it, to no avail. Once again Amad threw the radio to the floor, then stormed out of the cockpit and summoned Mahmud. "We are leaving ahead of schedule. I don't trust the situation," he said in Arabic.

Mahmud was standing two rows behind Peter, who understood what Amad had just said. Leaving? To go where? Peter wondered.

Suddenly, Amad jumped at Robinson, who was sitting in the front row of coach, and kicked him in the head with the heel of his shoe. Robinson took it hard and crumbled onto the floor. Clearly, Amad was taking his frustration out on Robinson.

Mahmud rushed forward; again, Peter saw his feet pass by. Damn it. If only he could do something, like trip him, he thought. Mahmud reached the front of the plane and asked Amad, "What is wrong?"

"The radio is not working. It did at first, but now there's only static."

"Let me try," Mahmud said, entering the cabin and picking the radio up. Sure enough, it was all static. This angered Mahmud as well. He threw it down and conferred with Amad.

"We have no choice but to go early," said Amad.

"Do you suspect that the Americans are not doing as we have ordered?" asked Mahmud.

"Something is not as it should be."

"We should go then."

"Yes, we shall go. You throw out the other two bodies and get secured. I'll get us under way."

Mahmud trudged down the aisle again. Peter was getting tired of watching Mahmud go up and down. It only added to his anxiety.

Amad re-entered the cockpit with an urgent sense of mission about him. Up until now he had seemed in complete control; now he appeared rushed and nervous.

Robinson struggled to get back into his seat. He was still dazed and in pain. The young man sitting next to him helped him into his seat.

In the cockpit, Amad ordered Green, "Prepare to take off. We will inform you of our destination once we are in the air."

Damn, Green thought to himself. He was so sure that their best chance was still here, on the ground in Miami. He had to try. "It's not that simple. There are preflight checks, walkarounds, and — "

"None of that matters," shouted Amad. "You will start up the engines and be ready to go in five minutes, or I will kill your copilot right here in front of you, and then your passengers one by one. Now, let's go!"

Green looked down in compliance. "All right," he nodded, speaking in a way so as not to ignite Amad.

Just like the Americans, thought Amad. They'd always capitulate to save a few worthless pagan lives.

Ann Howard entered the conference room. Already present and discussing the main event of the day was her senior editor, Bob Hearn, and a handful of assistant editors. There appeared to be no real order to the discussion, mainly because the star reporter hadn't arrived yet.

Hearn called the room to order. "Okay, let's get this sorted out." Everyone settled down. Ann Howard stood at one end of the table, like a general in front of her troops.

Hearn continued, "It's an addendum to your story, Ann. Do you want it?"

"I'll cover the story from the Miami end. I booked a flight to Tampa with a connection to Fort Lauderdale."

Some of the other staff reporters thought Howard was just a little too sure of herself at times. But, as usual, Hearn knew she would want the action, and because of her experience and what she had done for this paper, she deserved it.

"Great," Hearn concurred. "Keep me apprised." He ordered a young editor, "Get all the background on this Army of Allah. Dig up all the old stories. Let's get to work."

Howard departed, followed by Hearn. She quickly gathered some things from her office and darted out of the building, bound for her story.

Peter watched Mahmud drag a dead stewardess past him. He was disgusted by what he saw, and those others who dared to peek felt nauseated. Mahmud and Amad were taking no more chances that someone else might jump from the plane. They figured they needed every warm body they had for bargaining leverage. Mahmud left the body by the door and went to retrieve the last corpse.

Pritchard called Berry. "Mole, this is Fox."

"Fox, this is Mole."

"They're going to try and take off. You must expedite this at once. Go in now!"

"That'll compromise our element of surprise. We'd risk too many casualties."

"Don't let that plane get off the ground. Can you get a scope on them?"

Berry said in a hurried fashion, "Two, can you get a scope on the one in the cockpit?"

A male voice responded, "Affirmative, Mole. This is Two. I've had him sighted several times. If he stands still for two seconds, I can take him out. Over."

"Three, how about from your angle? Can you see hostile number two?" asked Berry.

Another male voice answered, "Mole, this is Three. I can't get a clear fix on him. He moves up and down the aisle too fast. The timing is too close to call."

"Fox, you copy?" asked Berry.

"I copy," answered Pritchard. "Damn it."

Shell watched as they stabilized Collins, who was still out cold. Perhaps his panic would pay off, although he might never fully recover. He might be uncomfortable for the rest of his life, if not paralyzed. Nevertheless, he would live, which might not be true for the other passengers still on the plane.

The coroner explained, "This one's been dead for a couple of hours. Same for the other one."

There wasn't much information to be gathered here, thought Shell. The steward, he figured, was killed in the takeover, and perhaps the passenger panicked or attempted to jump one of the hijackers. Beyond that, Shell thought he had better snoop elsewhere.

The FBI agent standing there said to the coroner, "Do what you have to do. Let's keep this area clear for any others who may come our way, God forbid." The agent gave the coroner a concerned glance and walked off. Shell gathered up his tools and disappeared out a side door.

Ann Howard was airborne and en route to Florida. She was scanning articles her paper had run on the Army of Allah, many written by herself. She was thinking about the prisoners the federal government was holding. She had already read a copy of Pritchard's statement that had come in over the wire, and wondered what he planned to do. Could they actually negotiate with these people and release the prisoners? She would know soon enough, once one of their reporters got to the prison and monitored it from that end.

Information was still sketchy from Miami. No one was even confirming that InterAir Flight 243 was on the ground there. The Cubans were maintaining that the flight was not on their soil, nor had it even contacted them. Major airline travel into the Miami area was a mess: either cancelled or diverted. Everyone who was anyone could figure it out, so why wouldn't the government just acknowledge it? Basically, she reasoned, the government was denying the passengers' loved ones the right to know what was going on.

Pritchard was at the back of the tower room on the phone with the Attorney General when Roth said, "Sir, they're opening the door."

Pritchard swiveled around to watch the monitor, but that was like watching it secondhand, so he lifted his binoculars to his face while balancing the phone against his shoulder. "Holy Christ," he mumbled. "I think they're making a run for it."

Mahmud dragged the final body over to the door and half dumped, half pushed it out. It just wouldn't fall by itself, so he had to shove it with his foot, using all the power he had. Amad guarded him near the cockpit door.

The body fell out onto the tarmac with its own definitive thud.

Mahmud stepped back and pressed his gun up against Robinson's head. "Move," he shouted. Robinson was slow to get up, so Mahmud kicked him in the abdomen. Robinson buckled slightly as Mahmud forced him up onto his feet. Robinson grimaced in pain from the blow. Mahmud forced Robinson to stand at the open door as he stood behind him with the gun against the back of Robinson's head.

Amad reached in, grabbed the headset from Green, and spoke into it. "Show the Americans this Marine. Tell them we will throw him from the aircraft at twenty thousand feet, alive." He threw the headset down. "Close the door," he said to the copilot. Amad guarded Luna, who closed the door.

Mahmud stepped aside and forced Robinson down onto the floor where he kicked him hard, again in the stomach.

Peter and all the other passengers near the front of the plane could hear the impact of Mahmud's foot as it came into contact with Robinson's stomach. They could hear the air escape from Robinson's lungs.

Once the door was secure, Amad followed Luna into the cockpit and shouted at Green, "Get it under way. Now!"

Green and Luna hurriedly completed a few preflight checks. Both knew that they could get airborne and fly with no real problem. Of course, they were so accustomed to doing all their walkarounds and other checks that they would have felt more secure doing them, but in this situation there was clearly no choice. Green fired up the engines.

Berry could see Unit Three at the tail cone of the aircraft. "Three, move in now. Get in there!" He watched as the two men made their way under the belly of the plane. One man from the unit reached the front wheel well, while the other stayed low on the ground directly under the belly. Five other two-man units rushed up to the tail cone of the aircraft from the runway perimeter. They took up positions near the tail cone and waited to move in.

Suddenly, the plane began to move forward slowly and turned to the left.

"What are you doing, two-four-three?" asked Horacio, with Pritchard bearing down on him like he was going to grab the microphone himself. There was no answer. "I ask again, two-four-three, what are you doing?"

The plane was almost turned around on the tarmac facing in the opposite direction.

One agent under the plane's belly moved with the plane, while the other was precariously close to being chewed up by the front strut. The others stayed behind the tail cone and remained out of sight from anyone on-board the plane.

Green said, "We are departing. Clear the airspace. We will contact you when airborne. Over."

"You are not clear for takeoff," said Horacio. "I repeat, you are not clear."

"Then clear us," demanded Green. "We are taking off whether clear or not."

Amad grabbed the headset from Green and spoke into it. "I do not like the situation here any longer."

Pritchard slammed his fist down on the counter. "Jesus," he slurred.

The plane completed its turnaround. Green pressed switches and checked some gauges. Amad watched him and Luna like a hawk.

"I must instruct the passengers," Green said to Amad.

Amad nodded his approval.

"This is your captain speaking." Green's voice broke the stillness that had pervaded the whole aircraft. "Please fasten your seat belts. We have been instructed to take off immediately. Our destination is not known at this time."

Many passengers began expressing more fear, if that was possible. Peter didn't know what to think. Had something gone wrong, and these clowns now wanted the plane airborne to blow it up? No, that didn't make much sense. They could blow it up on the ground and ensure the destruction they had planned.

Pritchard spoke into the phone in a defeated tone. "I'll let you know as soon as we know." He hung up. Frustration was eating at him. He radioed Berry, "Mole, this is Fox."

"Go ahead, Fox," answered Berry.

"Let it go. Abort the mission. Repeat, abort it."

"I copy, abort?"

"Roger. Pull everyone back. Where's the lead man?"

"He's already in place."

"Pull him out also."

"I copy, pull him out. Three, this is Mole. Did you copy that?"

"Mole, this is Three. We copy," said the man in the front wheel well, who immediately dropped to the ground. He let the plane pass over him.

Pritchard and the others in the tower raised their binoculars and watched as Flight 243 picked up speed. "Let's only hope that your unit can be redeployed and has a second shot. God only knows where this bird will land," Pritchard said to Berry. He mumbled to Roth, "Get me Key West."

Roth punched some numbers into the phone and handed it to his boss. Pritchard spoke into the mouthpiece a second later. "General Banks, Pritchard. Get that tail. Follow that plane. I'm passing you off to a tower official who'll give you the info." He handed the phone to Horacio, who spoke to the Air Force General at Key West.

"Alert the Coast Guard," said Pritchard to Roth. "Tell them to stand by. I want to know what's in the area."

Green put the throttle down and sent Flight 243 racing down the runway. If they had anything going for them, it was that they truly did have clearance. Horacio was bluffing. There wasn't another flight in the area — could anyone believe this was Miami? They closed the airport only during hurricanes. Anyhow, they lifted off with no difficulty. They had enough fuel to hop around the Caribbean. Beyond that, they would need more.

Standing outside the hangar with the other airport officials and crew members, Shell watched the plane lift off and sail away into the sky. Where did they think they were going? It was anyone's guess. Nothing more could be done at this end. Shell slipped away.

In the press room the static image of Flight 243 on the video monitor flipped, then faded to black. The reporters sensed that things were not right and began to file out of the room. They were annoyed that they hadn't gotten the scoop. This waiting game could not go on. They would be given information or, by God, they'd file lawsuits!

Onboard her flight, she picked up the phone on the seatback in front of her as she read through her file. "Bob? This is Ann . . . When? . . . Okay. I'll call you from the airport." Howard wondered for a moment where Flight 243 could be heading. She hadn't a clue, but would most certainly be headed that way when she found out.

Sluggishly, Harry entered the house just as Joan and Katharina motioned to him to hurry. He took off his jacket and stood by Joan, who was still glued to the television.

The same anchor told the Murrays and the world, "There seems to be some confusion as to what is happening in Miami. We are getting unconfirmed reports that Flight 243 has taken off. This information comes from our Miami affiliate, even though we never received official confirmation that Flight 243 was in Miami at all. We are standing by to go live to WMIA. We are also getting some reports that one, and possibly two passengers have been shot and thrown from the plane. Of course, we have not seen that happen since receiving the live picture of InterAir Flight 243."

"What do you think?" asked Harry.

"That live picture didn't have any life," said Katharina, "It seemed, in a way, unreal."

"You mean they didn't show it take off?"

"No. The screen went blank almost ten minutes ago. They couldn't tell us anything new, until now," said Joan.

Kasim scurried along the crowded Cairo street. He was praying that Amad and Mahmud could still pull it off. They had been trained well, he reassured himself, and they knew all of the contingency plans. He was sure they would follow the plan and move at the preselected time. However, it was now clear that they were on American soil, and that the Americans were definitely up to something. They were not expected to move for over two more hours. He hadn't seen the latest update from CNN, but would shortly.

He approached a storefront where, ironically, the proprietors sold cheap souvenirs to foreign tourists, many of whom were American. Without knowing it, Americans were indirectly financing and supporting terrorists.

Kasim sauntered into the shop and went directly to the back room to find twenty-three of his young soldiers waiting for him. The television showed CNN in the background.

A man in his mid-twenties informed Kasim, "They have departed."

"Then they must suspect," said Kasim. He settled everyone down. "We will hit, and hit hard, with everything at our disposal. The targets will be chosen from our primary list. Thereafter, we will move ahead with our contingency plan, the Mother of All Attacks, albeit a year in advance. We will accelerate all logistics. You will await your orders at your usual locations. At this time there is nothing further. Understood?"

Everyone nodded in agreement. "Go," said Kasim. The group dispersed.

Peter watched Mahmud make his way back up the aisle just after takeoff. Mahmud began shouting at Robinson and kicking him repeatedly in the abdomen. Robinson wanted to fight back, but knew that if he did, he would probably be shot immediately.

Maxine stood up to see what the commotion was all about, fearing the worst. It took only a split second for her to confirm that it was her husband being beaten mercilessly. She screamed, "No!" and fell over the woman sitting beside her. Another woman, sitting on her other side, grabbed her by the arm and tried to stop her. The woman said, "They'll kill you too."

"My husband needs me. I must help him."

"There is nothing you can do," the woman said.

"I must try," protested Maxine, breaking the woman's grip. Maxine got to her feet and started moving up the aisle towards her husband and the relentlessly brutal Mahmud.

Mahmud stopped kicking Robinson when he heard Maxine pleading. Abruptly, he turned and saw her approaching.

Tears streaming down her cheeks, Marine begged, "Please stop! My husband never hurt anyone. Please!"

At first Mahmud couldn't believe that this stupid woman would try such a stunt.

Amad stepped out of the cabin and stood by the door to watch.

Peter watched Maxine's feet pass by and thought, this is one brave woman. She will probably get herself killed on account of it, but in situations like this, what did it matter when your loved one was being brutalized?

Mahmud raised his gun in the direction of Maxine. He took aim. Robinson, on the floor, saw what was happening and struggled to get up, but collapsed from the agony of his battered stomach.

Suddenly, a man shouted, "This is not what Allah wants!" He stood up from where he was sitting, just to the right of Maxine. He stepped into the aisle in front of Maxine to block her path. She didn't know what to make of this.

Mahmud hesitated on the trigger and looked over at Amad, who was curious about the event. Amad stepped forward, slowly pushed Mahmud's gun down, and asked, "Who are you?"

"I am Mohammed Al Raman," replied the man. "I am a Muslim." The man was fifty years old and dressed in a suit and tie.

"You are an American," countered Amad.

"I am. But I am also an authority on Islam. I'm a cleric."

"This is not possible."

"This is not sanctioned by the Qur'an or by Allah. This is wrong." He waved his left arm, indicating the entire plane and the hijacking.

Amad had had enough. He wasn't about to stand here in the middle of his operation and debate with this misguided man. However, he had to get in a lick. "You cannot be an American and a Muslim. You are therefore a traitor to Allah."

"You are mistaken and misled. You are seeking to murder innocent people in the name of Allah. That is blasphemy against his good name."

Amad stepped closer. He was getting angry with this distraction. His voice was strained. "You do not know what you are talking about, foolish old man. I tell you now to sit down."

"Can't you see that this is wrong? This is not what is written."

Amad walked up to the man and pistol-whipped him across the head. The man fell backwards onto Maxine, and they both crashed to the floor. They landed near Peter. He wanted to jump up and help, but he restrained himself. He buried his head, not only because he was instructed to do so, but in shame.

"Well, you are wrong, clergyman!" said Amad, fuming. Angrily, he turned to Mahmud, who stood there in disbelief. "Get them back to their seats, and get on with your task." Amad returned to the cockpit and slammed the door.

Mahmud lunged towards Maxine and the Islamic cleric who was bleeding slightly from his forehead. "On your feet!" he shouted to them.

Maxine began to stir. The cleric moved slowly at first, then assisted Maxine.

Peter listened helplessly.

An Air Force reconnaissance aircraft caught up to Flight 243 almost immediately after takeoff from south Florida. Captain Ron Waith took up position just above the aircraft and watched. He radioed in and waited.

Pritchard, his assistants, Roth, Horacio, and the other officials all watched the radar screens and listened to the radio for the hijackers' next move.

Pritchard was distraught at not getting the bastards, here, on his turf. No matter — he would use the all-powerful and far-reaching arm of the Federal Bureau of Investigation around the world and catch those who were responsible. They knew the group, and they would go after them, come hell or high water. This group, at least, was based in a friendly country, not like the fugitives in Libya.

Berry and his team were now in the hangar, handling the debriefing. Berry was upset that his men didn't have the opportunity to prove themselves. They were all disappointed at this turn of events, just when they were so close to making their move. In any event, they were placed on standby, awaiting their next orders. Berry was told in effect to wait and see where Flight 243 landed.

In the cockpit, Green asked Amad, "We need a heading so we don't cross into other flight paths."

Amad instructed him, "You will fly to Port-au-Prince."

Green looked at Luna and said, "Take the stick." Green took out his flight book and studied it. Luna took the controls. Amad watched them carefully.

As Green plotted a course to Haiti, he realized his options were limited. There was not much else to choose from, and trying the same stunt twice might not work, so he figured he had better fly to Haiti and not take the chance. Hopefully, they would refuel and fly to another

location after a few hours on the ground there, if this ordeal
was not concluded by then. He wrote down some headings
on his notepaper and checked the instruments. Finally, he
took the controls back from Luna. Green forced the plane
to bank around, since they had been flying over the Atlantic in no particular direction. He banked it around hard,
pointing it back towards the Bahamas. Amad studied
Green's moves from over his shoulder.

Captain Waith pulled up and away slightly to allow
Flight 243 room to turn. He banked into the same direction as the plane just below him. Then he radioed what he
was seeing to Key West, even though they were following
the action closely with their state-of-the-art technology.

Ann Howard's flight landed in Tampa minutes later.
She was up and out of her seat before the plane had come
to a complete stop. As soon as the door was opened, she
rushed through the tunnel. At the nearest pay phone she
dialed Bob Hearn at the paper.
"Bob? Ann. Nothing? Okay ... I'm on a hop to West
Palm Beach. I'll call you when I'm airborne." She hung up
and set off down the concourse.

Mahmud forced the pleading Maxine back to her seat.
Again, he thought about shooting her, but refrained because they needed every passenger for leverage. He shoved
her along, and at one point slapped her across the back of
the head because she wasn't moving fast enough.
Peter's adrenaline began to surge at the thoughts racing
through his mind. He had to do it — do something! — but
he was uncertain if he could anymore. It had been more
than twenty years since he had pulled a stunt like this one.
The time for indecision was over. If not him, then who? If

not now, when? He tentatively gave himself the go. Slowly, he unbuckled his seat belt and let it lie loosely in his lap. The two men sitting next to him didn't know what to make of this move.

The veins in Peter's neck were pulsating. He tried to maintain a steady breathing rate. At some point the window of opportunity had to open, and he needed to be ready to identify it and act. There could be no thought at that point. Peter couldn't let this insanity go on any longer, not if he saw that opportunity. Clearly, whatever was supposed to have happened back there on the ground hadn't.

Dion Robinson wanted to get back to his wife, but was reassured and attended to by another passenger next to him. He was in too much pain to do much of anything, and he realized that. Still, he wanted to try, but his seatmate held him back.

Mahmud began walking up the aisle again, only now he was losing it. He had let his mind wander slightly, and lowered his gun and his head as he walked. The words of the cleric echoed in his mind. He must try to block those thoughts; certainly they were planted there by the evil one for the express purpose of helping to destroy this mission!

Mahmud's feet were alongside Peter in the aisle now. Peter raised his head and sat up slowly in his seat, his back wrenching in pain from being in the same position so long.

Mahmud was just past Peter. Peter's adrenaline was now exploding. Before Mahmud could react, Peter stood up in the aisle and had his left arm around Mahmud's neck and his right hand around Mahmud's forehead. Without hesitating, and with precision and remarkable force, Peter snapped Mahmud's head to one side, breaking his neck. A distinct cracking sound could be heard for rows around. Peter performed as naturally and smoothly as if he were dancing with an old friend.

He placed Mahmud's body in the seat where he had been sitting, then took Mahmud's gun and placed it into the small of his back between his belt and shirt.

The two male passengers who had been sitting next to Peter kept quiet. Though they knew what was happening, they welcomed their new seat partner without protest.

Quickly, Peter walked up a few rows and instructed a male passenger, "Get to the rear of the plane, now." Without hesitating, the man did as he was told. Peter took his aisle seat, three rows behind first class. He bent over in his seat in the same position as before, his back protesting in pain. He extracted the pistol from the small of his back, checked it out, then concealed the weapon in his lap. He waited in this position.

Kasim was enraged as he paced around the room in a fury. He hated the American government and Western culture. How dare the American government keep its people in the dark! He thought they had the right to know. Wasn't it against their laws not to inform their people? Of course, it angered him more than it angered any particular American citizen at this time, except those who had loved ones onboard the plane.

His army was now mobilizing and awaiting the word. He would give that word as soon as he knew the outcome from the West Indies.

Kasim was an only son. Just before his father had died, he had married Kasim's older sister off to a local merchant. Kasim hadn't had much to do with her or her family since.

Kasim's father had died in the Six-Day War against Israel. His mother was still alive and lived with her sister's family in Cairo. Kasim sent her money, although she never knew what he did for a living. He told her he worked for God, and she asked no questions.

Kasim's family had been very poor. His parents had scratched out a living as street merchants. At the age of nine, Kasim was forced to begin working the streets in Giza, selling trinkets to tourists, to help support the family. Dreaming of a better life, he was a ripe candidate for induction into the Army of Allah. Poor and disillusioned, he felt owed by "the powers that be." He was recruited into the Army of Allah when he was nineteen. He had seen his share of "ugly Americans" and had come to resent them, thinking they all were wealthy and lived off the blood, sweat, and tears of the Third World — even though Americans accounted for only a small part of the tourist business in Egypt. Nevertheless, he soon began to raise money for the Army of Allah by setting up and running street franchises that in turn sold to foreigners.

In the beginning, the Army of Allah was strictly religious in nature. Out to accumulate wealth, they recruited and preached until they saw the revolution in Iran and the subsequent spread of fundamentalism. Then they aggressively sought out contacts with others throughout the world who shared in their struggle. Recently, they had begun to actively seek the overthrow of their own secular government, which they believed was indirectly a puppet of America and Israel. They concluded that Israel controlled America and, ultimately, them. In addition, the accord that Sadat signed with Israel, mediated by the United States, was the impetus that set that control in motion. Sadat was killed because he was thought to be a traitorous enslaver who capitulated to the enemy. That was what had put Kasim and the Army of Allah in motion.

Since then, they had been planning, preparing, and accumulating funds to hit the Egyptian and American governments. Only recently had they begun to get serious in their fight against the United States. Being partly funded, supplied, housed, trained, and guided by other Middle Eastern groups and governments, the Army of Allah had begun to get more involved. They were beginning to identify and carry out acts against American interests, both international and domestic. Everything was fair game in this war. American businessmen and business ventures overseas, including oil fields and production — as well as the obvious targets such as embassy personnel and military targets in the area — were all included as potential hits.

There was not much Kasim could do about the current situation at this time, however. He could only wait and watch CNN, along with the rest of the world. But as soon as this battle was over, blood would flow, he vowed, and the war would escalate. The ultimate battle was at hand. Sweat poured off his face and his stride reflected his anger.

8

*A*mad thought it was time to authorize radio contact. He instructed Green, "You will now contact Port-au-Prince."

Green complied by tuning the radio to their frequency. He fiddled with the radio and another instrument.

After a few tense moments Green radioed, "Port-au-Prince, this is InterAir Flight 243."

The cabin had a strange disquietude about it. Many passengers realized — after the whispers made their way around — that Mahmud was dead, and that a brave and somehow adept passenger had taken action.

Robinson managed to get buckled into his seat with the aid of the passenger who had restrained him earlier. He slouched over in his seat, his gut in agonizing pain. There was probably some internal bleeding and it was essential that he get to a doctor as soon as possible, although he knew the futility of that idea.

Maxine was back in her seat. She was somewhat comforted by the woman next to her, who whispered to her what had just transpired. Still, these words of reassurance didn't calm her. She still felt that the worst was yet to come. She'd be damned if they thought she wouldn't try again to save her husband. Maxine would rather die trying to save him than do nothing at all.

Amad was assured that everything was on track to Port-au-Prince. Green had made radio contact and, although Port-au-Prince was hesitant about receiving them, Haiti probably felt it should do the United States a favor since the U.S. had done so much for it. Amad decided to check on Mahmud and assist him in torturing the American Marine.

Amad opened the cockpit door and edged out. He closed the door behind him and looked for Mahmud. From Amad's vantage point at the front of the aircraft Mahmud's body couldn't be seen, so Amad stepped into the aisle near the second row and looked toward the rear of the plane. He called out, "Mr. Lincoln."

There was no answer. All he could see was the tops of the seats, since all the passengers had their heads down as ordered. It was a cramped position, and some larger passengers had to rest their heads on the seatbacks in front of them.

Amad waited, thinking perhaps Mahmud was in the rear near the galley or something. Perhaps he had needed to use the restroom. As he waited, he became edgy. "Mr. Lincoln," he shouted a second time. He had his gun up and pointed towards the rear.

Peter couldn't get a good fix on the situation. He wanted to peer around the boundary of his seat, but knew Amad was looking in his direction and that the element of surprise — that window of opportunity — was not there yet.

Amad shouted, "Mahmud!" The look of confidence, even the arrogance of control that he had displayed up until this point, began to fade. His expression turned to alarm. He didn't know quite what to do at this point, except find

Mahmud. He had to be sure there was nothing wrong with him, because if there was, his orders were to immediately blow up the entire plane. Of course, he had to be sure before he did something unnecessary. Then again, even after all the training — knowing his orders and the possibility of suicide — in his own mind he hadn't truly contemplated that outcome. Could he really do it? He had never believed it would come to that. So he waited. Hesitated. He backed up a couple of feet. "Mahmud!" He waited.

The passengers grew more anxious in the silence. There was no response from Peter, their unknown hero. Blood pressures maxed out.

"Mahmud! Where are you!" A bead of sweat rolled down the side of Amad's face. His expression changed to fear. The shoes were changing feet. He backed up, his body almost pressed against the cockpit door. He stood there contemplating his next move.

The plane seemed very quiet, though the usual hum of the engines could be heard. Amad was feeling alone, and for good reason, though he didn't yet know the true extent.

Peter acted methodically. He knew that bullet holes in the fuselage at this altitude could cause decompression. He peered around the border of his seat, with his pistol pointed in Amad's direction. He fired two quick bursts before Amad realized what was happening. One round struck Amad in the abdomen and the other in his shoulder. It had been some time since Peter had fired a weapon, and it showed. Peter knew that Amad had explosives strapped around his waist, so he had to be accurate. So far he had been lucky, but not as accurate as he would have hoped. He was aiming for Amad's head. He certainly didn't want to prolong this scene, but that was just what happened.

Amad returned fire in Peter's direction. The thought of blowing himself up didn't cross his mind at this point — he reacted instinctively with his gun. Peter fell to the floor as three rounds whizzed over his head. Two rounds hit the fuselage near the rear of the plane, and one went into the floor behind Peter.

Peter fired off three more rounds, two of which struck Amad in the chest.

Amad fell back against the cockpit door and commenced to fire in all directions. Four rounds went up and pierced the fuselage above and around him in a semicircle.

A few seconds later the plane began to dive. Decompression was immediate. The oxygen masks for the passengers ejected from their compartments, and the passengers placed them over their faces as thicker air began to escape the aircraft and thinner air entered. The bullet holes expanded somewhat.

Amad fell to the floor and dropped his gun. Peter struggled to crawl toward him. Many passengers began to scream as the plane's angle of descent increased rapidly.

In the cockpit, Green saw his instrument panel fail almost completely. The altimeter was spinning downward quickly. Twenty-five thousand feet, twenty-two, twenty. He struggled to control the plane. Unknown to Green, several of Amad's bullets had severed some wiring and punctured all primary and backup hydraulics. Miraculously, he could still control the flaps on the right wing. The left wing's controls and its engine had completely failed; however, Green managed to hold the plane somewhat steady. He tried to activate the manual reversion for the ailerons, to no avail. The left wing would not respond at all. In fact, the left wing began dipping even more.

Peter rushed Amad. In spite of the searing pain he was feeling, Amad scrambled to get his gun back. Why he didn't just activate the explosives strapped about him, he wasn't sure. The will to live and not to give up if you didn't have to was evident.

Just as Peter was about to plant a bullet in Amad's head, Amad regained possession of his gun. He was lying on the floor with his head pointed in Peter's direction. Amad sat up and shot at Peter. Instinctively, Peter dropped, but not before Amad had knocked Peter's gun from his hand.

Amad fell backwards slightly as he shot, in part due to the descending plane and the force of gravity pulling him backwards. Peter was now on top of Amad, tackling him. They wrestled for control of Amad's gun, since Peter's gun had been knocked too far from him and it would have taken more time to get it back than to get to Amad.

As Peter struggled for Amad's gun, Amad managed to fire off some more shots, this time in the direction of the main passenger door. Several shots hit the window and the door. More thick air escaped through the open window.

Green began to bring the nose of the aircraft up slightly, although they were still descending rapidly.

The bullet holes in the door's window expanded with the impact, and anything that was not secured was being sucked out.

Peter and Amad were sucked up to the door, and crashed into it with a hard impact. Peter lost his grip on Amad's arm, the one with the gun. All the better, as Amad's arm was pulled through the open door window.

Amad wailed in agony. The air was being blocked from escaping by Amad's arm and shoulder, which were plugging up the hole. The pressure from the escaping air began to rip and tear at his flesh. Because the hole was plugged, Peter was able to crawl back and grab onto the aisle seat.

Finally, the force was too much for Amad's arm. It was torn completely off at the shoulder. He was in such shock and pain that he couldn't do much of anything. The hole was now open, and the air was again escaping from the plane so quickly that unsecured objects were being thrust at Amad like projectiles launched from a cannon.

Struggling, Amad reached around and tried to detonate the explosives strapped to his waist. When Peter saw what Amad was attempting to do, he let go of the seat leg and got to Amad in a split second as the air sucked him towards the door.

Peter belted Amad across the head, but couldn't get enough of a grip to knock him out. Peter opened the latch to the door and pushed the door open, using all of his strength to hold onto a nearby seat. He couldn't strap himself in because of the suction, so he just held on with all his might.

The door was sucked open. Amad grabbed Peter's left foot with his one good arm as blood from his severed arm spurted out. The agony didn't bother him as much as the terror of being sucked from the plane.

Peter began kicking at Amad, first in the head. When that didn't jar him loose, he tried kicking him on his good arm. Finally, Amad lost his grip and flew towards the open door. He tried to hold onto the door frame with his one hand, but he just didn't have the strength. In a split second, just as his grip failed him and he was exiting the aircraft, he triggered the explosives. He was disintegrated instantaneously.

In the explosion, a sizable portion of the fuselage immediately around the door frame disappeared, as did the door itself; however, most of the blast occurred outside of the plane. Still, the explosion was large enough to knock the plane into another sharp dive, just as Green had been beginning to stabilize it. Peter almost lost his grip, but managed to hold onto the leg of another first-class seat.

Green tried to pull the nose of the airplane up. They were losing altitude quickly. The plane was falling and circling to the left. Green held it as steady as he could. He had no idea what had happened in the cabin, but that was not his concern. Stabilizing the plane, or bringing it down to rest upon the Atlantic, was. Luna assisted him, but rode it out for the most part. Green was calling over his radio, "Mayday! This is Flight 243. We are going down." He struggled to hold the plane together. "Mayday, mayday!"

"Two-four-three, this is the United States Air Force, bravo-two-niner," said Captain Waith over the radio. "I have visual contact. I'll follow you down. We have you. Bring her down, and we'll pick you up."

This was meant to reassure Green and Luna, but the greatest task at hand was not to totally ditch it. Green tried to hold steady, but the left wing was dipping too much. He told Luna, "Instruct the passengers to prepare for an emergency landing."

Luna announced to the passengers, "This is your copilot. Please brace yourselves. Discard all sharp objects, place your heads down, and cover your heads with your hands." Little did he realize that most of the passengers had been doing this for some time. "When we come to a stop, please use your seat bottom for a flotation device," he continued. "The Air Force is with us and will pick us up as soon as we're down."

Peter struggled against the pain he was feeling and the vacuum force working against him, laboring to get into the seat that he was holding onto. He slowly pulled himself up off the floor and buckled himself into the seat. There was nothing more he, or anyone, could do — except brace for the impact.

The plane continued its left downward spiral. Green miraculously held it so it didn't completely nose-dive.

Actually, he had a somewhat favorable angle of descent. Nonetheless, the impact was going to be brutal.

Maria was a complete wreck. She had just gotten off the phone again for the fifth time with Harry and Joan. They had nothing new to tell her. John from the State Department didn't know anything either.

Maria paced around the restaurant with Alberto, Oscar, and a group of close friends who had gathered. They had closed the restaurant and were glued to the television, waiting for news.

Maria had amazing strength under pressure. Having been through her mother's untimely death from cancer and her father's death in a plane crash, she had experience in such matters. However, this dilemma was on an even deeper level. This was a person with whom she shared her soul. There was nothing Maria wouldn't do to protect Peter from danger.

As several friends talked quietly, the television — tuned to CNN — blared, rehashing what was already known. Finally, the news anchor came on. "We have this update now concerning InterAir Flight 243. The Federal Aviation Administration, along with the Federal Bureau of Investigation, in a joint statement have confirmed that Flight 243 has indeed departed Miami. They do not know the new destination of the flight. They have confirmed two fatalities so far. This is all the information we have at this time. We will make more information available as it comes in. Now let's go live to our affiliate in Miami."

Maria looked at Alberto and Oscar, who looked back with the same stress and anxiety that she was feeling.

Kasim was somewhat relieved. He assumed that Amad and Mahmud had realized that something was not right and had begun Phase Two of the operation, albeit early. If that were the case, they should make their way to Port-au-Prince just a couple of hours ahead of schedule, unless this crazy American pilot tried another stunt. But how could he do it again? He would be risking the entire wrath of Allah and his angels, Kasim's brothers. At this point there was no need to proceed with a mass campaign of terror. The operation seemed to be back on track. He could do nothing but wait it out with the rest of the world. He was, like many others, at the mercy of the great American propaganda machine. Kasim sat in his chair at the trinket shop and watched the events unfold on CNN.

Peter braced himself and covered his head with his hands as well as he could. The impact, although it would be on water, would still be violent — depending on the angle with which they struck. He could feel the gravitational force of the earth pull at the plane, like a giant magnet attracting a small piece of metal. Peter concluded that this pilot had skillfully maintained a favorable angle of descent, considering that the left wing was dipping severely.

The plane picked up speed as it continued its descent. The noise of the air rushing through the open side door made an excruciating, eardrum-piercing, whistling sound.

Most passengers braced themselves, believing that they would survive. Some said their prayers and reaffirmed their faith, while others remained in too much shock to do much thinking of any sort. Everyone kept their heads down.

Green was doing everything he could to maintain the angle of descent he had managed to obtain. The sheer force of gravity, and the plane's velocity, were straining Green and Luna. To add to the terror, it was a clear day over the Bahamas and they could see for miles. They watched the mighty Caribbean Ocean approach their cockpit windows all too quickly.

Upon impact the plane spiraled to the left and the nose sliced into the water. The front one-third of the jetliner was submerged in the sea. The impact sheered off much of the left wing, which slammed back into the side of the fuselage. A dozen passengers, who were sitting next to the windows behind the wing, were crushed. The woman who had originally been sitting next to Peter in the rear was decapitated instantly when she sat up on impact. The seat where Peter had originally sat was cut into two by a section of the left wing.

All the passengers on the right side of the plane were virtually unscathed, except for minor injuries from flying debris.

Green and Luna were knocked unconscious from the tremendous blow of impact.

Peter was thrown back into his seat, and his back and neck took a substantial hammering. He was barely conscious, but came around quickly as water came rushing through the open door. Within seconds the plane began filling with water.

There was a lot of moaning and crying. Peter could hear several passengers calling for help. Slowly, regaining his faculties, Peter struggled to his feet. He saw a few passengers ripping out their seat bottoms for flotation devices. He started walking slowly, the now-searing back pain attacking every time he moved. He passed two male passengers who were in shock and unable to disengage their seat belts. Peter quickly released their belts so they could get out of their seats.

Robinson crawled along the floor, calling out for his wife. He was in too much pain to be of much use to her, thought Peter.

"Maxine! Maxine!" shouted Robinson. "I'm coming, hold on!" His every word was a pain-filled moan.

Peter grabbed a seat bottom and intercepted him. "Take this. I'll find her. You go on."

"I can't. I can't leave her," said Robinson, struggling with Peter.

"I'll get her. I promise you."

Peter forced the young Marine to hold onto the seat cushion. He grabbed Robinson by the chest and dragged him to the open emergency door on the right, where passengers were swimming out. Peter cast him off. Robinson floated away in protest as the water gushed in.

There was total chaos as many passengers fought to get out. Peter had to climb over several people to get to the back of the plane. The plane was tipping at a steep angle towards the opened left side of the fuselage. Several people were swept away through the opening. Many knew how to swim, and managed to swim out and away from the sinking plane. However, a few who were either knocked unconscious or trapped between sections of the broken plane were drowned where they sat.

Peter arrived at the section where Maxine and several other passengers were trapped, being held in their seats by a portion of the broken left wing that had sheered its way through and caused the overhead carry-on baggage compartment to collapse upon them. Water was up to Peter's waist. Another male passenger joined him from behind; apparently one of the women who was trapped there was his wife. Together, Peter and this man struggled to jar loose the collapsed baggage compartment. It wouldn't budge.

Peter and the man were yelling at one another, but neither could hear the other. Peter climbed up onto one of the seats and pushed up a portion of the compartment with his shoulder. He had to ignore the back pain he was feeling; otherwise, he would fail. In the past he had been forced to overcome pain and complete his mission, so he could certainly do it again, he told himself. Peter and the other man managed to move the compartment about three inches, just enough to allow Maxine and the two women next to her to escape. They swam off down the aisle. They didn't stop to secure a seat cushion — there wasn't time. They had to get out of the plane immediately.

Peter and the other man moved to the next row, where three women were trapped, with the water fast approaching their shoulder level. Again, they managed to move the collapsed compartment, and the women swam off down the aisle. A split second after they released the compartment, the other man waved at Peter and swam out the open emergency door just over the right wing.

Peter looked over to where he had originally been seated and saw the decapitated woman in her seat, still clutching her crucifix. At least for her it was over. It wasn't over for him yet, he thought, and he would understand the truth of that before long.

Peter half swam and half paddled down the aisle. He saw perhaps at least a dozen more dead passengers in the coach class. Most were still strapped in their seats, awaiting submersion in a watery grave. He made his way to the front of the plane, which was now completely underwater. However, there was still a two-foot air pocket at the ceiling, so Peter could come up for air when he needed to. He managed to kick open the cockpit door and swam inside.

To Peter's dismay, the crew had never regained consciousness from the crash, and had drowned. Captain Green would never know that his valiant efforts had saved the lives of two-thirds of his passengers. His experienced hand had guided the plane down in such a manner that many lives had been saved. A few more degrees downward and more would have died.

There was nothing more that Peter could do. He held his breath and swam out of the cockpit and toward the side door, the same door he had forced Amad through.

Peter didn't realize until he was clear from the plane that it was completely submerged. He had to swim several yards up to the surface.

Breaking the surface, he realized where they must have crashed. The water was warm, somewhat calm, and it was a sunny, clear day. They must be somewhere in the Caribbean. He would learn later that they were actually just off the northeast tip of the Bahaman island of Andros, about forty miles from Nassau. He was surrounded by about seventy surviving passengers. They were floating around, many with seat cushions, some without. He swam towards a group of them and began treading water.

Captain Waith never lost sight of Flight 243. He circled around and watched several of the passengers emerge from the downed plane. Even before the plane hit the water he had radioed in the exact location.

The *USS JFK* was in the Straits of Florida. Immediately, several aircraft were dispatched, including rescue helicopters. They would be on the scene within minutes to make pickups and return to the aircraft carrier. The closest Coast Guard cutter was beyond the *JFK*; nevertheless, it began to steam towards the area as soon as it was put on alert.

The information was quickly relayed stateside. Officials in Nassau were notified. Nassau dispatched every available vessel. The government was responding with amazing efficiency. Several ships and helicopters were en route almost instantly. It would be only a matter of minutes before they began to reach the scene. The rescue was under way.

Captain Waith circled overhead so the survivors could see him and feel reassured.

As soon as Ann Howard landed in West Palm Beach, she was on the phone with her editor, Bob. "You're kidding ... How many? Nassau ... More planes ... Okay. When? ... Right. I'll call you when I get in." She hung up and rushed down the corridor towards another terminal.

Hearn was on top of things, and had her ticket already waiting at the passenger check-in. Shortly, she would be in the air again, this time heading for Nassau.

Hearn knew her better than he knew his own wife. Ann was one hell of a reporter. She wouldn't rest until she got the story. There wasn't anything more important to her. All else could wait. Sleep, food ... those could be had when and if there was time.

She lived for the story. She believed absolutely that the people had a right to know the story, the whole story, and nothing but the story. The truth? Well, hopefully the story had been verified, but sometimes the presses couldn't wait. If they printed misinformation, hopefully it was someone else's, and the *Sun* could be absolved of any liability. They could always print a retraction of an error, or a statement of misinformation from a third party. Again, this could be printed in time so it didn't cause anyone irreparable harm. Then again, if she had printed the truth and was certain of it, let the chips fall where they might. Things would still happen, with or without her story, for she believed a story would make its way around regardless.

Howard checked in and got her seating assignment for her flight to Nassau.

The place was abuzz with activity. Although it wasn't his area of operation, John Perkins hung out whenever he could and tried to stay on top of events as they unfolded. He knew William Kearny well. Kearny's area of expertise was Latin America in general, and the Caribbean in particular. Kearny was in his mid-forties and a middle manager of operations for the Caribbean bureau. He was at his desk when John entered.

"What's up?" asked John.

"Nassau has agreed to receive the survivors. The Pentagon is making the arrangements, and the first helicopters should arrive on the scene in less than fifteen minutes. The Coast Guard will arrive on the scene within the hour, and the Air Force estimates seventy to eighty survivors. That's all I have now."

"Thanks Bill. I'll inform Katharina." With that, John exited Kearny's office.

John had met Peter and liked him. They had even had a few cordial drinks after the divorce. Peter didn't really have any feelings toward John one way or another. He just thought John was a hard-working career diplomat who was dedicated to his country, and that was something Peter had admired. Peter took off with Maria shortly after Katharina had remarried; and Peter wished John and Katharina well. To be polite, John had invited Peter to come around whenever he wished. Peter hadn't taken him up on the offer. Instead, he had John fly the kids down to him in Cozumel when they had vacations. John had one child from a previous marriage, and knew how it was to go through a divorce.

John went back to his office and called Katharina.

Katharina, in turn, called Maria at the restaurant. Maria answered the phone. "Hello. Yes . . . Oh no . . . How many? That's a good number, although not for those less fortunate . . . I hope so . . . I'll try and get a flight to Nassau.

I've got to be there. Thanks Katharina." She hung up the phone and told the group what she had learned.

The sun was blistering. The saltwater quickly made the open wounds fester, quite painfully. Peter knew that many would not last long under these circumstances. By now he had stripped to his underwear, having tied off and inflated his jeans and shirt and given them to two women who had nothing to keep them afloat. He told them how to keep inserting air as necessary. Peter knew that sharks in these waters could gather by the dozens in no time, and that some were of substantial size. The potential smorgasbord their group represented worried him.

Peter swam over to a group of survivors who were staying together. He noticed the Islamic cleric, Al Raman, and asked, "Everyone okay?"

"We are not seriously hurt," answered Raman. "I am so sorry this has happened. Allah does not wish these kinds of acts to happen. It is against his good name."

"It's not your fault."

"I'm afraid it does not give my religion a good name."

Peter swam over to Robinson and his wife, who were treading water nearby. Even though Robinson was in worse pain than ever, when he saw Peter approaching he called out to him. "Over here!"

Peter swam over. "Are you all right?"

"There's a lot of pain," answered Dion. "I owe my life and my wife's to you."

"It's not over yet," Peter said, a flash of worry in his face and voice.

"You heard the captain say they were watching us," Maxine said, wanting to reassure herself.

"I did. Let's hope they get here soon," replied Peter. "We need to get everybody closer together and not let anyone stray off." He shouted, "Everybody! Listen to me. We must all stay close together so no one is left behind. They know where we are, and they are on the way. If we get closer together it will make their job easier." He had to say this, even though he wasn't quite sure how true it was. It was also necessary to get everyone as close as possible so that if the sharks did come, everyone could look out for one another. Peter watched as a few people responded and began to move in his direction. Others only looked on in confusion and shock.

"Come on! Everyone! Swim over here, together!"

More and more of the others began to swim over to where the floating crowd of Flight 243 survivors were assembling, as if they were about to board another flight.

Ten minutes later all of the survivors were gathered in a radius of several hundred feet. They looked rather peculiar floating there, resembling bobbing buoys. Not surprisingly, many said nothing because they were still in shock. Some believed their time was up. Most, however, held out hope.

It was very late in the afternoon. Harry and Joan had some food delivered to the house. They hadn't eaten since breakfast and were beginning to feel hungry. They had heard of the latest update from John, and this worried them.

The CNN anchor came on and announced, "We have an official update concerning InterAir Flight 243. The Federal Aviation Administration and the Federal Bureau of Investigation have confirmed that Flight 243 has crashed into the Caribbean near the Bahamas. They report that there are as many as seventy survivors in the water at this time. The Navy and the Coast Guard are in the area and should arrive on the scene momentarily. The survivors will be evacuated to Nassau."

This information was not news to Harry, Joan, or Katharina. However, it was news to Kasim.

He stood in front of a chair, his face full of rage. He bit down on his lip. He couldn't believe his ears. There were survivors? How could this be? Obviously, something had gone wrong and Amad and Mahmud had used the last resort, but how could there be survivors? There had been enough explosive material on one man to blow up the entire plane. The whole plane should have become a massive fireball thousands of feet in the air. There was no way anyone could have survived the blast, decompression, and fall. Kasim could not understand what had happened. He stormed out of the shop, lost in indignation and bewilderment, and walked into the street.

The streets of Giza had long since settled down for the night. Kasim made his way along. He was determined to put his campaign of terror and retribution into operation, and to accelerate the Mother of All Terrorist Attacks. He would, at the same time, continue to tune into CNN and await word as to what precisely had happened. The Americans were up to something, he concluded. They had obviously tried some stunt that the American media hadn't yet picked up. They would pay, and pay greatly, he told himself. He decided that his next battle, although it had been in the planning stages for some time, had to go on a year ahead of schedule. They could pull it off. They had the equipment, the personnel, and the in-country support. Hopefully, their American co-conspirators would agree to move it up by one year.

As the sun disappeared in the west, someone shouted, "Can you hear that? It's coming from over there." The middle-aged woman, battered and frail, gasped to maintain her breathing and not be overcome by the exertion from constant treading. She pointed due north. "Do you hear that?"

Several of the survivors thought she was hearing things, that she was losing her sanity in the face of this peril. They looked in the direction she was pointing.

"Yes, I hear something," said the man next to her. "Yes, I hear it."

Peter, who was near the south side of the group about a hundred and fifty feet away, raised his head and heard it also. "Yes, we hear it back here, too!" he assured the others. "It's a helicopter! I hear two, maybe more." If there was anyone who recognized the life-saving sound of a helicopter, it was Peter. He had waited for death to strike several times, in Vietnam and elsewhere around the world, lying at the edge of a landing zone. When he heard this sound, he knew exactly what it was.

The distinct chopping sound of the helicopter blades increased twofold every few seconds. Peter counted the sound of as many as four choppers.

A few moments later — moments that seemed like an eternity to those in the water — five Navy helicopters appeared from the north. They formed a circle around the passengers below.

Several frogmen jumped from the choppers. They inflated several life rafts, each of which could contain several people. They pushed the rafts towards the survivors.

The passengers began to enter the life rafts as the choppers lowered rescue cables with rescue baskets attached to the end. Two frogmen swam to each basket. They motioned for people to come near. The blades of the choppers cutting through the air made too much noise for anyone to hear any directions, so everyone had to rely on hand signals.

The frogmen began to place people in the baskets. In

moments all the survivors were either in a life raft or a rescue basket.

Peter was one of the last to get into a life raft. He was hugely relieved not to be treading water anymore, but his back was in much pain and was beginning to stiffen up.

The dozen frogmen steadied the rescue baskets and held the life rafts near. As soon as one helicopter was filled to capacity, it took off and headed towards Nassau.

Within a few more minutes, everyone was aboard. Just in time. Fortunately, the intense noise of the choppers had kept the curious sharks that had just arrived at a distance. The frogmen had radio communication with those above, so spotters aboard kept them well informed.

Exactly one hour after crashing into the Caribbean, the survivors of InterAir Flight 243 were bound for Nassau, the Bahamas. The Navy rescue helicopter Peter was on swooped off, picking up speed as it raced along. The survivors were given blankets to wrap themselves in. Peter nestled comfortably in a blanket himself, not knowing that his ordeal had only just begun.

9

*S*hell's flight landed in Nassau moments before the choppers began to arrive. He needed to quickly set up his identity and get answers to his questions. Known recently as Castillo, Martinez, and Estevez, Shell was now to be known as Rodriguez, a southern Florida businessman.

The choppers began landing at the Nassau airport. Survivors were transported to the nearby hospital. Shell needed to get to the hospital as soon as he could.

He came off the plane that had flown in from West Palm Beach, and made his way through the jet bridge with a businessman's briefcase in hand. Weaving his way through the crowd, he glanced down at his watch to check the time. Just as he was doing so, he bumped into another weary traveler who seemed to be in as much of a hurry as he was. "I'm so sorry, miss."

"Sure," responded Ann Howard, throwing him an agitated glance.

Shell didn't bother to say anything more. He hurried along.

Howard headed briskly in the same direction as Shell. Actually, they had been on the same flight. Howard was sure she had seen some helicopters and rescue activity over the Caribbean as they had descended into Nassau. There was no time to waste. She knew she would probably be one of the first reporters on the scene, and figured she had the whole story for her picking. She had her tape recorders ready and plenty of paper and pencils. Her first order of business was to find the pilot and crew and get some sort of official statement about what had happened. Then she would try to interview some of the survivors — those who were willing to talk, of course.

She had been in similar situations and had had some unruly sources in the past. One time she interviewed the victim of a serial rapist. The woman had gotten annoyed with Howard's persistent questions — questions that had seemed redundant — and had assaulted Howard. Howard had considered filing charges, but agreed with her attorney that the rape victim was not in control of her own faculties, considering that she was still badly bruised and in the hospital.

Howard rushed off down the concourse, practically chasing Shell.

The hours seemed to be growing longer and would stretch well into the night — a given with this job. Eugene Pritchard was in his jet, heading to Nassau, having just briefed the Attorney General, who in turn briefed the President.

First things first. The investigation was well under way. The Coast Guard was securing the crash site and Navy divers were recovering the deceased passengers. Their bodies were being flown to Miami as soon as they were recovered. They had to be identified, then the next of kin had to be notified before the bodies or names of the victims could be released. Survivors had to be interviewed and statements taken. Pritchard already knew who was responsible for this despicable act, but procedure had to be followed. Then the Bureau would go after the perpetrators. They would search the globe and bring those responsible to justice. These terrorists — as well as all other would-be terrorists — had to be sent a strong signal that American justice would be swift, calculated, and certain.

Pritchard never rested. While airborne he worked the phones, holding a succession of conference calls with other agents and government officials.

The last helicopter landed in Nassau. Peter disembarked with the rest of the surviving passengers. They were quickly directed onto a bus that was waiting to transport them to the hospital. Those with serious injuries were immediately transported via ambulance.

The bus departed as soon as everyone had boarded. Embassy officials were waiting for them on the bus. A woman from the embassy stood at the front of the bus and spoke. "My name is Tricia Compton . . . I am from the U.S. Embassy. We want to get all the information we can quickly, and get word to your loved ones. We want to get you on your way as soon as possible. We will have a remote telephone system ready at the hospital for your use. I am passing around a form that I would like you to fill out. It asks for some basic information. We have already been informed about the deaths of the terrorists, and would appreciate any additional information about the ordeal that you can provide." She passed out papers and pencils attached to clipboards.

Many of the survivors looked dumbfounded, and took the clipboards reluctantly, unsure how to proceed. A clipboard came Peter's way. He took it apprehensively. The first thing on his mind was getting some fresh clothes — after all, he was wrapped in a blanket, sitting in his wet underwear. Then he would call Maria. He studied the form.

Sure enough, they were simple, straightforward questions — such as name, address, phone number. At the bottom of the form was the penultimate question, a question Peter didn't answer. He had gotten more involved in this whole affair than he wanted, thank you, and wanted no more of it. He had done what he could. He wanted nothing more than to get to his mother's funeral before she was six feet under.

The question at the bottom of the form asked for additional information regarding the incident. It asked specifically about the terrorists, and for a description of the events that had taken place.

"Please hang on to your forms and we'll collect them when you depart the bus," instructed Compton. "We will get you into new clothes and attended to promptly. We will have food waiting for you at the hospital. We also have several officials standing by who will make arrangements for your transportation. It is my understanding that the Air Force will be flying in a transport plane for those who want to go Atlanta. You may book your flight with our officials to any destination stateside. All major carriers fly out of Nassau. We will also make available to you counselors, for those who wish to speak with a professional. I will gladly answer any questions you may have. I know there is nothing I can say to comfort you after what you have been through. Thank you for your understanding and cooperation."

The bus pulled into the hospital. Slowly, the survivors got off the bus, turning in their paperwork to Compton as they did so. She quickly checked the forms for completeness, and asked several people if they had any other pertinent information to offer. Many said no; few had written anything. Clearly, and understandably, they were too tired and frayed to provide information.

When Compton checked Peter's form, she said, "Thank you, Mr. Murray."

Peter had figured his name was on the airline's manifest, so he had better put down his real name and not draw attention to himself during an investigation.

"Do you have any information you could offer at this time, Mr. Murray?"

"No ma'am." He acted the part of a weary and tattered survivor.

"Thank you." Compton took the clipboard, and Peter and his fellow survivors moved into the hospital like sheep in a herd.

Inside the hospital, the expected chaos was evident. Hospital staffers hurried to attend to the survivors. Fortunately, most of them required only minor medical attention. Peter watched the activity from afar so he could design his escape. He saw where the hospital staffers were handing out clothing, and headed in that direction.

Shell pulled up in a taxi. He paid his fare and disappeared into the hospital. The major portion of the investigation would be handled by the FBI, not the CIA, so the CIA's authority was limited. Yet Shell was told to assassinate the terrorists if the opportunity presented itself. He slipped off down a side corridor and headed toward the laundry area.

Howard arrived in her taxi shortly after Shell's taxi had departed. She paid her fare and scurried into the hospital. Once inside, she was confronted by a hospital security guard and found herself having to talk quickly. She had to wait for an embassy official.

Finally, the official came. He was a middle-aged man,

dressed casually. He carried some papers and was not in the mood for a confrontation. "Yes?"

"I'm Ann Howard with the *Washington Sun*."

"Not now, Ms. Howard. It's too early."

"Not for the story, Mr. — ?"

"That's not my concern. You'll have to wait in the lobby until the survivors are released — and then only if they wish to talk to you."

He went on his way, leaving Howard perturbed by the way she was treated. She sneaked off down a corridor in the same direction that Shell had.

Howard ducked into a utility room where surgical greens and lab coats were stored. Startled, Shell dove beneath a gurney and managed to cover himself with a blanket that was nearby. It was very dark in this room, so chances were Howard hadn't seen him.

Sure enough, she hadn't. Howard located a penlight in her handbag and searched in the dark. She found a white lab coat and put it on over her clothing. She looked like a hospital staffer or — better still — a doctor or nurse. She searched her handbag again, and sorted through several artificial name tags she carried. Finally, she located one that said Ann Howard, Psychologist, Ph.D. She pinned it to her lapel. She adjusted herself, gathered up her belongings, and departed with a mission to accomplish.

Shell got up from under the gurney and got dressed in a lab coat himself. He was quite relaxed for someone who had been startled the way he was. Calmly, he strolled out.

Howard got right into the center of the disorder. She acted official and fit right in. She began talking with two passengers who were huddled together near the coffee and snack tables. The table offered muffins, donuts, and other quick treats. People passed by, snatching up some food and coffee, and went to mingle with others. Some made phone calls stateside.

Howard walked over to a man and his wife, both survivors, who were getting nourishment. The woman, Mrs. Simon, had bandaids on her face like a man who had gotten a bad shave.

"Hi. My name is Ann Howard," said Howard in a consoling tone. "I'm here to help you through this ordeal."

"I'm Mr. Simon, and this is my wife Edith," said Mr. Simon wearily.

"Have you gotten enough to eat?" she asked in her most sympathetic voice.

"Yes, thank you."

"Well, would you care to sit — perhaps out in the waiting room? We could talk there in private."

"Sure, that's fine," said Mr. Simon. The couple followed Howard into the waiting room. As they turned to sit, Howard reached into her purse and turned on her miniature tape recorder.

Howard sat on a sofa facing them. "Well, first of all, where are you folks from?"

Mr. Simon did most of the talking. It appeared that his wife was still quite upset from the peril. "We're from Dayton, Ohio."

"And you were on vacation?" Howard began taking notes. "I'm sorry, do you mind if I take notes to refer to later?"

"No, no. Go right ahead. Yes, we were on a vacation. Our children bought us this trip for our anniversary. We'd planned it for some time."

"I understand. Have you made arrangements for your flight back to Dayton?"

"We put in our request with the embassy. They told us to wait here while they make the arrangements. They said they would have a hotel room for us soon."

"Good. Now, I think we should talk about the flight and what you remember. Are you comfortable with that?"

Mr. Simon looked at his wife, who didn't signal anything one way or the other. "Yes, I guess that would be all right," he answered.

"Okay. Where were you sitting?"

Mr. Simon spoke slowly and recounted the whole affair. "At first, we were sitting in row 16 — uh, seats A and B. The terrorists moved us later, you see."

Howard listened intently to every word. She jotted down notes as Mr. Simon spoke. Her tape recorder captured every word.

Peter washed up and changed clothes in the men's bathroom. The clothes weren't exactly a perfect fit, but they would do for now. He left the restroom and made his way down the corridor. At the food table he picked up two muffins and a cup of coffee, then quickly went in search of a phone.

Walking out of the area, he passed the doorway to the waiting room. From where Mr. and Mrs. Simon and Howard were sitting, they didn't see him pass by.

Peter wandered into another section of the lobby, where he found several pay phones along the wall. He picked up the receiver and dialed an international operator. "Yes, please. A collect call to Cozumel, Mexico. San Miguel. The number is 86-555-3241." He waited while the operator placed the call.

Maria was packing her overnight bag when the phone rang. She bolted for it, running out of the bedroom and into the kitchen. "Hello!"

The operator said, "Will you accept a collect call from Peter?"

Maria screamed, "Peter?"

"It's me, Maria. Accept the call."

"Yes, yes. I accept the call." Maria collapsed into a chair by the kitchen table.

"Maria?"

"Peter."

"Maria, I'm fine. I'm in Nassau. I only have some back pain that we can take care of when I get back."

"I'm coming to you," she said with desperate urgency.

"You don't have to. I'm fine. Just wire me some money and I'll get to New York for the funeral."

"Are you sure? I can be there soon."

"I'm sure. That way I can have the money in a matter of minutes and be out of here and in the States in a few hours. There's no need for you to come."

"This was quite a scare, Peter. Your brother is petrified."

"Call him for me. I'll call him from the airplane with the information. Go to the wire office, and I'll call you there in about thirty minutes. Wire me five hundred."

"I can put the ticket on a credit card if you want. That would be faster, and you could pick it up at the airport."

"No. I'm slipping out of here and don't want a credit record. Okay?"

"Sure. I'll head out right now and wait for your call."

"Okay. Thirty minutes."

"Peter?"

"Yes?"

"I thought I had lost you."

"I thought I had lost me. It was close, I can tell you that. Many lost their lives, Maria."

"I'll pray for their families. I love you, Peter."

"I miss you, Maria. I never stopped thinking of you."

There was a moment of silence. Peter could hear Maria sniffle. He said nothing as she cherished this moment.

"I'll call you in thirty minutes. 'Bye."

" 'Bye," said Maria. She hung up and wiped a tear from her eye. She sat there for a few minutes to regain her composure.

She hadn't known Peter during the days when he would be gone for long periods at a time. Katharina had been the unfortunate soul who had anguished through those days and nights. Nevertheless, this event was just as terrifying, Maria thought.

Maria calmed down enough to place a call to Harry.

"So this man somehow managed to tackle Mr. Lincoln?" asked Howard.

Mr. Simon looked to his wife for what she knew. She didn't offer any information; she remained withdrawn.

"Lincoln, Washington, I couldn't keep them straight. Actually," said Mr. Simon, "I was in the window seat, and this man was in the aisle seat. I only saw him get up. I couldn't see how he got this Mr. Lincoln. I don't know how he did it."

For the first time, Mrs. Simon spoke. "Well ..." She spoke slowly, and Howard hung on every word. "I managed to look around the edge of my seat only a split second or so after the man had jumped Mr. Lincoln. It was all too fast, you see."

"Did the passenger — I guess we can call him a hero — did he struggle with Mr. Lincoln?"

Mrs. Simon thought about it for a moment, then finally said, "No, I don't think so. He sort of did the whole thing rather quickly. As a matter of fact, I believe Mr. Lincoln was already dead when I looked up."

Howard was intrigued. "But you said it was only a split second from the time this passenger jumped up until the time you looked."

"Wait a minute. Come to think of it, Mr. Lincoln's neck was quite limp, kinda hanging over backwards, like it was broken or something. You know, I once saw a person who had been in a traffic accident, whose neck was broken, and it looked the same way Mr. Lincoln's did."

"So this hero must've known what he was doing. Like he had done it before," Howard thought out loud. "He did it rather quickly, without so much as a warning to Mr. Lincoln?"

"Yes. At least that's the way I remember it." Mrs. Simon looked at her husband for agreement.

"Yes, well, I did see this man later in the water. He had a commanding way about him."

"Could you describe this man for me?" asked Howard, sensing that she had a story coming to her on a silver platter.

"Yes," responded Mr. Simon.

"Oh sure," said Mrs. Simon, at almost the same time.

Howard took copious notes as the Simons described Peter with remarkable accuracy.

Kasim marched back and forth as he spoke to his following. There were twenty men sitting, and ten others standing guard with automatic weapons. They were gathered in a tent at an encampment somewhere in a desert.

"We will hit all the primary targets," said Kasim militantly. "We will proceed to execute our Mother of All Attacks. You will be informed on a need-to-know basis. We do not yet know the circumstances surrounding the crash of the plane, but the American media should have the whole story shortly. When we know the circumstances — and we believe that it was perpetrated by the Americans — then we will carry out these retributions. Until that time, we will continue to train. We will expedite our logistics and get ready for our attack upon American soil." He paused, looking at those assembled before him. His red face had fury boiling within it. "Dismissed," he shouted.

Peter stood as he talked with Ms. Compton. The only thing he wanted was to get out of there. "I've made my own arrangements," he said.

"And there is nothing that you can add, Mr. Murray?"

"No. I'm sorry, I really didn't see much of anything. It all happened so fast, you know."

"I understand." She shuffled some papers and checked his one more time. "The FBI may contact you at some future time to follow up on this. They will need to reconstruct the event and may require some additional information. Is that okay with you, Mr. Murray?"

"Sure."

Compton studied Peter for a moment. He was well aware that she was scrutinizing him, and it made him want to pull away all the more.

"Have I met you before, Mr. Murray?" she asked.

"I don't think so, Ms. Compton."

"You seem very familiar to me for some reason."

"Many people say that. I must look like the average American Joe who lives next door or something."

"I guess you could say that, Mr. Murray. Well, thank you."

They shook hands. "Thank you for your quick and professional response," said Peter.

"That's unusual for us to hear, Mr. Murray. Rarely do those of us in government receive compliments."

"I understand, Ms. Compton." He smiled at her and slipped away. She stared after him, certain that she knew this man from somewhere.

Shell milled about the hectic hospital corridors, looking as if he belonged there. He was dressed as a janitor and carried some cleanser he had found in the utility room. He chatted in a friendly manner with several of the fatigued survivors. By bits and pieces, he put the story together. However, it wasn't until he met one survivor that he got the whole story in detail.

Mr. Miller, the man who was called first by Mahmud aboard Flight 243, offered his version of the story. He had been very still and frightened during the whole affair. However, he now offered his story easily and excitedly, as if he were a child telling another child about an adventure.

"You don't say," Shell was saying.

"He was some man, I'll tell you that," said Miller. "He sat there the whole time, kinda edgy-like. I could sense he was itching to do something. When he did it, man, I'm telling you, he performed just like a pro. He broke that man's neck like you would snap a twig or something. Then he took charge and shot the other terrorist, Mr. Jefferson, or something."

"Certainly quite an ordeal for you," responded Shell, now anxious to end the conversation with Miller.

"Yeah. I thought we were all going to die."

"Well, I must get back to work now." Shell edged away from Miller.

"Yeah, sure. Nice talking with you."

"Nice talking with you. You take it easy now."

"I thought I was," said Miller nervously.

Shell smiled halfheartedly at Miller and strolled off.

Howard essentially had most of the story. She had thanked Mr. and Mrs. Simon and found the same phones where Peter had phoned Maria minutes earlier. She dictated the story to Bob Hearn, who was taping it on his end. They would meet the deadline, scoop all the other media, and have the papers on the newsstand and people's

doorsteps almost twenty-four hours after InterAir Flight
243 had been hijacked. Of course, there were blanks still
to be filled in, such as names. That would come later.
Hearn had someone over at the airline trying to get a list
of the passengers. She hoped they would have the names
of the survivors for their late-afternoon edition.

"That's it, Bob," said Howard.

"Good. Well done. You've got to find that mystery
hero, Ann."

"I'm on it."

She hung up and went back to work. She rushed back
to the main lobby, where many of the survivors had begun
to gather after making their travel arrangements. They
had been told that the Air Force plane would be ready in
the morning to take those who wanted to fly the friendly
skies compliments of Uncle Sam. Howard began canvassing for survivors who seemed eager to offer information,
and spotted Maxine Robinson sitting in the lobby. She
looked drawn.

"How are you?" Howard offered her hand.

Limply, Maxine shook Howard's hand. "Better."

"I'm Ann Howard." She offered her badge. "Is there
anything I can do for you?"

"No, I'm okay for now. Thank you. Maxine
Robinson."

"Do you mind if I sit?"

"Not at all. Please."

Howard made herself comfortable next to Maxine, ac-
tivating her tape recorder as she sat down. "Are you waiting for someone?"

"My husband. He's in intensive care."

"Oh. How is he?"

"They say he should be fine. He had some internal
bleeding. He was beaten up pretty badly."

Howard scratched her head. "I don't understand."

"They beat him. Punched him in the face and kicked him several times in the stomach."

"The terrorists did this?" Howard moved a bit closer and looked around, scanning the activity. The waiting room was quite busy, with most of the survivors sitting or standing around.

"Yes. They singled him out because he's a Marine."

Another story was being spoon-fed to Howard. She had to act fast, because other reporters were beginning to gather just outside the lobby area, awaiting the meat to be fed to them also.

"I see," said Howard, acting concerned. "It's best if you talk about it. That's what I'm here for."

Maxine looked at Howard and took another sip of her coffee. "I don't even drink this stuff," she said, lifting her coffee cup. "Dion does, to wake himself up in the morning. You have to have something to wake you up that early." Maxine was drinking black coffee.

"What happened?" asked Howard.

Pritchard hustled down the corridor, followed by Roth. They arrived at the temporary central processing center that had been set up in a room adjacent to the emergency area. He was recognized and expected by everyone there. Compton went over to introduce herself.

"Mr. Pritchard, I'm Ms. Compton, from the embassy."

Pritchard shook her hand. "Pleasure to meet you," he said.

"I have all the information you may need to get your investigation started regarding the survivors," offered Compton.

"Good. Mr. Roth will handle that. What are you doing with the survivors?"

"Most of them have elected to be housed and flown out by the Air Force. A handful preferred to make their own plans."

"Where are those people?"

"Some are in the lobby. A couple have checked out. They left us with their addresses and phone numbers."

"Let me see that list."

She handed him the list. He noticed Peter's name immediately. The address and number were his brother Harry's.

"Peter Murray? Did you talk with Mr. Murray?

"Yes, I did. He was rather pleasant, calm. Not too shaken up, unlike many others."

"Where's Lockport?" asked Pritchard.

"Upstate somewhere. Near Buffalo, I believe. You know, come to think of it, he reminded me of someone I'd seen before. Who is he?"

"Colonel Murray. Iran-Contra?"

"Oh yes. I knew I had seen him before."

"He clearly doesn't want any publicity from this. I don't blame him actually. Poor man's character was assassinated back then." Pritchard threw Roth a glance. "We won't bother him. But send an agent out to check on him, and ask if there is anything we can do."

Roth nodded and sprinted to find a phone.

"I need to see the preliminaries you have," said Pritchard.

"Let's get a private area," Compton said, looking around at all the activity that had subsided considerably but was still not private enough.

The taxi stopped in front of the Western Union at Citibank on Thompson Boulevard in Nassau. Peter paid the cab fare with the pocket money the embassy had given each survivor. He entered the building and found a pay phone, where he asked an operator to place a call to Maria. The bank area was dark, but the Western Union portion was open as usual for business. There was a clerk behind the counter and one customer waiting for a wire.

Maria answered, "I'm here, Peter."

"Listen, I'm at Western Union on Thompson Boulevard. Okay?"

"I got it. That's it?"

"For now. I'll call you when I'm airborne, en route to the States." There was a slight pause. "Everything's fine, Maria. I'll try and get some sleep on the plane. Tell Harry to plan the funeral ASAP, and hopefully I'll be back home in a couple of days."

"I can't wait to hold you, Peter. I thought I might never hold you again."

"I know. But it's over, Maria. I love you, and I'll be home in a couple of days. 'Bye."

" 'Bye." The phone clicked on Maria's end. Peter hung up and approached the clerk at the counter.

Dugan was up late as usual. He had his jacket off and his tie loosened. The remnants of a fast food dinner cluttered his desk. A half glass of vodka begged to be finished. Dugan was reviewing top secret documents that sat on their respective envelopes on top of his desk. He read a variety of reports, ranging from simple intelligence gatherings to special operations in the field. Many Americans had recently been led to believe that the Agency had cleaned up its act. In many ways it had, but the Agency also took advantage of loopholes in the law and exploited them to undertake whatever it deemed appropriate for its mission. Of course, the respective congressional oversight committees had been informed, and they usually went along with most of what the CIA proposed.

Dugan could always make a good case for a special operation. His arguments usually persuaded the Congress. Of course, when he intoned national security — that elusive, universal term — it worked every time.

Lethargically, Conrad entered the room. He looked more haggard than Dugan. He carried some files loosely under his arm. "They confirmed the deaths," he said. "It's all there." He handed the files to Dugan.

"How?"

"Seems some passenger jumped them."

"Single-handedly?"

"Yeah."

"Who?"

"They don't have his name yet. He doesn't want to be identified."

"I don't blame him. Find out his name. Put it under wraps." Dugan shoved the files back to Conrad. "Let's get it kicked into high gear in Cairo. I want it over with. Approve all the back channel operatives we discussed before." He stared past Conrad as he continued speaking. "What's the Bureau up to?"

"The usual."

"Keep a close watch."

Conrad nodded his head and shuffled out. Dugan had worked with Conrad off and on for twenty years in a variety of intelligence operations. Both had grown to trust the other completely. Nods, winks, sighs, and the like — all were read like a book by the other. They knew how the other thought, and were, in fact, usually one step ahead of each other.

As usual, Bob Hearn was in his office late. The newsroom buzzed with activity as the biggest scoop to hit the *Sun* in years was unfolding. As Howard dictated Maxine

Robinson's story from Nassau, Hearn recorded everything she said. Several of his assistants came and went while he listened to Howard.

A young assistant burst into Hearn's office. He was a slick protege of Howard's. He handed a fax to Bob Hearn, who studied the paper.

"That's all I have at this end, Bob," Howard said over the phone. "What have you found out?"

"Jeff just handed me a copy of the manifest."

"Good work, Jeff. How'd you do that so fast?"

"I'm not at liberty to disclose my source, Ms. Howard."

"Good answer, Jeff."

"You can't find this hero, Ann?"

"No one can point him out. He could be one of the injured — which I'm checking on next — but I doubt it. The survivors confirm that he was okay in the water and was on the bus."

"Wait a minute." Hearn's glasses almost fell off his face. He pushed them back up onto the bridge of his nose.

"What is it, Bob?"

"There's a Peter Murray listed here. Round trip from Cancun. You think it could be the same Peter Murray?"

"You're kidding? That's it! The description would fit him. A little older, but they did say he was fit, tall, good-looking."

"This is all too incredible," said Hearn.

"Not entirely," countered Howard. "All the witnesses so far said this hero knew what he was doing. That's Murray, isn't it, Bob?"

"Sure sounds like him. Special black ops or something like that. How many people could jump up undetected and snap a man's neck that quickly?"

"Not many. I'll look around for him."

"You might want to try the airport, Ann."

"I think you're right. He doesn't want any part of this. That's obvious. I'm off, Bob."

"Right," said Hearn, switching off the speaker to the phone and disconnecting the call. "Jeff, find out where he lives. I think he moved to the Yucatan, near Cancun somewhere. He ran off with some Mexican woman. This is a great story, Jeff."

"I'm on it," said Jeff, racing from the office.

Hearn studied the manifest of InterAir Flight 243 again. Sure enough, there was Peter Murray listed among the rest, like the common man. Except his life was not — nor would it ever again be — common.

10

*P*eter's plane landed at Greater Buffalo's International airport early the next morning. He had been fortunate enough to need to make only one plane change in Newark, New Jersey, where he had a short, twenty-minute layover. Everything went smoothly on the flight; Peter even slept for an hour.

He was greeted by the whole gang as he emerged from the tunnel. Paul hugged his father, while Sarah held back. The children had been told about their father's ordeal only as it was concluding. Paul was showing excited concern, and Sarah was subdued.

Harry started to shake Peter's hand, but Peter hugged him. After hugging Joan, Peter kissed Katharina lightly on the cheek. They had both agreed that it was good for the children for them to show a positive demeanor towards one another. Katharina had no problem with the act. Peter, however, didn't feel comfortable with it. Even though he had gotten over Katharina, he still felt he had been betrayed. He would act civil for the sake of his children, but even though he still cared for Katharina in some way, he felt bitterness.

Peter and his family strolled down the concourse.

"Knowing you were involved in this and not knowing the details was the hardest part," said Harry. "The television kept speculating and that made it worse."

"I know all too well how they speculate, Harry."

Harry nodded.

"First order of business is a stop at the clothing store," said Peter. "I look like a sad clown in these oversized clothes."

"It's cool, Dad," said Paul. "That's the style now."

"I'll pass, thank you."

"How was it, crashing into the ocean?" asked Paul.

"I don't think your father wants to talk about that now," warned Katharina.

"No, it's okay," Peter said. "It was fast, but at the same time it seemed like forever, Paul."

They walked past an airport cafeteria. The aroma of fresh coffee filled the air. "You want some coffee, Peter?" asked Harry.

"Sure." Harry and Peter detoured into the cafeteria. "You read my mind."

A newspaper delivery man dropped off a stack of *The Buffalo News*. Much of the front page was filled with stories about the hijacking. Peter glanced at the paper but saw nothing unusual.

Outside the cafeteria, Joan waited with Katharina and the kids. "He doesn't seem the least bit stressed," said Joan. "He's so calm about the whole affair."

"He's like most men, Joan. He internalizes his emotions."

"Not Harry. The complete opposite, as you've seen at times."

The men joined them, carrying their cups of freshly brewed coffee.

"So, where was I?" inquired Peter.

"Crashing into the water," prompted Paul.

"I can't lie to you. It was terrifying, I have to say. The impact tore off the whole left wing of the airplane and the water came rushing in. Some people didn't make it."

The group approached the baggage claim area, but kept on walking since Peter had no luggage to claim. They walked to the parking lot and got into Harry's car. As Harry drove toward the house, the discussion continued.

"How long did it take for the plane to sink?" asked Paul.

"I can't say for certain. About five, six minutes ... maybe less. There's no real concept of time when something like that happens."

"Did you see any dead bodies?"

"Yeah. I did see some."

"How did they die?"

"Paul," interjected Katharina, "I don't think your father wants to get into all of that."

"It's okay," said Peter. "Most of them died from the impact and never had a chance or knew what happened. They died almost instantly."

"What about the terrorists?" asked Harry.

"Dead," answered Peter. "They died rather violently. Throughout the whole hijacking they acted cruelly, as if they were machines. In the end, they died like anyone else."

"How do people become such monsters?" asked Joan. "I really don't understand much of this."

"I don't know this group in particular, but in general, sometimes people become so fanatical about an issue or cause that they don't see others as humans any more, but as machines that represent their enemy. It's much like what I used to do, although, even though I acted like a machine at times because I had to, in the back of my mind I still knew that we are all human beings, fallible in many ways."

"But innocent civilians like that?"

"They don't see it that way. American civilians, to them, are the enemy, actually the financier for that which they probably think they're fighting against."

"I just don't get it," said Joan, confused. "How can anyone justify the violence?"

"It's like any other military campaign. One man's terrorist is another's freedom fighter, or something like that."

Joan shook her head in disgust.

Harry pulled into the driveway and stopped just short of the house. The day was pleasant, the sun shining, and the leaves on the trees turning color. Peter and his family got out of the car and headed for the house.

Across the street, in an unmarked car, sat Edward Sellers. Dressed in a sports jacket and tie, he was reading the morning *Washington Sun*. When he heard the car pull up, he folded the newspaper, got out of the car, and crossed the street. He called out, "Peter. Peter Murray."

Peter and the others whipped around to see Sellers approaching rapidly. "Eddy. You found me quickly," said Peter, not at all surprised to see his old acquaintance. "Harry, you remember Eddy Sellers, FBI." Harry nodded.

Sellers resembled a detective from one of those old Bogart movies, minus the hat. He even had Bogart's slow drawl. Peter and Eddy went back to the days when they were in the military together. When Eddy got out, he went to college and then joined the Bureau. They were the same age and had joined the war effort at about the same time. They both went into the Marines and through the same training unit; then they went their separate ways in Vietnam. Eddy got two purple hearts, while Peter somehow received none.

"It wasn't hard to figure out." Sellers had his copy of the *Washington Sun* folded under his arm. "Can we talk?"

"Uh ... sure. You guys all go in. I'll be there in a minute," Peter said, moving off to the side of the driveway with Sellers. "What's up, Eddy? I had to get out of there and attend my mother's funeral, you know."

"Have you seen this?" Sellers opened the *Washington Sun* and handed it to Peter. The headline read: HERO SINGLE-HANDEDLY STOPS TERRORISTS, SAVES MOST ON FLIGHT 243. HERO BELIEVED TO BE RETIRED MARINE LIEU- TENANT COLONEL PETER MURRAY.

Peter couldn't believe his eyes. He sighed, then noticed the author's name. Ann Howard. "How did she get this?"

"She's down there raking over the survivors. The Director wants to know if there is anything we can do for you."

Peter crumpled the paper up and handed it back to Sellers. "Now she calls me a hero? After all she said about me in the past?"

"Sells newspapers, Pete. Sold 'em one way, now sells 'em another."

"I don't want any attention. I want to bury my mother and get out of here."

"That's right, you're living in the Caribbean some- place, aren't you?"

"How the hell did you know that?"

"Peter, we're Bureau."

"Great."

"Maybe you should take a vacation or something. Go someplace for a while until this whole thing blows over."

"I might have to now. There's no way anyone else knows where I live, Eddy. I have no official records in my name there. The papers couldn't possibly find that out."

"I wouldn't trust them. You know how government leaks crap to the media all the time. It's a two-way street there."

Peter was agitated. "My kids, Eddy. Nothing happens to my kids."

"I'll certainly inform the Director. Maybe we can keep watch for a while till this blows over."

"Thanks, Eddy. I don't need any more of this."

"I understand. I'm close by if you need anything." He handed Peter his card.

"Thanks." Peter watched Eddy return to his car. He stood, fuming, as Sellers sped off.

At the airport in Nassau, Pritchard and his entourage hustled down the airport corridor to the Director's private jet.

Suddenly, Howard popped out of the shadows with a microphone in her hand, which she stuck in Pritchard's face. "Mr. Director, do you have a moment?"

"Actually, I don't, Ms. Howard." Pritchard kept moving, his people in tow.

"Are you certain who is responsible for this horrendous act?" She had to almost run to keep up with him.

Pritchard stopped abruptly and spun around. "Ms. Howard, the investigation is proceeding at a delicate pace, and anything I say one way or the other could seriously jeopardize our progress and people's lives. I hope that you and your paper will exercise extreme caution in printing any information you might have or obtain in the future."

Howard was stung by his words. "The American people have a right to know what you have done and will do about this catastrophe, Mr. Pritchard."

"Right." Pritchard turned his back to her and stormed off.

Howard stood there, aghast at the treatment she, a news professional, had just received. After all, she bristled, Pritchard was talking to the American people.

By now, most of the survivors were airborne on an Air Force C141 headed for Atlanta. Dion and Maxine Robinson and a few other survivors remained behind for medical attention.

The Navy, working with the Coast Guard, was retrieving the airplane's black box and the bodies of the other passengers. There was no sign of Amad's body, for obvious reasons, but they did manage to retrieve Mahmud's body. The evidence and the case were taking shape. The FBI knew for certain who was behind this action. It would only be a matter of time before they went after those responsible.

Pritchard flew back to D.C. He had to be there since everyone and his brother wanted information — information that he really couldn't give out at this time. Senators, House members, the Attorney General, and the President — all kept his phone ringing off the hook.

The sounds of automatic Chinese-made AK47's and American-made M16's ripped through the still air. They had a piercing effect upon the ear. All at once, human-sized targets made of cloth stuffed with fabric ripped into thousands of pieces.

Two dozen men lying in prone position fired away at the targets in front of them. Shortly after the firing ceased, a converted Toyota truck pulled up behind them and out jumped Kasim. He was dressed in standard military field garb — an outfit that was of old East German vintage, most certainly left over from those glory days when everything was easily definable in bilateral terms. Now, however, with so much uncertainty in the world, no one knew where anyone came down politically, nor where true alliances would lie if the balloon was to go up in various international trouble spots. For Kasim, nothing mattered but the emerging status of powerful and respected countries like Iran and Libya.

Confidently, Kasim knelt down over a young freedom fighter and tapped him on the shoulder. The young man stood up, his face aglow with pride.

"He has picked you," said Kasim. "You will gather up your belongings and come with me now."

The young man's face beamed with mission. He was seventeen years old, thin in mass but strong in demeanor. He had a full, rounded "baby face," and was still wet behind the ears.

The young fighter for Kasim's army grabbed his weapon and backpack and hopped into the Toyota with Kasim. As they were driven away, Kasim's other soldiers continued their target practice — practice accentuated by that crisp, distinctive sound of semi-automatic gunfire.

Peter sat in the back of the room next to Harry. The rest of the family lingered in the parlor, welcoming guests and keeping to schedule. The abundant assortment of flowers emitted that smell that is indicative of funeral parlors. Neither Peter nor Harry were especially emotional at this particular point in time.

"I didn't really care all that much about what Dad thought, to tell you the truth," said Peter.

"He always did question your motives, Peter," said Harry.

"How so?"

"You know, the whole Vietnam thing. On the one hand, certainly in the beginning, like many Americans, he thought you were doing your patriotic duty and all, but later he thought that you had lost all sight of the true goal."

"I don't really follow you, Harry. I suppose our generation will debate this issue until we die. Then, even the history books will remain controversial." Peter shifted in his seat.

Harry sensed his agitation and moved on. "What do you think you'll do when you get back to Cozumel?"

"I don't know. I guess we should take some time off and go somewhere, perhaps the mainland, and see some of Maria's family. We could hide out in the jungle or something."

"She called almost every hour."

"I knew she would."

They were both silent for some time. Their mother lay on her back in an open box, on display like an exhibit, not more than twenty feet in front of them. The whole setting made Peter a little uncomfortable. He had seen dead bodies in the jungle in all kinds of fashions — many missing body parts; however, it unnerved him when it was his own mother. He only wanted this whole nightmare to end so he could get back to Maria and his life in paradise.

"You know, Mother never said it, but I know she was grateful that you sent money to help pay her bills," said Harry.

Peter thought for a moment. "I know you had a different outlook on the matter, but I was so angry when Father died. I had no idea they had cancelled his insurance policies."

"Yeah, they cancelled him because he became a risk with his heart and all, a pre-existing condition they said. He put all he had in that shop, and when the government took it all for back taxes and left Mother with nothing, I didn't know what to do. I'll never forget the money you helped me find to get the shop up and running again."

"I never liked the apparel business. I think Father sensed that."

"Yeah, he did. He knew you had to get out of town and do something else, but he was disappointed that you didn't stick around."

"And have a heart attack like him? I worry about you, Harry."

"I work hard, but not like he did."

The next day, the procession moved along the highway at a crawl. Fittingly, the sky was grey and heavy black rain clouds threatened the day.

The motorcade arrived at the grave site. All the usual ceremonials were extended. The relatives and close friends gathered at the grave site and listened as the Reverend delivered his final sermon for Helen Murray.

Off in the distance, far from view, Eddy Sellers was standing next to his car. He watched the ceremony through binoculars. He had been tailing Peter since his arrival in Buffalo. The media were going absolutely nuts about this Peter Murray angle. Networks, newspapers, magazines, and television talk shows were offering tens of thousands of dollars for the interview of the moment. However, Murray was nowhere to be found. Harry had managed to keep the funeral low-profile, and it wouldn't be revealed until after it was over that Peter had been there.

The burial concluded, and the entourage departed slowly. Peter and Harry thanked the guests, and invited close friends and relatives to join them back at Harry's house.

Sellers watched as everyone departed. From a distance, he followed the limousine that carried Peter and his family.

11

Conrad raced urgently down the corridor, then bolted into a room where he was greeted by the staff present. Standing behind the monitors, he was briefed by the technical specialist, Mr. Owens.

"The base is being dismantled and will pull out within four hours, give or take thirty minutes," said Owens.

"What about Abdul Kasim?" Conrad asked.

"He was there earlier, but hasn't returned."

Conrad studied the satellite monitors that showed live coverage of Kasim's base in east-central Libya. Kasim's operatives scampered about, methodically striking the compound.

"Any idea where he went?"

"The truck drove due north, I assume heading towards Tripoli."

"Good enough." Conrad left the room abruptly. The staff went back to monitoring and interpreting the data it was compiling.

Conrad called Dugan on his secure cell phone.

Dugan answered the call from his limousine on the way to Capitol Hill for another briefing — briefings seemed to be all he did with most of his time since becoming Director of the Agency. "Give the green light," said Dugan.

"Double-check the information and contingencies. I'll brief the Hill. Got that?"

"Yes. I affirm, green light," said Conrad.

Dugan hung up as he sped towards the Hill.

Conrad placed calls to other deputy directors and field operatives. That which the company had been good at in days of old, a covert operation, was a go.

The Toyota trucks, customized for military use and painted in desert camouflage, pulled out from behind their shrouded settings next to a large sand hill and headed down the dusty desert road. There were eighteen of these rag-tag paramilitary trucks full of paramilitary warriors for hire. Most were distinctively Middle Eastern; however, a handful were clearly Westerners who were made up to look like the rest. They had heavy make-up on and were dressed in identical military fatigues — fatigues similar to those worn by Kasim's group.

The Westerners were clearly the ones calling the shots. Everyone was heavily armed. Several of the Toyota trucks had fifty-caliber machine guns mounted on top. The men had grenade launchers, AK47's, and American-made LAWs (light anti-tank weapons), M72A2's and 3's.

No one had any identification. Trucks and weapons had their ID numbers and all associative markings removed or destroyed. In the event that any one person or piece of equipment was left behind, there was no way anyone or anything could be identified. Their plan was simple: kill everyone, make it back to the rally point, and cross back into Chad.

They picked up speed as nightfall set in. A few miles down the road, the main force broke into two groups of nine vehicles each. One group turned down a side road and disappeared from the other group.

They were busy breaking down their positions at Kasim's base camp. One fighter heard the trucks approaching, but didn't think anything of it, or it didn't register for a moment — a moment that would cost him dearly. An LAW ripped through his truck and exploded upon impact, killing him instantly.

The next second the nine lead paramilitary trucks swarmed in and encircled Kasim's camp from one side, taking Kasim's warriors completely by surprise. The camp was for the most part disassembled, and the operatives were either snoozing in their trucks or lying around, waiting for the word to move out. There were thirty personnel who had remained behind and were scattered around, casually sitting or walking around the camp. It was nightfall and no one was prepared for a fight. Many weapons were inside or leaning against vehicles. There was no concern about an attack since they were in a friendly and supportive country. Besides, Libya's intelligence apparatus would have warned them of imminent danger. Nevertheless, clearly something had failed and they had been too lax in security.

An LAW was fired from each approaching Toyota. Most connected with an opposing target; a few missed their mark slightly, but nonetheless did collateral damage to anyone sitting nearby. Those not killed instantly by an LAW scrambled for cover. Kasim's people tried to return fire with their handheld weapons. However, the second group of trucks promptly appeared on the left flank and fired away with everything it had.

The fifty-caliber guns exacted heavy damage. Kasim's soldiers miraculously managed to kill off five of the invading soldiers, but they were too overwhelmed to stage a serious effort. The invading paramilitary force had the element of surprise and superior firepower. The slaughter was over within minutes.

After the dust had settled, half a dozen trucks moved in to finish off the wounded. A few members of Kasim's force were still alive. Groaning in agony, each was quickly finished off with a bullet or two in the head. Once they were certain that the task was complete, the invading paramilitary group departed and headed back the way they had come. The trucks disappeared on the southern horizon and into the dead of night.

Before they left, the invading force retrieved the bodies of their own dead soldiers and placed them in the back of one of their trucks. During the return trip, they destroyed the five bodies in the desert.

Howard was escorted to a table in the back of the restaurant. It wasn't particularly busy tonight. The waiter appeared right away.

"Can I get you something to drink, ma'am?"

"Yes. Coffee please," she said.

The restaurant was a simple, medium-sized, all-night coffee shop. Those who were there represented the ordinary night creatures. There were a few truckers at the counter, several middle-aged couples scattered about, late night lovebirds, plus an odd character — a greasy homeless man asleep in a nearby booth.

Sam sauntered in shortly thereafter, late by only a couple minutes. He saw her huddled at a table in the rear, so he didn't bother waiting for the hostess. Middle-aged, dressed in a polyester suit and tie, he looked like a cheap lawyer. He slithered into a chair at her table.

"Ann, it's been a long time," he said, taking out a cigarette and lighting it. "Want one?"

"No thanks, Sam. Yeah, it's been what, fifteen years?" asked Howard.

"Since the Kenny spy scandal."

"I appreciated that, Sam. That information helped elevate me in the ranks. It paved the way for my eventual Pulitzer." She took a gulp of her coffee, knowing it could be a long night.

"I read your story about the hijacking. You get right in there, don't you?"

"I have to. If I don't, someone else will. That wouldn't be good business for the *Sun* now, would it?"

"You're a good businesswoman, Ann. You know how to sell your product." He took a heavy drag on his cigarette. "What you want is information on Murray, right?"

"I only want to get his story."

"You and every paper and network in the country."

"How much?"

"I don't know yet."

"Sam, don't mess with me. I'll blow your cover wide open. I don't think the statute of limitations has run out on selling out your country. They'd hang you high."

"Relax, Ann. Who's threatening who?"

"You're a sleaze to your country, Sam. You'd sell it out for money. At least my profession is a public service."

"Give me a break, Ann. You're no different than the rest of us. That First Amendment crap doesn't fly here. Give me ten thousand. I need a down payment for a new car."

"I want to know where he lives and I want it in twenty-four hours."

"I'll call you. I want cash and I want it delivered when I deliver the info ... twenty-four hours from now." He smiled at her and snubbed out his cigarette. "You want to have dinner sometime?"

"Don't flatter yourself, Sam."

"You're a good-looking and intelligent woman, Ann. You need some recreation."

Howard finished her coffee and tossed a few bucks down on the table. She threw Sam a cross look, gathered herself together, and left the restaurant.

Sam sat there and smiled to himself. "Iceberg," he mumbled.

During his whole stay, Sarah hadn't said a word to Peter. She was obviously still upset about her parents' divorce a few years ago. Yet Peter hoped that someday she would come around. In the meantime, however, he didn't want to push her, since she was now a teen, and he knew how teens were.

He hugged his children — Sarah was unresponsive — his ex-wife, Harry, and Joan; then said his goodbyes. Peter boarded another flight, this time bound to where it all began. With a short layover in Atlanta, he would land in Cozumel by late afternoon. This time, because of normal flying hours and an available seat, he managed to get a flight right onto the island. Maria most certainly would be at the gate, pressed as close as she could get, he thought.

They watched Peter's flight lift off into the cloudy western New York morning. It quickly disappeared from sight. Peter had promised the kids a winter vacation on the island this Christmas. Sadly, for all those concerned, that would not transpire.

Katharina and the kids boarded their flight to D.C. a few minutes later. The kids had to be back in school, and Katharina wanted things to get back to normal. Little did she know, her children's routine would be upset even more.

Onboard the plane, Peter settled into yet another flight. He had a popular national news magazine to read, and luckily it predated his ordeal. Peter flipped it open and found the sports section. He began reading the latest news about the exclusive world of American football. He didn't care what anybody said, his favorite team was still the Buffalo Bills. Sure, they had lost all those consecutive Super Bowls, but — he would point out to young rowdy football fans that patronized the bar — the Bills had made it to the Super Bowl all those consecutive years. He had followed the team from the Jack Kemp and O.J. Simpson years through the Jim Kelly, Bruce Smith, and Thurman Thomas years. One thing he didn't like about so many sports fans — and he saw these types on vacation from the States — was how they jumped on the bandwagon. For years he saw Steelers T-shirts, then Forty-Niners T-shirts, then the Cowboys. Then it was Lakers T-shirts, then the Bulls. At least he had the same teams and stuck with them. And that went for the Yankees, too! He chuckled to himself about sports rivalry in general, and his hang-up in particular.

He noticed a passenger sitting across the aisle from him, reading *The Buffalo News*. The man had the paper opened and was reading something inside, but Peter saw the front page sure enough. There on the front page was a pick-up from the article that the *Washington Sun* had run two days ago, when he had landed at the airport. Because of their preoccupation with the funeral and all the arrangements, no one at Harry's house had even opened the paper or watched the news on television. So here on the front page was an article about the "mystery hero" of Flight 243. More distressing for Peter was a picture of Lieutenant Colonel Murray. The photograph was a file picture *The News* had of him fully dressed in his Marine uniform, from those dreadful inquisition days known as Iran-Contra.

Peter sank down in his seat slightly and turned his head to the other side. Great, he thought. Could he ever get out of the country now, without someone recognizing him? If he could only manage that, he would be home free, he hoped.

Peter sat there and closed his eyes, thinking for the longest time. Maria's image was etched on the back of his eyelids, and he couldn't get her out of his mind, not that he was trying to.

He wanted to read the article. Opening his eyes, he saw that the man had finished with the main section and placed it on his lap. He leaned forward. "Excuse me, sir. May I look at your paper?"

The man turned to Peter. Peter hoped the man hadn't paid too much attention to the picture or the story. Peter was several years older than the photograph; perhaps he didn't look like that anymore.

"Sure," responded the man. "Keep it, I'm through with it." He handed the paper to Peter.

"Thank you." Peter took the paper, nonchalantly unfolded it, and concealed his picture so no one else could see it. The source for the article was Ann Howard's story in the *Washington Sun*. He examined his picture. Remarkably, he didn't look much different today, except his skin was more tanned and he hadn't shaved in a couple of days.

The article was typical American journalism, full of supposition. The passages detailing the events aboard Flight 243 were larger than life. "What crap," Peter murmured to himself, but not quietly enough. The elderly woman sitting next to him gave him an embarrassed smile.

Peter smiled back at her and kept reading the article. Some of the sources were identified and some were not. Most of the details surrounding Peter's involvement didn't have a source noted. The primary source was Maxine Robinson who, meaning no harm, had told the whole story. In between Maxine's account was clever, fill-in-the-blanks material from Howard. The article wasn't false, but it was certainly larger than reality.

Peter couldn't believe the way Howard carried on about how he was a hero to those passengers, at least those who lived, and to America in general. What a farce, he stewed. This is the same reporter who had labeled him "a dangerous renegade who helped subvert the democratic process at home to supposedly save it abroad." He couldn't help but remind himself that she was one of those people who had helped destroy his career. Of course, he knew she would say it differently. He was responsible for his actions; she just reported them. Ha! What he had done wasn't that bad, he thought, and what she had done was blow the whole thing totally out proportion.

He folded the paper up and tucked it in the mesh magazine holder on the seatback in front of him so no one else could read this hyperbole. "Do you have the sports page, sir?"

Again, the man turned to Peter and politely said, "Sure, it's all yours."

"I couldn't stomach the sensationalism of reality today," said Peter.

"I know what you mean. I only skim it to see if there's anything related to my work." He handed the sports page to Peter.

"Thanks. What business are you in, if you don't mind my asking?"

"No, not at all. I'm in computers. I help companies maximize their computers' potential. And you?"

"Oh, restaurant management."

"Good. Well, enjoy."

"Thank you." Peter settled into his seat and began to do just that: enjoy his sports page.

His temper exploded. Kasim's face was red with ven-geance. It must have been the Americans. Who else had the logistics and intelligence? he asked himself. There was no evidence, but he could feel it burning within him.

Kasim crept into the building, as he had been doing for years. He was dressed in his Gallabia gown and Ghou-tra headdress, like many on the streets of his native Cairo.

The Americans had completely destroyed a third of his operation, but he still had two-thirds with which to make his next move. He entered the main room in the back of the shop. Tourists were buying trinkets in front, and the back was where he conducted his organization. He approached the elder he had conferred with earlier. "You know what has happened?" he asked.

"I do," the old man responded gently. He had a full white beard about his worn and weathered face.

"I have relocated the others," Kasim said.

The man listened with his head hung low.

"We are ready to proceed," continued Kasim.

"Very well." The man gently lifted a newspaper that had laid upon the table beside him and handed it to Kasim. Kasim took it apprehensively.

The newspaper was written in Arabic, but most capti-vating were the pictures, worth a thousand words. The story had been picked up by Reuters wire service. There was the same picture of Peter that *The Buffalo News* had run. His Marine uniform was completely visible, and that infuriated Kasim. The veins in his neck bulged as he read about how Peter had single-handedly taken out Mahmud, then Amad, and how many of the passengers, mostly Americans, had survived. He crumpled the pages as he turned them. He found the page where the story con-tinued, then kept reading furiously. The elder sat patiently. Kasim finished the article and crushed the newspaper. He threw it on the table next to him. "Where does this American live?"

"I do not know," said the man. "I am getting tired. I shall retire." The man got up slowly. Kasim assisted him. The old man sluggishly journeyed into an adjoining room and closed the door.

Kasim stood there for a moment; then he turned and stormed out.

The sun hadn't risen yet. The morning dew was heavy upon the grass and flowers, and the air was cool and refreshing.

Sam drove up to the gate at CIA headquarters in Langley in his late-model Lexus LS400. He had his necessary identification ready for presentation. "Good morning, Lawrence," he said to the guard at the gate.

The guard, in his mid-fifties and quite the typical-looking security guard — beefy, tall, and greying — greeted Sam in kind. "Good morning Mr. Ailes. Awfully early this morning."

"I have a lot of paper to push today, Lawrence. How's the wife?"

"Fine, thank you."

"And grandchildren?"

"Growing too fast, as always."

"Well, my regards."

"Thank you, sir."

Sam passed through the checkpoint. He maneuvered his Lexus into his reserved slot in the parking lot. He got out of his car, put on his jacket, picked up his briefcase, and strolled up to the entrance. He entered the building and took the elevator to his third-floor office.

Sam Ailes was a middle-management operative with a top secret security clearance. He had access to some of the most current operations as well as the archives via his desk-top computer. In the past, he had come across files that were related to Iran-Contra and some of the operatives in-volved, including Peter Murray.

He tossed his briefcase into the chair in front of his desk, then took off his jacket and did the same with it. He sat down and fired up his computer. He entered his access code and was onboard shortly thereafter. He punched in Peter Murray's name and a reference year, and waited while the computer checked its files. About ten seconds later, the files relating to Peter Murray popped up on his screen.

He scanned several files, most that didn't require a spe-cial security clearance. The files he sought regarding Peter Murray were old and declassified, and had been thor-oughly reviewed by the Congressional Select Committee years before. There were several files on his screen to choose from. Most provided basic information relating to Peter's involvement in the Iranian side of the affair. Ailes skimmed the information that was obtained through back channels, since Peter operated the Iranian side of the affair out of the Pentagon.

Sam picked a file that indicated it might be one of the last ones to be entered. He called it up and scanned it. There was nothing revealing, only that it highlighted some of Murray's Select Committee testimony and con-cluding documentation about the affair. The file didn't give Sam what he was after, so he closed it and called up another.

The next file Ailes scanned was added to the previous one as an addendum. Towards the end of the document, Sam discovered the following information:

MURRAY VOLUNTARILY RETIRED FROM THE MARINE CORPS AT THE RANK OF LIEUTENANT COLONEL. SUBJECT WAS OFFERED, BY

THIS AGENCY, JACK DUGAN, DEPUTY DIRECTOR, CIA, AN INTELLI-
GENCE ANALYST POSITION. SUBJECT DECLINED. SUBJECT WAS
LAST KNOWN TO BE LIVING IN COZUMEL, MEXICO, WITH MARIA
RIVAS, DAUGHTER OF MARINE GENERAL JOSEPH RIVAS, WHO DIED
IN A MARINE TRAINING ACCIDENT (SEE FILE NO. BEUI9OKE8JEDN).

Sam ordered a printout and closed the file. He tore off
the printout, folded it, and stuck it in his pocket. He had
thought about the fact that this inquiry into the file would
be noted on record. But it was one of hundreds — perhaps
thousands or more — of inquiries into the archived computer system per day. He was doing some research and
stumbled upon the file, and there was no big deal. He had
only the general location that Murray was believed to be
in, and it would be up to Howard to track him down.
Besides, he reasoned, the Bureau, the IRS, the Pentagon,
and God-only-knew who else probably had similar information on Murray's whereabouts. Sam was Howard's best
source in this business. She came to him because she had
no doubt that the company had this information. She was
right.

Maria was there, just as Peter had known she would be.
Alberto, Oscar, and half of Maria's cousins and extended
family were also there.

When Maria saw Peter emerge from the gate, she rushed
to him. They held each other in an extended embrace, or so
it seemed to others who wanted to greet him also. Finally,
after a long and heartfelt kiss that followed the hug, they
let up slightly so Peter could be hugged and greeted by the
others. Then they all headed to the restaurant.

The rear section of the restaurant had been reserved for
Peter and his party. The celebration would last as long as
Peter and Maria wanted — which, knowing Peter, would

be until mid-evening, when he would want to retire to the house with Maria.

Everyone congregated around a few tables at the back of the restaurant, where the regulars always sat. The main eating area was jammed with tourists. A live local band was playing both calypso and reggae. Music filled the air. Half a dozen patrons danced in the open area near the front door.

Maria stayed close to Peter, while Oscar and Alberto sat nearby. There were other friends and locals who knew Peter and Maria from the business community. The topic at hand was predictable.

"Even though I've had all that training and experience," confided Peter, "it never quite prepares anyone for something like this, Oscar. The biggest fear you have is no control over the events taking place. At least from a military point of view — and it doesn't matter what side you are on, offense or defense — you have some control over your environment and the events taking place. There are always contingency plans. In a situation like this, however, you have to react to the events as they happen. For me, I have to admit, I was as terrified as the others. I was running scenarios through the old stem," he pointed to his head, "but I felt a dire sense of helplessness the whole time." He sipped his drink.

Rolf Petersen, a German immigrant, walked over to where the group was sitting in the back. He was tall, with grey hair, and was in his mid-sixties. A retired automobile engineer with Mercedes of Deutchland, he now managed a local hotel.

"Peter." He reached over to shake Peter's hand. Peter took his hand in solid friendship. Over the past few years, Rolf and Peter had had some long nights at the restaurant talking about everything under the sun. Rolf was quite the conversationalist, something Peter admired greatly, since many Americans had lost their sense of the art.

"Rolf, I guess we have a lot of talking to do," said Peter.

"And not soon enough. May I?" his gesture asking whether he might sit and join the group.

"I'd be offended if you didn't."

"Thank you."

"I expected you sooner," said Peter.

"I was working the desk and couldn't get away. We're really busy now."

"What would you like to drink?" Maria asked politely.

"The usual, my dear. Becks." Maria darted off to get Rolf his beer. "How are you, Peter?"

"Shaken. I have mixed feelings."

"Well, I was watching CNN from the lobby much of the day, and I must say that your picture is all over the place — a good picture of you, I might add."

"Thanks, Rolf," Peter said in a sarcastic but friendly tone.

Rolf's heavy German accent was sometimes difficult for others to understand, but Peter, who had known many English-speaking Germans over the years, was used to it. Actually, Peter could speak some German, and when he and Rolf practiced, it drove Maria and the others near them crazy. Peter had picked up German while he was with Katharina.

"Looks like those media folks are going to beat this to death until it's time to move on to the next media event," said Rolf.

"Well, we're considering taking a vacation, to get out of town for a while until this cools off."

"Good idea. Where will you go?" asked Rolf.

"I don't know . . . maybe Brazil or Argentina," said Peter.

"That sounds good. You know," Rolf continued, "I was in Argentina. That was well after the war, of course. I visited distant relatives on my father's side." He thought a second, then said, "I still think to this day that they were ex-Nazi's or something. Otherwise, I couldn't understand why they went there, although I must say it is beautiful."

Peter nodded and sipped his drink. "What's CNN saying now?"

"Well, as you must know already, they have picked up that story written by Ann Howard of the *Washington Sun*. Do you know who that is?"

"All too well, I'm afraid, Rolf. I'll tell you about her sometime. I don't know how I've avoided talking about her before." Peter polished off his beer.

"Well, they've gone absolutely wild with this story, and everyone is looking to interview you, of course. Your picture was even in some Mexican publications."

"Great. Someone is bound to recognize me here sooner or later. I guess we'd better book our escape now."

Maria returned with Rolf's beer and drinks for others in the group, catching the tail end of the conversation.

"Shall we book that trip, Maria?" asked Peter.

"What do you think, Maya?" asked Maria.

Maya, Alberto's wife, was sitting at the far end of the table. She was in her early twenties and totally adoring of Alberto. Alberto stuck to her side like glue. "I'll get started on it tomorrow," she answered.

"Thanks," said Peter. "So they're saying pretty much what's been said already?" he asked Rolf.

"Except that they've gone into a complete re-telling of your wonder days in the military and your days with Iran-Contra and Congress. One pundit went so far as to say that this is your redemption for helping deceive the American people and helping the President betray constitutional law, or something like that."

"Fiction, Rolf."

"You'll have to tell me about it. I mean, it's better to get it straight from the horse's mouth, don't you think?"

Peter nodded and smiled faintly. "How many of Andy Warhol's fifteen minutes have I had now? I wish I could trade some in to someone who wanted their fifteen minutes. Damn."

"I understand. I'm afraid, as they say, that this story has legs now," replied Rolf.

It was only a matter of time before Peter understood just how deeply he was submerged in this mess.

They said their goodbyes, hugged a few friends, then walked to their house. When they got there, Peter closed the door and turned to Maria, who leaped into his arms. He was taken back slightly as the force of her weight knocked him into the wall. He had to quickly put his arms around her body and hold her so she wouldn't end up sliding to the floor. She latched onto his lips with hers, and ran her fingers through his hair, from the sides to the top to the back. He allowed her to engulf him with her passion.

He finally managed to make his way across the floor, carrying her as he went. He entered the bedroom and gently lowered her onto the bed. She wouldn't let go, so he toppled over onto her. She immediately began to undress him, without taking her lips off his. Once she had his shirt off, she began to apply herself to his chest, while he struggled to undress her. This ritual went on for several minutes until they were both completely unclothed.

Later, they had lost their sense of time. They were exhausted and couldn't move a muscle. Peter lay on his back with Maria beside him, her arm draped across his chest.

"I'm so glad you're home. Don't leave me again."

"I won't, I promise."

"I was thinking about my father and how proud he would be of you."

"You know, in a way he was like a father to me. When I first got to Vietnam, I was scared to death. As a young second lieutenant just off the boat, so to speak, he took me under his wing and saw to it that I had everything I needed. Then, during those inquisition days known as Iran-Contra, he came along and got me back up on my feet. I never really had the opportunity to thank him before he died in that crash."

"When he introduced me to you, I fell in love with you instantly. Of course I had to hide it from him."

Peter moaned his agreement.

"Dreams do come true, in the end," Maria said, kissing him once again.

"Yeah, that was a hell of a time with the divorce, Congress, and the media."

"What did that one senator say during the hearings? Something about saving the village?"

"Yeah, Parker. The old precept in Vietnam that in order to save the village, it had to be destroyed."

"That's it."

"What a jackass. Nothing could make me go back to all that."

Peter hadn't gotten much sleep since his ordeal had begun a few days earlier. He drifted off to sleep while Maria gently massaged him. She lay awake for some time, until she finally succumbed to her own sleep. Together, in the comfort of each other's love, they found their serenity. The world beyond their shores was too far away to bring distress.

Howard had taken the first flight out in the morning, made one stop in Houston, and then flown directly to

Cozumel. After passing through customs she went straight to the car rental and was on the road shortly thereafter.

It was Howard's first visit to Cozumel. She had no real idea of where she was going, except for what she could make out from her map. She drove past several large, high-class hotels along "hotel row" on the northwest side of the island. She pulled into the Plaza Las Glorias Cozumel, one of the last in the row, and checked in. It was an exquisite beachfront resort with all the Caribbean amenities. Although she probably wouldn't have time to enjoy them, she chose one of the best just to feel well accommodated.

Howard decided against asking anyone around the hotel if they knew the man in the picture she was carrying. She got back into her car and headed into town to start canvassing the area.

The tourist traffic was congested along the main drag on the west side of the island. In town, Howard made an illegal left turn and was chased by a policeman, who promptly gave her a ticket. She decided against trying to bribe the man — she didn't need any more hassle than she already had. She drove up another street, a side street, until she found a place to park. Then she began walking around the business district, asking the locals if they knew Peter Murray.

After stopping in two shops and getting no information, Howard went into a small tourist shop that sold trinkets and duty-free jewelry. She approached the clerk. "Pardon me, do you speak English?"

The young female clerk answered, "Yes. How may I help you?"

"I'm looking for this man. Do you know him?" She showed the clerk her picture of Peter, the same picture that had appeared in many newspapers and on television around the world.

Without thinking, the clerk said, "Yes, everyone knows Peter. How do you know him?"

"I'm an old friend, and I was told that he might live around here."

"His restaurant is Maria's. That's over on Ten Avenue Sur, near Calle Three Sur. You can't miss it. Where do you know each other from?"

Howard quickly fabricated, "From high school. We graduated together."

"How nice. He is such a nice man. I am sure he will be happy to see you."

"I know he will. Thank you so much for your help."

The clerk smiled and nodded.

Howard darted out of the shop. She trotted one block up Avenida Benito Juarez and turned south on Ten Avenue Sur. She saw Maria's Cantina straight ahead.

As she entered Maria's, tourists and regulars were enjoying a late-morning brunch. She waited by the hostess stand. The place was quaint with its Caribbean-style decor. There were shark jaws and other sea relics hanging about. As in Peter's house, a fishing net hung in one corner, and there was some antiquated scuba gear on display in another corner. Howard felt as though she had boarded Jacques Cousteau's *Calypso*.

Maria walked up to Howard and asked politely, "Good morning. One for breakfast?"

"Uh, yes." Howard followed Maria to a table and sat down. Maria gave her the menu and asked, "May I get you something to drink?"

"An orange juice."

As Maria went to pour the orange juice, Howard began looking at the menu. She peered over it to scope out the area. She didn't know quite how she would approach Peter.

The best way, she figured, was to play it straight, just walk up to him and beg for an interview.

Maria returned with the juice and asked, "Are you ready to order?"

"Yes. I'll have the huevos rancheros and a coffee."

"Anything else?"

"No, thank you."

Maria jotted down Howard's order on a guest check, gave it to a passing waitress, and went back to the business of being hostess. Howard sat and observed the activity in the restaurant. She saw no sign of Peter.

Maria led Rolf to a table next to Howard's. He sat down for his usual breakfast. "I have today off, Maria," said Rolf. "Where's the old man?"

Howard overheard and perked up when she heard Maria's name and the reference to her old man.

"Unusual for him, Rolf. He was up early and told Oscar he wanted to take the first scuba run. I haven't seen him like this for a long time."

"I hope he doesn't do it often. I'll have no one to discuss current events with in the morning."

"I think he just needed to get out this morning to take his mind off of everything that's happened."

"He's trying to cope with the trauma, I believe."

Maria nodded and went to seat another customer. Howard waited until she was gone. "Excuse me, sir."

Rolf strained to see who was talking to him. "Yes ma'am?"

"I'm vacationing for a few days here on the island, and I was wondering if you knew your way around?"

Rolf turned to get a better angle on his inquisitor. "Yes, I know my way around quite well. How may I be of assistance to you?"

"I see so many scuba diving operations listed in all my brochures, and I was wondering if you could recommend a good outfit for me. You see, I don't have all that much training, and I'm looking for a good instructor."

"Why yes, as a matter of fact, my good friend runs an outfit. He is one of the best and has reasonable prices too."

"That would be wonderful. Do you know the schedule for excursions?"

"They have one in the morning — I'm sorry to say it has left already — and one in the late afternoon that runs into the evening."

"Good. What's it called and where is it?"

"Cozumel Scuba Shop. It's on the main road just south of Chankanab National Park. The taxi drivers know it."

"Thank you very much. I'll check it out." Howard was eager to end the conversation there, but Rolf was interested in continuing it, since Howard was an attractive woman.

"Actually, I could take you down there if you like," said Rolf.

"Oh, thank you, but I'm here with my friend, and I'll be going with him. He's at the hotel. Thank you so much anyway."

Rolf felt a little dejected. He was puzzled about why she was eating her breakfast alone, while her friend was still at the hotel. It had sounded as if she were alone, he thought. Anyway, he left it at that. Turning back to his table, he began reading a copy of the local paper he had picked up on his way to Maria's.

12

*H*e walked through the streets with a sense of loss, feeling that the "good old days" he had known were gone forever.

He lived in East Berlin in the same old apartment his parents had lived in. At age sixty-three and still fit, he took any job he was offered.

His given name at birth was Otto Waltraut; however, he had used so many names since then that even *he* hadn't always been able to keep them all straight. He still maintained many fictitious passports with all sorts of aliases.

Waltraut sauntered across what was once no-man's land, the Berlin Wall, and into what was referred to as the western sector, West Berlin, now just another part of this ancient and glorious city. In the cold war days he traveled to West Berlin with some maneuvering. Now he could just walk right through what had been Checkpoint Charlie. No one even looked at him; how times had changed.

He entered a small drinking establishment and took a seat at a table in the back. The hostess asked what he wanted to drink, and he ordered a fine pilsner called Hacker-Pschorr from Munchen. As he sat there sipping his beer, he scanned the small room.

A short time later Abdul Kasim slipped in and stood near the bar. He was clean-shaven, dressed in a T-shirt and jeans, and blended in with the other foreigners who frequented the area. He searched the room, studying everyone there. He saw Waltraut sitting in the back, but he glanced past him. He ordered a Coca-Cola from the bar.

The minute Waltraut saw Kasim enter he knew who he was; however, he only watched Kasim from afar.

After a few minutes Kasim strolled over to a table next to Waltraut and sat down. Kasim sipped his Coke and waited another minute. "I don't know where the target lives at this time," Kasim said in English, looking straight ahead and speaking in a voice so soft that only Waltraut could hear. "But we will contact you with his name and where he can be found." Kasim continued to stare straight ahead, not looking at Waltraut. "We agree to your financial terms, and when we deposit the funds in your account we will notify you." Kasim took a swig of his Coke.

Waltraut didn't blink or move his head.

"That is all," said Kasim. He finished his drink, stood up, and left the bar. Waltraut nursed his drink for several minutes before he finally got up and left. He meandered back to his apartment and put Wagner's *Götterdammerung* on his Japanese-made compact disc player. He fell asleep reading *Investor's Business Daily*.

Jack Dugan sat in a conference room at CIA headquarters in Langley. There were department heads and other top officials discussing many areas of concern. Dugan would interject now and then. "Anything more to add on Colonel Murray?" he asked.

"Last we knew, Murray lived in Cozumel, Mexico, with his girlfriend, Maria Rivas," reported Will Ferrer, a special operations deputy director.

"Yes, I remember," said Dugan. "And the rest of his family? Didn't he have a German wife and a couple of kids?"

"They live in Chevy Chase," said Ferrer. "She married a State Department official, uh — John Perkins, Middle Eastern Bureau."

The door buzzer sounded. The room was a state-of-the-art secure room, with everything kept in full secrecy. A man near the door pushed a button, and a little video screen on his desk revealed that Conrad was outside requesting access. The man buzzed the door and Conrad entered.

"We've received confirmation that Kasim was in Berlin and was seen in the same bar as Otto Waltraut," said Conrad.

"That son-of-a-bitch gets around. Can't anybody get him?" No one answered that one. Dugan stewed a moment before he spoke again. "Otto Waltraut." He paused for a moment, then asked, "What was the nature of the visit?"

"The local informant was unable to ascertain any pertinent information," said Conrad.

"And Kasim?"

"Disappeared."

"Why'd I even ask?" Dugan signaled his unhappiness with a frown. Conrad knew how to read him. He quickly spun around and darted out of the room, off to gather more information. The man at the door secured it behind Conrad.

Dugan shifted uncomfortably in his seat. "Will, what do you know about this Otto Waltraut?"

"He's basically a gun for hire now. Former Stasi. I guess ideology is out, money is in." He smiled at that. "He turned up in Nicaragua in the mid-'80s, assassinating Contra leaders. No one really knew who he worked for, but we suspected Castro at the time. Lately, he hasn't done much of anything. He has a nest egg stashed away in Switzerland from jobs he's done, both with the Stasi and others, but he hasn't had a job that we've been able to identify for a couple of years or more."

"Get me his complete file. We need to get someone on him, and I want a report on everything he does as it happens."

"I'll get on it as soon as we're through here."

"No, do it now. I want this set up right away."

Ferrer nodded his head and got up to leave. "I'll have the file sent right up and have an agent on him in a few minutes." As Ferrer left the room, Dugan sighed and looked around at the others. He feared a hit on Murray.

Howard parked at the entrance to the Cozumel Scuba Shop. The shop was right at the water's edge, and several tourists were waiting for the next excursion to get under way. Most had already checked out their wetsuits and swimming gear and were getting dressed at this time. Howard was out of uniform and it showed. The shop was small and weather-worn.

Howard noticed the dock near the back. Then she spotted a pay phone attached to the side of the shop. She called Bob Hearn in Washington. He answered, "Hearn."

"It's me, Bob. Listen, I found Murray and I'm waiting for him to come in off his boat. He runs a restaurant and a scuba shop right here on the island."

"Good work, Ann. Be careful with him. He's not going to be happy to see you."

"I know, Bob. But the worst he can do is not talk to me."

"Okay. Keep me informed."

She hung up and waited by the shop.

The morning excursion had been successful. Peter had taken a group of thirteen divers, most of whom were experienced. The passengers were sitting around the boat, watching the beautiful scenery. Peter maneuvered the boat towards the dock, which was now visible and they were fast approaching.

On shore Oscar was busy getting ready for the next excursion. He had logged in sixteen people to go on this run. When he saw the boat coming in, Oscar went down to the dock. Peter pulled up to the dock with a smooth landing and Oscar secured the boat. The passengers disembarked and lined up at the shop window to turn in their equipment.

Peter shut off the engine, gathered up a few items, and made his way up to the shop. Howard spotted him right away but waited until he got closer. She was surprised to see how healthy he was. He was as handsome as ever, and his tanned skin and rough beard seemed to fit perfectly with his surroundings. He was at the window turning in some equipment when Howard approached him.

"Colonel Murray?"

Peter pivoted around and was shocked by what he saw. He couldn't believe his eyes — or his ears, for that matter — that voice that had pestered him in front of his home years before in D.C. He couldn't forget it. "How did you get here?"

"That doesn't matter."

"The hell it doesn't."

Hearn had been right: the tone in Peter's voice was hostile.

"I don't want the whole world media swarming around here. Now go back to your paper." He continued to check in equipment and categorize it.

"They don't have to. Tell me your story and no one will

follow."

"Look, Ms. Howard, I only want to be left out of this."

"That's impossible. You're part of it."

"Thanks to whom?"

"You were on the plane, Colonel. Look, if you give me your story, I'll be out of here today."

"My story? I read it already. It seems to me you've already printed it."

"Not from your point of view."

"I have nothing to add." He walked around to the side of the shop carrying some scuba gear. Howard tailed him.

"How did you kill the terrorists?"

Peter grew annoyed. His face tightened. "Look, Ms. Howard, those two men were soldiers who have generals somewhere. If you carelessly print all the details and continue to plaster my picture all over the world, do you think those bastards won't want my ass? Don't people like you have any sense of the harm you do?"

"People will do what they do, with or without us, Colonel."

"Right, Ms. Howard," Peter said sarcastically, walking back to the window with Howard in pursuit. He whirled around and stared her down. "That's the kind of arrogance that gets people killed. What the — Can't you just take a step back and see what you're doing? Not only to me, but to others?"

"You're still hung up on the past?"

"Hung up? You vilified me and helped ruin my career."

"You did what you did, Colonel. I only reported it."

"You dragged me through the mud and printed private details about my marriage."

"The people have a right to know about their public figures, or haven't you read the First Amendment lately?"

"The people don't have the right to know about my

intimate life. You think there are people out there who haven't sinned? Read your Bible."

"And what wasn't true, Colonel?"

"You stretched the limits of truth about my days in Vietnam, my involvement in Iran-Contra, and my personal life. I only carried out policy. I was a trooper carrying out the wishes of his superiors. I did nothing criminal or unconstitutional."

"But you did lie to Congress."

"We've been through this. Do I need to spell it out to you again?" He stacked scuba gear. "They asked a question. I answered it," he continued. "How was I to answer something that they didn't ask?"

"You withheld information."

"You're talking semantics."

"Semantics, my ass."

He couldn't believe she said that.

"There's a clear distinction between what is right and what is wrong," she said.

He was very perturbed, but maintained his composure under cross-examination. "You'd better take a look at who walks a fine line with the truth, Ms. Howard."

"I write it as I see it."

"Extrapolation?"

"That's subjective, Colonel."

"Why don't we write a story about your private life? I could be very subjective. Why aren't you married, Ms. Howard?"

"I'm not a public figure. Besides, that's none of your business."

"But my marriage was?"

"You were a public figure."

"You're a public figure."

"It was relevant to your situation."

"Relevant? You and people like you are absurd, lady."

"It went to your credibility, your state of mind."

"My credibility?"

"You were a married man. You were seeing your girl-friend at the time."

"We were just friends. I was very close to her father. I was never unfaithful to my wife, ever. You didn't check that out, and you didn't bother to print that."

"I wrote about what I saw."

"And it was very suggestive of infidelity. You painted me as the bad guy."

"So why did your wife file for divorce?"

Peter froze. He didn't want to dig up old wounds.

"Colonel?"

He stared her down. "This is strictly between you and me, and not the world. You print any of this and I'll kill you." He was serious.

She looked at him without flinching. However, under that Teflon exterior she was terrified.

"For my children's sake." The look of a madman stared at her. He waited for her agreement.

She believed his threat was sincere, knowing that he had killed before, and so she nodded in compliance.

"She fell out of love with me and had an affair," said Peter. "That's it."

Howard stood there frozen. She couldn't swallow. She couldn't move a muscle. She dared not blink and take her eyes off of him.

"Good day, Ms. Howard." He stomped into the back of the scuba shop and disappeared into another room.

Howard waited, fuming to herself. She bit her lip. Oscar had watched the exchange and wondered what it was about. Finally, she went and called Bob Hearn again.

"It's me," said Howard sullenly. "He's not cooperating,

but I think I can give you an interesting angle about the reclusive, disinclined hero."

"Okay, I'm taping. Give it to me straight and get outta there, Ann. There's no point in you being there."

Later, at the airport, while getting booked for one of the last flights off of the island, Howard ran into another reporter — one she knew very well — who worked for a national tabloid.

"June, what a pleasant surprise," said Howard.

"Ann, you've found Murray, haven't you?" asked June.

"The story's running in our late edition."

"Where is he?" asked June.

"I'll tell you if you tell me who told you he was here," said Howard.

"Okay."

"He's at Maria's Cantina. It's downtown, can't miss it."

"Thanks. A contact at CIA." June rushed off.

"CIA," said Howard to herself. "Bastard, Sam."

Before all was said and done, Sam would in fact give out the same information to half a dozen reporters, all of whom paid him well.

The story went out with the paper's late edition. It was a masterpiece of contemporary American journalism. It speculated about much of what Peter might or might not have been feeling about the incident on InterAir Flight 243. Howard went on about how he wasn't willing to talk about the whole episode because he was a modest hero who did what he had to do, and who didn't seek publicity.

The entire article bordered on fiction; however, Howard wasn't in the least bit worried. She had been through the legal aspects of creative story writing before, and knew that people like Murray wouldn't come after the paper for many reasons: time, energy, and the paper's extensive financial resources. Most people couldn't afford to fight the paper's lawyers indefinitely.

Howard also noted in passing that Peter owned and operated Maria's Cantina and the Cozumel Scuba Shop. No one who knew Peter had read the late edition of the *Washington Sun*, so there was no one who could warn him.

The next day Peter put the word out around town that reporters would be snooping around and no one should give them any information.

He snuck out with Maria through the back of the house, and they drove to the secluded northeast end of the island in a rugged Jeep Wrangler that handled the terrain very well. They disappeared for the day so that the reporters snooping around in town wouldn't find them. They took along enough food for a nice picnic, and scuba gear so they could check out some of the area. The shark population tended to concentrate on the Atlantic side in deeper cold water, so Peter and Maria didn't venture out very far from shore. Still, the day was magnificent. They enjoyed each other, the food, seclusion, and nature's wonders. They even made love on the warm, sandy beach.

"Do you really think they would come after you here?" asked Maria, soaking up some sun.

"I don't know," said Peter. "I don't know anything about these people and what they're capable of. To play it safe, I think we've made a wise decision to get out for a while. At least until this blows over."

"I don't want anything more to happen to you. I can't believe this has happened, after all that you've been through. I mean, here we are, on our own little island in the Caribbean, and this Middle East thing finds us here."

"I know. It's like I'm still burning bridges."

They hugged each other as they lay there on the sand. There they were, all by themselves, not another soul in sight. The ocean was before them and the plush jungle behind them. Peter closed his eyes and wondered, what else could happen?

13

O tto Waltraut's flight landed right on schedule. By the time he had changed flights several times, flown all over western Europe, and finally changed planes in Havana, he was exhausted when he landed in Cozumel. He went straight to the hotel and checked in; however, he there was no time for him to rest.

Waltraut's mission had taken shape rather swiftly. The money had been placed in his account right on schedule, and the phone call had come just a few hours before. The information was relayed, and he was airborne shortly thereafter. He checked out a Jeep Wrangler at the airport, then checked into his hotel, where he got a map from the desk.

He took the scenic drive along the main drag near the shore towards the south side of the island. Waltraut had located the Cozumel Scuba Shop on the map before leaving his hotel, so he knew where he was going. He approached the scuba shop and pulled over to the side of the road so he could scope it out. He sat there for five minutes and checked his map once again, then started up the jeep, pulled back onto the main road, and drove down the main highway towards the southern tip of the island.

It was the middle of the night and pitch dark; the moon was barely visible beneath the Egyptian sky. The weather was slightly overcast and cool. The Volkswagen van sped through the streets. Its driver was the young man who had left the base camp with Kasim. Kasim had inadvertently helped spare his life from the raid by the CIA-led band of mercenaries — at least for the moment.

As he rounded the curve and pulled up to the embassy gates, a bead of sweat rolled down his forehead and onto his shirt. Disguised as a common deliveryman, his van had been stolen just minutes ago from the commissary contractor.

The young soldier from Allah's army pulled up to the gate. The Marine guard halted him there. The gate was locked, and the Marine could enter and exit through a kiosk.

The Marine's buddy, his superior, stayed inside the kiosk as the junior Marine inquired about this late delivery. As a precaution, the senior Marine in the kiosk called inside the embassy and reported the approaching van.

The junior Marine, just shy of his twenty-third birthday, approached the young driver cautiously. "What is the nature of this delivery?" he asked.

The driver handed the Marine some papers; the Marine took the papers and stepped back. The delivery papers were from their regular food supplier, but the Marine knew there was no delivery planned for this late hour.

The van driver knew he had to make his move — because it was only a matter of moments before they tried to stop him — so he floored the van. It went forward, smashing into the wrought-iron gate.

The senior Marine in the kiosk saw what was happening and screamed, "Look out!"

The van bounced off of the gate and backwards a few yards, then exploded into a massive fireball. The young soldier driving the van died instantly, and the Marine at the gate was thrown backwards into a side wall. He was barely conscious and knew that he was seriously hurt, but he was in such shock that he was completely numb. He could not move to see that his legs were not there anymore. He had massive chest wounds to add to his misery.

The Marine in the kiosk was also hurt by the blast, but his injuries were not life-threatening. Several embassy staffers and personnel came rushing out to offer assistance. One man ran to the seriously injured Marine and comforted him, while another began ripping the young Marine's clothes off to get at his wounds. The Marine sat there, twisted against the wall, not moving. His eyes were all aflutter. "I can't see. How are my eyes?" he asked.

The man from the embassy didn't know what to say. He squeezed the dying Marine's hand. "Can you feel my grip?"

"Where?" asked the Marine.

The man squeezed tighter.

"I feel a little dizzy," sighed the Marine.

The other embassy official began applying crudely made tourniquets from his own shirt around the Marine's stumps just below his waist.

The senior Marine from the kiosk limped to the scene and listened to the exchange.

"I feel really warm," said the dying Marine. "Are you flashing a light in my eyes? I can see this light. It's rather bright."

The man squeezing his hand had no light in the Marine's eyes, nor did anyone else.

"Mom. What are you doing here?" The Marine grew silent. The man set the Marine's hand down and told the other man attending to the tourniquets, "He's dead." The man stopped what he was doing and sat down, in shock himself.

"His mother died last year," said the senior Marine. "He didn't make it to her deathbed before she died. He felt really bad about it."

Miguel, who had planted the plastic explosives and guns aboard Flight 243, was driving a boat across the channel. He approached the shoreline and flashed a series of codes with the light on the boat.

From shore, just inside the jungle line, lights from a jeep flashed back an answer.

Miguel pulled up to the sandy shore on the deserted and remote southeast side of Cozumel. He secured the boat and walked onto the beach. He located Otto Waltraut in the Jeep Wrangler parked inside the brush.

"Miguel?" asked Waltraut.

"Si. Eagle terminator?" asked Miguel. Waltraut nodded, then started up the jeep and drove down to the shoreline to help Miguel unload the cargo.

They unloaded some C4 explosives and diving equipment, placed it all in the back of the jeep, and covered it with a tarpaulin. Waltraut restarted the jeep and drove off into town. Miguel got back into his boat and motored around the tip of the island and back across the channel, headed for the mainland.

Reporters were still hanging out around town trying to get information. A few lucky ones had been able to buy some information about Peter and were now hanging out at Maria's.

Peter was holed up at the house reading a book when Rolf knocked on the door. Rolf had a key, so he let himself in after the short knock. Maria was at the restaurant.

"Help yourself to a drink and join me in the kitchen for a card game," said Peter.

Rolf knew very well where the drinks were located, so he got to work. After he had made his drink, he joined Peter in the kitchen.

"House arrest, Peter? Not an ideal picture."

"Thanks. We have a trip booked. We're out of here tomorrow night. I only have to hide out until then. Of course, what we had to pay was astronomical, booking it so late. They're swarming out there, aren't they?" Peter shuffled a deck of cards.

Rolf took a swig of his Jim Beam. "I had one at the hotel. A very aggressive young man, said he was from a TV show called *Hard Copy*. Have you heard of it?"

"No."

"He said it was a highly regarded TV news magazine. I told him I didn't watch much television, outside of the news and sports. He said I'd like it." Peter dealt a hand of gin rummy.

Waltraut was working late, with little sleep. He sat in his rented jeep across the street from Maria's Cantina and watched people come and go. No sign of Murray. Waltraut could plainly see the media lurking there, so it was obvious that Murray wouldn't show until they had cleared. Nevertheless, he decided to go in and check the layout.

The restaurant was filled to capacity. Most of the patrons were not regulars. They were either curiosity-seekers or members of the media. Waltraut had a Corona and waited for a while.

"I'll go stir-crazy sitting here. I'm a hostage in my own home," Peter said. "Oscar called. He can't take the morning run tomorrow. His uncle is sick on the mainland. I told him to go. Do you have the day off?"

"I do now," answered Rolf.

"How so?"

"My schedule is flexible. I believe that friends should always be there for one another."

"Thanks. Can you pick me up and smuggle me out of here and into the shop?"

"Absolutely."

They were silent while they played another hand of gin rummy. "The papers have been rehashing a lot of your past," said Rolf, breaking the silence.

"I guess I should come clean." They laughed. "You know how reporters make things bigger than they are," said Peter. Rolf nodded and arranged his cards.

"You know most of the story, Rolf. I'm still bound — by that elusive term known as national security — not to explain details of particular events. You understand."

Rolf nodded.

"As you know," Peter continued, "I went to Vietnam and played games with the foe. Charley, as we used to call him." He grinned. "While I was there, I was assigned to Maria's father's unit. We hit it off right away. Of course, I didn't meet Maria until fifteen years later. Anyway, we were involved in search and destroy missions. We would seek out North Vietnamese commanders and Vietcong, many times in North Vietnam and Laos. Our mission? Assassinate. It was war, and we didn't see it any other way. In war, you kill the enemy. And that includes his ability to command and control. You kill the enemy's hierarchy."

Rolf listened intently. He polished off his drink and poured another.

"Well, one thing led to another, and before I knew it, I was assigned to black ops — that's a super-secret operation, assassinations and the like. I'm not modest about my performance. I was good at what I did. I was a stealth killing machine. We would go into the jungle and sit for days, sometimes right under the enemy's nose, before we struck. I slit a few throats and broke a few necks with my bare hands in the blink of an eye."

Rolf gulped. They kept playing cards and Peter continued. "After 'Nam, well, I was sought out by the Defense Intelligence Agency. I was stationed with an intelligence brigade in Berlin. That's where I met Katharina. Later, I went to the Defense Language Institute. They desperately needed intelligence officers who could speak Arabic. I spent two years there, studying nothing but Arabic." He paused and sipped his tequila.

"At that time it seemed to me that I was getting my marriage back on track. We spent a lot of time together. Katharina and I even practiced German in between my Arabic lessons." Peter shook his head. "After that, it was all downhill, Rolf. I was relocated to D.C. From there, they started sending me out on missions, primarily to the Middle East, Egypt, Saudi Arabia, Kuwait. I was even in Iran before the Shah got the boot." He laughed and swigged down his drink.

"Damn, that was one hell of a mess. We completely blew that one. I even met Saddam Hussein — another mess, I hate to admit that one too — but we, I helped out a lot, supplied Saddam with goodies during his war with the beard, the other one, of course. Anyway, I was primarily in on intelligence-gathering, making contacts, logistics, armaments. That all led to Iran-Contra." He stretched the words out, letting them roll off of his tongue with a long drawl.

Rolf interjected, "I'm afraid I don't know much about this. What exactly did you do?"

"What I did, for the most part, was make the contacts with intermediaries, the Israelis, others, who in turn dealt with the Iranian officials who arranged the transfers. I also helped set up the accounts for the money transfers that were funneled back through Switzerland. That's it. You-know-who took it from there. I didn't have anything to do with the money after that. You see, in the military, you do your job and you don't ask questions. For one thing, you don't have a 'need to know.' As long as an order is legal, you carry it out.

"Now, as far as policy goes, the President makes the policy. Was it bad policy? That's for the American people to decide. The Administration said that the policy was to make contacts with moderate Iranian officials to help secure the release of hostages in Lebanon. The hostage-takers were influenced by the Iranians. That was what I believed. Well, if it was partly intended to fund the Contras all along — you see, Congress barred all government agencies from using their time or funds to help the Contras — but if it was always intended to fund them secretly, then it was ingenious. Illegal? Perhaps — and that's open for interpretation — but it was ingenious. I never laughed so hard when I found out that the Ayatollah's money was being used to fund the Contras. From what I now understand, not much of the money ever reached the Contras. I don't think to this day they know where all the money went." He shuffled the cards and dealt another hand.

"So why were you kicked out?"

"Well, I wasn't exactly kicked out. It was more like a pat on the back and a wink of an eye that it was my time to go. You see, before the shit hit the fan, I was completely covert. No one knew what I did, where or when. Not even my wife. Oh, she knew I was in defense intelligence, but she didn't know the details for obvious reasons." While Peter drifted off in own thoughts for a moment, Rolf played his hand, then poured himself another drink.

"Where was I? Oh, kicked out. So, I didn't want to have some desk job pushing papers for politicians in some corner office somewhere. I'm a field man, you see. Outdoors, as you know. Besides, I wasn't going to go any higher than I was. To go higher, well, there's a lot of politics involved. After I was dragged through the hearings, I just decided I didn't want it any more. I elected to retire, and ended up here. Of course, Maria had a large hand in that. Otherwise, I probably would have become a psycho somewhere, getting even with the world."

They folded the hand, Rolf taking it this time.

"As you've figured out, I wasn't around much for Katharina during all this nonsense. She was a lonely woman with needs, and she found another man who met those needs. It happens every day. This past of mine, well, it's crap I'd like to forget. But now this." He thought a moment.

"And this Ann Howard?"

"A bitch. She would stand on my front lawn and shout questions at me through my window. I'd walk down the street, and she'd chase after me and stick that damn microphone in my face. At one point I told her I was going to stick her microphone up her crotch." He chuckled. "Shit, well, that did it. After that she printed stories about my marriage." He was silent for a moment. "Needless to say, I was down in the dumps, until you-know-who rescued me."

"I can't even imagine a life like yours." They played some more cards and had another round of drinks.

"How good are you at misinformation?" Peter asked.

"Well, I don't know. What does it involve?"

"Lying."

"Oh. Well, you know me, Peter. I'm honest Abe."

"That's exactly why I'm asking, Rolf. The evidence is clear that Abe was so well known for telling the truth, when he *did* lie everyone believed him. The historians still fight over it today."

"I think I know what you mean."

"Wait here. Let's finish a drink or two, then you can go work on a few of those First Amendment hawks. Tell them I skipped out."

"Not a problem."

"See you in the morning at six?"

"I'll be here." They played cards for a few more minutes, then Rolf left to disseminate some misinformation.

At the restaurant, Rolf worked his way into the crowd. It didn't take him long to hook up with a young reporter and his producer from NBC. They made small-talk for a few minutes until the reporter asked, "Have you heard where Peter Murray might be?"

"Oh yes, I heard that Mr. Murray and his lady friend decided to get off the island," said Rolf. "So they've gone to London and will tour parts of England and Scotland." Rolf spoke in a fairly loud voice so he would be overheard by the others. The cantina area was noisy, with many customers and the reggae band playing, so Rolf had to speak up anyway just to be heard by those with whom he was talking.

"Are you sure of this?" asked the aggressive TV reporter.

"Positive. I overheard a friend of Mr. Murray's discussing it in the lobby of my hotel, you see."

"Thank you, sir." The reporter ran out the door. Several others standing nearby started buzzing with talk of Peter's escape. It didn't take long before the rumor was around the room. Many of the reporters hustled out right away.

Rolf stayed for a while and watched them leave. Maria was hiding in the back doing bookwork. Rolf popped in.

"Maria, hi. How are you holding out?"

"Pretty well, Rolf. I thought you were with Peter."

"We played a few hands, then he sent me here on a misinformation assignment."

"Oh?"

"Yeah. I spread a rumor around to the reporters that you and Peter had gone to London for vacation. It worked. Many have already left the restaurant and more are trickling out. I think it won't be long before they are all gone in search of you two."

"That's funny. I should still make a getaway out the back. Will you cover me while I make my escape?" Maria and Rolf left a moment later.

In response to the rumors that Murray had fled to England, some reporters were told to return home, others awaited orders, and a few did indeed go looking for Peter in Great Britain.

Alberto closed up the restaurant and locked the front door. It was almost four in the morning. He walked right past the jeep that Waltraut had been sitting in, and noticed nothing to cause him any alarm. Waltraut was standing behind a car on the far side of the street, watching Alberto.

When Alberto had turned the corner and passed from view, Waltraut crept down an alley with his duffel bag full of plastic explosives. He was quiet and very cognizant of every street dog sleeping and every alley cat scavenging. He approached the wall at the back of Maria's where the small, open outdoor patio area was located. He checked to see if anyone was watching. Then, when he was sure there was no one, he scaled the wall with his bag strapped to his back and lowered himself gently onto the patio.

He gained entry to the rear door by picking it. It wasn't exactly a high crime area, so the set-up was low-security: it was a simple door knob with a key hole.

Once inside, he went to work. He secured the plastic explosives to the underbelly of the bar, at the far end in a corner where it wouldn't be noticed. He attached a remote timing device to the explosives. He finished in less than five minutes, and re-secured the back door the way he had found it. Since he had picked the lock, all he had to do was close the door and lock it on his way out. He was over the wall, down the alley, and in his jeep within seconds. He drove off and returned to the hotel where he planned to get a couple hours of sleep. He left a wake-up call at the front desk, and set his alarm clock for insurance.

14

*I*t was well into the day as Kasim roamed the streets of Cairo. He knew he had to get out of Egypt soon. The Egyptian government had quickly established the link between the bombing and Kasim's group, and the media had already broadcast that information, so Kasim was, now more than ever, a hunted man.

He stopped by the same storefront where he had spoken with the elder earlier. He played for a moment with two children who were tossing a ball back and forth. It made him angry to see these young children chasing Western tourists around the streets, trying to sell cheap trinkets for a minuscule return. He blamed America's government and his own. The Americans still provided large sums of foreign aid to his country, and therefore kept their position at the "top of the chain," responsible in part for his government's continued existence. A more just society, through an Islamic and theocratic state, was the ultimate goal. There would be no more of this coddling the West for sustenance. Kasim sat down and watched the children play.

After a few minutes he went inside the shop, where he met with the elder he had conferred with earlier.

"It will be the Mother of All Attacks," said Kasim.

"And the American people?" asked the elder.

"Contemporary American mood, I believe, indicates that many Americans have a less-than-favorable view of this particular target. The plan is moving ahead as scheduled."

"And our American associates?"

"Ready."

"You trust them?"

"No, but there are no others with the same goal."

The elder nodded his head. "Very well."

They sat in silence for a minute. "We have come a long way, my son," the elder said at last. "From the early '70s until now, it has been a long journey. We have come from advocating passive resistance to armed confrontation. Allah did not wish it this way, but the Great Satan, the United States, is tricky. He is deceitful and clever. He tricked Sadat into making a false peace with the Zionists. Now, with the help of our brothers in the region, we will establish a state like Iran. It is written."

Kasim nodded, but seemed distant. His thoughts were on the mission. He kissed the elder's hand and departed swiftly.

Rolf was punctual this morning. "Ready?" he asked Peter.

"Yeah." Peter got into the back seat of Rolf's car.

"Here, put this over yourself." Rolf handed Peter a blanket. Peter concealed himself.

Rolf drove off. "I think I was pretty successful with my assignment last night," said Rolf.

"Oh?"

"Yes, many reporters began to depart after I had told one of them that you and Maria had gone to England. I would not put it past some of them to actually go there looking for you."

"I think you're right, Rolf," Peter said from under the blanket.

Rolf drove to the scuba shop, where several customers had already gathered. He pulled up and parked. Peter opened the shop and attended to the customers. He checked out equipment to those who needed it, which was most of them, although a few had their own gear. Rolf helped himself to some gear and attended to a few patrons.

Waltraut pulled up in his jeep only minutes after the shop had opened. He was prepared with his own gear. He made his way over to the counter where Peter had just finished helping a customer. Waltraut noticed Peter right away. There was no mistaking the Colonel from the picture he had clipped out of the newspaper. Waltraut moved up to the counter.

"Good morning. May I help you, sir?" Peter asked politely.

"Yes, one ticket please," said Waltraut.

Peter gave him a ticket and Waltraut paid in cash.

Rolf, standing nearby, turned to look at the man with the German accent. His curiosity was activated.

"Do you need any gear, sir?"

"No, no. I have my own."

"Where are you from, friend?" asked Rolf in German.

Waltraut was taken aback at first, but maintained his composure when he heard Rolf speak. "Berlin."

"I see. I'm from the Munich area," said Rolf. Peter listened to the exchange, understanding every word.

Waltraut nodded and left it at that, but Rolf wanted to keep chatting. After all, they were in a friendly environment.

"You are on vacation, I see?" Rolf asked.

Waltraut played along, "Uh, yes. Yes, I'm on holiday."

Rolf nodded, expecting more conversation initiated by

this stranger. However, Waltraut was obviously not interested in this friendly dialogue, and left to fetch his gear.

Peter counted the manifest and saw that he had registered thirteen people — a good number at this early hour.

"I'll ready the boat and begin boarding. Can you check in any last-minute passengers, Rolf?"

"Yes, yes. Go ahead."

Waltraut went through his gear at his jeep. He checked to see that his German-made Stiffelmesser, or boot knife, was firmly secured in its hidden sheath near the lower leg of his wetsuit. It was, and he prepared to board.

Peter readied the boat. "We're ready, folks. You may board now." All the divers, including Waltraut, boarded Peter's boat.

"Let's go, Rolf," Peter called out.

Rolf was closing the shop when a car pulled up. A middle-aged couple jumped out and ran over to Rolf. They stopped him just before he closed the shop.

"Is there still time to buy a ticket?" asked the man.

"Yes, of course," said Rolf. "Do you need any gear?"

"No, we have our own, thank you," the man answered. The couple looked rough and tough, and it seemed to Rolf that they were experienced. They paid cash for their tickets, grabbed their gear, and followed Rolf down to the boat.

Waltraut took a seat on the port side while the late-arriving couple settled on the starboard. Rolf untied the lines and hopped in. A moment later the boat was heading for the pristine reefs off the southwest side of Cozumel Island.

Dugan was in his office by six in the morning, reading classified and declassified reports. Even though the Cold War was over, it seemed that it was business as usual —

even more business than before. With the break-up of the Soviet Union, there was a more pressing need to keep track of the military hardware. In days of old, their mission was to get as much information as they could on the hardware, estimate its size, and determine its deployment — but they didn't have to worry about it falling into the hands of every nut who could come up with the cash. In the old days, when the Soviets sold or gave hardware to client states, the U.S. could more easily keep track of who had what. Now, however, with the former Soviet states strapped for cash, every middle-management bureaucrat whose palms needed greasing pilfered anything that could be sold.

Conrad darted in and interrupted Dugan's mundane but essential reading. "Waltraut was seen boarding a plane in the Canary Islands, believed to be heading to the Caribbean."

"Then our suspicion was correct." Dugan leaned back in his high-top chair and rubbed his tired eyes.

"It seems that way, sir," said Conrad. "We're on top of it." Conrad sprinted out, and Dugan sat and thought for a moment about this lunacy.

Harry and Joan had had enough of the media. They were heading out for a vacation in a secret destination. They needed the space to lie low until this madness with Peter and Flight 243 blew over. Reporters were constantly hounding Harry for the story of Peter's life and his whereabouts. Each time Harry would respond that he had nothing to say, yet that didn't get rid of them. Didn't they understand that no meant no? At what point, wondered Harry, did this become harassment?

A few reporters who were still hanging around watched the Murrays pack their car. Harry had succeeded in getting the police to issue warnings for them to stay off his property and on the public sidewalk.

A reporter from a tabloid sneaked up on the front lawn as Harry packed the car. "Mr. Murray, could you tell us where your brother went in England?" he asked.

"No, I cannot. And don't you understand that you're trespassing?"

"Is that because you don't know, or is it because you do know and won't tell us?" the man persisted.

Harry approached him calmly. "If you don't get off my property, I'll remove you myself."

"Did your brother tell you any details of the hijacking?"

"Do you understand what I'm telling you? Do I need to get my shotgun to make the point?"

"Are you threatening my life, Mr. Murray? I'm only doing my job."

"Get off my property now, or I'll have you arrested."

"Okay, okay. Don't get so excited." The reporter smirked at Harry's irrationality, and walked leisurely back across the lawn to the sidewalk.

As Harry, Joan, and their three children made their escape, Harry watched in the rear view mirror as a few determined reporters followed.

Peter anchored the boat near the usual spot. Four other diving boats were already there with their groups. Most of Peter's passengers were outfitted by this time and ready to make their plunge.

"We'll depart this location at ten o'clock," said Peter over the loudspeaker. "Please check in when you return so we know that we have everyone. The sunken boat is about thirty yards off the port bow. It's active with undersea life. There are plenty of natural wonders to see in all directions."

The couple who had arrived late took their time getting dressed for their dive, although they appeared to know what they were doing. Waltraut was also slow to get ready. Several divers jumped in and began their exploration. Peter was almost ready for his dive, dressed in a flat grey wetsuit. He waited until Waltraut and the couple were suited. "About ready?" asked Peter.

"Yes, yes. Go right ahead," said Waltraut.

Peter looked at the couple, who indicated that it was okay with them for him to proceed. So, with that, Peter took the plunge.

The water was crystal-clear blue. Tropical fish, in an abundant array of rainbow colors, swam about curiously. The fish didn't seem to mind the Homo sapiens or their intrusive behavior, unless the intruders got too close or attempted to interfere with their path. Then they would scurry away to a safe distance and keep watch from there. The coral reef undersea life was incredibly active and extensive. The divers were clearly enjoying every bit that the ocean offered.

Peter swam down to the ocean floor and explored some coral formations. He swam past the sunken boat, a boat three times the size of his. He had been down here many times; however, he was always awed by the absolute beauty that this unspoiled corner of the world possessed. He made this dive every time he came out because he loved it so well.

Waltraut dove nearby. He saw the grey wetsuit and knew it was Murray. Waltraut circled around the area and waited for an opportune moment to move in on Murray. The "late couple" had followed Waltraut just seconds later and were nearby, exploring the undersea life.

Up top on the boat, Rolf listened to the local radio station. He found a diving magazine in the cabin and flipped through it. The sun was up, and the day was turning out to be another picture perfect Caribbean day.

Below, in the water, the coral reefs begged for exploration. Many reefs contained cliffs, caves, and escarpments. Always curious, Peter swam in and around the caves and cliffs. He was not surprised to encounter a barracuda treading in a static position under a cliff in the shade. It seemed to be sleeping and suspended in motion. Peter swam by. The barracuda paid Peter hardly any attention.

Waltraut kept a close eye on the grey wetsuit. After he saw Murray disappear in the coral caves, he checked to see if anyone was nearby. When he was sure no one was, he swam down towards Murray, pretending to be a curious tourist.

Peter swam out and greeted Waltraut. Waltraut waved back at him. Peter motioned for Waltraut to come closer, and pointed at some unusual coral just below a cliff. Waltraut nodded and moved closer to see what Murray was so excited about. Waltraut nodded again at the sight. Peter motioned for Waltraut to follow him. Waltraut trailed along.

They came to a deep crevice that revealed some orange and blue coral. This was it. He had to do it now. Killing came naturally to Waltraut, who, like Peter, had killed more than once. He reached down beside his leg, just under his wetsuit, to where the dagger was hidden. He extracted the dagger slowly and smoothly, concealing it close to his side.

Peter was just about to the spot he wanted to show his customer: an unusual coral formation at the bottom of the crevice. The formation resembled the face of a large man. Its shape was indeed striking. Murray motioned for Waltraut to come closer, which he did, dagger gripped firmly by his side.

Waltraut swam up beside Murray and nodded at the sight. Peter turned to look at another coral formation nearby. When he did, Waltraut moved closer. He had planned a surprise move, much like Peter's move on Mahmud aboard Flight 243. Waltraut planned to come up behind Murray and go for the silent kill by thrusting his five-inch blade into Peter's carotid artery. Peter would bleed to death quickly — Waltraut calculated it would take about twelve seconds. Then Waltraut planned to return to the boat, throw Rolf overboard, and make his escape.

Waltraut raised his dagger and lunged forward. He grabbed Murray with his left hand placed firmly on Murray's forehead. Peter didn't know what had hit him, but natural instinct told him to react. He grabbed Waltraut's hand with his own left hand.

Just as Waltraut brought down his right hand with the dagger firmly gripped in it — as he was about to stab Murray's neck — he stopped suddenly, unable to move a muscle. He went into a strange convulsion, dropped the dagger, and began descending to the ocean floor, paralyzed.

Peter turned to see what was happening and quickly realized what was to have been his fate when he saw the glistening knife blade. The sunlight that penetrated the water illuminated the blade as the knife sank to the ocean floor, along with Waltraut.

Peter turned and saw the late-boarding couple behind him. They signaled that everything was okay, although Peter wasn't so sure. They each held a peculiar-looking underwater gun. The woman signaled for Peter to go to the surface.

Peter looked back at Waltraut's body, now resting on the ocean floor. A few bubbles from Waltraut's mouth scurried to the surface but, when no others followed, it was clear that Waltraut was dead. A small school of tropical fish went to investigate the scene.

Peter promptly swam to the surface and over to the boat. Rolf saw him approaching and went to assist him into the boat. "You're back early, Peter. You still have time."

Trying to catch his breath, Peter spoke through gasps for air as Rolf helped him up in. "I was almost daggered by an assassin."

"What?" Rolf's eyes went wide, his expression one of confusion and disbelief.

The couple popped up behind the boat. The man identified himself. "Colonel Murray, I'm agent Shell and this is agent Clemmons. We're CIA."

Rolf's head was buzzing. He looked at Peter, who reassured him. "Rolf, it's okay now, I think."

They helped the agents up into the boat.

"We've been tracking Waltraut. That's the man from Berlin, er — the body at the bottom of the sea," said Shell, the senior agent. The agents took off their gear. "We picked up his trail after he met with Abdul Kasim in Berlin a couple days ago," Shell continued. "We lost his trail momentarily, and picked it up again only late last night. We had guessed correctly where he was headed, and we were already on our way here."

"This Kasim, don't tell me — he's from the group that hijacked Flight 243?" asked Peter.

"That's correct," said Shell.

Peter had to sit and think this through. "Damn, that guy bugged me back at the dock." He looked up at Rolf, who agreed by nodding his head nervously.

"He was, I can say this now, an ex-East German secret agent. He was looking for sustenance from wherever he could get it. He's been suspected of several hits in the past for international groups."

"Damn, I didn't think they would find me this fast. What else can you tell me about this hit?"

"Not much. We didn't know how he would conduct the hit until we met up with everyone this morning."

"You cut it close," said Peter.

"I agree." They were all silent for a moment while they thought about what had happened. "How much longer before you head back in?" asked Shell.

"Not for a couple of hours yet." Peter was agitated. He looked out at the ocean and nervously scanned the horizon.

"You should make plans to relocate for a while."

"Yeah," Peter sighed.

"The FBI and the Egyptian authorities are aggressively seeking Kasim and those affiliated with his group."

"And where are they based?"

"Primarily in Libya. They also get financial and material support from Iran."

"Iran." Peter said that like it was an old associate.

"It brings back all those old demons, Colonel?"

"I thought that was all behind me."

"I'm sorry it has come to this. We can set up a line if you like and keep you informed of events in this case. I can give you a private line to the Director. He was personally concerned."

"We may need that." Peter rubbed his face in his hands. He hated to put Maria though all this. He knew that the restaurant and scuba shop would be in good hands until this blew over, but where would they go, what would they do, and how long would this nightmare last? Would these people hold vengeance in their hearts forever? Would they continuously seek out the death of one retired Lieutenant Colonel Murray, USMC? Peter had to get Maria and get out of there for now, anyway. By the time he had rounded up his customers, it was time to head in.

Abdul Kasim sat in his Cairo shop making plans. He unfolded a map of Washington, D.C., and studied it. He took out a yellow highlighter and marked the White House, the Capitol, the Pentagon, and the State Department. Then he unfolded a map of Virginia and highlighted Leesburg, Virginia. He looked at his D.C. map again and highlighted the Jefferson Memorial, the Lincoln Memorial, and the Washington Monument. He sat there for the longest time studying the locations.

Rolf drove Peter to the restaurant. "Please keep me informed, Peter," said Rolf. "I want to help in any way I can."

"I will Rolf. Thanks." Peter ran inside the restaurant.

Peter met Maria in the middle of the restaurant near the bar. They embraced. "Let's talk on the patio," he said. They walked out back and stood on the patio, where a few customers were eating lunch.

Under the bar, in the corner, the bomb that Waltraut had placed there ticked silently. The timer was an elaborate and sophisticated set-up. Waltraut was the only one who could disable it by remote control. The remote control was in a duffel bag in his jeep back at the scuba shop.

"We have to get out of here now," said Peter.

"Why? What happened?"

"Two CIA agents came down to the shop and told me about a plot by the terrorist group to attack me here. We both knew it was coming." Peter didn't want to alarm her with any of the details.

Maria was quiet for a moment. She shook her head. "Will it end?"

"I don't know. We'll have to reassess the situation later, from afar. We might have to put out the word that we sold out and moved. Hopefully they can get these people before anything else happens."

"How did they find us?" she asked, perturbed.

"Most likely, the front page."

"That's who I mean. Was it that Ann Howard?"

"My guess, yes. That's not important now. What is, is that we catch a flight now. It's only a matter of time before they're here." They stood in silence for a minute.

Maria squeezed his hands tightly. "I love you, Peter. I'll go anywhere and do anything for you. Give me five minutes to tell Alberto. I can't believe it has come to this."

"I'll throw some clothes in the jeep and bring it around back. Five minutes."

They embraced. After a moment, Maria let go and walked urgently back into the restaurant, through the same back door that Waltraut had passed through the night before, carrying his bag of death.

Peter watched her go. He saw her warm, loving smile and watched her every move. Her beautiful black, shiny hair, full-bodied, swung around with a bounce. There was so much life to her movement. As he watched her, it seemed to Peter that he was watching a movie in slow motion. He felt sluggish; his vision was blurred. Suddenly he felt a strong sense of foreboding. It seemed that he was frozen in a time continuum.

Maria had just entered the restaurant when it exploded in all directions outward, with a push from a fireball. The entire building was immediately engulfed in flames.

Peter was thrown backwards by the blast. He saw total darkness, as though night had fallen under his eyes. A nearby table, chair, and fragments of the building were strewn about — under and on top of his body. The other restaurant patrons on the patio were tossed in the same manner, as though they were cottonwood fluffs blowing in the wind. All were knocked unconscious and wounded with lacerations, hematomas, and broken bones. None felt the pain, yet.

The restaurant burned. People screamed and began running in every direction. There was hysteria and mass confusion. A man rushed out the front door of the restaurant, totally engulfed in red hot flames. He collapsed on the sidewalk, flesh falling from his frame. His body twitched for a few minutes, then there was no movement. Smoke billowed up into the sky and could be seen as far away as the mainland in Playa Del Carmen. Several local vultures circled in curiosity.

People came running from adjacent buildings to assist. Two men jumped the back wall of Maria's and saw Peter bleeding on the ground. They bypassed him since it looked like he was dead. They helped the others who were beginning to stir.

15

Senator Jay Buchanan walked through the corridors of democracy with an arrogance of supremacy. Although many of his colleagues respected his political experience and intelligence, at the same time, both sides of the aisle disliked his tactics, which could be divisive — not only to the opposition, but to his own party. In days of old, many freshman senators feared him and would never have dared to cross him. Now, at any rate, many welcomed the opportunity to openly debate with him on the Senate floor. He, of course, would have liked to take the insolent, disrespectful ones out back for a lesson or two.

In his time, Buchanan had seen the complete deterioration of the moral fabric of American society. He longed for those great 1950s, when the world, and America in particular, were easily defined. He was determined to reverse this moral decline at any cost. No more speeches on the Senate floor to a bunch of crooked cowards.

Senator Buchanan was from South Carolina. He was a tall, Southern gentleman who occasionally drank like the dickens in the back room with the "boys." His face was weathered, and his white hair and bushy eyebrows seemed amalgamated. He looked down at most people, like a hawk from on high. He had served in government in one capacity or another for thirty years, the last seventeen in the U.S. Senate. Reaching into his middle seventies, he was about to embark on yet another term. His reelection now was all but certain. His challenger, although she had put up a good fight, wasn't ready for or up to the task. So Buchanan said. Actually, it was probably more accurate to say that South Carolina wasn't ready for a woman senator.

His staffer pulled his Cadillac Seville up to the east side Capitol entrance, used by the senators and congress members. Buchanan climbed into the back seat and was driven away.

As he rode, he read through an independent publication he subscribed to, written by a political pundit who was an alternative to the mainstream media. He glanced up occasionally to watch the city inside the beltway disappear and the green countryside of Virginia appear before him. He would be in Leesburg shortly.

The Reverend Jimmy White greeted Senator Buchanan at the front door of his house. The Reverend lived in a large, Southern-style plantation house that was well kept. His Lincoln Continental limousine was parked in the long paved driveway. White was in his middle sixties, a little stout, and always seemed to have a five-o'clock shadow. He was well taken care of by those who sent him money via his electronic pulpit. He usually wore an expensive white suit and a hat that resembled something a member of a barbershop quartet would wear.

Like Buchanan, White was fed up with the state of affairs that had beset the country — in large part, they both believed, because of the government, the politicians. White was in fact emperor of his own hard-line religious empire, which garnered its main support from rural and small-town America by way of the idiot box. He had money, power, and thousands of foot soldiers at his beck and call. His evangelical network was called "Glory to God," or GTG-TV.

Recently, he had been forced to use some of his money to hire an attorney for a follower who had shot and killed an abortion doctor in Georgia. Some of his followers had interpreted Jimmy's teachings as advocating the execution of abortion doctors, although Jimmy had never come out and said this directly. He didn't have to — the message was clear nevertheless.

White was one of seven children born to a poor Virginia tobacco farmer. They were brought up in the strictest of ways. His father would take a good switch to the children when they deserved "a little fear of God," or so he would say.

Young Jimmy made his parents proud when he told them he wanted to be a preacher. His father supported young Jimmy, who was very good with that hell, fire, and brimstone — even as a young boy standing on the front porch practicing for the neighbors. His father had forced his brothers to support Jimmy while he went through the training to become a "man of God." Three of his four brothers had complied. His older brother Carl, however, had left home, the farm, and the old man, and put himself through the University of Virginia. He received a scholarship from the University of Southern California School of Law. After passing the bar, he went on to become an associate law partner for a prestigious law firm in Los Angeles as a criminal trial lawyer. Later, he was appointed to the federal bench in San Diego.

Carl had little to do with his family after that. Jimmy didn't even inform Carl when their father passed away, a victim of liver disease from many years of tipping the whiskey bottle. In fact, Jimmy grew to hate Carl even more because of the line of work Carl had chosen. Jimmy once said to Carl that the people he represented should simply be executed, "for God to sort out later."

Jimmy's wife, Rose, was in the kitchen helping the staff clean up after dinner. Their two children were grown. Their son had become a preacher and had two children; their daughter had married a businessman and had three children.

Buchanan followed White into his study.

General Harvey stood and greeted the Senator. "Good to see you again, Senator."

The Reverend fixed the Senator a drink — straight bourbon, the way he liked it — and poured himself a glass of red wine.

General Harvey was a Pentagon Joint Chief, and a member of Jimmy's organization, Glory to God. Like the Reverend and the Senator, he too had gotten fed up with the state of moral affairs that had beset the United States. He was disgusted with gays in the military, women in combat, and shrinking defense budgets, and longed for the glory days when there was godless Communism as an easily definable enemy.

"They've moved it up by one year," said the Reverend.

"Can they be ready?" asked the Senator.

"They assure me they can be."

"Our intelligence informs us that they are planning a hit. We have all of our installations on alert," said the General.

Buchanan thought it over a minute, while Reverend White studied the General.

"Can they handle everything themselves as planned?" asked the Senator.

"Everything," answered Jimmy. "There's no need for you to concern yourself with any of the details. It'll be set up and take place at the same time, although exactly one year to the day earlier. The only thing you need to do is not be there. Have you worked that out?"

"I have," said Buchanan. "Can you have all the candidates ready for a special election shortly thereafter, Jimmy?"

"We're ready. Of course we'll re-run most of those who are expected to lose this time around."

"Good," said Buchanan.

They looked at one another with total confidence in what they were undertaking.

"This is on order from God," said Jimmy, reassuring the Senator and the General.

The Senator nodded and grunted an agreement. "I have no doubt," he said. "We'll restore this great country to what it was, a God-fearing land. General, will you be ready?"

"Yes. I'll be at the Pentagon. The other Joint Chiefs will be on the floor in place. I'll be the senior officer of the entire military at that time."

Jimmy raised his glass and the others followed suit. As they clinked glasses Jimmy said, "Glory to God. Amen."

"Amen," echoed the General and the Senator.

Jimmy White's evangelical organization stretched from the shores of the Atlantic to the Pacific; from the Dakotas to Brownsville, Texas. His members belonged to a secret citizen militia. Like many of the several independent state militias around the country, they had been stockpiling weapons for the big day when they would be called forth to defend their land and freedom. Or, better yet, they would be ready to take over when the government crumbled — which, according to White, would be soon. Many had not only been called to arms by Jimmy White and his massive tele-evangelical apparatus, but had also been influenced by the tentacles of shortwave and regular broadcast talk radio — radio that had been to the far right of center these last few years. Nevertheless, some members of militias had gotten restless with advocating, and had recently acted violently with direct intervention to spark the civil war that, in their minds, was inevitable.

The dusty 1986 Oldsmobile Cutlass drove north on Route 5. Juan was only a couple of miles out of Mexicali, one of those "chalky" Mexican towns. Everyone was out and about, with business as usual being conducted wherever there was a shady spot.

The American border and customs checkpoint at Calexico would be like any other for Juan. He was twenty-five and an American citizen. This was his car, registered in his name, and he was visiting relatives. He had crossed here hundreds of times, having gone back and forth between Mexico and America with ease.

He stopped at the kiosk.

"Where were you born?" asked the border guard.

"Los Angeles," said Juan.

"Anything to declare?"

"Nothing."

"And what was the nature of your visit to Mexico?"

"To visit relatives."

The guard briefly scanned the inside of Juan's car, and then waved him through. Juan drove into California and stopped just outside the small town of Calipatria. He waited in the desert sun at a prearranged site for his rendezvous.

They arrived exactly an hour later: two men, both Anglos, and both from Jimmy White's ministry. Juan stood watch as the men crawled under his car and removed two cylindrical tubes that were about three feet long. They had been attached to the frame with brackets.

The men reattached the tubing to brackets underneath their own Toyota Camry. Juan got into his car and drove off, and the two men did the same. Juan had no idea what he was smuggling. He was paid too much to ask any questions. He figured it had to be narcotics, but there was no way for him to be sure, and he actually didn't want to know.

Pritchard was up early, as always. His wife sat with him and ate breakfast, as she often did. They were reading several papers at once, the *Washington Sun* among them. The news was standard this day, reporting on the rising murder rate in the nation's capital. Pritchard had to get to the office to oversee the continuing investigation of the Army of Allah and their leader, Abdul Kasim.

The phone rang and Pritchard answered it right away. "Yes?" His expression changed to one of horror. His wife, seeing his expression, knew something was wrong.

"Are they sure?" the Director asked. "For chrissake . . . I'll be there in half an hour." Slowly, he placed the phone receiver back in its cradle. He looked at his wife. "They killed Colonel Murray. Blew him up, along with several other tourists in his restaurant on Cozumel Island."

Ann Howard arrived at the *Sun* early. She grabbed a cup of coffee from the community percolator, and hurried to her office to begin work on follow-up stories to the hijacking.

Bob Hearn saw her come in, but waited until she was at her desk before he approached her. He hadn't shaved in a couple of days and looked ragged. He slowly made his way to Howard's desk, carrying with him a clipping from the wire service. "Ann?"

Howard turned and said, "Good morning, Bob. Jeez, you look terrible." She took a sip of her coffee.

"This came in over the wire late last night." He handed the wire to Howard. She read it, but didn't show much emotion. She was speechless, however, as she sat back in her chair.

"Do you want to write it?" asked Hearn.

"No. No, I guess I shouldn't."

"You're not responsible for any of this. It would have happened anyway."

Howard thought a moment. "I suppose you're right. Although, you had better turn over the rest of this assignment to someone else. Perhaps I should take my vacation now."

"Take your time." Hearn returned to his office and sat there thinking about the affair. Howard straightened her desk and decided to leave a few minutes later. She put the whole affair out of her over the next few days, as the story faded from the headlines.

He lived a dangerous life. He knew that what he did could get him killed immediately if he were discovered. He was a thirty-seven-year-old Libyan national who needed extra money to support his family of seven. He worked for the Libyan secret police as a middle manager, and information came his way. He was involved in the financial and logistical support for the Army of Allah. In fact, he had just come from a meeting with several of Kasim's lieutenants, some newly elevated after the attack in the desert. He didn't know everything that Kasim's organization planned. Actually, he knew very little. His job was only to assist and provide support for them while they were on Libyan soil. His need-to-know was limited.

He drove to the restaurant for his rendezvous with his Russian contact, a fifty-two-year-old former KGB officer who now worked for the new Russian foreign intelligence apparatus. Concurrently, the Russian also worked for the Central Intelligence Agency. He had worked for the Americans during most of the last fifteen years of the Cold War. The Americans paid better.

"They are planning an attack on American soil," said the Libyan in Arabic. "It will take place in the near future."

"You have no more to go on?" asked the Russian.

"No. I did overhear that the target is to be an American landmark, but I do not know any more than this."

"Okay. Keep me informed." The Russian got up and left. The Libyan waited for a few minutes before leaving to return to his duties.

The Russian relayed the information to his contact in Casablanca, and from there it got back to Langley in short order.

16

*T*he sun was directly overhead, and the day was hot. Friends and relatives had gathered and were waiting for the ceremony to begin. Harry and Rolf silently stood together off to the side. They watched the crowd mill about. It was quite a drive: two and a half hours from Valladolid to the cemetery in Merida, Maria's hometown.

The graveside ceremony was about to begin. The motorcade slowly made its way up the roadway and stopped nearby. Rolf and Harry painstakingly made their way over to the hearses, where they waited for the officials to open them.

Rolf was one of the pallbearers for Maria, and Harry was a pallbearer for Peter. They carried the caskets up the small hill. Tears welled up in Rolf's eyes as he helped place Maria's casket over the open grave and on the mechanism that would lower it below. He stepped back and joined the crowd of mourners.

Harry did the same with Peter's casket, although he held back his tears. He stared at the ground as the priest conducted the final ceremony for Maria and Peter. The priest gave an inspiring speech and, as he spoke, both Rolf and Harry felt the same sadness. Such a tragedy, for all those involved. How had it come to this? Rolf wiped tears from his eyes with his handkerchief.

When the ceremony was finally over, Rolf, Harry, and a few of Maria's close relatives stood somberly at the graves, in complete silence except some quiet sniffling. They waited until the attendants lowered the caskets into the ground and began shoveling dirt into the graves, then turned and wandered back to their cars. No one said a word as everyone drove off.

During the drive back to Chichen Itza, still no one spoke.

Director Pritchard knew it must be something quite urgent. The Director of the CIA didn't normally call and ask to see the Director of the FBI in a secure room immediately. So he cleared his afternoon appointments and rescheduled a briefing regarding an important meeting about the corruption charges of a popular congressman.

Director Dugan was buzzed in. His driver/bodyguard stood guard just outside the office door. Dugan closed the door and hurried over to Pritchard, shook his hand, and said, "Gene."

"Jack," said Pritchard. "Can I get you something? Anything to drink?"

"No thanks," said Dugan. "I received this just two hours ago and thought you should see it right away." He handed Pritchard a large file folder with CLASSIFIED: DIRECTOR'S EYES ONLY stamped on it.

Pritchard opened the envelope and read the document it contained. Dugan waited patiently until Pritchard finished reading.

"What do you think the target might be?" asked Pritchard.

"We don't know. I think they're planning to hit targets that directly represent the government. Landmarks, perhaps the financial district again. They want to hit targets that strike at the very heart of our system."

"Christ. We'll be a police state soon. You going to see the chief?"

"Yeah. I think you should be there too. We all need to come up with a strategy to deal with this. A complete national security brief."

"You guys heard from our friend Kasim?"

"Last we knew he was in Libya."

"I thought maybe you got him in that hit on his camp."

Pritchard studied Dugan. Dugan didn't blink, but did stare him down.

"Forget it," said Pritchard. "Anyway, we've got to get in there and get this son-of-a-bitch. I'd appreciate anything else you can come up with." Pritchard handed the file back to Dugan.

"Otto Waltraut was assassinated in Cozumel just before Murray's restaurant blew up," said Dugan. "We tried to save Murray, but Waltraut was one step ahead of us." He sighed, then continued. "I knew Murray personally years ago, when he doubled for us on loan from the Pentagon. I want this asshole as much as you do."

"We had Murray under wraps while he was stateside. Howard got to him and helped bury him. There wasn't much more we could do. It sickens me."

With that, Dugan nodded slightly, turned, and left the office. Pritchard sat at his desk and stared at the wall.

The heat of the jungle had soaked their shirts well before they reached the small house just off the dirt road. The house was nestled in thick growth, and was slightly better kept than most in the area. Two cars, one a late-model Nissan, the other a Toyota, were parked in the driveway.

Harry and Rolf walked to the front door, knocked, then entered. Waiting inside were Oscar and his family.

Oscar introduced Harry to his grandmother, father, mother, and four brothers and sisters.

"Can we see him now, Oscar?" asked Rolf.

Oscar nodded.

Harry and Rolf followed Oscar into the back bedroom. Lying upon the bed, wrapped in heavy gauze and looking like death incarnate, was a wounded Peter. It had been four days since the explosion and he was still unconscious. A private nurse stood when the men entered. She was there to administer the multitude of antibiotics and other medical items that were laid on trays and in boxes.

There was no life to Peter's body except for shallow breathing. His eyes were bandaged closed, his face was stitched up, and his left arm was in a cast. An IV bottle dangled overhead from a rack, and a tube was inserted in his wrist. Peter had been sedated since the explosion.

"Well, as you know," said Rolf, "he has no life-threatening injuries, but he will be sore for some time, I'm afraid. This is Nurse Lupe. I brought her in from the island."

Harry nodded to the nurse, who responded with a slight smile.

"There is something that none of us can do, however, and that is heal his heart," said Rolf.

Harry sat in a chair in the corner of the room. "What worries me, Rolf, is what he'll do now. I know this man all too well. I'm afraid *this* time his life is over. Peter Murray is dead, so to speak. Last time, he had Maria to pull him through. This time, well . . ." Harry's eyes watered.

"We will have to revive him and get some solid food in his system before too long," said Rolf. "I think we should bring him around tomorrow."

"Yeah, you're right. I'll break the news to him then." Harry wiped his eyes. "By the way, how did you manage the cover-up of Peter's survival?"

"We had the necessary contacts with local officials. They handled all the legal details of staging Peter's death and gave us the casket. You see, Peter had a lot of friends here, and everyone gave without compensation. And to think that this is Mexico." Rolf chuckled under his breath at the irony, considering how corrupt Mexico was. "The priest didn't know that Peter wasn't in the box. Maria — " Rolf choked up. It was a moment before he could continue. "I know Peter would have given his life for her and for the others. Poor Alberto too. He was Peter's loyal and trustworthy sidekick."

"I know I'm just a simple man who leads a simple life, but this just doesn't make any sense to me," said Harry. "Peter saved those lives on that plane. Was that a bad thing to these monsters?"

"I can only say that it is a very complicated subject."

"How complicated is civility? There must be a better way for these people to achieve their goals." Harry looked at the floor.

"Actually, there is. It's called democracy. But even then, extreme elements aren't satisfied when they don't get their way."

Harry nodded but still wasn't satisfied with Rolf's explanation.

Rolf drove Harry to the Hotel Mayaland in Chichen Itza a few miles away. Harry thought he had walked onto the set of a Humphrey Bogart film. The hotel was a flashback, so it seemed, to the 1930s or '40s. It was on the site of one of the most famous of Mexico's Mayan ruins, where a large pyramid rose from the earth to the sun. Rolf had reserved a room for Harry for an indefinite stay.

Harry checked in and went to meet Rolf in the downstairs bar.

"Have you informed his ex-wife and children?" asked Rolf.

"Yeah, only what you told me on the phone. I'll call and update them tomorrow." Harry's drink arrived, and he downed it in one shot. He'd never drunk like this before, but it didn't seem to bother him.

"I realize Peter's life here is over," said Rolf.

"I can't imagine him staying now," said Harry. "He was the happiest here that he'd ever been, so he said more than once — the last time at Mother's funeral, to be exact."

"He had no need for anything more than what he had here," said Rolf.

"I know it. I know too that Peter won't let this pass. I'm worried about his head, as well as his heart."

They had had a voluminous catch, and the fish hold was filled to capacity with fresh halibut. The crew of four sat around and waited — for what, they didn't know, except what the captain had told them, which was that they were waiting to rendezvous with another vessel.

Captain Clark was an upstanding man in the community, a leader to his men, and a member of Reverend White's fundamentalist group, Glory to God. When he was asked to pick up some cargo from another member at sea and deliver it to a dock where another member would be waiting, he obliged without question. He believed he was doing God's work, and he didn't need to know exactly what he was transporting for the church.

A fancy and expensive cabin cruiser came in due order. Clark's crew lashed the two boats together. Two Anglo-American men onboard the cruiser appeared. Each carried a box that was three feet by three feet. They handed the boxes over to Clark's men, then returned to get more. They came back topside a moment later, each with two oblong crates, and passed them over right away. This went on for more than ten minutes, until Clark had two dozen cardboard boxes and wood crates stowed away on his fishing trawler. Some of the cargo was large, some small. Quite a load, thought Clark's crew. Nevertheless, everyone did their job and never questioned the activity.

Each boat cast off its respective lines and went its separate way. The cruiser headed back out to sea, while Clark's trawler docked and unloaded the cargo in Puget Sound. It was promptly loaded onto a moving truck, and arrived in Virginia three days later.

They were slowly taking him off the medication that had relegated him to an unconscious stupor. They had already taken the bandages off of his eyes. Harry, Rolf, and the nurse watched as Peter slowly came around.

As he struggled to consciousness, it took several minutes for him to open his eyes and understand who was standing before him. His eyes opened slowly and remained open for a moment, then closed again. It was a few minutes before he could open them again briefly and refocus. This process went on for twenty minutes. Harry and Rolf waited patiently.

Finally, Peter's eyes stayed open. Harry went over and stood by him, waiting for him to say something. Certainly, as he focused his eyes, Peter would see Harry standing there.

Peter's right hand moved slightly and Harry took it in his own right hand. Peter squeezed Harry's hand. Although, understandably, it wasn't his usual grip, it didn't bother Harry in the slightest.

Finally, Peter's lips began to move. Harry leaned down to listen, but couldn't understand what Peter was saying. All that came out were wisps of air, due to his grogginess and weakness. Peter kept trying, and finally there was no mistaking what he was trying to say. The sound coming from his lips took the form of a word, although the consonant "m" sound was slurred. "h — aria?"

Harry looked at Rolf, who nodded somberly in return. There was no stalling now. Harry had to tell him. Peter licked his lips and partially closed his eyes, then reopened them as Harry leaned in towards his right ear. "I'm sorry, Peter," said Harry. "Maria didn't make it."

Peter closed his eyes tightly and pursed his lips together. His eyes remained closed and his grip on Harry's hand got stronger. Harry backed off a bit until Peter finally let his hand go. Peter's hand fell to the side of the bed. Rolf and Harry stepped back towards the door. Peter kept his eyes closed, his fist now clenched, and his breathing rate steady, but deeper.

Harry, Rolf, and the nurse stayed for another half hour, but Peter never reopened his eyes or moved in any way. Finally, Harry and Rolf left the room in despair. The nurse moved her chair just outside the room and resumed her watch by the door.

Peter was coming around more and more, but chose to lie still and sink into depression. He really couldn't have moved even if he had wanted to. There was pain in his arm and back. His mind wasn't all that clear yet, but there was no mistaking the words that Harry had spoken.

Images flickered through his mind. He could see the pictures in his head as if they were happening before him right then. He could see Maria smiling as she sat on the boat with him, her shiny black hair blowing gently in the Caribbean breeze. Why couldn't he have died, so he could be with her right now? Better still, he would have given his life to spare hers.

It took two more days before Peter was strong enough to get up and walk around. The whole time, even when Harry or Rolf were there, Peter said nothing. There was no conversation, no small-talk, nothing at all. Harry and Rolf had agreed to wait until Peter was ready to talk. Harry watched the nurse give Peter some painkillers and a sleeping pill.

At the Mayaland Hotel, Rolf joined Harry for a drink. He had several newspapers under his arm.

"Here's the *Sun*," said Rolf. "Listen to this. It says here, quote: Colonel Murray served his country with honor and distinction. He was a hero to the American people even in retirement, unquote. Can you believe this? It's a full front page of Peter's life. How strange. It's not written by that Ann Howard. It's written by a *Sun* staff writer. It goes on and on in such a patronizing way." Rolf crumpled the paper by his side. "After Peter told me about Ann Howard and the *Washington Sun*, I can't read any more of this."

"Let me see," said Harry. Rolf handed the paper to Harry. "My God, you're right. It goes on about him being a decorated Marine and Vietnam veteran. We should burn these papers and not let Peter get access to any media. He'll want to kill someone." Harry skimmed the story. "I don't see anywhere how the terrorists were led to Peter. Someone should write about that part of the story."

Harry and Rolf read most of the stories contained within the several papers. They drank and stewed as they did so.

Peter sat in a large, mesh, tent-like bug apparatus near the house Oscar's family lived in. He stared straight ahead and didn't blink, twitch a muscle, or move his head. His eyes were black and blue from the explosion. His face was scratched and swollen and his left arm was in a sling. He was a static figure, seemingly lifeless. He was a shell, with only his memories now. An orange drink, still full, sat on a table next to him. He didn't even look around when he heard Harry and Rolf walking up the roadway after a walk through the neighborhood.

Harry and Rolf went inside the bug tent. They sat down quietly in their chairs and read magazines. Harry mostly looked at the pictures. They said nothing. The three of them sat there for almost an hour before Peter finally stood up, took his one crutch that he was using for his bum knee, and limped out of the mesh tent. Harry and Rolf followed him down the roadway. They kept their distance as Peter hobbled along.

"He's now refusing to take any painkilling medication," said Rolf. "I don't know what he's up to."

"I think I do," said Harry. "The trauma of this whole mess has made him take leave of his senses."

"Why would he punish himself like this?"

"I'm afraid he needs professional help, but he'd never agree to it."

Peter stopped at the edge of the roadway. He stood staring at a trash heap.

"What's he looking at, Rolf?"

"I don't know." Rolf walked closer and discovered that Peter was fixated upon two vultures that were fighting over some garbage that had been tossed from a house and onto a garbage pile. Vultures like these were common in these parts.

Peter stared, the scene reminding him of the time he went on a secret fact-finding mission to Honduras with the Defense Intelligence Agency and the CIA in the mid-'80s. He was driving with some military personnel along a roadway near the border of Nicaragua early one morning when his intelligence patrol came upon a recently deceased horse near the shoulder of the road. Several vultures were already beginning their feast. When they drove back the same route a few hours later, the insides of the mammal were missing. Peter had been able to see in one end and out the other. There was absolutely nothing in between. As sickening as it was, Peter had thought nature had an effective way of disposal. Now, watching these vultures on the garbage heap, Peter wondered how much different these creatures were from his own species. At least animals generally only killed when they needed to fill their bellies, were in imminent danger of losing their lives, or to defend their offspring. Then again, vultures usually only cleaned up the scraps left over from others. Not so with his kind. His kind killed out of emotion or to achieve political ends.

"Peter?" said Rolf.

Peter turned and saw Rolf standing before him. They stared at each other for more than thirty seconds. Peter's stare seemed vacant to Rolf, as if Peter were looking right through him.

"Are you ready to talk?" Rolf asked.

"I'm sorry Rolf," Peter said somberly, "there's nothing to talk about." Peter turned and continued hobbling. Rolf waited for Harry.

"What do you think?" asked Harry.

"It's obvious that he is extremely traumatized."

"Do you think we should get him professional help?"

"Like you said, knowing Peter, he would refuse. I suggest we stay here as long as it takes for him to come around, and then we can talk to him."

They followed Peter, silent for the longest time as they watched Peter limp along. "Harry? I have an idea," Rolf said at last.

"Go ahead. Anything."

"His children."

Harry thought for a minute, then finally replied. "Yes."

The Russian double agent previously seen in Libya with the Libyan informant now waited at a small roadside cafe. He had gone through two soft drinks and was getting concerned. He had been contacted about this impromptu meeting just the day before, and had checked into a local hotel for a two-day stay.

After finishing his third drink, he left the roadside watering hole. He got into his cheap, rundown car rental and drove back to his hotel.

When he got to his room, he found his informant sitting at the table with his back to him. He instantly froze in his tracks. As he began to back out of the room, two men came out of the bathroom, and two more men from the balcony. The Russian was surrounded.

One of the men who had come in from the balcony turned the informant around in his chair. He was dead, shot through the head. The Russian went for his gun, but it was too late. One of the men discharged a round into the back of the Russian's head, and he fell to the floor, instantly dead.

Dugan's cell phone rang just as he was teeing off on the fourth hole at the Gulf Shores Country Club in Naples, Florida. With Dugan was Senator Jay Buchanan. Buchanan had already made a fine shot, a shot that Dugan had to beat. Dugan hooked his golf ball and made a terrible shot. His ball landed in a nearby water trap. "Damn." He activated his phone. "Dugan."

"It's Ian," said Conrad over the phone.

"What is it?"

"Our informants in Libya are unaccountable."

Buchanan studied Dugan's expression of displeasure.

"The Russian and the Libyan?" asked Dugan.

"Yes."

"How long?"

"Two days now. The Russian missed his dropoff in Morocco. He never showed up there, or in Vienna."

"Christ, this operation is getting worse by the day." Dugan kicked at a divot. "We need to get the whole team assembled and put our heads together. These sons-of-bitches are moving on something, and we're dancing around in the wind. I'll be there first thing in the morning. Set up a meeting in the conference room at seven-thirty."

Dugan clicked off the connection and jammed the phone in his pocket. He turned to face Buchanan and prepared for a Mulligan.

"Anything wrong, Jack?"

"I don't know yet. It's related to Abdul Kasim and the Army of Allah situation I briefed the Senate Intelligence Committee about."

"Yes, yes. What's the latest?" asked Buchanan, watching Dugan closely as he made his second tee-off.

The limousine drove up to the abandoned tobacco barn late at night. The Reverend Jimmy White waited for his driver to open the door before he got out.

At the entrance to the barn, White was greeted by one of his foot soldiers, a young man named Billy, who was very enthusiastic and flabbergasted to see the Reverend in person. It was always an honor, so many thought, to shake the hand of the man who had a direct line to God.

Jimmy went into the barn and was greeted by the property's owner, Frank Wills. Wills was a proud tobacco farmer who had watched the continuing decline of a business that had been in his family for two hundred years. He was sick and tired of those government boys in Washington and their anti-smoking legislation. Hell, he was tired of government intrusion overall, for that matter. He figured that if the people chose to smoke, the government had no business interfering. But if someone asked him if the people had a right to smoke marijuana, or use other narcotics, "Well, that's different!" he had said.

"How's the operation, Frank?"

"Right on schedule," said Wills. "Everything is going according to plan."

"Good, good." They walked farther into the barn, where half a dozen men were checking over some of the merchandise. The cylindrical tubes had been delivered without incident from the desert of Southern California. The boxes had arrived from Seattle. The operation was taking shape.

Jimmy saw Mr. Assad, one of Kasim's lieutenants, standing over by the workers. Jimmy strutted over. "Mr. Assad." They shook hands and smiled with excitement. "I hope you are satisfied with the shipments."

"Yes, very much so." Assad was a plain-looking man in his middle-forties, casually dressed like any other American, in a sweatshirt and jeans. He was actually a resident alien who was in the country legally, at least he had been until a month ago when his visa expired. "We look forward to doing business with you once we are both established in our own lands. I'm sure our relationship will be one of continued cooperation."

"And our involvement with one another will be one of respect and self-determination," said the Reverend. "No more of this money for influence business. You will be free to go your own way, and we to go ours. As soon as we take control, we will cut off all of our aid to the Egyptian government, as agreed."

Jimmy sauntered off with Assad to the side of the barn. "Once we have you and all the hardware in place," said the Reverend, "you'll be on your own. We'll be here if you need us, but you'll run it from then on."

"I understand," said Assad.

"It will be totally up to your people to pull this off. You will need to be in position and watching your television to make your own determination of when the best opportunity arises."

"Again, I can assure you, we will be in position and will know the moment when we see it," Assad replied.

"Good." The Reverend shook Assad's hand with a self-assured, confident smile. He strolled from the barn to his awaiting limousine.

17

*P*eter hadn't shaved since the morning of his mother's funeral. It was well beyond the point where he usually let it grow. However, he was letting a thick, scruffy beard fill in around his face.

Over the last few years his skin tone had gotten darker from spending day after day out on the boat. Peter was sitting in a lawn chair soaking up the sun.

For the past hour Rolf had been watching him rest in his lawn chair and stare at the jungle that seemed to creep in around him. Suddenly Peter got up and went over to his workout station. He hadn't used his crutch in five days now. Peter had rigged a system to lift weights made from local limestone. He had even made a device that would let him do push-ups with his right arm, while his left arm remained in its cast.

Rolf watched as Peter underwent a strenuous workout, which went on for another thirty minutes, including stretching. Rolf watched with curiosity. "Another walk," Rolf predicted under his breath.

Peter finished stretching and began walking at a fast pace down the driveway and onto the road. Rolf couldn't keep up with him. The humidity was high, and the sweat rolled down his back. Peter disappeared into the historic archaeological site of the Mayan ruins. Rolf followed.

Peter climbed the steep steps of El Castillo — steps that had been built for feet much smaller than his — in the center of the Great Plaza. Much of this great pyramid had been restored and, as usual, there were many tourists about. It was probably one of the most popular archaeological exhibits in all of the Yucatan. A few tourists gave Peter puzzled looks as he ran up the steps.

Rolf spotted Peter at the top of the pyramid. He decided to wait at the bottom, knowing that Peter wouldn't stay put for too long. Besides, the angle of the descent was more frightening than the ascent for Rolf, and he didn't need any more excitement today. He waited in some shade under a tree near the base of the great pyramid.

Several minutes passed. Then several more.

Finally, Rolf got up to see where Peter had gone. He couldn't spot him at the top of the pyramid anymore. He walked quickly over to the Court of the Thousand Columns and searched, but didn't find Peter there either. He hurried back across the open field and approached the ancient, pre-Hispanic ballcourt, believed to have been built by the Toltecs.

Rolf stopped dead in his tracks when he saw Peter sitting on the grass with his legs crossed, Native-American–style, in front of some hieroglyphics. Exhausted from the heat and his strenuous walk, Rolf advanced sluggishly towards Peter until he stood five feet behind him.

Peter didn't even turn or acknowledge that Rolf was standing there, panting. He sat motionless, staring at a horrific scene etched into the wall before him. The scene depicted on the walls of the ballcourt was that of an ancient ball game, perhaps some sort of soccer, although there was still speculation as to the exact nature of the rules and objective of the game. The scene in front of Peter showed a player from one of the teams being decapitated.

Again, experts could only speculate as to the nature of this terrifying act. The best guess was that one of the players from the losing team — perhaps the captain — was beheaded, before the rulers, the elite, and the gods, for losing the game.

Finally, Rolf regained a normal breathing rate. He had been here several times and knew that Peter had also. Peter had seen this before. However, here Peter sat again, his hair growing longer, his beard becoming fuller. Peter's behavior worried Rolf . . . he was afraid that Peter had lost his mind.

Rolf wiped his forehead with a handkerchief that was already soiled with sweat. He wanted to say something to Peter but decided not to. He backed up and sat in the shade against the wall on the other side of the ancient ballcourt.

A group of visitors on a guided tour rounded the corner following their guide. They encircled Peter as their guide explained what they were seeing. Peter sat there, never once moving or looking to see the crowd that had gathered. Several tourists clicked away with their cameras, recording the strange mural on the wall.

The tour guide, a young man from the University of the Yucatan, began his talk. The tourists closed in to hear him speak; most ignored Peter, some thought he was peculiar sitting there.

"You can all see the player here who has been beheaded," said the guide. "We believe this to be a Toltec ritual, continued by the Aztecs. These were brutal people who brought savagery to this region. Actually, all evidence suggests that the Mayan peoples were gentle people until they were influenced by the Toltecs and Aztecs.

"We also believe they were responsible for what I will show you after the ballcourt. We will walk to the Sacred

Cenote, a sacrificial well, 110 feet deep and 190 feet wide — where it is believed that drugged maidens were sacrificed to the rain god, Chac. Of course, we won't go down into it, because there would be no way for you to get out. You see, the limestone walls are vertical and no one could climb out of it. How do we know they did this? Sometime back we excavated, from beneath thirty feet of water, many bones, idols, and other artifacts. But first, let us go look at the skulls." He walked towards the far end of the ballcourt, with his flock following closely.

Peter remained seated, staring through the wall — into what, Rolf could only guess.

President Myers had been elected two years earlier in one of the most contentious elections in United States history. The elections seemed, to most Americans, to get more negative and hostile every time. With recent presidential elections so negative and polarizing, this one topped all others. Myers won the popular vote with just over 51%, defeating a popular U.S. senator from the Midwest who was a decorated World War II hero. Senator Edwards lost on his platform of restoring basic American values, from God to family. The problem for him, in the end — according to most of the armchair quarterbacks, the pundits — was that he lacked a specific plan for change. Edwards had campaigned in generalities and attacked Myers, but had offered no specifics about his own plan for America. Then again, for the 49% of Americans who voted for him, that had been enough. They needed only generalities.

Myers, commanding in appearance — tall, greying, in his late fifties — strode into the meeting, late as usual. Pritchard was there; so was Dugan, the Secretary of Defense, the Secretary of State, and the rest of the National

Security Council. Everyone stood as the President entered, then sat after Myers had.

"Gentlemen," said Myers. He looked at his Chief of Staff, Victor Watkins. "Go ahead, Vic."

"Director Dugan will conduct this meeting, sir. Jack."

Dugan cleared his throat and spoke in a serious, measured tone. "Gentlemen." He had a file on the table in front of him, but he never referred to it because he knew this issue intimately. "Mr. President. We have received confirmation that the terrorist group run by Egyptian Abdul Kasim, now operating within Libya, is planning to hit an American target on American soil. Unfortunately, our source in Libya is missing and believed to have been compromised, so there is nothing more at this time. As you all are aware of, the last significant hit was the World Trade Center. As everyone knows, several other New York targets were planned but thwarted. We are conducting an extensive investigation at this time, but this puts us in delicate territory. The obvious suspects would be Americans of Arab descent, or those of Arab descent residing in this country, both legally and illegally. This is where we begin to get sticky with constitutional issues. We cannot round them up or violate their civil rights. On the other hand, someone — or some group internally — most likely would be charged with carrying this out."

"I see," said Myers. "Gene, what do you propose?"

"To start with," said Pritchard, "from the INS, we will need immediate access to the records regarding any and all immigrants from the region. We can then begin to narrow possible subjects. As Jack said, we are treading on sensitive constitutional ground."

"We're obviously talking about a national security issue here, Jack," said Myers. "People's lives are at stake."

"I agree. I need the A.G. to check the books regarding

this issue to see what authority we have in this area and what methods we can employ."

"Where is he, anyway?"

"At a crime conference in Dallas."

"Let's use everything at our disposal, but keep it all within the bounds of law," said Myers. "Call me with any developments." Myers got up from the table. "I have some congressional arm-twisting to attend to. Everyone back to work." He darted out of the conference room.

Kasim sat in a hotel room in Tripoli. He had temporarily moved his personal accommodations from a tent in the desert to a secure, well-guarded room. Much of his operation, however, remained in the desert, on the move every other day — just one step ahead of the satellites and insurgents, or so he hoped.

Mr. Fuad, another of Kasim's lieutenants, entered the room after being admitted by one of Kasim's bodyguards. Kasim's senior by three years, his role was primarily logistical and related support. He had a grotesque-looking scar across his left cheek, where fragments of a hand grenade had been imbedded years before during an experiment he had conducted for a terrorist operation.

Kasim rose from his chair and hugged Fuad. "Brother," said Kasim. "What is the latest?"

"We're about ready for the test," said Fuad.

"And the Libyans?"

"Not so good. Qaddafi may want closer oversight. He's worried about American retaliation."

"That is why we must proceed as planned."

"The shipments arrived from Seattle and California. Much of the hardware was in its original shipping crates. We will be ready when the target becomes available in January. Here is the map." Fuad spread out a map of

Washington, D.C. He also dropped on the table several photographs of the U.S. Capitol with its anti-terrorist barricades, the White House, the Pentagon, the Jefferson Memorial, the Lincoln Memorial, the Washington Monument, and the State Department Building.

"What about the vans?" said Kasim.

"They will be delivered to the Wills farm in Virginia shortly. We will get more pictures of the primary routes and the positions for the launches when we're in country."

"Good. Let's keep an elusive communication with the Libyans. We need to buy just enough time to get this operation into its active mode."

"I understand. I must get back now."

"Yes. Very good." Kasim hugged Fuad again, and Fuad quickly departed.

Kasim sat at a desk and studied the map of D.C. He placed a sheet of clear acetate over the map. Next to the map was a little black book he carried with him. He studied prominent locations around D.C. Also on his desk was a book from the U.S. Capitol Historical Society detailing the architectural layout of the Capitol building. Kasim's face lit up with a smile as he plotted his attack.

Peter's strength was returning in full force. He was now doing more and more push-ups, lifting his crudely made weights, and jogging before the sun came up each day. Rolf couldn't keep up with him at all anymore, so he let Peter go on by himself. Peter still hadn't said much, except for what his immediate physical needs were at any given moment.

Rolf watched Peter leave each morning and return an hour or more later. It was odd to see him doing all this physical exercise because his arm was still in a sling. When Peter ran, he strapped his left arm tightly against his chest with a leather strap. He was now eating only healthful foods, primarily fruits, vegetables, and high-protein meats. In stark contrast, he still hadn't shaved or cut his hair. Actually, he was intentionally letting both his hair and his beard grow for his mission. He was becoming a strong, muscular man once again on the inside, and a rugged-looking mountain man on the outside.

A disturbing characteristic about Peter — that concerned those around him — was his facial expression: there was none. There was no evidence of emotion. Peter's emotion had changed from one of deep sadness to seemingly none at all. He stared straight ahead most of the time, and when he did look at someone, it was as though they were invisible. Rolf was sure that the trauma had created a madman.

Peter was resting in the bug tent at noontime, with Rolf nearby reading a Spanish language magazine. Rolf heard car doors slam at the end of the driveway and looked over at Peter, who was sitting in his chair staring at nothing. Rolf got up and walked down the driveway to head off their guests.

Halfway down the driveway, Rolf intercepted Peter's children and Harry. He whispered some instructions and sent the children up the driveway. He hung back with Harry.

When Peter saw Paul and Sarah walking toward him, he sighed softly, then stood and walked out of the tent to meet them near the entrance. No one said a word. He hugged both children at the same time; Sarah was uncomfortable. All this time Peter's expression remained blank.

"Follow me," said Peter.

Paul did as instructed; however, Sarah held back. She looked over at Harry, who motioned for her to follow Peter. Reluctantly, she obeyed.

Harry and Rolf watched the threesome walk into the thick vegetation, Sarah tailing from a distance.

A hundred yards down the path, they came to where several trees had been recently cut down. Peter sat down on one of the tree stumps. He took a deep breath. "I didn't know you were coming," he said slowly.

"We had to miss school," said Sarah distantly.

"Well, I'll see to it that Harry gets you right back."

"I'll stay, Dad. She can go."

Peter's lips curled up slightly.

"I like the beard," said Paul.

"It's my new disguise. You can't tell anyone about any of this. For everyone outside the family, I'm dead."

"You might as well be," said Sarah.

Peter did not react.

"Uncle Harry thinks you might be going to get the terrorists," said Paul.

Sarah stood there, looking off in distance.

"I have to," Peter sighed deliberately. "There are a lot of things I don't understand, Paul, but one thing I do. And you must never forget this: There must be dignity and justice for all human beings. I don't know what to tell you except that I have to do this. I don't know anything about these people, and they know nothing about me. I have nothing against their beliefs. But, they must be held accountable for what they have done to others."

There was a long silence.

"There is nothing left here for me," continued Peter. "I must do it for Maria, Alberto, and the others."

"I hope you don't get hurt, Dad," said Paul.

"I have to be honest with you: I can't promise anything, but I'll try to not let you down."

Sarah tapped her toes impatiently. "Can we go now?"

"I'm sorry about Maria," said Paul.

Peter stood, patted his son tenderly on the back, and whispered, "Go back to the house and wait for me with Harry and Rolf."

Paul looked at him, confused. Peter signaled to him that he wanted to be alone with Sarah. Paul ran off down the trail.

"Where's he going?" protested Sarah.

"Back to the house."

Sarah stared him down. "What do you want from me?"

"Only that which you want to give."

"I want to go home." She turned to leave, and took two steps before Peter lunged forward and grabbed her.

"Let me go!" She struggled, hitting him about the chest.

He deflected her punches and held her arms tightly. Her strength was no match for his.

"Fuck you, Dad! I hate you! I wished you would have died with Maria." Tears streamed down her face. She began sobbing hysterically.

Peter held her firmly. "Sometimes people fall out of love," Peter explained. "Your mother and I did just that. That didn't and doesn't change our love for you."

"I don't get it. Why weren't you happy? What did I do wrong?"

"You didn't do anything wrong. We did. It has nothing to do with you." Peter released his hold slowly, and brushed her chestnut hair away from her face.

She shook loose. "It's not fair," she cried.

"There is so much that isn't. I can't explain."

"I only wanted you and Mom to stay together."

"I'm sorry, Sarah. But life is more complicated. Sometimes things just don't work out. It was nothing you did. It was between your mother and me."

Sarah sniffled and thought about this for a minute. Finally, "You really did love her?"

"Your mother? Of course."

"No, Maria."

He was taken aback by the question. He froze for what seemed to Sarah a very long time. At last, "Yes. Yes, I loved her very much." He stared around Sarah and into the jungle.

"I thought she stole you from us. I hated her."

"No. I didn't become romantically involved with her until after your mother and I had drifted apart."

Sarah was silent for some time. She wiped at her tears with her shirt sleeve. Then she sighed loudly and said, "I'm sorry, Dad. I didn't treat her nicely. I was so bad. Now she's dead, and I can't apologize."

"I think you just did. And I hope she can hear you."

"What can I do now?" asked Sarah.

"Just be there for your brother and your mother."

"What about you? Am I going to lose you for good now?"

Peter didn't know how to answer that.

"You don't have to do this," persisted Sarah.

"There's nothing left otherwise."

"There's us."

"I've arranged everything for you and Paul."

"We don't want money. We need our dad."

Peter couldn't answer.

"I'm hating the world more and more," said Sarah.

"Hate doesn't work, Sarah. You must try to understand the world and others. And if that's too hard, just try to get along."

She shook her head. "I just don't understand." Tears fell from her eyes again. She wiped them away. "I'm sorry I said those things to you. I didn't mean them."

"Apology accepted." He held her close and gently stroked her hair.

Peter walked up to Harry, with Sarah by his side. Her tears were beginning to dry.

"Take us to Maria," said Peter.

Harry nodded and said, "Okay."

Throughout the entire ride not a word was spoken, although the lack of expression communicated much. The mood was deeply depressed. Their car stopped on the dirt roadway near where Maria was buried. Everyone got out of the car. "Over there," said Harry, pointing toward the grave site.

Peter walked over to the grave with his children. He stood there, holding Sarah's hand tightly. When he let loose the grip, he kneeled down to be closer to the earth, the earth that now held Maria, cradled gently. The children stood near and watched Peter stare at the grass. Sarah glanced over at the headstone adjacent to Maria's and saw the inscription for Peter. Her mother and Harry had told her about the deception, but it still gave her the chills.

Peter stayed for another ten minutes, until he realized there was nothing more for him to do. He felt in his heart that only Maria's body lay in the earth, and that her spirit was somewhere else ... somewhere wonderful. He knew that he would never again set foot upon this ground. It was not necessary to return, for he knew that Maria's spirit would be with him wherever he went. It had been right for them to visit the burial site, but it wasn't something that would put him in close proximity to Maria. What would, was within his heart.

18

*T*he BTM 71A-guided practice missile was loaded into the M151E2 tubular-guided missile TOW 2 launcher. He positioned the tripod of this heavy anti-tank weapon firmly, making sure of its stability in the sand. He sighted his target about 600 meters away and fired. Three assistants aided him.

The flight motor ignited at twelve meters, sending the rocket soaring towards its target. The rocket produced the necessary noise and flash. A puff of smoke rose where the practice missile had hit the target. The target was a one-sided façade of a building about three stories high, thirty yards wide, and three feet thick, made of stone. The target didn't explode or collapse, but it had a white mark on its side where the practice rocket had hit.

It was just a simulation, but Kasim was pleased at how his men had mastered the device so quickly. He watched through binoculars as the next trainee positioned himself six hundred meters away, loaded his training device with the help of three assistants, sighted the target, and fired. Another direct hit.

Kasim had thirty men at the site training with these heavy anti-tank weapon TOW simulators. They had plenty of practice rounds to perfect their accuracy.

"I want the sixteen best on the primary team," Kasim said to Fuad. "We will have fourteen alternates on standby at the barn. So that's four vans, four in each. We'll have four rockets launched on the first command. They will immediately reload and fire their remaining rounds at will. We'll move to our live firing range and practice the drill several times with the training devices, then commence with a live fire on the structure."

"We are ensuring overkill," said Fuad.

"We must ensure that there are no survivors. I want the live fire soon. We must begin smuggling our soldiers to the front."

Kasim hopped into his truck and was whisked away by his driver. Fuad went back to the training range where the training rockets continued to strike the structural façade a thousand meters away.

Dugan looked at the satellite photographs again. He didn't like what he saw. The pictures showed the target practice in the Libyan desert that Kasim had witnessed just minutes before.

Conrad entered Dugan's office and bolted over to his desk. "We have an Egyptian agent setting up in Cairo now," said Conrad. "He'll be able to penetrate into Libya in about three weeks. Here's the file." He handed it to Dugan, who opened it and began scanning the documents. "As you can see," continued Conrad, "he's an experienced Egyptian soldier. He's been in and out of Libya on several occasions for different missions."

"Do we know where these TOWs came from?" Dugan asked impatiently.

"We're awaiting confirmation from sources, but all indications are — since they get most of their support from Iran — from that shipment to Iran in the mid-'80s."

"That's the one from the NSC, North and Company?"

"We believe so," said Conrad. "Probably one of those shipments during the height of Iran-Contra. There were several dozen TOWs in those shipments. We're checking the files now to confirm."

"Wonderful. Does it come back to haunt us or what?"

Conrad nodded, but said nothing.

Peter went out for his early-morning run. It was easier now since his arm had been out of its sling for almost a week. He had been doing push-ups with two arms and amazing his son in the process.

He ran down a path and was surprised when Paul jumped out at him from behind a bush. Paul chased him back to the house.

Later, Peter taught Paul infantry tactics. Paul got camouflaged and assumed the role of a bush. At the perfect moment, he jumped out and tackled an unsuspecting Peter.

After Sarah had calmed down, they agreed that the kids could stay a while. It was nice having the kids around, Peter thought. It gave him perspective.

Peter was some sight, this middle-aged, full-bearded, muscular man, running around the jungle wearing no shirt, only shorts and sneakers. He looked like a caveman with running shoes.

The next day after his run he stopped to stretch near the house. He saw Harry and Rolf playing cards with Sarah in the bug tent. It looked like they had just eaten breakfast. There were empty glasses and plates scraped clean. Peter watched Sarah learning to play poker.

Harry, Rolf, and Sarah stopped long enough to look up at Peter, standing there dripping in sweat. He was hardly puffing from the strenuous run that had to have been several miles long. He had "that look" in his eye — as if someone crossed him, he would not hesitate to snap their neck in a heartbeat. "It's time for me to go," said Peter.

Harry and Rolf looked at one another in dread. This was one of the few times Peter had spoken to them since the explosion, and it was to tell them he was leaving. "You know what I want to say to you, Peter."

"And you know, my dear brother, it's futile."

"I have to try, to save the sanity I have left."

Rolf put his cards down and listened intently to the conversation. He realized there was no stopping Peter.

"Do you really think you can do this?" asked Harry.

"First rule of the game is never say 'think.' After that, there's no debate."

"I don't want any more funerals, brother."

"Neither do I. But I can't promise anything. This is not about revenge. These people must be stopped. I will, at least, stop one."

"But you're not a policeman, Peter."

Peter tried to be patient. He knew Harry meant well. "No, but I have a particular and specialized skill. I have done this kind of thing before. Some I'm not too proud of; others I am. This, I must do."

He *has* lost his mind, thought Harry. He'll get himself killed for sure, and we'll have to bury him for real this time. With that, Peter turned and went into the house.

Sarah looked worried. "I don't like it, Uncle Harry."

"Neither do I, Sarah. Neither do I."

Harry, Rolf, and the children packed their clothes. Peter had very little to his name in terms of material things. In fact, "things" had never really meant much to him anyway. Now more than ever, they meant nothing.

Peter said goodbye to Oscar's family and thanked them for their hospitality. He hugged Oscar's mother and grand-mother, then stood in front of Oscar. "You tell Maya that there will be justice for Alberto's death," he said.

"I didn't tell you, Peter — " Oscar gasped. His eyes teared.

When Peter had seen grown men cry before, it was usually in the face of death. This sounded serious. "What is it, Oscar?"

"Maya is pregnant with Alberto's child."

Peter wanted to cry, but his expression remained blank, as it had been for weeks. "I'm glad you told me. I'm going to have Harry set up a trust fund for Alberto's child." He hugged Oscar, then walked to the car to join the others.

Rolf dropped them off at the airport. He got out of the car, helped the children with their bags, then cornered Peter. "Peter, I've known you for what, five years now? You know I pray there is a God, and that there is justice in the end for the unfortunate." He paused, and sighed. "I'm glad to have known you." He stuck out his hand and thought, this might be the last time he'd ever see Peter.

Peter shook Rolf's hand. "I'm glad for having known you, Rolf. I hope our paths will cross again. I wish there were more people in this world like you. I know it would be a better place if there were." Peter entered the airport con-course and disappeared from sight. Rolf stared after him.

Two hours later, Rolf was back on the island, and Peter, Harry, and the children were somewhere over the Gulf of Mexico.

Ann Howard was back at work covering the insider grind that was D.C. She was working on a story about the inner decision-making circles of Myers' White House. The recent rumor was that Myers had no discipline, had lost control, and that there were several loose cannons running things.

The Myers administration was the first in decades to get a handle on the budget — balancing it, in fact — as the economy grew and inflation remained in check. However, the focus of Howard's article was the disarray in the White House. Like most Washington insiders, she believed that people were more interested in the "process" than results. Process was more newsworthy than unemployment being down or the economy chugging along. It was dramatic, sexy, she reasoned. And it sold more copies. Of course, she had her White House sources for her story — or so she said. Myers never could understand who those sources were, since he had talked to most of his close aides directly about it. They all denied any knowledge about it. So who *were* these "close insider Administration sources"? Damned if Myers knew — or anyone else, for that matter.

Howard's vacation had been pleasant. She had spent three weeks visiting relatives in Texas, which had been quite refreshing. She had forgotten all about Flight 243 and Peter Murray. So had the media. The story was old — "ancient history" — and there were new stories to hammer over the heads of the American people. In fact, a popular, much-loved basketball hero's wife had recently been murdered. The media had been covering the story day by day and minute by minute since the basketball hero had been accused of the crime.

Hopefully Howard could finish her story about the Myers administration and slip it in during a lull in the basketball hero's story in order to get noticed. When this kind of story was hot, all other news took a back seat. Myers had actually taken a trip to Europe and the media had barely noticed. When one Washingtonian, who appeared to be a well-educated professional, had been asked on the street if he knew where the President was or what he was doing, he had to admit that he didn't. He said that when he read the paper or watched the news, he couldn't find any news relating to the President. Oh well, thought Howard. They would inform the people when and if anything important was taking place.

It was dark, and the temperature was dropping on this December night. Howard had put on her heavy coat to go out for dinner. She left the *Sun* building and walked down the busy street. Her favorite restaurant was in walking distance, and she would be there in short order.

A man watched her leave the building. He was the stereotypical "street person": dressed shabbily in clothes that were grimy, torn, and baggy. His long hair and beard were filthy. He was in serious need of a bath — if anyone got near him, they could smell his grime as well as see it. He wanted it this way, so he could get around without having people look at him too closely. He had hit the nail precisely on the head. Most Americans didn't want to look at street people; they looked the other way and ignored the annoying solicitous gestures.

He reached into his coat pocket and took out his Vietnam-vintage Special Forces knife which he had just purchased in a local Army surplus store. Its 6½-inch blade was sharp and glistened in the moonlight. He put it back into his pocket and crossed the street.

He took up a position right in front of her path. When she was within striking distance, he stuck out his cup and said, "Could you spare a quarter for an American down on his luck?"

Howard ignored him and kept on walking.

So far, so good. He had disguised his voice as well as he could, adding a little hoarseness. He followed her. "Please,

I just need a quarter and I'll have enough to buy a sandwich."

She ignored him and kept on walking, becoming a little perturbed.

"Please, why do you pretend I don't exist?"

"Get lost before I call the cops, creep," she said over her shoulder as she hurried along.

"Call the cops? I have as much right to be here on this sidewalk as you do."

She turned down another street. He kept up the pace.

"You don't have the right to harass me," she said angrily.

"I'm not harassing you. I'm begging."

"Bother someone else." She ducked into Rumors restaurant.

Her pursuer was stopped at the door by the host of the restaurant, who rolled his eyes and gave Peter a look of disgust.

"Dinner for one, please," Peter said to the host.

"Get lost, bum."

"What, my money's no good here?"

The host looked at him with even less patience. Peter took out a wad of cash and flashed it in his face.

"Who did you steal that from?" asked the host.

"I earned it. I'm a veteran, you know."

"Great. Another Vietnam nut case," said the host, a smirk upon his face. "You see that sign?"

Peter looked at the sign the host was pointing to in the window of the restaurant. It said: WE RESERVE THE RIGHT TO REFUSE SERVICE TO ANYONE.

"So you discriminate against veterans."

"Yeah, now you're catching on."

Peter's fun was over. He retraced his steps and sat against a building near the corner. He waited there.

It was getting late. She must be having some extravagant dinner in there, Peter thought. He could wait all night. He had to finish what he had started. As he expected, most of the people who passed by him only looked the other way.

Finally, he saw her leave the restaurant. Good, she was alone. In fact, she had eaten alone this particular night so she could work on her story. Even though she ate alone, many of the restaurant's patrons knew who she was. Many who knew her personally would come by during the course of the dinner and exchange pleasantries. Most were D.C. operatives working in government in some capacity; therefore, they had to stay on her good side, lest they be the subject of her next unflattering story. She backtracked toward the *Sun* building, ready to keep working on her story. She had more sources to phone, bribe, perhaps blackmail, maybe create.

Peter clutched his knife in his coat pocket and ducked into an alley. He peered around the storefront and saw her coming. It was late and the night was dark. Street and foot traffic were light; this was the perfect opportunity.

Just as she passed the opening to the alley, Peter stepped out and grabbed her with full force, placing his hand over her mouth to silence her. She tried to struggle and kick at him, but his strength was overpowering. He pulled her into the darkness of the alley, then pushed her against the wall of the building and stuck his smelly beard right in her face. She gagged at the smell. He took out the knife and placed its blade against her neck. She froze in terror.

He stared at her and spoke like a crazed lunatic. He disguised his voice to sound like Dennis Hopper. "I had a vision, man. An angel spoke to me and said that Ann Howard felt no remorse." He did, indeed, talk like a nut case.

Howard's eyes got even wider. She was petrified. Her hands trembled in fear, and it was clear that she had heard what he said, even though she didn't know what this wacko was talking about.

"The angel said that Ann Howard felt no responsibility for contributing to the deaths of several people," said Peter, salivating on his beard, "including two beautiful human beings, a man and a woman who were killed as a direct result of a story she wrote."

Her eyes scanned his face over and over. She saw only a dirty, shaggy, bearded man, but she felt she knew him from somewhere. Still, she didn't know what this insane fool was talking about.

"You are a vile creature, and there are eyes watching you." He was foaming at the mouth. "The ghosts of those you helped bury did not forget. You walk a fine line between the rights of the individual to enjoy the guarantees of life, liberty, and the right to be secure, and those that are set forth in the same document you cite for your defense." His heartbeat raced, his eyes stared, unblinking. "The angel who spoke to me was the angel of death. I know him personally." He stared at her for more than ten seconds.

She was completely frozen in terror and couldn't move, though her breathing rate increased considerably.

He was losing it, he told himself. He wanted to kill this bitch so badly, he could almost taste her blood in his mouth. He snapped. He saw Maria's image flash before him, and saw his mother praying for him in a pew at church.

Peter kept staring at Howard, and saw the fear of death in her horrified eyes. A drop of blood ran down her neck, where he held the knife against her flesh.

Then, he slowly removed his hand from her mouth.

She couldn't bring herself to scream or say a word. It was as if she was in a nightmare, paralyzed while being chased by an apparition. She couldn't move, even after he released her.

Peter dropped the knife to his side and backed up. Howard remained firmly affixed to the wall, her body as rigid as a board.

Peter stared her down. "An angel has spared you. God have mercy on your soul." And with that he jogged off.

Howard stood there, frozen in apprehension. Her hands trembled. After a considerable amount of time she finally turned to see where Peter had gone. She could see nothing except a dark alley. She gathered herself together and then took off at a brisk pace down the sidewalk, staying in well-lit areas.

She made it back to the *Sun* and sat down at her desk. Howard was still shaking, trying to make sense out of what had just happened. Damned lunatics, she thought. She sat, staring into space and blotting the small cut on her neck with a tissue. Finally, she went back to work on her piece and tried to put the incident out of her mind.

Peter was back at his motel in Arlington, Virginia — ironically, just down the road from the Pentagon, where he had worked for many years. When he had registered he had been clean and well groomed. Now, returning from his outing with Howard, he was absolutely filthy, and the desk attendant did a double-take. Peter saw the man look at him, so he flashed his room key. He told the attendant that he had accidentally fallen into some garbage. In truth, he had fallen into some, but not by accident. To prepare for his role, he had jumped into a garbage heap and rolled around in it to get the desired effect. The attendant smiled disingenuously and Peter ducked into his room.

Peter figured he didn't have any reason to see Howard again. There was only so much he could do to her, and he thought he had gone far enough. He told himself that if he saw her again, he didn't know how he might react, so it would be better if he steered clear of her. He had more pressing issues to attend to.

This time they were BGM 71A surface-attack guided missiles: live warheads. The structure was four-sided, a hundred meters square, and three stories high. The frame was wood, coated with three inches of concrete. It was crudely constructed, but would serve its purpose.

Six hundred meters away, on two sides of the structure, were four positions. Each position consisted of four men standing close to each other near a van. Each van, a run-down Volkswagen, had one TOW heavy anti-tank weapon system bolted down to its bed, loaded and ready. The men waited for their signal, each with an earpiece in his right ear and a wire attached to a receiver that was clipped to his belt.

Mr. Fuad stood watching from seven hundred meters away. He held binoculars to his eyes with one hand and a hand radio with the other. He scanned the four positions and saw that all of the sixteen primary men were ready. "Get back into your vans," Fuad said into his radio. Each of the sixteen men did as instructed. Fuad watched closely. "Back up one hundred meters," he directed. The driver in each van did so, then stopped. "All right. On my command, proceed!"

Each van moved backwards to its original position and stopped. The rear doors opened, and all four men in each van jumped out and took their positions, ready to assist the gunner in their van.

"Fire!" said Fuad.

Each of the gunners immediately fired his TOW missile at the structure. All four of the TOWs were direct hits, smashing and ripping into the structure. They exploded upon impact, causing severe damage to the structure. With the help of their assistants, the gunners instantaneously reloaded, sighted, and fired their second TOWs. All four of the TOWs struck and exploded what was left of the makeshift target.

Mr. Fuad lowered his binoculars and spoke into his radio. "Successful hits."

Behind Mr. Fuad about three hundred meters was parked a Toyota truck. Kasim stood in the truck's bed. "Very good," he said over the radio. "We are ready to proceed. Return to my tent for a final briefing. We will begin moving out tomorrow." Kasim got into his truck, and was driven off to his tent for the final preparation.

19

*T*owel wrapped around his waist and toothbrush stuck in his mouth, Peter switched on the TV after taking his shower. His physique was well toned. Those aggressive workouts in the jungle had paid off. He channel-surfed until he came across the "Glory to God" evangelical network. What caught his eye was the guest for this broadcast, Senator Jay Buchanan. "We must stand up and fight Satan's representatives, the politicians," said the Reverend.

Peter remembered the Senator from his days before the select committee, which Buchanan sat in on. Peter remembered the Senator not for what he did, but for what he *didn't* do. Buchanan hadn't had much to say one way or the other during those committee days. He never offered an opinion. He never chastised Peter, nor defended him. Peter had not understood the man or his motives. He had always felt that the Senator was supportive of the military — he was a hardened backer when it came time for appropriations — yet he hadn't defended Peter's actions. This had contributed to Peter's bitterness, the being "hung-out-to-dry syndrome," by those he had thought supported him.

Peter didn't like the way the boys at the Pentagon left him hanging either, and he didn't like the way some of the politicians lectured him on television. When the shit had hit the fan, Peter and a few other fall guys had been left with the mess.

As Peter got dressed he listened to the Reverend Jimmy White. Melodramatically, White said, "The time is at hand." White's eyes were closed, his hands were clasped tightly, and his head was tilted back. "I'm having a vision, God is speaking to me right now. He is saying that there will be a horrific event, one that will thrust us into unknown territory. We will be called forth to fill the void. We will be called forth to bring order out of chaos. We will be asked to provide leadership to a nation gone adrift in the ways of Satan."

Several of the people in the audience could be heard saying "Amen," "Praise Jesus," "Hallelujah."

Peter came and went from the bathroom. He could see an 800 number at the bottom of the screen and the words: PLEASE HELP. BE SAVED. SEND YOUR DONATION TO GOD. CALL NOW.

Peter shook his head and went back into the bathroom.

The Reverend began talking with Buchanan. Peter didn't pay much attention. "So tell us, Senator, what you see, what your vision is."

"Well," said Buchanan, "it's much in line with what you preach, Reverend. I think we need a government that is committed to God. We need a government that gets back to the essentials our founding fathers established. After all, they started with the Treasury Department, the State Department, and the War Department — nothing else. They didn't have all these other socialistic departments such as education, health and human services, and the like. I think we need to abolish these ineffective socialistic departments and get back to letting the people be the people. The schools would be free to teach only the basics, and God would be re-introduced into the classroom. Anything anti-God — such as tolerance of alternative lifestyles, women in combat, and the half-baked notion of man being evolved from monkeys — would be forbidden. After all, God had rules in the garden, and when man disobeyed, all hell broke loose." They both chuckled.

"We would no longer allow public schools to pollute the minds of young children," continued Buchanan, "which I believe is the reason there is so much wrong with kids today. We would bring back order, respect, and discipline to children's lives. Science would no longer receive government funding, except for medical research. We need to take back our government from the feminists, homosexuals, environmentalists, abortionists — and the politicians who coddle them. Mothers need to be at home with their children. And those animal freaks who are more worried about saving the whale, the owl, and God-only-knows what other vermin, would be put down. Why not save the American family? These exotic animals have no soul and can't be saved anyhow. God gave us dominion over all of earth's creatures."

Peter finished dressing, this time in casual jeans and a button-down shirt. He looked reasonably presentable with his uneven hair combed back over his head and his scraggly beard somewhat groomed. Still, anyone who had seen Peter's picture in the paper recently would have had to strain long and hard to recognize him now.

"So," said White, "we would restore God's country to what it was before all these socialists forced all their ideas down our throats." White went into his preaching mode. "I have had this vision, from God himself" — the audience went wild, the phone lines lit up with donors — "that God will intervene in our affairs and set us on the right path to follow. He can only do so much, he has told me, and we need to take fate into our own hands. We will be instructed to form a new government in the wake of this intervention from God. He has told me that the devil is sly. The devil has used our democracy against us to force his way upon us. Look at what we've got now: crime rampant in the streets; criminals; child molesters; homo-sexuals running wild and seducing our children; feminists destroying family values, taking our children away from us, and leading them over to Satan! We must not let this happen! We will stand and be counted. We will come forward and fill this spiritual void in this country. We will not let God down!"

"Hallelujah, praise God. Glory be to God!" the audience shouted enthusiastically.

Peter called the number the agents in Cozumel had given him. It was Dugan's private beeper number. He waited for Dugan to call him back, lying on the bed switching channels. There wasn't much to watch, despite dozens of channels to choose from. Peter couldn't believe the crap. All those situation comedies, all so the average American could come home and tune out from reality.

The phone never rang, so Peter called a direct number to the Agency that Shell had given him. A secretary answered.

"May I speak with the Director, please?"

"He's in a meeting and is unavailable. May I take a message?"

"No, thanks." Peter hung up.

Peter pulled up in his rental car and parked on the shoulder just past the entrance to the long dirt driveway of Dugan's house. The house was in a secluded area on the outer edge of Falls Church, Virginia. Peter knew his way around. He had personally delivered some important documentation here when Dugan had been a deputy director. It was dark out this night, blacker than coffee. The moon was hidden behind thick clouds. Peter sat and waited. It was ten-thirty.

The limousine turned right and headed for Interstate 495. It was almost midnight. Dugan's limousine turned south on 495, then took the exit to Falls Church and headed west for a few miles. They turned up the long driveway where Peter had parked. Peter watched the limousine turn out of sight. He got out of his car and walked up the dirt path.

The driveway led him to an old country house. Peter jumped behind a hedgerow and concealed himself. He watched the limousine stop at the front porch. Dugan got out, said something to his driver, and went into the house. The limousine came back down the driveway. Peter closed his eyes to protect his night vision and crouched down as the car passed. He waited a minute, then quietly and slowly snuck along the hedgerow until he reached the house.

Inside, Dugan took off his shoes, sports jacket, and tie, and fixed himself a drink. He had disengaged the house's security system and hadn't reset it after he entered. He usually didn't set it until he went to bed.

His house was a large, country-style dwelling that could have passed for Mount Vernon. It was well furnished with early-American furniture. Dugan went into the kitchen and fixed himself a cheese snack from the refrigerator. Drink and cheese in hand, he walked back to the living room, which was illuminated by just one light in the hallway. He set his drink down on an end table by his favorite recliner, sat down, and began looking through some papers he had brought home in his briefcase.

Peter stepped forward from the darkness. He knew that he would startle Dugan, so he spoke softly to ease the shock. "Jack."

Dugan turned and knocked his drink off the table. "What the—?"

Peter motioned with his hands that it was all right. "It's Colonel Murray."

Dugan jumped out of his seat and into a defensive position. He studied Peter, but couldn't recognize him because of his beard and long hair.

Peter threw Dugan his passport. Dugan caught it and examined it, while keeping an eye on Peter. "I don't believe in ghosts," said Dugan.

"I don't either," said Peter. "My death was staged. Sadly, Maria's wasn't."

"My God, it is you!" Dugan handed the passport back to Peter. "How did you get in here?"

"You forget, I did this for a living once."

Dugan took out his handkerchief and wiped the sweat from his brow. "Jesus, Colonel. I'm glad to see you, but how'd you stage this?"

"I had some quick-thinking friends in high places on the island."

Dugan kept his distance because he still wasn't sure what the Colonel had planned. "You met our two agents?"

"Yes."

"I'm sorry they didn't get Waltraut earlier, before, well — "

"Forget it."

Dugan wiped some more sweat from his brow. "God, I'm sorry."

"It's over now."

"You want a drink or something?"

"No, thanks. Sorry I made you spill yours."

"Ah — " Dugan waved it off. "Please, sit. That's quite a disguise." Dugan picked up his glass and ice cubes, which had scattered on the rug. They sat down facing each other.

"The beard's real," Peter continued. "I'll need it where I'm going."

"Jack? Everything all right?" said Dugan's wife from the top of the stairs.

"Yes, yes. I'm talking with an old friend." He turned to Peter once again, waited a moment for his wife to go back to bed, then said, "Kasim's organization is located in Libya. You know, we've tried to get in there and get the Pan Am 103 boys for years."

"That doesn't matter. I'm going in."

"And you want me to set you up?"

"With the background, profile, and all recent intelligence."

"Colonel, we have operatives in the area, working on this right now. You'd stick out and get killed."

"That's for me to worry about, not you. As you well know, I was in Iran before the Shah fell. I was in Tripoli before Qaddafi lost touch. I know my way around. I need your help, Jack."

Dugan shook his head in apprehension and considered the proposal. "This is highly irregular, Colonel."

"Jack, there's no discussion."

Dugan was silent. He could see that Peter was emotionally volatile, and that worried him to no end. But he also knew that Peter had been one of the best in the business. If he didn't give in to Peter . . . hell, he didn't want to think about it. "How long do you need?" asked Dugan.

"A week, at the most."

"Okay," he sighed. "Let me think." He paused. "We have an agent working on this now. Let me see what I can do."

"There can be no one but you who knows of this."

Dugan thought it over some more while Peter's eyes trained in on him. Dugan could see that the Colonel was determined to see this through. He knew that Murray had indeed traveled around the Middle East with the Defense Intelligence Agency and the National Security Agency. Still, this was irregular. Operations like this took time and preparation.

"How's your Arabic?" asked Dugan.

"Ready."

"You've been out of this business for years now. You're not thinking rationally. Remember, when someone becomes emotionally involved, they're pulled out. You know this, Colonel."

"Jack," Peter spoke slowly. "I'm going to do this, and I need your help. I'm not going to sit and argue with you. Yes, I've lost everything, and I am emotional. But this is something I have to do, or I'm dead inside. You know what I've done and what I'm capable of doing. My state of mind has never interfered with my objective."

Peter could see the doubt still in Dugan's eyes.

"I've always thought of you as an honorable and decent man, Jack," said Peter. "I trust you."

"You know I'm only worried about a clear head."

"Jack, need I remind you of all that I've been through, the situations I've been in before?"

"No, no, that's not necessary. Okay. Let me think." Dugan massaged his forehead with his left hand. "Okay, all right, I'll set it up."

"Good," said Peter.

"I'll let you try this, Colonel. No one will know but me. This is too sensitive to involve anyone else. Didn't you get my beeper number?"

"You didn't return my call."

"Oh, I left it in my office."

"I'll call you here tomorrow at midnight. I want all the files on this Kasim and his organization. I'll return them to you before I leave."

"What about passports?"

"I have a contact at State. Tomorrow, midnight." Peter walked out the front door, and Dugan sat for a couple of minutes thinking about what had transpired. Damn, we've all gone crazy, he thought, fixing himself another drink and downing it in one swig.

Fuad's flight had originated in Amman. He changed planes in Paris and had only a small carry-on bag. When he landed at JFK he went to customs and claimed political asylum. He filled out the requested paperwork and was given a hearing date with the INS. In less than two hours, he was on the streets of New York city, having checked into a hotel in mid-Manhattan for a couple days. He wanted to see the sights.

"On behalf of the airline, we would like to welcome you to Los Angeles," said the pilot over the speaker. "We hope your flight has been a pleasant one, and we know your stay in America will be enjoyable."

Another of the men who had been chosen by Kasim for the mission stood with the rest of the passengers and disembarked. His flight had originated in Algiers. He had changed planes in London and flown directly to Los Angeles. He went through customs as easily as Mr. Fuad had, and was also given a hearing date for political asylum. He was met at the airport by a member of Jimmy White's organization, with whom he stayed for two days before boarding a train for Virginia.

It was nighttime, and the boat was small enough so as not to draw unwanted attention as it neared the shore just off the coast of Pascagoula, Mississippi. The boat's driver was from the area and everyone knew him, so no one would suspect anything out of the ordinary. If he was stopped by the Coast Guard, or another authority, he would exchange pleasantries and be on his way.

He saw a light flashing the predetermined code from shoreline and headed in. On shore he was greeted by two men; both were fellow members of Jimmy White's Glory to God organization. They helped move the merchandise from his boat into their van. The merchandise consisted of several large wire-bound wooden crates. One of the men opened a box and inspected its cargo. Inside, neatly packed, were several BGM 71A TOW rockets. Satisfied, the men finished loading the rockets into their van. They thanked the boat driver, got into their van, and took off. The boat returned to sea.

Dugan had everything that Murray had requested. He had the files bound together and placed into a large manila envelope. He was sitting in his chair at midnight, waiting for Peter's call. The phone rang. "Dugan," he answered.

"It's Murray. Drive south on 495 to Annandale and west on 236. I'll flash my high beams three times. Pull over where you find a good spot. That's all."

"Right." Dugan hung up. He knew this was highly irregular for him to be undertaking, but he trusted Colonel Murray. Dugan figured Murray was only being cautious, and rightly so. Dugan did as he had been instructed.

Peter flashed his high beams three times and Dugan pulled over onto the shoulder just outside Annandale. Peter went over and got into Dugan's car. Dugan handed him the envelope. "Everything is in order," he said. "What is not there, I must tell you, is what is still unfolding at this time. We have reason to believe that Kasim is planning to strike at an American target here on American soil."

"When?"

"We don't know."

"Any idea what the target is?"

"Could be anything — probably a landmark, for symbolism."

"So that's why you're willing to let me do this?"

"One reason."

"And you need information?"

"Quickly. I know how good you are, Colonel. When we worked together for the NSA, I saw how professionally you conducted yourself and how dedicated to your country you were. That was why I tried to recruit you after Iran-Contra. I won't beat around the bush with this. Kasim's group has hit us and hit us hard, both here and overseas. They blew up a car bomb outside our embassy in Cairo and killed a young Marine. As you know, they killed thirty-eight people onboard Flight 243. They killed your Maria and ten others at your restaurant."

Peter didn't respond; his eyes remained distant and unfeeling.

"We want this asshole and we want him now," Dugan continued. "Get in there and get this information. In these files you will see their latest movements in the Libyan desert." Dugan reached into his pocket and pulled out a piece of notebook paper. "This is the code for an Egyptian agent in Cairo." He pointed at the paper. "This is where you can find him. He's setting up a one-man incursion, now for two men."

Peter looked at the paper and memorized the information. Dugan burned the paper in the ashtray with the car's cigarette lighter. "I know I don't need to explain to you the rules of the game. You remember them well?"

"I understand," Peter said.

"I don't have the files on a recent operation we initiated there. They don't exist, but I can tell you that Kasim's operation is continuously on the move. They fear attack and, as a result, the Libyans have beefed up security. However, as you will see on the maps and in the photos, they have pretty much stuck to a particular area, about a fifty-mile radius.

"As you know, Libya is a training center for many of these groups. There are three other groups operating in the same area. Some of them are outlined. The latest photos detailing Kasim's training camp are already outdated. They broke camp and moved again during the last forty-eight hours. That, in a nutshell, is all I have at this time."

"I'll call you in a few days and tell you where you can pick this up." Peter, bulky manila envelope in hand, got out of Dugan's car, returned to his own car, and drove off. Dugan watched him go and then drove home.

Back at his motel, Peter stayed up all night reading the documentation Dugan had given him. There was a picture of Kasim and an extensive background on him. Peter learned how Kasim had been recruited into the organization at a young age, and how his father had died in the war with Israel. He learned how the young Kasim had been a street merchant selling cheap trinkets to foreign tourists.

Most of the information was courtesy of the Egyptian secret police. The more recent information on their organization was compiled from various sources, including the CIA. The satellite photographs were stamped with dates ranging from several weeks earlier up through two days earlier. Dugan had left out the information regarding the TOW training because they had yet to analyze it.

The profile of Kasim's organization outlined its immediate political objectives: overthrow the secular Egyptian government and replace it with one closely resembling Iran's; and hit the Americans hard and often to weaken financial, military, and political support for the Egyptian government. He'd seen it before. Of course, they didn't do a good job of foreseeing the Iranian revolution. Perhaps the Egyptians and American intelligence could keep on top of Kasim's Army of Allah.

He studied the recent satellite photographs. Most of Kasim's activity was centered around Buzaymah in the southern Libyan desert near the Egyptian border. It would be an exhausting journey through the southern end of the Libyan desert and into the Sahara. Hot was an understatement; however, Peter had been in similar situations in the past, albeit at a younger age. It was amazing but true, how putting "mind over matter" really was important. It did work. He thought nothing of the desert and the heat. He finally succumbed to sleep at five in the morning, and slept until noon.

John Perkins strolled into the coffee shop at eight o'clock. He carried a large manila envelope under his right arm. The hostess seated him in a booth at the back of the restaurant. He ordered coffee and waited.

Peter had parked in a place where he could see Perkins enter. After he saw that Perkins was settled in a booth, he entered the restaurant and joined him. "John."

"That you, Colonel?" asked Perkins.

"It works, doesn't it?"

"Fooled me."

"What do you have?"

Perkins opened the envelope and took out some documents. "I've got everything you asked for. You have the pictures?"

Peter handed Perkins half a dozen passport-sized current photos of himself. Perkins looked them over. "Damn, you look good. Your skin is nice and brown, and your beard really does the trick. These are good. They'll work well."

"I plan on leaving in a few days. I have to go before I turn white again."

"I can have the passports in two days."

"Good. We'll meet here in exactly forty-eight hours." Peter shook Perkins' hand, took the manila envelope, and left.

20

It was before breakfast when President Myers shuffled into the conference room dressed in his sweats and slippers. The meeting had been called to order with only an hour's notice. The entire national security team was there, including Dugan.

Secretary of Defense Stuart Williams — a seasoned defense establishment analyst in his mid-fifties, who had served in defense-related positions for twenty years — started the meeting. "Our intelligence has confirmed that the terrorist organization run by Abdul Kasim is responsible for the attack at our embassy in Cairo. Intelligence has concluded that Kasim's organization is planning a hit here on American soil."

"Jack?" said Myers.

"Our agents in Libya were compromised," said Dugan. "We're not sure whether Kasim knows that we're aware of what he's up to. He probably thinks we know very little, because the agent wasn't privy to much information to begin with. You all know Kasim's profile. Because of his history, I believe he'll go forward with his plans. It's probably as big as the World Trade Center bombing, and he has to go through with it because he's running the operations end of the organization now and he's on a power trip. He has to prove his worth to his elders in order to gain full control someday. He's worked all of his life for this moment. We're working on establishing another link in Libya. It will take a couple of weeks to set up."

"What do you think should be done now?" asked Myers.

Dugan replied, "I think we should first present our evidence to Libya's ambassador to the U.N. We should inform Libya that we will take appropriate action — without warning — if Kasim is not handed over to either the Egyptians or to us within forty-eight hours."

"What action do you propose if Libya doesn't cooperate, since it never has?"

"We can have up-to-the-minute satellite confirmation on the whereabouts of Kasim's main camp. We should call in an air strike."

"I don't think we should be too hasty in our actions," said Secretary of State Gregory Northwood. At sixty-three, Northwood was older than most of the group, and was considered overly cautious by some, indecisive by others. "We should exhaust the use of every available diplomatic avenue first."

Dugan had never like Northwood. He always second-guessed Dugan and usually won the President's approval. That was why many on the outside thought there was disarray in the decision-making of this White House. Because of the obvious tension between Dugan and North-wood, many thought it was Dugan who was leaking to the press. He wasn't.

"What do you think, Adam?" Myers asked his National Security Advisor.

The National Security Advisor, Adam Rosen, usually didn't have much to say unless he was directly asked for his opinion. He had his Ph.D. from Princeton and was very knowledgeable about history; therefore, he could talk for hours once he got started. "On the one hand, Mr. President, we need to send a strong message to Libya that we mean business when it comes to them harboring terrorists and allowing them to operate there with impunity for their actions. On the other hand, we should take our case before the world and show what Kasim's group has done, and continues to do, so that we can go ahead at a later date with an air strike. Although, I must add, on the other hand — "

"Stuart?" Myers turned to Williams, cutting Rosen off. After all, how many hands did he have? Besides, the President wanted to get back to bed; the bags under his eyes were beginning to show again. Myers thought, This is one hell of a job! Why would anyone want it?

"We could be ready for an air strike in a couple of hours," said Williams, "but I think we should use our other resources first. We should state our case, present the evidence, and put pressure on Libya. We can always revisit the options later. Although I believe we must inform the Libyans that we will strike, and strike hard in full force, if in fact Kasim's group commits another act."

"You agree, Greg?" asked Myers.

"I fully agree," said Northwood. "Give me some time to get this together. I'll need everything you have, Jack, Stuart," he said, looking at them.

"Let's get into position in case we need to resort to an air strike. What do we have in the Mediterranean, Stuart?" asked Myers.

"The USS Coral Sea is in the western Med now."

"Good. Then that's what we'll do. Let's keep this under wraps, gentlemen." Myers quickly left the room. The others went home to shower, shave, and eat breakfast, for their day had already begun.

Peter had time to spare, so he took a walk around the Mall. He was dressed casually in jeans, a sweatshirt, an overcoat, and sneakers. If anyone recognized him it would be surprising.

The way in which D.C. was laid out, especially around the Capitol and the Mall, always impressed him. It was a beautiful city, despite the vermin that slithered around there, according to the Reverend Jimmy White.

At the reflecting pool near the statue of Grant on his horse, Peter sat. He had a clear angle on the Capitol, especially from the west side where he could see the House Chamber. A light snow fell.

Peter watched the hustle and bustle that was D.C. A few tourists walked through the park taking pictures. Most of the tourists came through the area from spring through summer, but there were always a few wandering around no matter what time of year it was.

One of the tourists, camera in hand, clicking away, was Mr. Fuad, fresh from New York city after seeing the sights there. Peter looked at Fuad long and hard. He knew that the man was an Arab, perhaps an Arab-American. Peter noticed Fuad's distinct and unmistakable scar. He also realized that Fuad was clicking away speedily with his camera.

Mr. Fuad had already done the main tour of the White House and was stopping to take some pictures of the Capitol before taking the main Capitol tour. Congress wasn't in session because of the holidays, and anyone could go on the tour and actually sit right in the Senate and House Chambers.

Mr. Fuad walked on, stopping often to take a couple of pictures. He was, in fact, counting off the meters as he approached the Capitol, methodically taking two pictures every ten meters, all in a straight line.

Fuad had done the same meter count up First Street; Capitol Street South, from one thousand meters down to five hundred meters; and up New Jersey Avenue. This angle, from Maryland Avenue near the Garfield Monument, was his last leg.

Peter watched Fuad and the other tourists disappear from immediate sight. He still had time, so he took the long walk to the other end of the Mall to look at the Vietnam Memorial, "the Wall." He had never seen it before. He had been out of the country for years now and had never gotten around to it. In reality, he had avoided it, for it was part of his past from which he still felt estranged.

He looked at the directory and searched for several names of Americans he had known — two of whom he had seen killed just inches from him. When Peter found the names inscribed in the polished black granite, he couldn't help thinking that fate was a strange phenomenon. In one instance he had been so close to taking the bullets, but instead his buddy to his right flank did. In fact, Peter had moved out of that exact spot only seconds before the onslaught of bullets cut down his friend. It could have just as easily been Peter's name up there on that wall, but it wasn't.

It was time to move on. There was something else that burned in his soul that he had to do now.

The C4 plastic explosive material was packed in two boxes. The boxes were hidden under a suitcase and other personal items in the trunk of Wayne Lewis's 1994 Cadillac Seville. Lewis drove up to the customs official standing in his little kiosk on the U.S. side of Niagara Falls.

"Where were you born?" asked the customs official.

"Rochester," said Lewis.

"Do you have anything to declare?"

"No, nothing."

"What was the nature of your visit to Canada?"

"Business."

The official did a quick scan around the inside of Lewis's car, and Lewis was back on the road. The whole process took ten seconds. After all, Lewis was dressed like a businessman and everything appeared normal. Lewis was in Virginia and at the barn by nightfall.

"Ladies and gentlemen, we will be landing in Philadelphia shortly. Please return to your seats and fasten your seat belts at this time," said the captain.

He did as instructed. He understood just enough English to get done what he had to do, and that was to get through customs and call the number he had been given. After that, all he had to do was sit back and enjoy the short ride to Virginia.

And it was just that easy. His entry was easier than those of the others before him. Luckily, he had a tourist's visa that had been issued to him in Cairo. His passport number and name were written down and photograph was taken. Customs was giving this information to the FBI. It was now the FBI's incredible job to keep track of the hundreds of asylum-seekers and thousands of tourists who entered the States every day — a job they didn't have the resources for at this point.

He came into the main tent for the meeting, sat down, and waited for his leader. Several of Kasim's other lieutenants, some newly promoted in rank, filed in and conversed with each other.

Late by more than thirty minutes, Kasim finally arrived in style. He was dressed in what appeared to be an

American military aviator's flight suit, Western-style sunglasses, and a scarf much like the one Qaddafi wore. He carried his maps and papers in a camouflage military-style map case wherever he went. He snapped at Lieutenant #1 and called the meeting to order. "What's your report?"

Lieutenant #1 stood, saluted Kasim, and said, "We now have nine in country, including Fuad, six of which have reported in at the barn in Virginia. The others are due to check in over the next five days. They will be going in at intervals, and everyone should be there and checked in by the end of next week. They have already begun to check out the area. Fuad has all the photographs assembled. We are right on schedule."

"Good," said Kasim. He pivoted around and barked at Lieutenant #2, "The diversion?"

"We believe target number four would be best," said Lieutenant #2, "for it would pull them off considerably, plus it has cherished historical significance."

Kasim fumbled with his maps on a table that was set up where he was standing. He found the map he needed, placed the corresponding acetate over the map, and studied it. He found target number four on the map, the Jefferson Memorial. "Good. I want the call placed five minutes before we hit."

Peter took a different route back, and stopped at the Jefferson Memorial. He read the inscription engraved upon the memorial that was encircled above Jefferson's larger-than-life full body statue inside. The inscription read: I HAVE SWORN UPON THE ALTAR OF GOD ETERNAL HOSTILITY AGAINST EVERY FORM OF TYRANNY OVER THE MIND OF MAN.

Peter stood there and thought about that Jefferson quote, admiring the fact that Jefferson was indeed larger than life then, and now. He looked around for a few more minutes before heading back to his motel.

Kasim was alone in his command tent, having dismissed the meeting. He sat there studying his maps. He knew he could pull this battle off, but had doubts about whether he could win the war with his own country's government any time soon, although eventually he felt he would. In one way he knew that his group still hadn't won over the hearts and minds of the Egyptian people, and for that, he knew there was a long and hard struggle ahead.

It was ironic, in a way, that he found himself agreeing with Vladimir Lenin in one respect. He had read some of Lenin's works, and disagreed with most of Lenin's views, but he agreed with the idea that the people didn't know what was good for them, and that they needed to be led. Without a central brain to make decisions for them, the people would make bad choices. This was evidenced by Western democracies in general, and American democracy in particular, he reasoned.

In Kasim's case, this meant his people needed to be led by Allah, not only spiritually, but governmentally, or theocratically. He therefore believed that his group must attain power by riding in on the hand of Allah and establishing his order. The people would acquiesce — they wouldn't revolt against God — and he would have won the war against evil.

Kasim looked at the notes in his black book. He had scribbled on a page Reverend Jimmy White's name, along with some other inconsequential information. He wondered if White's group could pull off their end of the deal. Kasim had to rely on White. Kasim would uphold his end of the deal, and White, through his operatives — candidates waiting in the wings — would take power, conduct a sham investigation, and inform the American people of false conclusions to protect Kasim's organization.

Kasim gathered up his maps and notes and returned to his private tent where he could nap. He settled down on his cot and picked up the book he was reading: a book on General George Patton. Reading English gave him an opportunity to continue advancing his understanding of the language, so that when he took over power in Egypt, he would communicate more fluently with the new American government. Plus, reading about Patton made Kasim feel larger than life, much like the General.

Kasim finally fell asleep in the late afternoon sun. He needed rest, because the camp had to move again tomorrow. They had been at this site for too long, four days. He caught a few hours of sleep and was driven back into Tripoli, where he met with some Libyan officials and briefed them on the status of his struggle. He feared the Libyans would become impatient and perhaps intimidated by the Americans and their threats, so Kasim tried to convince them to give him more time. Of course, they did.

Ann Howard sat at her desk trying to finish her piece on the Myers White House. She couldn't stop thinking about her unpleasant encounter the other night; the dirty, thick-bearded face of that homeless man kept haunting her. She replayed his voice over and over in her mind. "Sounded artificial, come to think about it," she said out loud to herself.

She got up from her desk and went to the archives room in the basement, where she looked up several articles on the bombing and death of Colonel Murray. There were headline stories, sidebars, photographs, and follow-up pieces. She found one article, with an accompanying picture that showed the cemetery where the Colonel and

Maria were buried. She thought to herself for a few minutes. "Did I see a ghost?" she asked herself out loud. A nearby clerk overheard her and gave her a strange glance. "I don't believe in ghosts," Howard said.

"Everything all right, Ms. Howard?" asked the clerk.

"What? Oh, yes. I think so." Howard photocopied a couple of the articles and was on the next flight out of town.

Once again, Peter waited in his rental car outside the coffee shop. Hopefully Perkins had everything in order so Peter could leave the day after next. Everything was moving along easily. Having the right contacts in the right places helped.

John Perkins drove up and parked his car. Peter got out of his car and went over and tapped on Perkins' window. Peter was carrying a large shopping bag.

Perkins unlocked the door and Peter got in. "Everything in order?" asked Peter.

"Yes," said Perkins, handing Peter the documentation. Included were three passports. Peter looked them over. One was Egyptian, one was Libyan, and one was American to get him into Egypt. All three were a little weathered, for effect. The recent picture of Peter with full beard, long hair, and brown skin adorned each document. Perkins handed Peter two other documents, local Egyptian and Libyan papers for citizens of each country who would otherwise not have a passport. These documents also had Peter's current picture.

"Good," said Peter. "Any trouble?"

"No. I had to put in the pictures and type myself so my contact at State wouldn't figure this out." He watched Peter secure the documents in his jacket. "I have no doubt that you know you know what you're doing, but I can't help wondering how you're going to pull this off."

"John, let me worry about that." Peter paused for a moment. "I've never had anything against you, and I hope it's reciprocal. All I ask from you is that you keep this to yourself and that you take care of my children. If I don't make it through this, then make sure my children understand, especially when they mature. Look after them."

"I understand."

"Give these Christmas presents to them," said Peter. He handed Perkins the shopping bag full of gifts.

Perkins took the bag.

"My trust fund for them is financially intact. I gave Harry power of attorney over my other assets, and he knows what to do. It's all for the kids."

"I don't know what to say, Colonel."

"Say merry Christmas." Peter offered his hand for a gentlemen's goodbye. They shook hands and Perkins said, "Merry Christmas."

Peter got out of the car and into his own. Perkins watched him drive away.

Howard's flight was smooth, but the drive after it wasn't. Her taxi driver drove like a maniac and scared her half to death. Nevertheless, they made it to Merida alive. Howard inquired on the whereabouts of the graves and found them in short order.

There they were, Maria's and Peter Murray's. The more Howard replayed her encounter with the homeless man over and over in her head, the more convinced she became that Peter was not in that grave at her feet.

She went back to Cozumel Island and checked out Maria's Cantina. It was boarded up with scars from the explosion and burned wood from the blast. Still, she wanted more answers.

She wandered into a dozen shops, restaurants, hotels,

and bars trying to find someone who would answer her questions. At her next hotel, she noticed the man behind the counter in the office. She was sure he was the man she had talked with at Maria's that day. She called out to him, "Excuse me, sir."

Rolf looked up and almost had a coronary when he saw Ann Howard standing there. Shortly after Peter's departure Rolf had seen a picture of Howard and realized that she had been the one in the restaurant that morning. If he ever saw Peter again, he planned to tell him.

"What does she want?" he mumbled to himself. Rolf went to the counter and stood opposite her. "Yes, may I help you?"

"I was wondering if you could tell me a few things about Peter Murray. I'm doing some research on his life and had some questions."

Rolf couldn't believe it. The nerve of this woman! "You're Ann Howard, aren't you?"

"Well, yes," she said, taken off guard.

"You spoke to me at the restaurant that morning?"

Oh no. He had her. She had better play it straight. "Yes, yes, that was you there that morning. I remember now."

"How could you deceive me like that? Don't you have any ethics?"

"I was doing my job, sir."

"Look lady, Peter and Maria were very close friends of mine. I feel I helped lead you to him and because of that helped cause their deaths, and I feel terrible about the whole thing. I'm beginning to despise reporters as the lowest form of life, so I think you had better go. I have nothing to say to you."

"What happened to the Colonel would have happened with or without me. Anyway, I don't think he died," she said, watching for his reaction.

"Don't be ridiculous. I was at the funeral. He's dead. Now if you please . . ." He went back into his office.

Howard could usually tell if someone was lying by looking at their eyes, and she saw deception within Rolf's. "Thank you, sir. You've just confirmed what I was after," she said to herself as she quickly left the hotel. She got back into her cab and returned to the airport.

Onboard her flight, she called Bob Hearn. "It's Ann."

"Where are you, Ann?"

"Bob, I don't have time to explain. I have reason to believe that Colonel Murray is alive." There was silence at the other end of the phone. "I don't think he died in the restaurant bombing."

"You're saying it was all staged?"

"At least his death."

"How do you know?"

"I found a friend of his in Cozumel who was less than convincing."

"You have to be sure about this, Ann."

"I'm going to confirm my suspicion. I'm going to see his brother in New York."

"This could be big, Ann. Keep me posted, but we won't go on this until you've confirmed it."

"I'll call you when I do." She hung up the phone and began writing a rough draft for her next piece.

"Jack, it's me," said Peter into the pay telephone. "Go to the Motel Virginia, Room 21, just past the Pentagon on 395. The key's under the flower pot near the sidewalk. You'll find your envelope under the bed sheet. You'd better get here before check-out at noon."

"Colonel, your contact will be waiting. He's been told to expect an American agent, but was not told the identity, for security. Good luck."

"Thanks, Jack. I'll let you know what I find out." Peter got into his rental car and drove to Washington Dulles International Airport. After boarding his flight, he relaxed back in his seat as the 747 luxury liner took off for Cairo, with a short stopover in Amsterdam.

Frank Wills' barn was isolated enough so that his neighbors couldn't see or suspect that anything unusual was going on. Most of Kasim's operatives had arrived; there were only three more to check in. Most of the equipment had already arrived, all without incident. The only thing they awaited was their shipment of M16 rifles, and those would arrive soon.

The barn now housed Kasim's men. They were being well fed and looked after, some thought even better than they had been in the desert at their training camp, although they did not voice this thought. That was something to keep to yourself, lest you embarrass Colonel Kasim.

Wills had set up a small recreation area behind the barn where the men could get some fresh air. The area was secluded, and the men understood the need for their confinement.

Not far away, parked in another barn on the Wills Virginia farm, were five Ford vans. They had been gutted, with only the two front seats remaining inside each one. They were large utility vans, with full side panels and no windows. Their exterior paint had been stripped and three men were now repainting them. One of the vans was almost done. It was beginning to look like a Bell Atlantic telephone company van.

Mr. Fuad strolled into the barn with Reverend White at his side. "As you can see, we are right on schedule," said the Reverend. Fuad, who understood English well, nodded and grunted to himself.

"As soon as the vans are ready, you can take your drivers around and show them the route," continued the Reverend. "And as we have suggested, each and every operative should know the route, someone else can take over just in case something happens to the driver."

"Very good," said Fuad. He and the Reverend left the barn optimistically. The Reverend got into his limousine and was driven off.

Harry knew he had seen her someplace before. On television perhaps? Yes, one of those talking head pundit shows. He was sure of it.

"I would like to ask you a few questions about your brother, Colonel Murray," said Ann Howard.

Harry didn't know what to say, except that he didn't want to talk about it, for obvious reasons. "What magazine did you say you were from?"

"Well, it's part of the *Washington Sun.*"

"I have nothing to say to that rag. Now, if you please — "

Before Harry could close the door, Howard blocked it with her foot. "I believe your brother is alive, Mr. Murray."

Harry, like Rolf, was not good at lying or acting. His face revealed the truth, despite the words which came from his mouth. "I don't know what you're talking about. My brother died, thanks to your kind. What did you say your name was?"

"I didn't, actually."

"Wait a minute. You're not that despicable Ann Howard are you?"

She was hurt by that remark, but didn't show it. "Why yes. Yes, I am."

Harry lost all patience with her now. He opened the door. "I advise you to get your foot out of the way before I break it when I slam this door shut."

She slowly removed her foot, but not before giving Harry a little smirk. "Thank you, Mr. Murray. You have confirmed what it was I came here for."

Harry didn't know what she meant by that. "And don't come back here, or I'll call the police!" He slammed the door in her face.

Howard gathered up her things and returned to her rental car. She drove back to the airport.

21

P eter landed in Cairo and went through customs, using his American passport and a visa that Perkins
had arranged for him.

The official took his passport and visa and looked them
over. "What is the nature of your business?" he asked.

"I work in the tourist business, and I'm making arrangements with an American company to bring in more tourists
to help expand your economy."

Satisfied, the official stamped Peter's passport and
waved him through.

Peter had only one carry-on bag. Right away he exchanged some of the cash he was carrying for Egyptian
pounds.

Peter found a thirty-day rental locker and deposited his
open-ended return airline ticket inside. He took out a pair
of pants, a shirt, socks, and shoes from his carry-on and
placed them into the locker also. He stuffed three hundred
dollars and his American passport into one of the shoes.
He closed the door and set the combination according to
Maria's birthday.

Outside the airport Peter got into a cab and headed to
a hotel. It was well into the night so Peter went to bed and
slept for ten hours.

The next morning, he went shopping and found some clothes that made him look like the common man on the street. He wore a Gallabia over his body and an Egyptian-style Ghoutra on his head. He seemed to blend in rather well, with his thickening beard, which he colored darker now, and his tanned skin.

Peter walked around the streets and practiced his Arabic language skills, although a few Egyptians, when he talked with them, looked at him long and hard. He didn't think that they suspected anything, since they never seemed to question his performance.

He walked around the city and noticed some Christmas decorations celebrating the birth of Christ. There were many Coptic Christians who lived in Egypt. It seemed to Peter that the Sunni Muslim majority coexisted peacefully in this secular state. He wondered what would happen if Kasim did get his way. It just depended upon the character of the government, because he knew that in other Middle Eastern countries, including Iran and Iraq, there were minority religions or sects, some treated well and with respect, others which were not.

Peter went back to his hotel and rested.

Walter Hudson was a well-known cattle rancher. His trucks went in and out of Mexico across the Texas border at several points daily. He knew the inspectors and officials, and they knew and trusted him. They rarely gave his trucks any hassle when they went through. They had to inspect them, but they were usually very relaxed about it. After all, he was Mr. Hudson.

Hudson was also a good friend of the Reverend Jimmy White. They went back many years, and shared many of the same values of traditional American life. He sided with the Reverend on every issue, and stood shoulder-to-shoulder with him, prepared to assist in any way he could to win this cultural war.

One of his trucks had made an early morning run into Ciudad Juarez in the Chihuahua state of northern Mexico. Hudson did business there regularly. The truckload of cattle was delivered for local distribution throughout Mexico. Upon the truck's return to El Paso, Hudson's driver made a prearranged stop alongside a road just south of Ciudad Juarez, where he picked up several long, flat crates. The crates were transferred into the truck by two Anglo-American men, who placed them in the front of the trailer under some pallets.

On its way back into Texas, Hudson's truck, supposedly empty upon return, was waved through after the inspector briefly opened the rear door to the trailer and saw that the truck was empty except for ordinary-looking pallets. The border patrol was primarily looking for illegal aliens or drugs. Clearly, there were no illegals or contraband aboard this truck.

A few miles north of El Paso, the truck stopped on a side road. The crates were unloaded by the same two men who had loaded the crates in Mexico. The tractor-trailer driver headed back to Hudson's ranch, not knowing what he had just delivered.

The two men opened the crates and inspected them. Everything had arrived in order. There were thirty-five M16 rifles packed inside. They put the crates back into their truck and took off.

At Fort McClellan, near Anniston, Alabama, a lowly MP soldier in training stood guard. He was waiting for the truck to deliver the ammunition. The company was due in an hour or so, for the recruits to qualify on their M16's.

The truck pulled up with several crates of live ammunition for the M16 rifles. Two sergeants unloaded the boxes and piled them near the range shack. One of the sergeants and the private stayed to guard the ammunition while the other sergeant got in the truck and drove off.

Many of these stateside American military installations — and some overseas, for that matter — were easy to enter and drive around in. There were open access roads all over the place.

The civilian truck drove up and kept its distance. One of the two men inside looked through his binoculars and scoped out the range area. He saw the private sitting on a counter near the range shack, and watched the sergeant enter the portable potty.

They made their move. They drove forward and stopped near the range shack. The men got out of their truck and walked up to the private. The bigger man pulled out a handgun, pointed it at the private, and said, "Don't say a word."

The private didn't understand what was happening as the two men started loading the ammunition into their truck. "You can't take that!" exclaimed the private.

"Shut up," said the man with the gun.

The private now got it. He put his hands up and kept quiet. The two men finished putting the boxes into their truck just as the sergeant came out of the portable potty. They got into the truck and drove off.

The sergeant came running up to the private. "What's going on here, Private?"

"Those men held a gun on me and stole the ammunition."

"What?"

The truck was long gone.

A few miles outside the fort, the men passed off the

boxes of ammunition to another awaiting truck. The second truck sped off toward Virginia.

It was nearing the end of the year, and for the Western world it would be the end of an era, Kasim planned. Kasim was counting the days until the attack. A new dawn would rise at that time.

He had returned to his hotel room in Tripoli. His main camp was on the move again. One of his lieutenants, #2 from the meeting at the desert camp, arrived. "We are ready for the target, Colonel."

"Yes, I have chosen one that will make the Americans mad indeed." He pulled some notes out of his little black book. He tore a page out and handed it to his lieutenant. "I want this target hit as planned. Both principals will be there at that time and I want you to carry it out."

The lieutenant looked at the notepaper and said, "I understand." He saluted Kasim and hurried out.

Kasim lay down to rest and stared at the ceiling, remembering his childhood. He thought about those days rummaging through the streets, begging tourists to buy his crappy little knickknacks. Many of them would say, "No thank you, little boy." He would run after them and tug at their shirts, and continue the pressure until they bought the damn thing just to get rid of him.

Kasim thought about his mother, left widowed by the war with Israel. Damned Zionists — and those who supported them — would regret it, he stewed. Sometime after he had come to power and aligned with countries like Iran and Libya, they would take Palestine back with a vengeance, and damn anyone who stood in their way. All those peace accords with Israel lately would be nullified. More than anything, all his Arab brothers in the region who were making peace with the Zionists were misguided. To appease evil was unforgivable. He was sure Allah had not meant it to be this way.

Peter roamed around Giza in his disguise — ironically, near Kasim's shop — near the great pyramids. Later, he went into a nearby shop and saw a middle-aged man behind the counter attending to three tourists.

After the man had finished serving his customers, Peter went up to him and said in Arabic, "I would like to see the Sultan of Jade."

The man looked Peter over for a moment, then said, "Just a minute." He went into the back of the shop and came out a few seconds later, followed by another man.

The first man went to help a tourist who had a question about some merchandise. The second man scrutinized Peter for a moment. Finally, he smiled, nodded, and said, "Please," motioning towards the back room.

Peter nodded slightly and went into the room. The man followed him. "I am Mohammed Al Qadir," he said. He extended his hand for Peter to shake. Qadir was one of the men who had observed the thwarted attack on Kasim weeks earlier.

Peter shook his hand and studied him for a moment. Qadir was slightly shorter than Peter, in his mid-forties, and looked younger than his age. "They didn't tell me your name," said Qadir, "but now that I've seen your face, I know who you are."

"My disguise didn't throw you?"

Qadir shook his head. "I know about Abdul Kasim and what he has done. I know what he has done to you. Please, sit down." He motioned for Peter to sit in a nearby chair. Qadir sat across from him and continued. "I have the highest access to my government's intelligence and what your government communicates to us. Your CIA informed me that an unexpected agent must accompany me on my journey. There was no explanation for this. I was only instructed to accommodate this agent. I knew this was irregular, but when I saw your face just now in the shop, I knew who you were, even though you are dressed the way you are. I met you once before, in 1983 during a joint exercise."

Peter nodded his head and said, "Yes, I remember. You were in charge of security."

"Yes, I was. I never forget a face, Colonel. Well, enough." Qadir sighed and adjusted himself in his seat. "You see, we have been after Mr. Kasim — 'Colonel,' as he is known to his people — for many years. He spends most of his time in Libya and Iran, but he does slip into Egypt at times. He is clever and is always one step ahead of us. The clever ones make mistakes too, though. We almost had him several weeks back, but he managed to escape again. The only way we can get him now, we figure, is to go into Libya and abduct him."

"That is why I am here."

"I know this, and I know how good you are. You are more than welcome to come with me. I am honored."

"Thank you. There is nothing I need to explain to you. I must say, however, that I will not leave here until we get Kasim. I wish to take him alive. I would be honored to deliver him to your government. He has murdered Americans and must be brought to justice. Killing him would not give him the punishment he deserves."

"I agree. There need be no more words between us regarding Kasim. We have a mutual job to do."

Peter nodded in agreement.

"We have much preparatory work to do," continued Qadir, handing Peter a piece of paper. "We will meet at this address tomorrow night at twenty hundred hours.

Until then, please enjoy our fine city."

"Thank you, I will. And I will meet you then." Peter shook Qadir's hand and exited the shop, determined to see this madness through.

The morning edition of the *Washington Sun* said it all. Dugan almost fell out the front door of his house when he reached down to pick up his copy.

The headline read: FORMER MARINE LIEUTENANT COLO-NEL PETER MURRAY BELIEVED TO BE ALIVE. Dugan nearly bumped into a wall walking back into his house while reading the article. "How does she know this?" he said to himself. The article, written by Ann Howard, went on about how she had reason to believe, but no definitive proof, that Murray was alive and traipsing around Washington, D.C. She speculated that the Colonel was out for revenge for the death of his girlfriend and the others killed in the blast at his restaurant on Cozumel Island. "Damn," Dugan mumbled.

Kasim was handed an Arabic news-wire translation of the *Washington Sun*'s article. As he read it, his face became red. He placed the article on a table and said to his messenger, one of his lieutenants, "How could this Murray possibly come after me?"

His lieutenant shook his head from side to side.

"This Murray can't just walk in here! He couldn't just walk into Libya. Although," said Kasim, thinking it over, "once in the American intelligence business, always in it. He has contacts. Perhaps he can get in as an American businessman or something like that. I had better get back into the desert and stay with the camp. At least from there we can control the situation, and a raid into Libya like the one by the American mercenaries is less likely now. Get someone in Washington and here in Tripoli to look around for Murray. When you find him, kill him. Allah's had enough of his interference."

They went over their plans. Peter and Qadir walked along a Giza street, the same street Kasim had walked many times in the past.

"As you can see," said Qadir, "getting to the border from here, and having our transportation waiting on this side of the border to bring us back to Cairo, will be easy to execute. Once in Libya, I'm afraid we'll be on our own."

"I have no doubt that we can weather the elements. Taking the camp at night will be the challenge for both of us. But it is the best way I can see," said Peter. "There is no other way."

"Good. We will discuss more of our plan tomorrow. Now, however, I want to show you around. Come, we will have a meal."

Peter didn't object to Qadir's hospitality; he was grateful. They strolled in the marketplace. The exchange of goods was plentiful. Qadir and Peter got away from the predominantly tourist area and into the heart of Cairo, where Qadir could let Peter practice his Egyptian persona.

They came upon a traditional Egyptian restaurant (passing a Kentucky Fried Chicken along the way). They sat down and ordered.

"I have been asked to extract any information I can from Kasim about a possible hit on American soil," said Peter.

"I know. We've been notified and will cooperate fully." They were silent for some time.

"I hope you won't mind my line of questioning," added Peter.

Qadir indicated for Peter to go ahead by raising his hands slightly. Peter continued, "You are a Muslim."

Qadir nodded his head.

"Kasim's organization seeks to establish a theocratic state more so than Iran," continued Peter.

"Yes. But Allah does not want people forced into submission. He wishes for people to be brought over with kindness and reason. As you know, in Christianity, as well as other religions, there are different interpretations. That is why you have Catholics and differing Protestant ways. The same is true with Islam: there are Sunnites and Shi'ites and other interpretations as well. Of course you know all this. As for Abdul Kasim, I believe what he is attempting to do is not spiritual, but political. His way wishes to rule over people, not guide them religiously.

"The people of Egypt cultivate different religions. We live in peace with one another, side by side. As in your country, I believe that people should be allowed to practice their religion without governmental interference. And, I believe, likewise, that government should not be subjugated to any particular religious belief. All evidence indicates that Kasim's organization wants to subjugate the people. I don't believe he's as religious as he pretends to be."

"How strong do you expect his support to be?"

"Minuscule, if that."

Peter nodded.

"I also believe that justice is most important," continued Qadir. "The Qur'an says that Allah loves those who act in justice. These terrorist acts, that many people in the West know, unfortunately are all they hear about Islam, and that is sad. It is not what Allah wishes. These acts of terrorism are blasphemy against him."

Peter nodded in agreement. "Yes, I wish more understood."

"Like Kasim," Qadir continued, "I also lost my father in the war with Israel. He was only a regular conscript. I believe that justice was served when we made peace with Israel, thanks in great measure to your government at the time. I believed that it was important to get beyond the animosity. I also praise the peacemakers elsewhere in the region who are getting beyond their hatred. We cannot go on fighting each other forever. If we do, eventually we will destroy each other, and there will be nothing left for anyone."

Peter knew that he was referring to the nuclear bomb, a bomb that some countries in the area either had already, or were developing or planning to develop in the near future.

"I understand," said Peter. "I believe that humans are determined to fulfill prophesy, even though we have it within our power to prevent it, or prove it wrong."

"Then perhaps that is why it is written, because humans are fallible, and prophecy is written because it is inevitable."

"But I believe God gave us the intelligence to see that outcome and work to prevent it."

"I agree," said Qadir. "Therefore those who strive for peace, as the Qur'an says, will be rewarded."

Their meal arrived, and they ate while chatting about everything under the sun. They talked more about religion in a friendly and constructive manner. Peter already knew something about Islam, having studied it while learning Arabic at the Defense Language Institute, and Qadir knew much about Christianity and Judaism. How ironic, they both thought, that all three religions were so alike in so many ways, from the aspect that they all believed in the same one God, to the way in which humanity should be viewed and treated by all.

After their meal, they retired for the night. Qadir went home and Peter returned to his hotel. They still had preparations to make and plans to go over. Hopefully, Peter thought, they could be on their way within a few days. He was anxious for this to be over, although he also knew how important preparation and planning were in any mission. Of course, no matter how much planning was done, there were always events beyond your control that sprang up and threw a wrench into the cog. Peter knew that fact well, and would experience it again.

22

*T*he utility van drove around D.C. with its new markings painted on the side. The markings read: BELL ATLANTIC. They drove down Pennsylvania Avenue, past the Capitol, and as close as they could to the White House, since the White House had installed barricades on Pennsylvania Avenue there. That wouldn't matter to them; their plan compensated for this fact.

They blended in with the rest of the hectic D.C. traffic. They were getting acquainted with the streets and surroundings that pertained to their mission's success. Mr. Fuad drove, and Mr. Assad was his passenger.

They doubled back down Massachusetts Avenue, cut over to the Dwight D. Eisenhower freeway and circled around the Jefferson Memorial. They stopped in the parking lot and examined the area.

"What do you think?" asked Fuad.

"It'll be easy," said Assad. "It's a good choice. You know that this Jefferson was a slave owner."

"No, I didn't. They honor such a man?"

"He wrote their Declaration of Independence."

"And we will write ours, beginning here, that night." Mr. Fuad smiled. Assad nodded.

"I have received word from Colonel Kasim that Colonel Murray is alive and in D.C. someplace," said Fuad.

"We have been instructed to keep an eye out for him. When we find him, we are to kill him immediately. Colonel Kasim is doing the same in Tripoli. This creature has caused us too much distraction."

Assad and Fuad departed the city, heading west for the Virginia countryside. At the Wills barn outside Leesburg, they drove into the holding area where their soldiers were gathered. They got out of their van. "Gather around, everyone," shouted Assad.

The group of operatives came close to hear Assad. "We will begin our practice runs tomorrow. I will have a schedule for you. Each van will drive to your position, familiarizing yourselves with the route — and that means all four onboard will know how to get there and return. We have gone over the traffic laws. I cannot overemphasize the fact that you must drive the way Americans do, not the way you do at home. Everyone knows the contingency plan if, by chance, you are stopped."

On a wall near where Fuad stood, there were enlarged photographs of the Capitol, from four different angles. They were marked by position, numbered 1 through 4. An acetate sheet was overlaid on the map of D.C., highlighting the positions. Next to the photographs were other maps of D.C., and a large map of northern Virginia with four routes highlighted to and from the Capitol and the Wills farm.

Mr. Wills stood near the door listening, although he didn't understand one word of Arabic.

"We're fast approaching our zero hour," continued Assad. "Everything has gone according to our plans, because we have the Great One on our side guiding us through this. Each and every one of you has been chosen by him for this ultimate battle against the Great Satan. If you die in the execution of this task, you have been chosen to go straight to heaven to be with him. You will not fail. It is written, for Allah said: As for those who are slain in the cause of Allah, he will not allow their works to perish. He will vouchsafe them guidance and ennoble their state; he will admit them to the Paradise he has made known to them."

Wills was joined by one of his farm hands, the young man who had been honored to shake the Reverend Jimmy White's hand earlier. In his middle twenties, he was tall, and chewed some of Wills' best tobacco. "Whaddaya 'spose they're talkin' 'bout, Mr. Wills?" asked the young man.

"I don't know, Billy. I guess their plans. One of them just came back from a drive around D.C. Their disguises seem to work."

"D'ya know what they plan on hittin'?"

"No, I don't. But it must be big. Reverend White says the Lord has instructed him on what to do. I think things will change, Billy. We'll be running God's country soon."

Billy nodded and spit out some chew. The residue dribbled down his chin.

Senator Buchanan got out of his car and into Reverend White's limousine that was parked in front. The road was a country dirt road that was seldom traveled.

"I'm afraid he's getting too close to figuring something out."

"How so?" inquired Jimmy White.

"I think they're talking about taking Kasim out," said the Senator, shifting in his seat.

"Is that legal?"

"Jimmy, you're talking about the CIA."

"Right." Jimmy corrected himself. He thought it over. "Just him?"

"I think so. I know Dugan better than anyone. He lets

the wheels turn for a while before he discusses his theories with anyone."

"What do you propose?" asked the Reverend, knowing the answer already, but wanting to hear it from Buchanan for assurance.

"It would be made to look like an accident."

Reverend White thought about this for a minute. He took a deep breath and said, "We're doing the Lord's work. My conscience is clear. The end justifies the means. In other words, this is justifiable homicide. God Almighty will sort out those who will be at his side and those who won't."

"You can handle it, then?"

"Yes," said Jimmy self-confidently. "I'll handle it."

It was hot, and there wasn't much to see out here, so Peter laid back and closed his eyes as the desert passed by. He was riding in the lead vehicle with Qadir and a driver. They had been flown from Cairo to an outpost in southeastern Egypt, where they were picked up by military vehicles. Their camels and equipment followed in another truck. It was a long journey indeed. Peter stopped keeping track of time; he had, in fact, lost all sense of it since that day at the restaurant. Time meant nothing to him now.

They came upon another secret Egyptian military outpost not far from the Libyan border and stopped to get some more supplies. Qadir made contact with an official while Peter waited near the truck. He took a sip of water from his water pouch; the water was even hotter than the pouch felt. Nevertheless, it was water, and out here in the desert it didn't matter whether it was warm or cold, so long as it was wet.

Peter was dressed like Qadir, in a gown-like Gallabia and Ghoutra. They looked like two dusty nomads who had lost their way. Peter's hair was long and full, as was his beard, both of which were collecting dust and sand. The skin on his face and hands was already beginning to look like parchment. Studying himself in the mirror before leaving on this insane undertaking, he thought he looked like Charlton Heston as Moses crossing the desert.

Qadir returned to the truck. "They've moved again," he said, "although it is still within our area of concentration." He handed Peter two satellite photographs. One showed a bunch of small dots in the desert, while the other showed that the dots were now in another location, about twenty miles from the first one.

"We will be dropped off seven kilometers from here," continued Qadir. "This base will be here when we return. It will be up to us to get back here on our own." He handed Peter another map to study. "Look this over. Familiarize yourself with it, for we must leave it here. To minimize exposure, our next journey will not be along any traditional caravan route."

Peter took notes in his book and coded the entries. He noted the location of the Egyptian military camp. As he studied the map, Qadir packed some other supplies into one of the trucks.

Qadir and Peter boarded the lead truck. They traveled for several more kilometers before the two trucks stopped in the middle of nowhere. Along the way there was little to note — no landmarks or other distinguishing formations were visible. It would be quite a challenge to find their way back to the Egyptian military camp.

It was late in the afternoon, and the sun's harsh rays were beginning to soften. Qadir, Peter, and the two drivers disembarked and began unloading their equipment.

Peter prepared his camel. Because of its hump it would be a challenge for him to ride. Most of the packs that Peter and Qadir loaded on their camels were water pouches, mainly for their own consumption. The camels had been replenished with water outside Cairo before they had departed the previous day.

As Peter secured his pack on his camel, it spat at him. "Thanks," he said, wiping the spit from his robe. "You and I are on a life-threatening mission, and I would advise you that we need each other to survive this." The camel Peter had named Tut looked at him and pursed its lips. As he finished readying Tut, Peter wondered if the camel somehow actually did sense the task at hand.

Both Qadir and Peter had been issued a Fairbairn-Sykes commando-style knife and had strapped them into their sheaths under their gowns. These were the only weapons they had. Peter checked to make sure his knife was securely fastened. It was.

Qadir had a few last words with the two drivers. Then they got into their trucks and departed. Peter and Qadir watched as the trucks disappeared over the horizon. They were alone. Nothing but the desolate sea of sand and the open sky awaited them. "Shall we?" asked Qadir.

Peter nodded, got up on his camel, and followed Qadir westward. Both men carried compasses. Peter checked his and made a note in his log. He calculated the return trip, from this point, by doing a back azimuth. There was a small ridge ahead of them which they were approaching, and an Egyptian marker near a caravan intersection just behind them that read: Cairo, 700 kilometers. Peter wrote this information down, sketched a simple map, closed his small logbook, then looked ahead and concentrated on the horizon.

At various points along the way, when a discernible natural marking presented itself, Peter recorded their progress. Qadir did much the same, since they both knew all too well that if they became separated, each would need his own map, written by his own hand, so that each could understand his own notes.

As Peter rode along, bouncing atop Tut, he thought about how he had tended to lose track of time lately. He didn't know exactly what day it was, only that it was the second week of January.

The minutes turned into hours. The scenery was much the same. There was nothing to do but stay on your camel, look for anything remotely different about the surroundings to record, and think. Peter thought about his children and the kind of world they were growing up in. That disturbed him greatly, as it did many parents who cared.

Peter watched Qadir riding on his camel. Here was a man who came from a different culture. What a history. Egypt was in the Old Testament of the Bible. What an empire. Egypt dated back thousands of years, at least in human history. Nomads had roamed these deserts for at least that long. Peter wondered about his own significance in the scope of time, as Tut trotted over these ancient sands. He realized that his time on earth was insignificant; it amounted to the equivalent of one grain of sand that Tut stepped on. That single grain of sand was his time on earth.

Memories of Maria entered Peter's mind. He became even more bitter as he contemplated how her time amounted to only a fraction of one grain of sand. There was no doubt in his heart that he wanted to kill Kasim. He could actually tie the bastard down and torture him to death slowly. However, Peter would not become like Kasim. He knew that abducting Kasim and returning him to the authorities so justice could be served was more important. Still, Peter could easily rip out Kasim's heart if he didn't control his inner beast. He had to maintain control over his emotions. He had to let his head rule.

They moved at a slow pace, following the sun. Several hours later, they saw a caravan approaching. There were at least twelve camels, each with a rider and a pack. As they got closer, Qadir and Peter could see that the people in the caravan were simple nomads. They stopped to chat.

The caravan's leader, a man in his seventies, conversed with Qadir, while Peter kept quiet.

A young boy, perhaps fifteen years of age, studied Peter. Although Peter was dressed like the others, and had a full, dusty beard that he had darkened, the boy wasn't sure about him.

"How is your travel, my friend?" Peter asked in Arabic.

"Good, sir. Thank you," said the boy, more convinced after Peter's performance. He looked away as Qadir and the caravan's leader broke off their conversation.

Peter's camel followed Qadir's as the rest of the caravan passed them. The sun was now setting on the horizon.

Kasim was back at the camp, which had just recently moved to its present location. The activity at the camp was getting smaller with every passing day. There were only twenty men now present, carrying on with logistical oversight and communications with their field operatives in Virginia, and now with their small contingent in Berlin.

"Colonel Kasim?" a young messenger called through the open tent.

"Yes, what is it?" Kasim answered, sitting at his makeshift desk studying his maps and overlays. An assistant first lieutenant stood over him.

The young messenger entered the tent and handed Kasim's lieutenant a communique. The lieutenant opened it and read it out loud.

COLONEL KASIM, FROM LIBYAN INTERNAL SECURITY PO-
LICE, STOP. THE AMERICANS ARE THREATENING AN AIR STRIKE
IF ANOTHER ATTACK IS INITIATED BY THE ARMY OF ALLAH,
STOP. BE ADVISED THAT COLONEL QADDAFI IS CONSIDERING
A RELOCATION OF YOUR OPERATION, STOP. BE ADVISED THAT
YOU ARE REQUESTED TO HALT ANY AND ALL PRESENT OPERA-
TIONS.

The lieutenant handed the paper to Kasim. Kasim
crumpled it up and tossed it into the trash. "You are dismissed," he said to the young messenger.

"I beg the Colonel's pardon. I was instructed to ask the
favor of a reply."

Kasim gave the young man a cross look, but stopped
himself short of any action. He knew the young man was
only doing his job, so he took out a paper and scribbled
down his reply.

FROM COLONEL KASIM. I UNDERSTAND. I WILL AWAIT
FURTHER ORDERS.

He signed the note and gave it to the messenger. The
messenger departed for Tripoli, and Kasim went back to
his maps and overlays.

"You are not concerned, my brother?" asked Kasim's
lieutenant.

"We must stall Qaddafi. He will thank us dearly when
we have succeeded in our task."

"You do not think the Americans will attempt to bomb
us here?"

"It is irrelevant if they do. Nothing can stop what we
have put into place."

"And the Berlin hit is necessary?"

Kasim was agitated. "It is, my brother. We must keep
the Americans off guard, responding to our actions, not
preempting our main objective."

"Forgive me. I understand."

"Although, I have an idea," said Kasim, his face lighting up. "We need some friendly public relations. I think I know how to obtain that."

Kasim's lieutenant looked puzzled.

At sundown they relaxed for a couple of hours. They found a small sandstone overhang where the camels rested also.

Peter entered the location in his log. "How far past the border do you calculate we've come?" asked Peter.

"I estimate about twenty kilometers." Qadir sipped water from his satchel.

"We should make good time under the cover of night."

They were silent for some time. Finally, Qadir asked, "I hope you don't mind me asking you this, Colonel. Why did you leave your profession so early? I know you were good at what you did."

"Politics, essentially. I wasn't going to go anywhere after Iran-Contra, professionally."

"All that you had done for your country wasn't appreciated?"

"I got my pension and some medals. How else does a country show its appreciation?"

Qadir pondered that while Peter made designs in the sand with a staff he had brought along. He did look like Moses in search of something.

They rested a few more minutes until the sun disappeared completely. As the moon peeked out from behind a cloud, they got on their camels again and continued their westward journey.

They kept moving until the sun came up. They found a sand dune wall and set up a lean-to. They made a lean-to for the camels, who obliged and lay down for sleep.

Peter slept until just before noon, the hottest time of the day. He awoke and found Qadir still sleeping. The camels were happily resting in the same positions they had been when Peter had fallen asleep. Peter decided to let Qadir sleep a while longer.

He took out his log and studied his entries from their first day's travel. He looked out from under the lean-to and saw nothing but endless desert looking back at him. There wasn't much to note at this location except the dune wall to his backside, so he recorded what he could, including his headings, and pocketed the logbook.

Qadir began to stir after an annoying sand gnat buzzed at his nose. "There's the Al Kufrah Oasis and one near Rebiana, as well as water at various springs," said Qadir, "so we may encounter some pests."

"According to my calculations," said Peter, "we should be in range tonight."

"Yes, I think we will."

23

Mr. Todd was a clean-cut man in his mid-thirties. Dressed in a suit and tie, his eyes continuously scanned the room nervously. He was escorted into the judge's chambers by a United States Marshall for the Federal District Court in San Diego. After the Marshall departed, Todd paced back and forth several times before the judge came in. It was eight o'clock in the morning and the judge had about an hour before court was in session.

Judge Carl White was a tall, healthy, grandfatherly figure, now pushing seventy years of age. He wore a well-tailored suit. He walked cautiously over to the man and shook his hand. "Mr. Todd, how may I help you?" asked Judge White. "Please, sit down."

Mr. Todd was a member of the local school board. He had recently been elected, along with several others who all belonged to Jimmy White's Glory to God organization. He was a prominent local businessman who truly believed that with their majority on the board, they could bring God back into the schools and get rid of the tolerance-based left-wing indoctrination they believed was destroying their society and stealing their children from them.

Mr. Todd sat, then shifted nervously in his seat. "I may be in great danger, Judge. I came to you because I know you are Reverend White's brother."

Judge White sat down slowly in his chair upon hearing his brother's name. "Go on."

"I was just excommunicated from Glory to God. I worked in the San Diego chapter." Todd got up and paced in front of Judge White's large oak desk. This made Judge White somewhat nervous himself. His head moved back and forth, following Todd like a spectator at a tennis match would follow the ball.

"Three weeks ago I was instructed to pick up a man at the airport and drive him to Virginia. I'm not racist, Judge, but the man was an Arab. He was rather pleasant, despite the fact that we couldn't really communicate. We drove almost the whole way without stopping. When I dropped him off at this barn in Virginia, I noticed there were about fifteen or more Arabs camped out there. I also happened to see — and I was in the army, Judge — some type of military hardware in crates there. I believe they were missile launchers.

"Well, I was given a room at a local motel and told to drive back to San Diego. I had no idea what this all meant, but I know that the Reverend, your brother, is preaching about an intervention from God. The more I thought about it, the more it bothered me."

Judge White leaned forward. His face tightened.

"I didn't know who to come to with this, Judge."

"That's okay, Mr. Todd. Please, continue."

"Well, it bothered me all the way back here. I am a devout Christian. I believe in all that Christ stands for. I truly believed in what your brother preached. When I got back, I began to ask a lot of questions about the matter, despite having been told to forget about it. As it turned out, I asked too many questions. They got to my wife and told her that I was evil, had lost the faith, and was controlled by Satan. God only knows what else they told her.

I tried to explain to her what I saw in Virginia, but she wouldn't listen to me.

"Then I got threats over the phone. Death threats. I was told that if I talked to anyone about anything, God would call me home. Call me home? Can you imagine? My wife has moved out, and I was told to resign from the school board or further measures would be taken. Further measures?"

"Okay," said Judge White. "You need to check into a hotel and lie low. Leave a message at this number so I know where I can reach you." He scribbled down a number and handed it to Mr. Todd. "I'm going to be in Washington for a judicial conference this weekend. Let me talk to my brother and get some facts. Where is this barn?"

"Leesburg. It belongs to the Wills Tobacco Company."

"Okay."

"I just thought someone should know about this. Your brother has been talking about a new order in this country. I mean, I have mixed emotions. I believe we need God back in our national life and all, but I'm worried that people will get hurt."

"You did the right thing, Mr. Todd."

"Thank you, Judge."

Judge White watched him go. He sat and thought about what this meant. He had court today, then nothing planned until the weekend and the conference. What in God's good name was his brother up to? He decided to check out Mr. Todd's story by going to the barn and confronting Jimmy before he went to the authorities. He was a cautious man, and he wanted facts before he ruled. He prepared for his court session.

Howard's story wasn't going anywhere. She couldn't get any follow-up material. She followed the Director of

Central Intelligence into a restaurant in D.C. He was with his driver/bodyguard, Kenny, and a staffer. The three of them sat down and ordered lunch.

She walked up to them and, as always, never hesitated. "Mr. Director?"

He almost spilled the water he was sipping.

"May I?" She sat down before Dugan could respond. His bodyguard, Kenny — who was an expert in hand-to-hand combat — knew who she was, but was, nevertheless, edgy about her being here. He could roust her from here in a split second if need be. He looked at Dugan for instructions. Dugan raised his hand slightly to indicate that it was all right, at least for the moment.

"Ms. Howard," greeted Dugan. "What can I do for you?" He was polite, knowing who had the real power in this town. He didn't want to tick her off and have her go write an unflattering piece about him. After all, this Administration was already being hammered by the media.

"I know you knew Colonel Murray. I wonder if you might tell me where I could find him."

Dugan knew it was coming, but he had to stick to his story. "I would hope at God's hand."

"Look, Director, let's not play games with one another. If you are withholding information — "

"I'm legally authorized. It's part of my job, you know."

"Not in this case."

"Let the man rest in peace, Ms. Howard. Don't you think you've done enough damage?"

"I'm a reporter, Mr. Dugan. I only report on the facts."

"Now *you're* playing games, Ms. Howard."

"Okay, okay, let's cut through the crap. Is Murray working for the Agency?"

"No. Murray is dead."

"Is he seeking revenge for the death of his girlfriend?"

"No. Murray is dead."

"Thank you, Director." With that, she got up and strutted out the door, knowing full well the Director was lying. Dugan had done a good job, but she knew he was a professional liar.

Howard had done her research. She went through the archives and found out that Murray's wife had remarried, one John Perkins, State Department employee and career foreign service officer. She had contacts at State, so it wasn't hard to find Perkins. She followed him home to see where he lived.

She watched Perkins park his car in the garage, then went home, got some sleep, and was back at his house early the next morning. She took instant pictures of Paul and Sarah as they got on the school bus, then followed the bus to the school.

While she waited in the office to be helped, she noticed a classroom register that a child had delivered to the office, apparently after the teacher had taken attendance. She chose a name from it and told the office secretary that she was the child's parent. She was given a thirty-minute visitor's pass to visit the classroom. She used it to locate Paul on the yard minutes later at recess.

It was an unseasonably warm winter day. It didn't take her long to spot Paul, who sat on a bench with some other kids waiting to play handball. She started onto the yard and was stopped by a yard aide. "May I help you?" asked the aide.

Howard flashed her visitor's pass. "I'm visiting my child's classroom."

The aide nodded that it was okay. Howard went over to Paul. "Hi, Paul."

Paul nodded, more interested in the game.

"I'm Buddy Wilhelm's mother, in Room 23." She sat on the bench. Paul slid over as another kid got up to take his turn.

"Yeah, I know Buddy," said Paul.

"Yes. That's right. How's your mother?"

"She's good."

"Good. How's your father doing?"

"John?"

"Oh, he's your stepfather, isn't he?"

"Yes. We call him John. I call my real father Dad."

"I see. And how's he doing these days?"

Paul caught himself and looked at Howard. "He died."

"I thought I read in the newspaper where they thought he was alive."

Paul looked at her for moment, then jumped up and played his round of handball. Howard sensed he wasn't telling the truth by the way he was acting. Paul finished his turn and took his seat on the bench again. Howard hovered over him. "So when was the last time you saw your father, Paul?"

Paul looked at her with an unsure expression. "I don't know."

"You don't know what?"

"You said you were Buddy's mother?"

"Yes."

"I don't want to talk about my dad."

"Why not?"

"Because."

"Did he tell you not to?"

Paul didn't say anything. He watched the handball game and slid over a notch on the bench as space became available.

"Is your father going after the terrorists?"

He remembered his father telling him in the jungle

never to tell anyone about his faked death and what he planned to do. "You're not Buddy's mother, are you?"

She didn't answer.

"I'm going to tell my teacher." Paul jumped up from the bench and raced across the yard, in search of his teacher who had stayed in the room correcting papers. Howard made a dash for her car in the parking lot. She got out of there as fast as she could.

It was daybreak in the desert. They were standing in the middle of the area where just two days before Kasim's base camp had been.

"It was certainly a camp," said Qadir. "And according to my notes, it should have been Kasim's camp, from that last satellite photo we got at the outpost when we departed."

Peter picked up a spent AK47 cartridge. "It won't be hard to track them from here. There are tracks all over the place."

"Yes. We should locate them tomorrow or the day after."

"I agree. Let's find a spot to set up for today," said Peter.

They found a ridge and dug in. They ate the Meals-Ready-to-Eat packets they had gotten at the Egyptian outpost. These American-made military food packets were making their way around the world. They could last for some time, although when Peter first became acquainted with them in the early '80s, he had thought they were awful. They had been improved and weren't so bad. Still, living off these things altered the digestive system some-what. At times it seemed you could go for days without having a bowel movement. Fortunately, when militaries in the Middle East ordered these meals, they didn't receive the ham or pork patties, so there wasn't any need for Qadir and Peter to exchange packets. Qadir had beef stew and Peter had a chicken patty; each had a potato patty.

After they had eaten, Peter watched Qadir pray and read from his Qur'an. As Peter studied Qadir and his religious ceremony, Qadir felt Peter's eyes upon him. "You are not religious, Colonel?" Qadir asked in English.

"I don't know."

"I do not understand."

"I don't worship," said Peter.

"But it is within you?"

"In a way. I believe what is important is that a person's heart is pure."

"I agree."

"And what he does is important."

"Yes. Allah takes such things into account. Do you have children, Colonel?"

"Yes, two from my first marriage — actually my only marriage. I was planning to ask Maria to marry me."

"I'm sorry," said Qadir.

"It's okay," said Peter, waving it off.

Qadir continued. "Children, I believe, are a gift from Allah himself."

"Yes, mine are," said Peter. "Mine are. And your children?"

"Four," said Qadir. "Three girls and a boy, who I'm proud to say is following in his father's footsteps."

"And the girls?"

"In my footsteps? Oh, no. Traditional."

Peter nodded.

Qadir went back to his Qur'an. Peter lay on his back looking up at the stars that filled the sky. As the grains of sand had reminded him of how small he was, the stars seemed to reiterate that point. Although he didn't know it yet, he was larger than the biggest star. The molecular constituents that made up his flesh and bones, and all human bodies, were from the stars. He didn't yet know how important he was in the larger scope of human history, and in God's eyes — but he was soon to learn.

Kasim was furious with the news he had just been handed. "Those contemptuous Americans," he fumed, slamming the communique down onto his desk.

His lieutenant stood over him and waited for an order. Kasim finally barked at him, "We proceed as planned, despite the fact that the American Secretary will not be a target at this time. We can hit the subordinates and have just as much effect. I want it done anyway. That is my wish."

His lieutenant saluted and quickly left the tent. He had the message relayed to their operatives in Berlin later that day.

Kasim sat at his desk, fuming to himself. He looked at his maps of D.C. once again. Everything was in order. There wasn't anything more to do. He rolled up the maps of D.C. and put a rubber band around them. Then he rolled up his acetate and put a rubber band around it. He placed these items off to the side upon a field table. His black book also sat there upon the table.

Another messenger entered the tent, saluted Kasim, and handed him a Libyan newspaper. The messenger departed while Kasim furiously scanned the article. It was a pick-up from the article that Howard had just written for the *Sun*. The paper speculated that Colonel Murray was alive and in Libya somewhere, looking for the terrorists who had killed his girlfriend. The article speculated that the terrorist Abdul Kasim was responsible for the bombing that day, and that it was, in fact, Kasim that Murray was seeking.

Kasim called together his top two lieutenants. "I don't know how good this Murray is, but it appears that he is in

Libya somewhere looking for me. We will stick to our original plans. However, I want to be ready for this Murray. I want more standing guards around the clock. Place two more guards at my tent. Go!" One lieutenant departed with his orders while the other remained.

Both of Kasim's lieutenants performed their jobs without question. They would, when tasked, salute Kasim and go about their assigned tasks. They regarded Kasim as their leader, their father, and a representative of God. It never crossed their minds that Kasim didn't receive his authority from God himself.

"We are so close, my brother," Kasim said to the lieutenant at his side. "I can feel his hand upon us. I know Qaddafi's support worries you, but I assure you that once we finish off the Americans, he will be more than willing to help us in our crusade against our own misguided countrymen. He will relish the thought of helping to bring down the government that made a deal with the devil, the Zionists."

"I agree, my brother," said Kasim's lieutenant. "I agree."

24

The Judge's flight landed at Dulles. He rented a car and drove to Leesburg. When he found the Wills tobacco farm, he pulled off to the side of the road and used his binoculars to watch what was happening.

He saw nothing unusual for more than ten minutes. Then he saw a utility van with Bell Atlantic markings enter on the far side and pull up to the barn door. The door opened and the van drove in. The Judge could see that the van was driven by an Arab and that, when the door to the barn opened, he was greeted by several others. Clearly, they were hiding from something. However, the Judge wasn't about to trespass. He did represent the law. So, he quietly left the scene and drove to his brother's house, not far away.

Judge White was a man who tolerated no nonsense. He was straightforward in his courtroom — he tolerated no running around an issue — and he would be the same way with his brother.

As he drove up to his brother's well-kept country estate, he knew full well that his brother was worth millions of dollars. If it weren't for the devil, Jimmy would have nothing. He'd be out of business. Still, wealth never intimidated Judge White. He truly believed in the American constitutional precept that under the law, everyone was equal, despite the fact that those who had more money could afford better lawyers. He was proud of the fact that he administered justice equally.

Jimmy's wife, Rose, answered the door.

"Hello, Rose," said the Judge.

She said nothing. Her mouth dropped open. She was shocked to see her brother-in-law standing at her door. It had been more than twenty years since she had seen him.

Rose's shoulders were stooped over, and she was dressed in a simple black skirt and a plain white blouse. She ducked into the house, leaving the screen door still separating the Judge from the inside of the house. Judge White could hear her calling to Jimmy, "Reverend! Come quick."

How odd that she called him Reverend, thought the Judge. She had always called him Jimmy, from what he could remember.

Seconds later the Reverend appeared at the door with Rose behind him. "You can go about your business," Jimmy said to Rose. She disappeared into the house.

"What can I do for you, Carl?"

"I wanted to stop by for a little talk. May I come in?"

Reluctantly, Jimmy opened the door and let Carl in. "In the den," said Jimmy, motioning down the hall.

The Judge found his way into Jimmy's den. Jimmy followed Carl apprehensively and closed the door gently behind him. "What do you want, Carl?" he asked coolly.

"I want to know what you're up to over at the Wills barn."

The Reverend's face turned red. The Judge could see it immediately, and would know right off if Jimmy was lying.

"The Lord's work. It doesn't concern you. You best be leaving."

"Not until you tell me what it is that you're doing with those people over there, and why there are Atlantic Bell vans there."

The Reverend knew his brother had him. "What we are doing, my dear long-lost brother, is saving people." The Reverend began to preach, as if he were preaching to his flock. "What we are doing is paving the way for the Lord. He has spoken to me in a vision. He said, 'Prepare the way.'"

"Jimmy, I'm not one of your parishioners."

"Do not interrupt when the Lord speaks through me." Jimmy began to back up as he continued. His voice cracked, and he seemed like he was about to cry. "He has spoken to me on high. Oh, my dear brother. You have gone astray. You are one of his lost sheep. I have prayed for your soul, my dear, dear brother." He had his back up against the den's door now. "You know not what you do. I pray he will forgive you for your sins."

"Jimmy. Jimmy! Stop this. I'll have to go to the authorities."

"Dear brother, I pray for thee. You should not have come here. Don't you see, you are being used by the Prince of Darkness? He has put you up to this."

The Judge moved toward the Reverend, but before he could get to him, Jimmy slipped out the den door and locked his brother inside.

"Jimmy! Jimmy! Let me out of here! Jimmy! For God's sake, get ahold of yourself." The Judge pounded on the door. He moved away from the door and started looking around for another way out. The only way was the window. He went over to it and looked out. It was a short drop, but he could make it. As he started to open the window, the Reverend threw open the door to the den and entered, looking possessed.

The Judge turned and faced his brother, and was terrified by what he saw. The Reverend was holding a double-barrel shotgun, standing twenty feet away. He pumped off a round, hitting the Judge in the chest.

At the end of the hallway, hiding in the shadows, Rose gasped in shock.

Judge White fell to the floor. He was still alive, but barely.

The Reverend walked over to his brother and pointed the shotgun at him. The Judge clutched one hand to his chest and held the other up for mercy. He cried, "Jimmy, what have you done?"

"I have saved you, my dear brother. You were interfering with his work. May God have mercy on your soul." The Reverend pumped off two more rounds from less than three feet from his brother.

Rose jumped. Aghast, she ran up to her room, where she closed the door and hid inside.

Judge Carl White died instantly upon receiving the second round of gunshots in his chest. The third shot had opened a large exit hole in his back.

Reverend White dragged his brother's body out the back door and to the garden. He put a sheet over him while he dug the grave where Carl would rest, becoming part of God's great earth.

After placing his brother's body in his grave, Jimmy said a few words and filled in the hole. He went back into the house and cleaned up the mess.

It was nearly four in the morning when he finally went upstairs and into his room, just across the hall from Rose's, and went to sleep.

They found a favorable area and tied up their camels. It was the dead of night, but they saw clearly what they believed to be Kasim's operation no more than two-thirds of a kilometer due north by northeast. They backtracked another third of a kilometer and concealed most of their provisions, including their transportation. Then they went back to the sand ridge and got a good angle on the activity in front of them. They lay, camouflaged in desert fatigues, watching the camp with night-vision goggles.

The occupants of Kasim's camp weren't trying to be inconspicuous. There were bright lights and several vehicles coming and going regularly. It was sort of a military operation; then again, it wasn't. Qadir and Peter lay there for three hours watching the activity. At four in the morning they saw that the camp had folded up for the night. There were several guards in the area walking in circles. Some sat down and fell asleep.

Qadir and Peter waited and watched the inactivity for two more hours, carefully noting the positions of the guards around the camp. The whole time they lay there they were absolutely still, uttering not a word to each other.

At first light, Peter and Qadir snuck back to their outpost and prepared to turn in for the day. They had the camels lying down, concealed under their lean-to's, and their belongings and themselves buried in the sand. Peter took the first watch while Qadir slept. From what Peter could hear, there wasn't anything going on at the camp, but he kept his eyes and ears open.

Peter went over the plan of attack in his head, making plans for which guards he would take out and which ones Qadir would handle. He felt certain it would be time to make their move early the next day. They couldn't chase Kasim around the desert for long with their limited supplies. They had to strike, obtain their objective — Kasim — and get out.

Assistant Secretary of State David Eisenberg was driven in a modest-sized Mercedes limousine through the busy Berlin traffic. As he sat in the back seat he read through a stack of briefing papers on his lap. He was a last-minute replacement for Secretary of State Northwood. Northwood went back to the Middle East for breakthrough meetings with the Syrian president.

Eisenberg was here to meet with Sanford Hayes, the American ambassador to Germany, and their German counterparts, regarding the diminishing American military presence. It was a minor matter, but the Secretary of State had planned to meet with his German counterpart — they were old friends. In addition to the meeting they were to make some opening statements for public relations, set their negotiators to work, then depart. However, peace was breaking out all over the Middle East, so the Secretary had to be in Syria during these delicate stages of negotiation.

Eisenberg's driver/bodyguard pulled up to the German government building in what was once referred to as West Berlin or the American sector. How odd, how things had changed so quickly, thought Secretary Eisenberg, who at the age of fifty-four was old enough to have known all about the Cold War, its implications and ramifications. Hopefully, the world had learned its lessons of the 20th century and could move into the 21st in better condition. However, reality also indicated that since the break-up of the old world order, the new world order was uncertain, with many divisions once again breaking down along ethnic and religious lines. Perhaps nothing had changed.

Secretary Eisenberg was greeted by the American ambassador, Sanford Hayes, and German ambassador Landauer. They went to the conference room in the German government building and began their meeting.

The security consisted of German polizei and a few officials from the American embassy. This was not a high-level
meeting, so it didn't require extensive security measures.

Four hours went by. The meeting was on schedule,
with progress being made. Finally, the meeting adjourned
for lunch. Ambassador Hayes, Secretary Eisenberg, and
Ambassador Landauer prepared for lunch, guests of the
German government at a fine Berlin restaurant. They left
the building and walked to the sidewalk. An official German government limousine waited at curbside. The driver
opened the doors for the men to enter.

Then three men jumped out of a car that had pulled
up alongside the curb just behind the limousine and
opened fire with their Israeli-made uzi's.

It was all over before the driver could react. He tried to
reach for the automatic gun he had strapped under his
armpit, but they cut him down before he could get it out
of its holster.

Ambassador Hayes was the first to die. He tried to run
back into the building, but was shot full of holes from his
backside. Two plainclothes German policemen at the
main door returned fire and managed to kill two of the
assailants.

However, as the Secretary and Ambassador Landauer
scrambled to get into the limousine, they were shot and
killed by the third assailant. The Secretary and his German counterpart were slaughtered while struggling to
close the limousine door. The third assailant was executed
on the spot shortly thereafter by an American State Department security guard as he came running from the
building. The State Department security official stood
there in disbelief. Now, why would anyone go and do a
thing like this? These guys weren't big fish. Damn, it
didn't make any sense.

The mood within the White House basement National Security Council emergency command center was somber. Many gathered there had known Ambassador Hayes and Secretary Eisenberg personally, so the news had affected them deeply. Undersecretary of State Dan Bright had just arrived, carrying with him a cable he had just received from Secretary of State Northwood, who was in Syria at the moment.

Dugan was there, as was Defense Secretary Williams. National Security Advisor Adam Rosen entered with President Myers at his side. The door was secured and the meeting was called to order by Myers. "Gentlemen, please be seated."

Everyone sat. No one said a word.

"I'll let Adam brief you," said President Myers.

"As most of you know, Ambassador Hayes, Secretary Eisenberg, and Ambassador Landauer were killed a few hours ago. We have extensive, irrefutable evidence that Abdul Kasim's group is responsible. Jack, you have those photos?"

"Yes." Dugan removed the photographs from a manila envelope and passed them out.

"These photos confirm that Kasim's operation is located in the Libyan desert," continued Rosen, "approximately thirty-five miles north-northeast of Rebiana. Mr. President."

"Jack, how long before they bug out?"

"Sometime tomorrow," said Dugan, "if they stick to their pattern."

"Stuart?" asked Myers. "How soon can we strike?"

"We've been on standby," said Williams. "We can deploy the F-111's within the hour, and we have the *Coral Sea* in the Med now. It'll be by the book, and there will be nothing left for the satellites to photograph after we're done."

"Everyone agreed?" asked Myers.

Everyone nodded. The room was quiet. Dugan knew Kasim had to be stopped. He thought about Murray and Qadir running around in the desert. This retaliation had to go forward. Murray and Qadir were expendable if they happened to get in the way. If the air strike got Kasim, so be it. If Murray and Qadir happened to get Kasim out before the air strike, so much to the good. In any event, the air strike had to proceed. It was a political statement to terrorists, including Qaddafi, as well as retaliation for their dead countrymen.

Myers broke the silence. "Secretary Bright. What did Northwood say?" he asked.

"He concurs," Bright answered, "and says he would advise a surgical air strike in retaliation."

"Jack, what's going on with this son-of-a-bitch?" asked Myers.

"Now I believe it's spite. There's no other explanation."

"What do we have on the possible hit domestically?" asked Myers.

"We're compiling data from customs and the Bureau, but nothing definitive. We have no evidence to support any attack domestically. Customs has nothing, INS has nothing. There's no evidence one way or the other."

"What about that McClellan incident, Stuart?"

"We've determined that the ammunition was stolen by American males in their thirties," said Williams. "Probably paramilitary militiamen looking for some ammunition for their assault rifles."

"The only thing we can do is tighten security and keep everyone on alert," said Dugan.

"So no domestic connection at all?" asked Myers.

"Last I knew the Bureau was doing all they could to keep an eye on the Arab-American community without violating civil and constitutional rights," said Dugan. "Plus, you know how it would play if they found out we were even watching them at all. We see no evidence of a domestic hit, but we should, of course, keep our guard up."

"Okay, let's get this over with," said Myers. "I've got to get back to the phones and strong-arm the Hill on the budget bill. Keep me up to date as developments arise. I'll call a press conference and brief the world on this madness when it's confirmed that it was carried out. I want you there Stuart, and you too, Dan. Let's get to work." Myers was buzzed out, followed by Rosen, Williams, Bright, and the others. It would be a long night indeed.

25

Since her story had gone out, the frenzy had picked up again. Reporters were scouring the streets of D.C. in search of Murray.

Howard was one step ahead of the competition. Bob Hearn had received an offer from Kasim's organization to be flown to the Libyan desert and interview Kasim for his side of the story. Howard couldn't believe the opportunity.

She was on her way out the door when she saw Katharina Perkins walking up the sidewalk with Paul and Sarah Murray.

"Ms. Howard, I'm Katharina Perkins. And this is my son Paul, whom you've met from what he tells me."

Howard locked her front door and walked toward her car. She said nothing. Katharina and the children followed.

"Paul, is this the lady who talked to you at school yesterday?"

"It's her."

"What do you want, Mrs. Perkins?"

"For you to leave my family alone."

"I'm only doing my job."

"Your job? Is it your job to lie to and use children?"

Howard said nothing as she packed her bag in her car.

"I'm thinking of filing a lawsuit."

"Don't waste your time, Mrs. Perkins."

Howard got into her car to go, but Sarah stepped forward and got in the way so Howard couldn't close the door.

"Get out of my way, kid."

"You're a bad person, Ms. Howard," Sarah said solemnly. "Just leave my father alone."

Howard was stung. "Why you insolent little shit," she said, pushing Sarah away so she could close the door.

Paul jumped forward and spat on the driver's window just as the door closed.

Howard jammed the car into reverse and backed up. She peeled out and sped away, leaving Katharina, Paul, and Sarah standing there, furious.

Peter wasn't able to get much sleep, due to the intensity of the heat, so he lay there mentally preparing himself for the mission. The sun would disappear soon, and hopefully he could doze off for a couple of hours then. Later, they would have to move out and get into position.

Qadir re-checked his maps and calculations, something Peter had done several times while Qadir slept. Neither had spoken for some time now. They thought it best if they didn't, in case someone was near or there were listening devices in the area trying to detect intruders. Actually, there was nothing left to talk about, anyway. They had gone over the plan of attack several times, quizzing each other about procedure, rendezvous, and location points. All that remained was to execute their abduction.

Peter did, in fact, catch three hours of sleep. They moved out shortly after he awakened. The sun had already set, and the night was turning very dark. For most of the way over to the sand ridge that overlooked Kasim's camp they combat–high-crawled.

They made it to the ridge where they had stayed the night before. They stopped there, watching and waiting. Several hours passed while they monitored the camp's activity. With their night-vision goggles, Peter and Qadir watched the camp bustling with activity. It seemed that there was always someone coming or going. Peter had seen Kasim walking around several times, and had pinpointed his personal quarters and his command tent.

Peter spotted a camouflaged van arrive. He exchanged perplexed looks with Qadir; neither of them had seen a van like this one before. They watched four people get out of the van. Three were Kasim's soldiers, carrying their AK47's at the ready.

Peter's heart almost stopped when he recognized the fourth person, also clad in military fatigues. He took his telescopic night-vision gear off, rubbed his eyes, and put the goggles back on to make sure he had seen what he thought he had seen. It was Ann Howard!

Qadir looked over at Peter. Peter shrugged his shoulders. He was furious, but didn't show it — he couldn't let his emotions surface.

Howard had flown into Tripoli and on to a Libyan base not far from Kasim's compound. She had been blindfolded during the last leg of the trip.

Kasim sat at a table in his command tent. Howard was escorted in and sat facing Kasim. Kasim's guards removed her blindfold.

She had two tape recorders and two notepads. "Mr. Kasim," said Howard. "I am grateful that you have allowed me the opportunity to interview you, so you can present your side of the story."

"My pleasure, Ms. Howard," said Kasim, practicing his English.

"First of all, can you tell me how you feel about Colonel Peter Murray?"

"Yes, I must say that I'm sorry for his loss. I have lost in much the same way. But I must say that it is not me he should be seeking. I had nothing to do with the attack on his restaurant in Cozumel and the death of his girlfriend. I must also add that our taking of the American jetliner was not meant to happen the way it did. We had no intention of killing anyone, and it was Mr. Murray who interfered and caused the deaths that took place."

"I see. So what you're saying is that Colonel Murray is responsible for the loss of life?"

"That is what I'm saying. We are a peaceful people. We only wish to be involved in the political process in our homeland, but it is the Egyptian government who persecutes us."

Peter and Qadir watched and waited. Peter thought about taking a snipe at Howard when she emerged from the tent. Another time he might have; however, he didn't have a rifle and he couldn't blow their cover if he did. He checked his watch. They waited. The moon was out, and the night was bright.

It was close to three in the morning when Howard and Kasim came out of the tent. Howard shook Kasim's hand. He took her hand and kissed it. Peter's adrenaline surged. He might just kill her if he got the chance again.

Howard departed under escort in the van. They blindfolded her again for the return trip.

The camp had settled down. There was no activity, and the half a dozen guards still on duty were sitting down near their posts, as most had done the night before. Peter and Qadir waited until three-thirty in the morning. Peter signaled to Qadir to move out. They began low-crawling on their bellies towards their destination: the camp and Kasim.

The tankers had already left their base in Italy. The four F-111's were airborne, having taken off from their base in England. The tankers were airborne for refueling the F-111's. The mission was clear: decimate the entire area. Produce overkill.

Every operative had done the route three times now. They rechecked their weapons of massive death and went over their plans once again. Many, dressed like casual Americans in jeans, sneakers, and T-shirts, had even gone on tours of the White House and the Capitol. They couldn't believe how easy it was. Sure, they had gone through metal detectors and other security checks, but they had waltzed right into the tours! Some had even sat with the rest of the tourists in the House Chamber balcony; this, of course, three weeks ago during the holiday break, when Congress wasn't in session. Nevertheless, some had gotten a good view of the layout, even though they weren't allowed to take pictures inside the chambers.

Many now became restless for this "Mother of All Terrorist Attacks" to commence. It was almost time for Allah to call the Americans home.

Kasim retired for the night. His security guards were posted in full force. Two stood guard right outside the opening to his tent. Two more stood guard near the head of his bed just outside his tent; they could actually hear Kasim snoring. Another two were on the other side, and two more were opposite them. In effect, there were two guards on each of the four sides of the tent. There was no way anyone could get to Colonel Kasim without being met by heavy resistance.

Kasim had rolled up his acetate and placed his black book next to it on his side table. His other maps were nearby.

They continued low-crawling at a painstakingly slow pace for quite a distance. Qadir and Peter blended in so well with the desert floor that if one looked closely, the most they could see were two camouflaged desert snakes slithering through the sand. Both were well versed in what they did. Neither spoke a word to the other. Like Kasim's men in Virginia, Qadir and Peter maintained their focus.

The camp was quiet; there was no activity anywhere. They stopped low-crawling. Peter looked over at Qadir and nodded. Qadir nodded back and gave Peter a thumbs-up sign.

Qadir took out his knife, put it between his teeth, and resumed low-crawling towards the camp. Peter did the same with his knife, and headed in the opposite direction.

The F-111's soared through the night sky. The pilots went through last-minute checks of the instruments. The plan was simple. Two F-111's would fly in formation and release their smart bombs. They would be immediately followed by the other two, who would release all they had for an added follow-up measure.

The United States aircraft carrier, the *Coral Sea*, had already launched four F/A-18 Hornet escort fighter aircraft that would be used to shoot down any Libyan attack aircraft that scrambled in time to threaten the F-111's. The F/A-18's would rendezvous shortly with the F-111's. An AWACS aircraft, with its flying radar capability, was airborne, keeping track of the air traffic information and relaying that information to those friendlies who needed to know.

At the White House, in the Situation Room, and at the Pentagon, the activity was bustling. Electronic maps blinked; brass and enlisted alike were scurrying.

Peter checked his watch. He was in place and awaiting the precise moment to begin his maneuver.

Two minutes later, at exactly four in the morning, Peter moved in. Qadir did the same on his end.

In the satellite room at Langley, Dugan sat with Conrad and others watching live satellite pictures of Kasim's base in the Libyan desert.

"Sir, we have some unusual movement," said one of the technicians.

Dugan perked up when he saw what the technician had spotted.

"Here, and here," said the technician, pointing to the screen where they could see two nondescript specks moving slowly through the sand towards the camp. Dugan fidgeted in his seat. Poor bastards, thought Dugan. This time, for sure, Colonel Murray was dead.

As Peter had expected, many of the guards dozed in and out of consciousness. Peter snuck up behind his first unsuspecting victim, sleeping in his chair near the outer compound, and stabbed him in his carotid artery. The guard convulsed, and blood squirted out of his neck as he gasped for air. He fell to the ground in agony. Peter took the AK47 off the dead guard, strapped it to his back, and moved on.

Qadir had just done much the same with his first objective, a guard half asleep at his post. He, too, confiscated the guard's AK47. Qadir moved on.

All four F-111's had now armed their smart bombs. They would be over their target momentarily.

Kasim snored away in a deep sleep. He had visions of power dancing in his head.

Peter was upon his second target. He snuck up and took the guard by surprise, although this guard was not asleep. The guard, in fact, reacted with a short burst of rounds from his weapon before Peter silenced him forever.

The plan had now changed. Peter would have to use the two confiscated AK47's to defend himself. He took up a position and waited for the other guards to come investigate.

Qadir heard the shots. He knew that his plans had now changed also. He would immediately proceed to Kasim's tent and prepare to intercept Kasim when and if he emerged from his tent, which was likely since the shots had been fired.

Kasim was roused by the two guards at the door to his tent. He awoke from his deep sleep, disoriented at first. He didn't show any alarm when told the news, but he did whisper to himself, "Murray."

Peter heard a buzzing sound in the distance. It was definitely the sound of approaching aircraft. But whose? They hadn't heard any aircraft whatsoever since they had begun this operation, and the Libyans didn't have any air bases in the area.

Kasim gathered up his black book, his maps, and the acetate. Shielded by four bodyguards, he scurried out of his tent.

Qadir rounded the corner and came face to face with Kasim and his guards. Qadir jumped and rolled behind a tent, but not before the guards had spotted him. Two of the guards opened fire in Qadir's general direction. Kasim jumped behind the other two guards and pushed them out in front of him.

Peter saw three guards round the corner of a tent not far away, heading in his direction. They didn't exactly approach him in a military formation or maneuver. It would be a turkey shoot. At the same time, he could hear those jets approaching in his general direction. Imminent danger first, thought Peter. He waited, waited — and just before the three were practically in front of him, he squeezed the trigger of one of the AK47's and swept a burst of rounds from left to right. All three guards went down. One, however, was still moving, so Peter rushed him and squeezed off a quick burst of rounds at point blank range, thus finishing the guard off.

The two lead F-111's had a fix on the target. They waited, fingers on the release buttons.

Qadir pinned down the two guards as Kasim hid behind the other two on the far side of a tent. Now everyone could hear the approaching F-111's. No one knew what it meant, yet.

Dugan and his crew were on their feet. They saw the fire-fight unfold on their video screens in front of them, but only Dugan knew what was truly transpiring. Only Dugan knew it was Murray. Those who smoked lit one cigarette after the other. Those who didn't, well, they were smoking too — second-handedly, of course. Everyone's adrenaline was exploding. Dugan's blood pressure soared and his face turned red.

Peter's mind raced. What was going on up there? he wondered. Could it be? Dugan knew he was here, damn it! Why would they go and order this now? Peter waited, listening.

He could hear the aircraft almost directly overhead. Wait! He could now hear what sounded like two more aircraft closing in from the north, just a few minutes behind the first two. Damn it! It is. "Shit!" he said to himself.

Two more of Kasim's guards were approaching Peter's position. Peter saw them coming, but decided to make a run for it in the opposite direction. He had to hold his night-vision goggles on his head as he ran so they wouldn't fall off.

The two guards saw Peter running in the opposite direction and lost sight of him in the darkness; they didn't have night-vision goggles. Still, they kept chasing him.

Kasim could hear the aircraft almost overhead. He, too, had figured it out and began running through the sand as fast as he could, leaving his guards to fight it out with Qadir.

The smart bombs were released. They dropped with tremendous speed, like attacking hawks, towards their objective.

The first target, Kasim's command area, exploded into a massive fireball. A direct hit. A large crater opened up where the tent had been a split second earlier.

The second target, Kasim's personal sleeping quarters, was similarly demolished.

Altogether, the two bombs destroyed half the camp. Those guards who had remained in the area disappeared from the face of the earth forever, scattered like dust.

Peter hit the sand hard, much like the Marine he was. His night-vision goggles were pulled from his face by the percussion of the bombs that had passed over him. The first two bombs exploded just a couple hundred yards from him. Luckily, they hit on the far side of the compound, the opposite side from Peter. In any event, Peter's head rang.

The two guards who were in hot pursuit of Peter also hit the sand, albeit involuntarily. They dropped their weapons from the force of the blasts. One guard was knocked unconscious.

The first two F-111's soared past the compound. They banked hard to the west, circled around, then headed north. The two follow-up F-111's closed in on target.

The F/A-18's from the *USS Coral Sea* had to turn and intercept two approaching Libyan aircraft which had scrambled after the F-111's had entered Libyan airspace. The Navy fighter aircraft engaged the Libyan aircraft.

Qadir was only yards from the crater. He was knocked out by the blast.

Kasim had managed to get farther away, but he too was knocked out from the percussion, and had lost his black book, maps, and acetate in the process.

Peter stirred enough to hear the other two F-111's almost overhead. He went to get up, but the pain in his back once again seared. He had thought he had licked the back pain brought on by the crash of Flight 243. However, it was recurring and in full force.

He had to get up. This next round from above could be worse, and probably much closer, he reasoned. He gritted his teeth, tolerated the pain, and got to his feet. He ran as fast as he could manage, away from what was left of Kasim's camp.

Dugan and those around him couldn't see much anymore. The explosions had lit up their screens and, together with the fire and ensuing smoke, caused obscurity. They could only sit — or stand in this case — and wait for things to clear before they could see more.

However, they would have to wait even longer. The two follow-up F-111's had just locked onto their targets and released their smart bombs.

Peter heard the incoming whiz of the just-released bombs rushing toward the ground just behind him by a few hundred yards.

One of the guards who had been chasing Peter collected himself and ran after Peter once again, leaving his unconscious comrade lying on the ground.

Peter dove into the sand once again. He had been trained to time the hit of a bomb immediately after hearing the whiz.

Because the pursuing guard couldn't see Peter, or wasn't trained to take cover from incoming fire, he didn't dive into the sand before the bombs struck. The blast threw him by several yards, causing him to crash to the ground hard enough to break both arms.

The percussion of the blast rushed over Peter and caused the sand to kick up over him. He was practically buried in two inches of it. It was enough to ring his bell a second time — this one was harder, however. He lay there trying to regain his faculties.

The two follow-up F-111's banked hard to the left and circled away.

Dugan and his crew couldn't see anything on their screens now. They would have to wait until after the dust had settled to see the effects.

The F-111's were called home to their base in England. The F/A-18's easily shot down the two Libyan challengers in not much of a duel. The *Coral Sea* recalled their aircraft, and the tankers waited to refuel the F-111's over the Mediterranean. Mission accomplished.

It was unusually quiet on the ground, except for the crackling of the fires which were consuming anything that wasn't blown up on the periphery of the camp. Large craters adorned the area. Most of the camp was destroyed. Very little in the way of material was left unscathed. Most of the camp's inhabitants were killed; a few guards had escaped like Peter, and were gathering their faculties at the periphery.

Qadir was alive but unconscious on the north side. Kasim was also unconscious.

Peter was conscious, but barely. He rolled over onto his back and tried to focus his eyes on the starlit sky above him. His back ached more than ever.

The guard who had been chasing Peter was unconscious and had several broken bones. His comrade, several yards behind him, was unconscious and covered with sand. His breathing rate was shallow.

Not much stirred.

After several minutes, Dugan and his crew could see the craters and debris scattered about, but no signs of life. They sat until they felt certain that nothing was moving.

Dugan then reported on the attack to the White House. He told Myers that he believed Kasim was out of business, and there wasn't anything to be concerned about as far as Kasim hitting any more targets, internationally or domestically. The Pentagon called the White House and told the President that the mission was a success.

Later that morning, President Myers announced the events live from the press room. He promptly turned the session over to Secretary Williams, National Security Advisor Rosen, and Joint Chiefs Chairman Leahy.

As the President was speaking to the world, Dugan headed home for some sleep.

The car came out of nowhere. It struck the driver's door and pushed him into the next lane, thus smashing into another car there. All three cars were entangled and twisting every which way.

Dugan's driver, Kenny, regained some control, but the car that had struck them swept back and crashed into them again. It pushed their car across the beltway. The car that had struck the Director's limousine stabilized itself and sped off down the beltway.

Dugan, in the back seat, braced himself as well as he could. The limousine was out of control. Moving at sixty miles an hour, it rolled over and was propelled sideways by another car that had been in the lane to the right. It struck hard.

There was a chain reaction, and before it was over, twenty cars had crashed into each other and three had flipped, including Dugan's, which rolled down an embankment.

Dugan, who didn't have his seat belt on, was tossed around inside the limousine and knocked unconscious. Kenny was trapped and had to be extracted with the Jaws of Life.

Dugan was rushed to George Washington University Hospital, where he lay unconscious with neck and head injuries. Kenny was admitted but, miraculously, wasn't severely injured, and was expected to be released within a few days.

26

M r. Fuad took his last ride around the District of Co-
lumbia. He checked out the area one last time. He
had not heard the announcement made by the American
president about the raid in the desert on the camp. Fuad
drove in one of the Bell Atlantic company vans. He was
alone as he drove down Independence Avenue past the
Capitol.

He made a right turn onto Third Street and a left on
Constitution Avenue. On his way back, he drove near the
White House and turned past the old Executive Office
Building. He was back at the barn in Leesburg later that
evening.

Howard was in Tripoli when she saw the President's
announcement on CNN. She sat and reflected on the fact
that she had been there only minutes before the attack.
She could have died.

Anyway, she hadn't. She had the interview of the century and was on her way back to D.C. She had already
dictated much of the story to Bob Hearn over the phone,
and would write a follow-up article when she returned.
She would plot her next move and try to find Murray.

His head was in excruciating pain, and his back ached as he slowly regained his focus. The stars in the sky above slowly became clear. The moon's light illuminated the area. Sluggishly, Peter sat up and got a fix on his surroundings. He remembered he had night-vision goggles, but he couldn't find them. He saw the smoke from the small fires still burning in what had been, only minutes ago, Kasim's operations camp. It seemed like the dust had settled, so he slowly got to his feet, his back protesting the order. Numbly, Peter made his way, AK47 in hand, back toward the ruins of the camp.

Kasim began to move. He brushed sand from his chest and rolled over onto his back. It took him several minutes to sit up and focus his eyes. He looked around for his belongings but couldn't see much of anything. He began to sift through the nearby sand.

Three guards who had been on the outer edges of the camp and escaped death, as Peter had, began to stir. They couldn't find their weapons — they had been stripped from their hands by the percussion and were nowhere to be found.

Qadir was one of the lucky ones who had been on the camp's periphery. He began to move, albeit rather slowly, since his head was still numb. He checked himself over to see if he was intact. For the most part he was, although he was extremely sore and could feel small cuts on his face.

Peter limped along. He saw a mound of sand moving slightly, so he stopped. When he saw that the mound was one of Kasim's guards, he executed him on the spot by severing his carotid artery.

Several yards further, Peter saw another freshly made sand mound. This one, however, didn't move. He cleared some sand off of it and slit the guard's throat anyway.

Kasim lifted a rifle off of one of his dead guards, and continued to search about. He found his black book and acetate. He still couldn't locate his map case. He secured the book and acetate in the pockets of his fatigues.

Peter stood at the edge of one of the craters, where debris smoldered. He discovered a couple of human limbs and determined that anyone who had been close to the camp when the bombing began was dead. He headed towards the spot where Kasim's command tent had been, on the other side of the compound.

Still looking for his map case, Kasim came upon a man who began to move. He moved closer to investigate. "Get up and help me search," said Kasim.

The man didn't move any faster, so Kasim shoved the man with his foot. "Let's go."

As sand fell off the man, Kasim realized he wasn't dressed like one of his guards. "Murray," Kasim mumbled to himself. He panicked and reacted by immediately shooting a burst of rounds into the man. Qadir died instantly.

Kasim searched Qadir's body and realized that this man was an Arab, not an Anglo. This made him more agitated. He kicked at Qadir's body and scanned the area for other activity. Murray was here somewhere, Kasim was sure. He could feel it. His heart rate increased.

When Peter heard the shots he dove for cover. He couldn't see anything beyond his immediate position, but knew that the shots were no more than a hundred yards in front of him. He took cover and waited, but heard nothing else, so he slowly got up and inched closer to the shots.

Kasim walked away, leaving the dead Qadir. He had to get out of there; he panicked. Picking up speed as he walked faster and faster, he looked over his shoulder continuously, then disappeared into the darkness.

Peter was on the scene not more than three minutes later. He knew he was on his own when he saw Qadir's body full of bullet holes. He looked around and figured that whoever had done this must be close by. He had no time to waste, nor to mourn. Quickly, he followed Kasim's trail in the sand.

Kasim trudged through the sand. He was not entirely up to the task of maintaining a constant speed; his head ached immensely. He slowed down, and had to stop and catch his breath several times.

Peter wasn't more than four minutes behind Kasim, although he didn't know it yet. He knew that the Libyans would be swarming the area soon. He had to catch up to this man and find out for sure who it was. After all, he didn't come all this way for it to end like this. At the same time, however, his back pain seared. Peter struggled to put the pain out of his mind.

Unlike Kasim, Peter kept up his pace. It was a moderate pace, but it was steady. The sun would be up soon, and then it would be more difficult to continue under these circumstances. He had to do this — for Maria, and for the others. If he didn't succeed, then he might not be able to go on at all, he told himself. He had to do this, or die.

Kasim stopped to catch his breath. He propped himself up against a wall of rock and sand that was half his height. He stood there gasping for breath. His body was in pain, much like Peter's. His back ached, his right arm was bruised and sore, and his head pounded.

Peter spotted Kasim from about thirty yards away. In order not to be seen, he fell to the ground with a thump. "Damn, that hurt!" he said to himself.

Kasim thought he'd heard something. He turned and

looked in the direction the sound had come from. He couldn't see much — it was still dark. The ground was lit by the moon; still, he couldn't make Peter out there in the sand. He decided to be cautious and take cover behind the mound he was leaning against. After a short time he looked around and again couldn't see anything unusual. His mind must be playing tricks on him, he reasoned. So he began to walk again.

Peter saw Kasim's shadow moving, coming from behind the rock. Peter high-crawled towards Kasim. He calculated that he wasn't more than thirty yards from Kasim, so he decided to take a shot. Peter lay back down in a prone position, took aim at the man's right leg, and squeezed off a round.

Kasim went down as the bullet ripped through his kneecap, screaming in pain. The acetate fell from his hand and rolled off to the side.

"Throw your weapon down," Peter shouted in Arabic.

Kasim was in pain. He couldn't get a good view of the man who had shot him. He had, in fact, already dropped his AK47 to his side to clasp his knee with both hands. "I dropped it," Kasim said in agony.

Peter took no chances. He low-crawled towards Kasim until he could see the weapon off to Kasim's side. Peter got up and kicked it away further. He pulled out a set of military-issue black handcuffs, and said, "Roll over and put your hands behind your back."

Kasim did as instructed. Peter handcuffed him. "Roll over," ordered Peter. Again, Kasim did as instructed. Peter reached into his field pack and pulled out a compress. He ripped open Kasim's pants and applied a compress to Kasim's wound. Peter then took out a small rope and tied up Kasim's legs.

"Murray," said the hog-tied Kasim.

"Kasim," said Peter.

"You're Satan himself," Kasim said.

Peter said nothing; he just looked at Kasim contemptuously. He finished tying off Kasim's legs rather tightly — perhaps too tightly — but it didn't concern Peter.

Peter searched Kasim, while Kasim wrenched in agony. Peter found Kasim's little black book and put it in his own pocket. "Don't go anywhere," he ordered.

Peter walked off in the direction of the smoldering camp. As he approached the camp, he noticed the three guards who had survived. They stood around assessing the scene. All were shell-shocked.

As far as Peter could tell, no one had a weapon. Nevertheless, Peter took cover and then squeezed off a round, striking one of the guards in the chest. The others started running, which provided Peter with easy shots. He took the other guards out like he was shooting ducks at a carnival game.

Peter returned to his own encampment and found the two camels still lying where they had been left, content to do nothing but lie there. Peter roused them and secured some equipment, then returned to Kasim.

Peter got Kasim up onto Qadir's camel and lashed him on. Kasim protested. "Forced extradition is illegal."

Peter said nothing. He led the camels off towards the east, with Egypt beyond.

"You will never get away with this," Kasim screamed in agitation.

Peter maintained his focus on the journey ahead and ignored Kasim. He consulted his travel log for the return trip.

Kasim became even more agitated lying there tied up on the camel like a deer on the hood of a hunter's car. "This is about your woman isn't it, Colonel Murray?"

Peter still said nothing. He tuned out the taunting as Kasim went on endlessly, trying to provoke him.

Mr. Fuad and Mr. Assad went ballistic. They rounded up their hit squads and made the terrible announcement.

"The Americans have bombed our headquarters in Libya," said Assad.

The men went crazy, screaming for retribution. The anger was pronounced and predictable.

"We are now truly on our own. Colonel Kasim is presumed dead. He sits with Allah himself now."

The men enthusiastically agreed.

"We must stay focused on our mission from Allah and carry it out regardless. We must stay on schedule." Assad looked at Fuad, who grunted and nodded his concurrence.

It was daylight. Peter knew they hadn't reached Egypt yet, and wouldn't until early the next morning. They trudged on.

Kasim fell off of his camel. Peter heard the thud and turned to see Kasim lying there in the dust.

Peter got out his first aid kit and went over to Kasim, who was sitting up. When Peter tried to attend to Kasim's injured kneecap, Kasim kicked sand in his face and said, "I don't want your mercy."

"I must attend to your injury or it'll get infected. I have the proper medications to prevent that."

Kasim spat at Peter. The dribble ran down Peter's arm. Peter stood there and remained calm. God knew that with the rage he was feeling he could rip this man's eyes out with his bare hands. However, he kept his emotions in check.

"I must keep you alive so you can stand trial, be convicted, sentenced to death, and executed," Peter said calmly. "I want you to live to see that day."

"I do not understand you, American."

"And that is your misfortune."

"There is only one justice, and that is Allah's. You have no authority."

With that, Peter repacked his medical kit and attended to his own personal needs. So be it, he thought. He took some prescription-strength painkillers for his aching back. After that, he rechecked Kasim's handcuffs and put him back on the camel. Then Peter climbed onto Tut and headed east.

The Libyan military forces were on the scene assessing the damage late the next morning. They had been there only an hour when they discovered fresh tracks heading off towards the east. A detachment large enough to be considered a military police squad — three trucks — picked up the trail. They found Kasim's acetate blowing in the wind, and the squad leader retained it.

27

Increasingly, the American public had tuned out, for a variety of reasons. Sadly, the American people had stayed home from the polls in large numbers — large enough to considerably alter the political make-up of the country. Even though the public might not be interested, the President was required by the Constitution from time to time to give information of the state of the Union. So he worked on his speech.

Though his recent approval rating was in the doldrums, he had met the job head-on and produced results. Unfortunately, the American people, wanting instant gratification, didn't see it that way. And Congress, well, their approval rating was even lower. Nevertheless, he polished his speech, trying to forget that he would lose in the television ratings to reruns of *Roseanne* on independent stations that didn't even carry his State of the Union address.

National Security Advisor Rosen entered the Oval Office.

"Adam, please sit," said Myers.

"Thank you, Mr. President."

"What's the verdict on this Kasim?"

"All indications point to the fact that his operation has been discontinued. According to our intelligence, a likely hit upon American soil is nil."

"And customs, the FBI?"

"Haven't found any evidence to support a domestic terrorist act by Kasim's organization or anyone else."

"So we can put this behind us and move on?"

"I think so, Mr. President."

Peter slouched over his camel in the hot mid-morning sun. Kasim passed out.

Peter got off of his camel, took a drink of water, and walked over to Kasim. He looked at Kasim and remembered the black book he had taken from him. He fingered through it. His eye caught an unusual entry, that of the Reverend Jimmy White, an address in Virginia, and a phone number, again apparently in Virginia. On the next page were names and phone numbers for Senator Jay Buchanan, General Harvey, and Frank Wills under the heading "Frank Wills, Tobacco Growers Inc." There were crudely drawn diagrams that made no sense to him. He wanted answers to his questions now.

He shook Kasim's body and Kasim sluggishly awakened. It was clear that he needed medical attention; he was lethargic and his wound was blood-soaked and dirty.

"What's your business with Reverend White?"

Kasim squinted up at Peter, but refused to answer.

"Does this have to do with the terrorist attack in the United States?"

Again Kasim didn't answer; he just smirked.

Peter shook Kasim hard. Kasim hid his pain from Peter. He would never give this man the satisfaction of seeing him squirm.

"What about Senator Buchanan?" Peter persisted.

"You will rot in hell," said Kasim.

"Perhaps," said Peter. "But that is not relevant now."

"Torture will never make me talk. Don't waste your

time. Curse you, you arrogant Yankee."

"I'm not going to torture you," said Peter. "But I will keep you alive long enough for the Egyptian secret police to torture you." Peter secured the black book in his pocket. He checked to make sure the rope was securely tied from Kasim's camel to the pack he sat on. Then he got back on Tut and headed them all toward Egypt.

The squad-sized element was hot on their trail. They raced across the desert in search of those who had escaped Kasim's camp.

Peter was sure they must be closing in on the Egyptian border. If his calculations were correct, they couldn't be more than ten kilometers away.

Kasim moaned in pain. The rope slipped off of him and he fell onto the ground again.

When Peter saw what had happened, he stopped his camel and went to put Kasim back up on his camel. Since Kasim appeared to be knocked out cold, Peter decided to administer medication to Kasim's injury. He got the medication out of his pack and began to attend to the injured knee.

Peter untied Kasim's feet and separated his legs. He unwrapped the bandage that was soaked with blood, and began to clean the wound.

Kasim pretended to be unconscious. Then, at the most opportune moment, when Peter turned to get a clean bandage from his pack, Kasim kicked Peter upside the head with his good leg.

Peter crashed onto the hard sandy ground. The kick in the head hurt. He fell onto his back. Because of the pain in his back, Peter couldn't move. It was just too disabling. He lay there trying to regain his senses.

Kasim managed to sit up. He slid over toward Peter and began to kick at his head.

After receiving three vicious kicks, Peter blocked the blows with his hands. Kasim then rolled over onto Peter and began to bite at Peter's arms. He got in a good bite and pulled a small chunk of Peter's flesh away from his lower arm.

Peter struggled back, managing to get in a strong punch at Kasim's face, sending Kasim onto his back. Peter, in worse pain than ever, managed to get up and go on the offensive. He tried to pin Kasim down, striking him in the face several times. Kasim fought back and grabbed Peter's knife, extracting it from its sheath. Kasim did a good job at this, despite the fact that he was still handcuffed.

Peter sensed the loss of his knife and stopped Kasim just as he was about to level it into Peter's chest. Peter, who had the advantage with both his hands free, struggled to regain control of the knife.

As Kasim's advantage diminished and Peter regained control, Peter brought the knife down and leveled it into Kasim's left side. It penetrated Kasim's flesh by a few inches. Kasim shrieked in agony. Peter pulled the knife out.

He rolled Kasim over onto his backside and sat back down to regain his breath. Kasim was bleeding profusely from the knife wound. Peter was so angry that he grabbed Kasim by his collar and shook him as he spoke. "You fool. You want to die!"

Through his agony, Kasim huffed, and said, "I would go straight to Allah's side."

"What the hell do you have to do with the Reverend White?"

"It is written by Allah himself. There is nothing you can do to stop what is written. It will happen with me or without me."

"I'm not going to kill you, you son-of-a-bitch!"

"You know I had your woman killed, and all those other people, on authority from high."

"This is not about revenge or religion."

"Curse you and your unjust and illegitimate laws. There is only one law."

Peter had had enough of Kasim and his insanity. He punched Kasim hard in the face, knocking him out cold. Peter wrapped Kasim's knife wound and once again tied him onto the camel and moved out.

According to Peter's calculations, they had crossed the border and were back in Egypt. The relentless sun dehydrated Peter rapidly; he constantly replenished his system with water.

After an hour Peter stopped his camel in its tracks and checked his log. He was sure the Egyptian base had to be close by. All his markings and notations suggested that the base should be right on this spot, but it wasn't. As Peter got off of his camel, he fell to the ground in the process. He took another hard hit, this time dislocating his shoulder. It hurt him badly. His head still ached; his back was much worse. Struggling against the pain, Peter got himself up off of the ground and checked on Kasim.

Kasim was alive, but severely dehydrated. His skin seemed to be shrivelling up right before Peter's eyes. Kasim's knee wound had coagulated, but his knife wound didn't look good at all. Peter tied another bandage around the knife wound and poured some water over Kasim's face. Kasim slowly regained some slight consciousness and licked the water at his lips. The will to live was still there, in all his delirium, thought Peter.

Peter made himself a crude sling from a torn rag and tied it around his shoulder. It would do for now, he told himself. He looked around at the sand floor beneath his feet. He checked his log once again. It had to be here! Damn it! He walked around the location in circles for some time, until he fell to the ground in exhaustion.

The sun was taking its toll. Despite the fact that Peter had been blotting his face with a water-soaked rag, his lips cracked and gruesome sores began to appear on his face.

When Peter had fallen onto the ground, his face had disturbed the sand and revealed a spent piece of brass. He lay there looking at it. Damn! He finally understood that he was lying on the former site of the Egyptian military outpost. Why had they bugged out? His mind raced.

His energy was draining quickly. Peter was paralyzed. He lay there, swallowing the sand dust that blew at him.

The Libyan squad crossed the border and drove into Egypt. They followed the trail that Peter and Kasim's camels had left in the sand.

It was well into the afternoon. The sun was too much. The combination of heat and intense pain that Peter was feeling was beginning to make him very weak. Peter forced himself to sit up, then crawl over to his camel. He sat there in front of Tut for a few minutes before finally passing out from the heat. His frame slumped over into the sand, and Tut just stood there. Qadir's camel, with Kasim draped upon it, stood next to them.

When Myers read the Howard article, he couldn't believe the crap he was reading. His Chief of Staff, Victor Watkins, sat across from him in the Oval Office.

"Listen to this," said Myers. "Kasim said, and I quote: We are a peaceful people. We have been wrongly implicated in these terrorist attacks. I believe that the Americans and

their Zionist cohorts have staged these events — even per-
petuated them — to bring about a war against our people.
We wish only to live in peace and practice our religion like
those in America do. We have nothing against the American people. It is their government that we take issue with.
Unquote. Can you believe Howard gave this monster a
forum?"

"I believe it, knowing her character," said Watkins.

"I'm glad this lunatic is behind us," Myers said, crum-
pling up the newspaper.

He didn't know how long he had lain there, but Peter
slowly regained consciousness. The sun beating down on
him was so intense that he began to hallucinate. He
thought he saw Maria standing over him, wanting to help
him up. As he sat there her image faded away. Peter looked
over at Kasim, who was hunched over his camel in the
same position Peter had left him in.

Through his pain, Peter found the strength to get up
on his knees. After his head stopped spinning, he found a
water satchel and poured some water over his lips and
face. He made his way over to Kasim.

Kasim was dead, having roasted and bled to death in
the unrelenting sun. Just as well, Peter thought. He could
go his way with a lighter load, for now it was only survival
that interested him.

He cut Kasim loose from his camel. Kasim fell to the
ground. Peter got back onto Tut and headed northeast.

They knew they were several kilometers into Egyptian
territory. Any further and they might get caught and cause
an incident. Still, the Libyan squad leader persisted. "We
go a little further," said the leader. They proceeded deeper
into Egypt.

A kilometer later, they discovered Kasim's body rotting in the heat. The squad leader inspected the body, but didn't recognize that it was Kasim's. "One of them," he said. "A little further."

They drove off in Peter's direction.

Peter was slumped over Tut, barely conscious, when he heard the sound of trucks approaching. He hoped they were Egyptians.

The Libyans had spotted him. They moved into high gear.

The patrol sped down a caravan route. As they rounded a bend in the trail, they drove up towards Peter and came face to face with the Libyans who had approached from the opposite side. The Libyans were had. They spun around and tried to retreat, but were hotly pursued by the Egyptian patrol new on the scene.

The Egyptians opened fire on the fleeing Libyans. They managed to destroy most of the small Libyan squad. However, one truck escaped back into Libya.

The Egyptians went back to retrieve the unconscious man on the camel. They put him inside their military truck and headed back to base camp.

The Egyptian military had Peter transferred to a hospital in Cairo. Peter slowly came out of his stupor the next day and saw an Egyptian commander, a man in his fifties, standing over him.

"How do you feel, Colonel Murray?" asked the commander.

"I don't know."

"You were brought here yesterday. You have no life-threatening injuries, I am pleased to report. We found Abdul Kasim's body shortly after we found you. Where's Colonel Qadir?"

"Kasim got him. I'm sorry."

"I am sorry too. He was a fine man. I'll inform his family, then."

"What happened to your base?"

"We moved out the night of the American hit. We had to pull back."

"Why did they strike?"

"Retaliation for killing American and German government officials in Berlin."

"Berlin?" asked Peter, confused.

"Yes. You were carrying this when we found you. What does it mean?" He handed Kasim's black book to Peter.

Peter took it with his uninjured hand; his other arm was in a sling. They had cleaned Peter up, but with his scraggly beard and parched skin he still had a wild caveman look. "I don't know what it means yet," said Peter. "Have you examined it?"

"Yes, but we don't have a clue. It seems he had contact with some Americans."

"You haven't notified anyone that I'm here?"

"No. Per our agreement, your mission and whereabouts are still classified. Only I and one other person know of your situation here."

"Then I'm through here. I need to get this book back to Director Dugan for analysis."

"I'll consult with the doctor, but I don't see why you couldn't be discharged momentarily. We have what we were after, Kasim, unfortunately at a heavy price. Colonel Qadir was one of our finest, a leader of men."

"I had nothing but the highest respect for the man. He did his job for his country and his God."

"Thank you. I'll note that at his ceremony."

Peter nodded. The Egyptian commander left the room and Peter studied the black book. He saw the names of Reverend White, Buchanan, Harvey, and Wills again. He studied the diagrams again, in detail. One of them was a square, with four lines drawn from different angles, all intersecting the square. The lines were labeled in Arabic: N.J., S.C.S., 1., and MA.

An Egyptian military doctor entered the room. "Colonel Murray?"

"Yes?"

"I'm your doctor. Doctor Gebel. You were very lucky, Colonel Murray. Since you arrived yesterday afternoon, you have made a quick recovery. If you wish, I don't see any problem with your leaving for the States tomorrow."

"Thank you. I must get back as soon as possible."

With that, Doctor Gebel left the room and Peter went back to the black book. He couldn't figure it out, so he set it aside. His mission was complete. He had no desire to do anything except deliver this information to Dugan and be on his way. Where to was anyone's guess. He'd had enough of this madness.

28

Peter returned to the locker in the airport and picked up his ticket, clothes, and cash. He went into the restroom and changed into his casual clothes, but he still looked like Moses minus the robe and staff.

Peter had no problem getting booked on a flight to Frankfurt, Germany, where he would have a layover and a plane change for Dulles.

Peter had an hour and a half to kill at the airport in Cairo, so he grabbed some breakfast in the lounge and watched CNN on the television. The news had follow-up stories about the air strike in Libya a couple of days ago.

It was early morning and still dark on the east coast of the United States. Most of Kasim's soldiers in Virginia were too restless to sleep, so they tossed and turned on their cots at the Wills barn. There were still a few hours before the sun rose in the eastern sky. Some knew very well that the sun had already risen over the region where many of their homes and families were.

Mr. Fuad was raging inside. He hadn't gotten much sleep because of the presumed death of Kasim and the impending attack that he had yet to launch. Fuad knew he had to keep a clear head and maintain focus on the mission. He was, like Peter, a professional, and knew that emotion had no place in an operation like this. Yet, he took great satisfaction in the thought that he would be helping cause the destruction of the American government. Like Mahmud aboard Flight 243, he also felt that in the long run he was doing the Americans a favor, and that they would eventually thank him.

Fuad turned on his flashlight and studied his maps and diagrams of D.C. once again. Planning and rechecking were part of life in a military operation, and that was exactly what he felt he was engaged in: a war. After all, they were part of Allah's army.

Peter checked his watch and saw that it was about forty-five minutes until his flight, so he made his way to the gate. He waited for ten minutes until his section of the plane was allowed to board. His arm was in a sling and his face was swollen. He had some bruises where Kasim had kicked him, and several small cuts. His drooping eyes gave him a sickly look. Some fellow travelers did double-takes, but, to be polite, most didn't stare.

Just as he was handing his ticket to the gate agent, the commander who had been at the hospital the day before took him by the arm. "Excuse me, sir."

Peter stepped to the side and let the other passengers board. "What do you have?" Peter asked.

"We had a reconnaissance patrol gathering data concerning Kasim's base and the American raid on it. They found this in the desert near where the Libyans met our patrol." He handed over Kasim's rolled-up acetate. "I examined it and had it photographed this morning. Perhaps it will aid you in your investigation. I can't seem to make any sense out of it."

"Thank you, commander." Peter shook the Egyptian commander's hand and boarded the plane. The Boeing 747 was airborne within minutes.

Jack Dugan began to come around. His vision was blurred and he felt the pain immediately. For those who were standing by him, seeing him come out of his coma was an incredible relief.

President Myers had stopped by, wanting to be there when his long-time friend came out of it. He had his State of the Union speech ready to go and figured he had time to spare.

Dugan couldn't talk yet. He saw his wife, the President, and First Lady standing over him.

"Don't try to talk, dear. You still need plenty of rest. And we're going to get out of here and let you do just that so you can make a speedy recovery," said Dugan's wife.

Dugan's head was in a brace so he couldn't nod, but he managed a smile.

Peter studied the acetate during his flight. It had the same diagram that was in Kasim's black book, albeit at a larger scale; and there were some other unusual markings there also. From the square, near the four intersecting lines, were two lines off on a tangent, running parallel with one another. In the left bottom corner was a circle that seemed to be all by itself. Peter translated the Arabic letters; the circle was abbreviated: T.J. The original intersecting lines running away from the square had the same abbreviations the black book had. This obviously was an overlay to a map, most likely an American city.

Peter sat there thinking about what had happened to him in the desert. He agonized over the fact that Dugan had allowed the bombing to proceed while he and Qadir were there. It was typical, he stewed. And even after all that Peter had been through in the past with Iran-Contra, he knew he still had to keep his promise of giving Dugan the information he had. He used the telephone in the seat-back in front of him. It took some doing, but he finally got wired through to the private number Dugan had given him. It rang and a beeper sounded.

Dugan's beeper was on his bed at home, attached to the belt he had worn the day of the accident. It beeped away. There was no one to hear it.

Peter waited in his seat for thirty minutes before placing another call, this time tracking down Dugan's office with the assistance of an operator in Virginia.

It rang twice and a secretary answered. "Director Dugan's office."

"Yes, please . . . I need to speak with the Director."

"I'm sorry to say, sir, he was injured in an automobile accident."

"How is he?"

"He's recovering, but he came out of a coma just this morning and is not fully alert yet. May I take a message?"

"No, this is urgent. Let's see. How about Ian Conrad?"

"Well, he's unavailable. Who is calling, please?"

"Murray, Peter Murray."

"I'll forward the message and have him return your call. It'll take a few minutes."

"I'm on an international flight over the Mediterranean. I think it would be easier if I called him."

"I'm sorry sir, but that's not possible."

Peter hung up.

"We will be landing in Frankfurt shortly," the captain announced over the intercom.

Senator Buchanan collapsed in his office in the Dirksen Senate Office building. He fell to the floor clutching his chest. His aides called the ambulance and he was rushed to Bethesda. It was a performance worthy of an Academy Award. He complained of chest pains, and the doctors decided to run all sorts of tests and admit him for observation. He ordered his staff to take the rest of the day off.

General Harvey reported to work in his Pentagon office as usual. He was next in the chain of command after the Joint Chiefs, who all planned to be there tonight. When all hell broke loose, well, he would be right there to keep the military in line, per the Reverend's instructions.

The President had a light schedule for the day. He had a handful of minor appointments and briefings, but beyond that, his main focus was getting ready for tonight.

When Peter got to the gate for his connecting flight, he learned that the flight had been delayed by an hour, so he went into a nearby lounge and waited. His arm felt better, so he took it out of its sling. He massaged it and exercised it a little.

In the lounge, he watched CNN. The anchor came on and explained, "We will carry the President's State of the Union address here on CNN live, beginning at nine eastern time."

Peter perked up hearing this news. He pulled out his plane ticket and checked the date. It read: January 25. Peter then checked Kasim's black book and the diagrams it contained. He drew his own diagram of the Capitol and other landmarks in the area. He compared his drawing to Kasim's and realized they were similar. He flipped a few pages past the diagrams and found what he realized was a date scribbled next to Reverend White's name. 1-25. "That's it. Holy Christ!"

Peter rushed over to a pay phone and dialed an international number. He was finally patched through to the FBI's headquarters at the J. Edgar Hoover building in D.C.

A switchboard operator answered. "FBI."

"I need to speak with the Director."

"And who may I say is calling?"

"Peter Murray."

A secretary answered. "Director Pritchard's office."

"I need to speak with the Director, please."

"He's not in right now. May I take a message?"

"It's very urgent that I speak with him. I'm at a pay phone in Germany and I'm about to board a flight to Dulles. Can you get him for me?"

"I'm sorry, sir. That's impossible."

"How about a deputy director?"

"I need to know the nature of the call."

"I'm not at liberty to discuss it."

"Then there are special channels and procedures to follow, sir. Who is this again?"

Peter hung up. He knew he couldn't get anywhere with the secretary. He paced by the phone.

He dialed the international operator again and was patched through to the Capitol police. "Listen very carefully to what I am telling you. There will be a terrorist bombing tonight during the President's State of the Union address."

There was silence on the other end.

"Hello?" asked Peter.

"Who is this?" asked the police officer.

"I can't tell you that. But I have uncovered a plot to blow up the House Chamber."

In the Capitol police office, they were tracing the call. The Capitol police officer looked at his buddy. He'd heard these threats many times before, from every nut case that had access to a phone. Nevertheless, each call was taken seriously.

"Do you understand what I'm saying?" asked Peter.

"Who is planning to do this?" asked the officer.

"The Army of Allah," said Peter.

"The army of who?"

"The Army of Allah." Peter hung up.

He waited a couple of minutes, then got connected to the Secret Service and patched through to an officer.

"Who is this?" asked the officer.

"Look, there's no time. I was on a mission for the CIA and have uncovered a plot by Abdul Kasim to blow up the House Chamber tonight. Do you understand?"

"Hold on, please," said the officer.

Peter hung up. He dialed the FBI and gave them the same information, then the CIA, the Park police, and the Washington D.C. Police Department.

He waited a few minutes and called the CIA again. He got Dugan's secretary. "I just need to know where I can speak with him."

"He's not to be disturbed, sir."

"Dammit. Listen, he was the only one who knew about the mission I was on. I believe that the Army of Allah, led by Abdul Kasim, is planning to bomb the House Chamber tonight during the State of the Union."

There was dead silence on the other end.

"Hello?" asked Peter.

"Sir, are you making a threat on the President's life?"

Peter hung up.

"I should know better," he muttered to himself as he made his way to his gate.

One agency called another, and soon the whole town was abuzz. They had bomb-sniffing dogs everywhere, and before long the Capitol police had turned the Capitol upside-down. They found nothing. The various agencies compared notes and determined that it must have been a prank by some lunatic who wanted to see the State of the Union speech disrupted. As the national government had slipped even more deeply in the polls, there were more and more bomb and related death threats, mostly aimed at the President, some at other officials. Increasingly, most of the threats were proving to be just that: threats.

His flight was delayed yet another hour. Now it appeared that if it went as scheduled, he would be landing at Dulles during the dinner hour.

At the Capitol, the respective agencies decided that since everything had checked out, there was no reason why they couldn't go ahead as planned. They would beef up the already tight security, but democracy wouldn't be derailed by pranksters and terrorists.

Dugan was sitting up and feeling much better. He could even talk, so he started to order the nurses around. That was just part of his charming personality. His wife sat with him as he read through several national news magazines and local newspapers.

There wasn't much Peter could do but sit back and enjoy his flight. He tried to take his mind off of events by watching the in-flight movie, a recent Arnold Schwarzenegger flick. It showed Arnie taking on the bad guys, getting shot at but not hit, and winning in the end. Peter looked down at his sore, aching shoulder.

They were ready to move out. Each unit was assembled, with their vans topped off and all the M16's aboard. Each van had a M151E2-guided TOW tubular missile launcher with TOW 2 mods attached to a tripod and bolted to the floor. Each operative was wired into a headset and had completed an audio check to ensure that they could hear Fuad's command when he gave it.

29

*P*eter's flight landed at Dulles after the dinner hour. He called the CIA again. And once again he got a secretary. "I need to speak to whoever's in charge."

"Just a moment." She put him on hold. They were tracing the call.

"This is Deputy Director Kinsley, for special operations. How may I help you?" Kinsley was surrounded by electronics specialists who worked fast at their job.

"I need to speak with Jack Dugan. Just tell me what hospital he's in. He can clear all this up."

"I must know who is calling."

"Tell him it's Murray."

"Murray who, sir?"

"Peter Murray."

The other end went silent. Finally, "Last I checked, sir, Peter Murray was dead."

"Look, he didn't — I didn't die. The Director knows everything. It was staged. Just check with him, goddammit!"

More silence.

"Look," continued Peter, "I'll give it to you straight. I've uncovered evidence that Abdul Kasim from the Army of Allah had a plan to blow up the Capitol building during the State of the Union tonight."

Again there was silence on the other end. Finally, the deputy director answered. "Abdul Kasim is also dead, sir."

"I know," said Peter. "I was there."

"Are you threatening the President of the United States?"

Peter froze and was silent. "No, I'm not," he said after a moment. "Listen, just call the Director and tell him that Murray called and said that Kasim's hit on the Capitol goes on with or without him." He hung up the phone and started walking down the concourse. He was trying to think while he rushed along.

"What?" the airport security officer asked into the phone. He handed the phone to the senior officer and said, "Says he's CIA and there's a man calling from a phone on Concourse D who's threatening the life of the President."

The senior officer took the phone apprehensively.

"What?" asked the airport security officer who was patrolling Concourse C.

"I repeat," said the radio dispatcher over the officer's handheld radio, "Look for a suspicious man on Concourse D. He's threatening the life of the President."

"Do you have a description?" asked the officer.

"No. He made the call to the CIA from a pay phone there."

"Roger," said the officer. "The CIA?" he mumbled to himself. He turned off of Concourse C and walked up Concourse D.

Peter stopped at another pay phone and called the FBI. "This is very urgent. I must speak with the Director."

"I need to know who you are and what it's in reference to, sir." They were tracing the call.

"Look, tell him it's Peter Murray and I've uncovered a plot to bomb the Capitol tonight during the State of the Union."

Again, silence from the other end.

"If you'll hold, sir, I'll get the Director. I have to page him, and it will take me a couple of minutes. Please don't hang up."

Peter didn't like it. He stood there as calmly as he could.

"We just received a call from the FBI," said the voice on the officer's hand radio, "he's on a phone near Gate 10."

"Roger." The officer started to run. "The FBI?" he said to himself. What was this all about?

Peter was edgy. He rocked up and down slightly on his heels. This was taking too long. He thought of Eddy Sellers. He disconnected the call to the FBI. He punched in some numbers and got an operator in Buffalo. "Yes, I need the FBI." He waited while the operator placed the call. "I need to speak with Eddy Sellers." He waited while the FBI switchboard operator rang Eddy's number.

"Sellers."

"Eddy, it's Murray. Peter Murray."

"What?"

"Eddy, it's me, Peter."

"Is this a joke?"

"Goddammit, Eddy, my death was staged. I'm alive and I was working for Jack Dugan."

"What are you talking about?"

"Listen to me, Abdul Kasim planned on bombing — "

"Hey, you!" the officer called out as he ran. This had to be the man they were seeking. After all, this man at the phone had a scraggly beard and looked like a wreck.

Peter turned to see the officer running towards him. It

took a moment to register, but when it did he dropped the phone and began running in the opposite direction. He forgot to pick up his carry-on bag, the one with his identification.

"Freeze!" yelled the officer, running to catch up with him. He had his hand on his gun in the holster.

Peter zigzagged down the concourse, dodging in and out of the people walking around. The officer pulled his weapon from its holster and yelled, "Freeze."

He said that already, Peter thought as he picked up a little speed.

"He's running down Concourse D away from the terminal," the officer said into his radio.

Peter ran down a flight of stairs and out a door. He emerged on the tarmac near a plane that was being readied for flight.

"He's on the tarmac," said the officer over his radio, and kept running after Peter.

Peter turned a corner and ran into three security officers who had their guns drawn.

"On the ground, face down, now!" yelled one officer.

There was no place to run, so Peter did as instructed. He kneeled down, favoring his injured shoulder. His movements weren't quick enough for the senior officer, so the officer kicked out Peter's arms and forced him to the pavement faster. Peter wrenched in agony. The officer wrangled Peter's arms behind his back, and his shoulder snapped. The officer handcuffed and searched him, then hauled him off. The officer didn't find Kasim's black book because Peter had concealed it in his shoe.

President Myers finished his dinner with the First Lady, and the Chief of Staff and his wife, and got into the presidential limousine for the ride up Pennsylvania Avenue.

Mr. Fuad did a final check of the five vans. He checked to ensure that the TOW launcher tripods were securely bolted to their respective van floors, then had the men mount up and wait for the move-out signal.

Dugan had enough strength to make his way to the bathroom. His wife helped him, then sat back down next to the bed and watched the news. From the bathroom, Dugan could faintly hear the news on TV, but couldn't make out what was being said.

The local television station anchor came on and said, "We are following a breaking story that is still unfolding at this time. Details are sketchy. Apparently there has been some type of disturbance at Dulles International Airport only minutes ago. Sources tell us that a man was running through a concourse with a gun, threatening to kill the President. We have a van on its way, and we expect pictures momentarily from the airport as they transfer the man to police headquarters."

Dugan came out of the bathroom walking quite well. He was beginning to feel much better. He would be sore for many days to come, and had learned his lesson about wearing a seat belt. Actually, it was government policy, but who paid any attention to government directives anyway, especially those in government?

His wife sat in her chair reading *The New Yorker*.

"What's going on?" Dugan asked.

"Oh, they caught some man who was threatening to kill the President."

"Who?"

"They don't know yet."

Peter stood at the bars in the holding tank at the airport. He was still cuffed. He tried to talk sense with the airport security officer, who stood there not believing a word.

"Look, I'm not trying to kill anyone. My shoulder is injured. Can't you take these cuffs off?"

"Not until we sort this out," said the Officer.

"This is all a misunderstanding. I must speak with the CIA Director. He can straighten this out."

The CIA Director? thought the Officer. This bearded, scraggly-looking man knows him personally? Right. "And when I have lunch with him tomorrow we'll discuss it," the officer said sarcastically.

"I'm Peter Murray. Don't you know who I am?"

"You know how many crackpot Peter Murrays have been turning up since Ann Howard's article?"

"Did you find my carry-on bag? It has my identification in it."

"Not yet."

President Myers was at the Capitol getting ready. He was with his Chief of Staff going over the speech one last time in the room that presidents use for such occasions.

All five vans were on the road, heading for D.C. They broke off and took different routes so they wouldn't draw unwanted attention.

The Virginia police came for Peter. They took him outside to an awaiting police car. As he was transferred and put into the car, the media were there and the video cameras recorded his image. They shouted questions at him and he yelled back at them. "I'm Peter Murray. Someone call the CIA Director, Jack Dugan."

They placed the protesting Peter into the police car. The car drove off. Peter felt defeated.

After the car had left, the media scrambled and the buzz was centered on the Peter Murray angle. Questions brewed.

An airport security officer finally located Peter's carry-on bag. Someone had turned it in to the lost-and-found. The officer threw it on the captain's desk, where it awaited the return of the captain.

All five vans had entered the city limits. Right on schedule, they made their way along the surface streets.

President Myers was ready, and it was almost on the hour. He waited for his escort.

Outside, on the Capitol grounds and the nearby surface streets, security was tight. Roads were blocked off and police officers stood guard. A small army of D.C. police officers, Capitol police, Secret Service, and other security guards were in position. There was no way anyone could get close enough to bomb this place.

30

Dugan waited for the President's speech. The local station was wrapping up its programming and getting ready for the national feed.

"Tonight at eleven," said the anchor, "a man was apprehended after threatening the President's life." A short video clip showed the scraggly-looking Peter being shoved into a police car outside the airport security office.

Upon seeing it, Dugan sat up in his bed, his eyes wide. "What the — ?"

His wife sensed the distress. "Jack?"

"Give me the phone, Nancy."

She passed it to him. He punched in some numbers frantically. He waited. Finally, "Ian, listen. That man they got for threatening Myers' life? . . . Oh, you haven't heard? Well, at Dulles, they apprehended Colonel Peter Murray . . . What? . . . My head's fine. Look, I sent him to Egypt with Qadir . . . Yes. Yes. Where are you now? . . . On the 395. Okay, look, the Virginia State Police have him. Get over there and get him out. I'll get on the line here. Go." He hung up and punched in another number. He waited. A secretary came on. "This is Jack Dugan, I need to speak with Pritchard. It's urgent."

Pritchard took the call on his cellular phone. "Who? ... Agent Sellers got a call from whom? ... Wait, I have an emergency call coming through." He pushed a button, and answered, "Pritchard ... Jack, how are you — ... What? ... Murray? ... You sure? ... Right ..." He clicked off the line. He punched in some other numbers as he got out of his limousine and jogged towards his private FBI jet that was waiting on the tarmac in Atlanta.

Everyone was there: the Vice President, the Speaker of the House; the President pro tem of the Senate, the entire leadership from both parties, every congress member and senator (except Senator Buchanan), the entire Joint Chiefs of Staff, the Supreme Court, and the entire Cabinet; as well as family members, including the First Family in the balcony above.

"Mr. Speaker, the President of the United States," yelled the doorkeeper above all the murmur. Everyone began to clap as the President made his way to the rostrum. On the way, he shook hands with friend and foe alike.

Van #1 got off of Highway 395 and made its way to Maryland Avenue. It stopped at Seventh Street and waited.

Van #2 made its way to Third and E Streets and took up position.

Van #3 stopped at South Capitol Street and Virginia Avenue.

Van #4 parked at New Jersey and E Street.

All four vans waited for Fuad's command.

The fifth van turned down Fourth Street and stopped; Fuad got out. The van continued on as Fuad found a bench on the Mall and sat down. He took out his portable television from his small duffel bag and tuned it to the State of the Union. He waited.

"It is my highest honor and distinct privilege to present the President of the United States," said the Speaker of the House of Representatives.

The entire chamber stood up and clapped; the partisans cheered. Myers waited for the applause to subside.

The fifth van pulled over near the Memorial. It was under renovation or something, the driver figured, but that wouldn't matter shortly. He waited, looking around and seeing that it was relatively quiet. There were a few people meandering about.

"Are you in position number five?" Fuad asked over the handset.

"Yes," answered the driver.

"Proceed," said Fuad.

The driver drove over the curb and floored the van. He got right up to the backside of the Memorial.

Inside, the light cast a shadow across Jefferson's face, presenting an ominous ambience. Jefferson's face seemed forlorn.

The driver got out of the van and ran as fast as he could. A moment later, it looked like the Fourth of July. The van exploded into a massive fireball. Windows at the Bureau of Engraving & Printing and the Department of Agriculture shattered out. Several windows at the White House shook violently as the percussion of the blast passed by it.

At the Capitol, all of the security detachment saw the red-hot fireball plume skyward. The calls were immediate.

Numerous D.C. police cars near the Capitol were dispatched instantly.

In the House Chamber, some people thought they heard a bang, including the President. But Myers went on.

"Mr. Speaker, Mr. President, members of Congress, distinguished guests . . ." said the President.

Conrad didn't bother to park his car. He rushed right into the station. Dugan had called and told them to expect him. Just inside the station, Peter was sitting handcuffed on a bench under heavy guard.

"Colonel Murray?"

Peter stood, but the police pushed him back onto the bench, which only aggravated his shoulder more. "Yes," said Peter.

"I'm Deputy Director Ian Conrad. What's this all about?"

"Call off the State of the Union for chrissake. Kasim said it would go forth with or without him."

Conrad didn't know what to say. "Are you sure, Colonel?"

"Goddammit, do it!"

"There's been some kind of an explosion at the Jefferson Memorial," said an officer, rushing in to where all the top brass were listening to the exchange between Peter and Conrad.

Conrad looked at the officer in terror. The officer looked at the top brass in shock. Conrad looked back at Peter, confused.

"It's happening! Get 'em out of there!" screamed Peter.

Conrad fiercely punched in some numbers on his cell phone.

A few D.C. squad cars and security detachments on the outer periphery of the Capitol, near surrounding streets, were pulled off of detail and ordered to the Memorial. Still, the State of the Union address went on, as the Constitution mandated.

"Thirty seconds," said Mr. Fuad over his radio.

"What?" asked the Secret Service agent in his office. "Who?" He handed the phone to his supervisor.

The police quickly took off the handcuffs. Peter rotated his injured shoulder around to the front of his body and kneaded it gently. Then he pulled Kasim's black book from his shoe. He opened it and pointed out to the police captain the entries Kasim had written there. "These people have something to do with this. You'd better check it out," said Peter.

The captain took the book from Peter and quickly dispatched several units.

"This is the Deputy Director of the CIA, Ian Conrad," he said into his phone. "We have been presented with clear evidence that the House Chamber is targeted for a terrorist bombing. I'm handing the phone to Colonel Murray. Do what he tells you." Conrad handed his phone to Peter.

Peter spoke as fast as lightning. "This is Murray. I'm sure you know who I am. Listen very carefully to what I'm saying. I was on assignment from Jack Dugan. Abdul Kasim — I'm sure you know that name too — has planned to blow up the House Chamber tonight. He has operatives here, and it's already started. Get everyone outta there now!"

"Ten seconds," said Fuad over the radio. "Nine, eight, seven, six, five, four, three, two, one. Move out and commence firing."

Van #1 sped up Maryland Avenue.
Van #2 sped up First Street.

Van #3 sped up South Capitol Street.
Van #4 sped up New Jersey Street.

Peter and Conrad rushed out of the station and hopped into Conrad's car. They sped off towards D.C.

Van #1 skidded to a stop at Third and Maryland Streets. Three operatives inside jumped from the rear and opened fire on the unsuspecting police standing there.

Van #2 turned east on Independence and skidded to a stop just before First Street. Three operatives jumped out and fired their M16's at the police, who were standing there with no idea of what was happening.

Van #3 came to a stop at C and South Carolina Streets. Three operatives jumped from the van and slaughtered the police standing there.

Van #4 stopped at New Jersey and C Streets and did the same.

"Let me outline for you the main objectives as I see them," the President said to his attentive audience. You could hear a pin drop.

Van #1 turned around as its three operatives cleared a path. It backed up Maryland Avenue and stopped at First and Maryland, just northwest of the Garfield Monument.

The driver jumped from the driver's seat, ran to the back, and hopped into the back of the van while the others covered him. The driver readied the TOW missile launcher.

By this time vans #2 and #4 had done the same. Van #2 backed up First Street and came to rest just South of the Garfield Monument. Van #4 had its rear door opened facing the House Chamber on New Jersey Avenue.

Van #3 met some resistance initially, but it quickly overcame this and killed all the police in its way. It backed up South Capitol Street and stopped several yards south of Independence Avenue.

The Secret Service agent ran down the aisle as though his life depended upon it. He had to hold his earpiece as he ran so he could hear what was going on.

Several people turned and began to murmur.

The President trickled off his sentence. "So, I believe that we can all come togeth — "

The agent ran up to Myers and whispered in his ear, "Code red." He practically pushed the President down the aisle amidst gasps and confusion of everyone present.

Another Secret Service agent emerged from the Speaker's lobby. He forcibly hurried the Vice President out the opposite side of the House Chamber.

The place was in an uproar. Everyone stood up and the chatter in the Chamber increased in intensity.

Yet another Secret Service agent ran to the rostrum and said, "Everyone: calmly, and in an orderly manner, evacuate the building."

The place went wild. Everyone started rushing the exits. It was every person for themselves. Senators and members of the House pushed and shoved their way through. The Supreme Court Justices would be the last ones to exit, unfortunately.

The crosshairs illuminated the target. "Fire!" The TOW missile shot out of its launch tube. At about twelve meters, the flight motor ignited and the TOW missile flew towards its target at about two hundred meters a second.

It smashed into the west wall of the House Chamber. A terrific explosion sent debris in all directions.

Three seconds later, a second missile impacted on the south wall. The explosion rocked the House Chamber.

Those not killed or injured screamed in bloody horror. Some escaped through the east entrance. Many people in the balcony jumped or were sent over the railing by the force of the blast and crashed onto the floor. It was a stampede to get out.

Having heard and seen the shootout from the other side of the Capitol, dozens of police officers and security agents came rushing toward the disturbance.

Dozens were met with gunfire upon entering the area. Some managed to take up positions and return fire.

Miraculously, plenty of people had already escaped. There were many still struggling to get out.

A third missile slammed into the House Chamber on the west side. A fourth smashed through on the south side. Scores of those still inside were blown to bits. A few people climbed over the dead and debris.

Van #1 was under attack by the police. Vans #3 and #4 had police moving in on them. Van #2 was preparing to make another launch. The driver, who was also the gunner, sighted the smoldering House Chamber. He squeezed off a missile. The TOW missile's flight motor ignited at twelve meters, sending it soaring ahead. It worked like it was supposed to. Hughes Aircraft Company, the TOW missile manufacturer, would have been proud. It smashed into what was left of the west wall, and exploded right on cue.

President Myers had been stuffed into his awaiting limousine on the east side of the Capitol. It had peeled out at breakneck speed, not stopping for any light or other vehicle. As the presidential limousine turned onto Pennsylvania Avenue, it plowed into a civilian vehicle and pushed it out of the way.

The Vice President was evacuated from the Chamber.

Those who had survived, well over three hundred people, had made it out onto the Capitol grounds. Many of them injured, they scattered in all directions and disappeared down adjacent streets. Complete pandemonium reigned.

All four vans were under attack, and it was unlikely that they could get off another missile. Every one of the operatives had to engage the onslaught of D.C. Police, Secret Service, and Capitol police. A SWAT unit was on its way.

However, van #3 was reloading and preparing another launch. Just as the gunner sent the TOW missile down its launch tube towards its target, the van was met with a hail of bullets and ripped apart. Nevertheless, the final TOW missile slammed into the rubble and exploded on impact.

Dugan had to get out of this place. He had gotten dressed just before the first missiles hit and the television screen went blank. He couldn't sit around not knowing what was going on. He made his way to his car, followed by his wife.

Conrad and Peter came in on Highway 66. They could see the smoldering fire near the Jefferson Memorial on their drive into town. They crossed the Theodore Roosevelt Bridge and made their way up Constitution Avenue. They could see smoke and fire rising above the Capitol.

After they passed the Ellipse, traffic came to a complete stop. There was just too much congestion, confusion, and panic in all directions.

The driver of van #2 was trying for another launch. He struggled, but just couldn't quite do it by himself. Their position was overrun shortly thereafter, and all four operatives were gunned down.

A D.C. SWAT team arrived in choppers. They rappelled down and began engaging the assailants. Sadly, with all the confusion, some advancing police units were shot by friendly fire.

It was certain to the driver of van #1 that he was going to be overrun. His brothers in arms had just been killed. He decided to make one last effort for Allah, knowing full well he would ascend only moments thereafter. He rushed a SWAT unit that had just deployed around his van and shot straight out while sweeping his M16 in every direction. He was riddled with a hail of return rounds from the SWAT unit. He did, indeed, die quickly. Ascension, however, was open for debate.

Conrad and Peter couldn't get anywhere in their car, so they got out and began running up the Mall. After a considerable run, they realized they couldn't really do anything, and that the authorities were in control of the situation, so they stopped near a fence and caught their breath. They watched the activity from a bench at Seventh Street and Madison Drive.

The crackling of the automatic weapons reminded Peter of Vietnam. Despite all of his misgivings about the U.S. system, he was sorry. The fire in the distance reflected off of his face, and he thought about Maria.

"We fucked this one up," said Conrad. "Jesus Christ, we fucked this up!" Peter looked at him and said nothing. There was nothing more to say.

Fuad came running down the Mall. Even though he was dressed in civilian clothes, he stuck out like a sore thumb. He still had his radio connections strapped to him and his black duffel bag in his hand.

Peter spotted him and remembered his face from the day he had seen Fuad taking pictures. He saw Fuad's scar and it all connected. "Give me your gun," Peter ordered Conrad.

"What?"

"Give me your fucking gun!" yelled Peter.

Conrad grabbed his 9mm Glock and handed it to Peter, who took it and kept it at his side. When Fuad was right in front of him, Peter pointed the Glock straight at Fuad. He said in Arabic, "Where do you think you're going?"

Fuad froze in his tracks, not knowing what to do. Then he panicked, and reached into his jacket with one hand.

Before Fuad could extract what it was he was going for, Peter squeezed off three rounds, striking Fuad's chest. Fuad went down hard.

Peter and Conrad rushed to Fuad's side. He was still alive, barely. Peter reached into Fuad's jacket and took out a handgun. He gave it to Conrad, who nodded, in shock.

"I'm going straight to Allah's side," said Fuad.

"No, I'll dance with you in hell," said Peter. Peter handed the gun to Conrad, threw him a tired glance, and walked off down the Mall. Conrad stood there and guarded Fuad, who died seconds later.

The police had the situation under control. Not one of Abdul Kasim's operatives had given himself up. They had all rushed forward and been shot in a hail of death.

The same Virginia police who had Peter in custody only minutes earlier now swarmed the Wills farm. They apprehended Frank Wills and his young assistant, Billy. They found Mr. Assad and the alternates inside the barn, watching the media cover events on television. They were completely unsuspecting. They had Assad, Wills, and everyone else cuffed and carted off; then they had roped off the area. They knew they had hit the jackpot when they discovered the leftover military hardware and enlarged photographs of the Capitol and the Jefferson Memorial, with the positions marked off for the vans and the Jefferson Memorial highlighted. Of course, the spare M16's and TOW missile launchers and assorted spare parts added to the obvious.

The media had been alerted and was there to video the apprehensions. A reporter announced the event live over television. "We have been told that tobacco grower Frank Wills, and several men of Arab descent, have been apprehended in connection with the bombing minutes ago at the Capitol. We are told that inside this barn," the camera panned away from the reporter and showed the barn in the background, "are photographs of the Capitol building, and military hardware. I'm told we're going back live to the Capitol now."

It was a tragic, gruesome scene inside the House Chamber. More than 150 people had lost their lives, including the First Lady and two of the First Lady's Secret Service detail who had tried to save her.

Four Supreme Court Justices perished, three Joint Chiefs, five cabinet secretaries, the President's Chief of Staff, the Speaker of the House, the Senate majority and minority leaders, several House leaders, twenty senators, and dozens of House members. Several family members in the balcony also perished. It would be many hours before all the bodies could be removed and identified.

President Myers made it back to the White House Situation Room and immediately ordered this great, old federal city sealed.

General Harvey took the order, but couldn't believe who made the call. He couldn't do anything but carry out the President's orders. The army had the city blocked off and surrounded a few hours later.

After Harvey got the orders out, he informed his Chief of Staff, Colonel Lee, that he was relieving himself of duty. The Colonel didn't understand, as General Harvey locked himself in his office.

Minutes later, the Colonel was knocking at Harvey's door. "General Harvey? There are some Secret Service men here to see you." There was no answer. The agents looked at the Colonel, who shrugged his shoulders. "General Harvey?" The Colonel knocked on the door again.

Inside, the General sat at his desk. He held a Bible with one hand and a gun in his mouth with the other. He pulled the trigger.

The media were interviewing those who would talk. Ann Howard was right there in the fray. She mingled with the survivors who were being treated on the Capitol Plaza and in nearby parks. The person she really wanted couldn't be found, and when asked about this, people only gave her blank stares. "Has anyone seen Colonel Peter Murray?" she asked a small group of congress members. No one answered, and she went on to the next group.

The Virginia police pulled up in six squad cars at the Reverend's house. Jimmy White was sitting inside, watching events unfold on television. He sat in his favorite chair, grasping his Bible in one hand and holding a shotgun across his lap. Terror filled his eyes. He had just watched the report come in from the Wills farm, and had seen Wills and Assad handcuffed and carted off. He heard the reporter talk about the maps and equipment inside.

An anchor came on and said, "We have confirmed that the President is, I repeat, is back at the White House and is not harmed. The Vice President is also safe and over at the Pentagon." Jimmy White's eyes teared. "Initial reports indicate that the majority of those in the House Chamber have survived," continued the anchor, "but we must add that at least a hundred, perhaps more, have died."

The doorbell rang. Jimmy jumped out of his chair like a crazed animal.

Rose peeked around the corner from the top of the stairs. She, too, was clutching her Bible in horror.

The Reverend scurried to the door and asked, "Who is it?"

"Virginia State Police," came a voice through the door.

"What's this about, officer?" asked the Reverend.

"We need to talk with you, Reverend."

"About what?"

"Could you please open the door, Reverend, so we can talk face to face?"

There was silence. And more silence.

"Reverend? Reverend White?" The police captain looked at his sergeant. "Break it down," he ordered.

The sergeant used a sledgehammer and broke open the Reverend's door quite easily.

They rushed inside, with guns covering one another. They searched the first floor but found no one.

They rushed upstairs and came upon a locked bedroom door: Rose's.

"Reverend? Reverend White?" called the captain. They heard the blast of a shotgun from inside the bedroom. The captain hollered to his sergeant, "Break it down."

The sergeant broke the door down. They found Reverend White standing over the body of Rose White, dead from the point-blank shotgun blast. The Reverend raised the shotgun slightly at the officers.

The officers froze. "Put it down," yelled the captain.

Reverend White looked maniacal. His face was contorted, his eyes wide and glassy. He ranted, "Forgive them Lord, for they know not what they do."

"Reverend White," screamed the captain, "put the shotgun down!"

"Give us strength so that we may overcome evil," continued the Reverend.

The Reverend pointed the shotgun at the officers. Yet, the officers held. Many knew the Reverend personally. How could they shoot a man of God? How had it come to this? thought the captain.

"I have tried, my Lord," continued the Reverend. "You know how I've tried to do your work here on earth." He leveled the shotgun at the captain. As he took aim he was shot by several of the officers. White fell to the floor.

The sergeant went over to the dying Reverend and took the shotgun from him.

"Reverend, what in God's name have you done?" asked the captain, kneeling next to Jimmy White.

"That's right, my son. In God's name." The Reverend passed away in the captain's arms. The captain looked horrified. He looked up at his sergeant and the other officers in the room, and at the lifeless body of Rose White, still clutching her Bible. He shook his head slowly in disbelief.

Senator Buchanan rushed out of Bethesda. Like the Reverend, he had also seen the events unfold on television. The Senator listened as the media reported that they had information from the authorities that was leading them right to the source and quickly. Buchanan wondered, What the devil went wrong? Why had God let them down?

He got into a cab and went back to his D.C. home. He hurried to pack a suitcase. He was panting hard now. He heard a loud knock at his door. "Secret Service, Senator. Open up."

Buchanan went into total shock. Sweat had built up on his brow. The knocking turned into pounding. It startled the Senator, and he looked around in a panic. He clutched his left arm. His chest felt like an elephant was sitting on it.

The pounding was heard again. "We're breaking it down, Senator," came a voice from outside.

Buchanan collapsed and fell to the floor.

Buchanan had had a heart attack, but the Secret Service managed to save his life and have him transported to Bethesda, where he recovered and would stand trial months later.

Conrad stayed at the bench near the body of Fuad. He waited for the authorities to arrive and retrieve the body. He had re-holstered his gun and was gazing at the smoke and embers that rose above the Capitol. He rubbed his eyes in disbelief.

Peter walked slowly along the Mall, and up the steps to the Lincoln Memorial. He stood for the longest time at the feet of Abe, as Abe's eyes looked down upon him. As Abe's face had expressed its sadness for the four years he was president, Peter had that same look in his eyes. A tear welled up in Peter's eye and rolled down his cheek.

Finally, he turned and walked slowly back down the steps, seeing the same aftermath and ruin Conrad saw. He paused and looked up at the cool night sky. Then, Peter headed toward his children's home in Maryland.

ABOUT THE AUTHOR

J.C. Arlington served with the United States military and was stationed in Egypt, Honduras, Europe, and the United States. He has a degree in political science. Currently, he and his wife are living somewhere on God's green earth. This is his first novel.

To order more copies of *Dance with the Devil*,
please call Bookworld Services at:

1-800-444-2524

Have your credit card ready.
Discounts available for quantity orders.

Dance with the Devil by J.C. Arlington
ISBN: 0-9648398-0-6
Ingram Title Code: 051246
Distributed by Bookworld Services, Inc.
1933 Whitfield Park Loop
Sarasota, FL 34243

DANCE WITH
THE DEVIL

*...A fast paced and riveting political thriller
that is right out of today's headlines.*

...Religious zealots hijack an American passenger
jet in order to force the American Government to
release prisoners held in connection with the
World Trade Center bombing.

*...This novel moves so fast you won't be
able to put it down until you've read the
last word!*

...Only one man, Lieutenant Colonel
Peter Murray, U.S.M.C. (ret.) –a disgraced
Iran-Contra scandal operative–reluctantly
takes action.

...Later, Murray discovers that the same
militants, assisted by fundamentalist American
citizens, are trying to overthrow the U.S.
Government!

*...Dance With The Devil mixes religious
fundamentalism and politics, and presents
the reader with issues and events that are
currently being debated
and taking place
in America.*

OCEAN FRONT PUBLISHERS
$6.95 U.S.A. (Canada $7.95) • Printed in U.S.A.

ISBN 0-9648398-0-6

50695>

9 780964 839809

www.ingramcontent.com/pod-product-compliance
Lightning Source LLC
Chambersburg PA
CBHW070900260626
47162CB00007B/2516

* 9 7 8 0 9 6 4 8 3 9 8 0 9 *